About

Diane Gaston's dream jɔ... ...ꞁꞁꞁꞁꞁꞁ ꞁꞁꞁꞁꞁ ꞁꞁꞁꞁꞁ write romance novels. One day she dared to pursue that dream and has never looked back. Her books have won Romance's highest honours: the *RITA* Award, the National Readers Choice Award, Holt Medallion, and Golden Heart. She lives in Virginia with her husband and three very ordinary house cats. Diane loves to hear from readers and friends. Visit her website at dianegaston.com

Regency Whispers

Regency Whispers:

Forbidden
Passion

DIANE GASTON

MILLS & BOON

First Published in Great Britain 2024
By Mills & Boon, an imprint of HarperCollins*Publishers* Ltd
1 London Bridge Street, London, SE1 9GF

www.harpercollins.co.uk

HarperCollins*Publishers*
Macken House, 39/40 Mayor Street Upper,
Dublin 1, D01 C9W8, Ireland

ISBN: 978-0-263-39773-4

This book contains FSC™ certified paper and other controlled sources to ensure responsible forest management.

For more information visit: www.harpercollins.co.uk/green

Printed and Bound in the UK using 100% Renewable Electricity at CPI Group (UK) Ltd, Croydon, CR0 4YY

BOUND BY
A SCANDALOUS
SECRET

To the memory of my Aunt Gerry,
who was endlessly energetic, efficient and,
it seemed to me, could do just about anything.

Chapter One

Lincolnshire—December 1815

Genna Summerfield first glimpsed him out of the corner of her eye, a distant horseman galloping across the land, all power and grace and heedless abandon. A thrilling sight. Beautiful grey steed, its rider in a topcoat of matching grey billowing behind him. Horse and rider looked as if they had been created from the clouds that were now covering the sky. Could she capture it on paper? She grabbed her sketchpad and charcoal and quickly drew.

It was no use. He disappeared in a dip in the hill.

She put down the sketchpad and charcoal and turned back to painting the scene in the valley below, her reason for sitting upon this hill in this cold December air. How she wished she could also paint the galloping horse and rider. What a challenge it would be to paint all those shades of grey, at the same time conveying all the power and movement.

The roar of galloping startled her. She turned. Man and horse thundered towards her.

Drat! Was he coming to oust her from the property? To chase her from this perfect vantage point?

Not now! She was almost finished. She needed but a few minutes more. Besides, she had to return soon before someone questioned her absence—

The image of the horse and rider interrupted her thoughts. Her brush rose in the air as she tried to memorise the sight, the movement, the lights and darks—

Goodness! He galloped straight for her. Genna backed away, knocking over her stool.

The rider pulled the horse to a halt mere inches away.

'I did not mean to alarm you,' the rider said.

'I thought you would run me down!' She threw her paint-brush into her jug of water and wiped her hands on the apron she wore over her dress.

He was a gentleman judging by the sheer fineness of his topcoat and tall hat and the way he sat in the saddle, as if it were his due to be above everyone else.

Please do not let this gentleman be her distant cousin, the man who'd inherited this land that she once—and still—called home.

'My apologies.' He dismounted. 'I came to see if you needed assistance, but now I see you intended to be seated on this hill.'

'Yes.' She shaded her eyes with her hand. 'As you can see I am painting the scene below.'

'It is near freezing out,' he said. 'This cold cannot be good for you.'

She showed him her hands. 'I am wearing gloves.' Of course, her gloves were fingerless. 'And my cloak is warm enough.'

She looked into his face. A strong face, long, but not thin, with a straight nose that perfectly suited him, and thick dark brows. His hair, just visible beneath his hat was also dark. His eyes were a spellbinding caramel, flecked with darker brown. She would love to paint such a memorable face.

He extended his hand. 'Allow me to introduce myself. I am Rossdale.'

Not her cousin, then. She breathed a sigh of relief. Some other aristocrat.

She placed her hand in his. 'Miss Summerfield.'

'Summerfield?' His brows rose. 'My host, Lord Penford, is Dell Summerfield. A relation, perhaps?'

She knew Lord Penford was her cousin, but that was about all she knew of him. Just her luck. This man was his guest.

'A distant relation.' She lifted her chin. 'I'm one of the scandalous Summerfields. You've heard of us, no doubt.'

The smile on his face froze and she had her answer. Of course he'd heard of her family. Of her late father, Sir Hollis Summerfield of Yardney, who'd lost his fortune in a series of foolish investments. And her mother, who was legendary for having many lovers, including the one with whom she'd eloped when Genna was almost too little to remember her. Who in society had not heard of the scandalous Summerfields?

'Then you used to live at Summerfield House.' He gestured to the house down below.

'That is why I am painting it,' she responded. 'And I would be obliged if you would not mention to Lord Penford that I trespassed on his land. I have disturbed nothing and only wished to come here this one time to paint this view.'

He waved a dismissive hand. 'I am certain he would not mind.'

Genna was not so certain. After her father's death, Lord Penford had been eager for Genna and her two sisters to leave the house.

She stood and started to pack up her paints. 'In any event, I will leave now.'

He put his hand on her easel. 'No need. Please continue.'

She shook her head. The magic was gone; the spell broken. She'd been reminded the house was no longer her home. 'I must be getting back. It is a bit of a walk.'

'Where are you bound?' he asked.

Surely he knew *all* the scandals. 'To Tinmore Hall.' She gave him a defiant look. 'Or did you forget that my sister Lorene married Lord Tinmore?'

He glanced away and dipped his head. 'I did forget.'

Genna's oldest sister married the ancient Lord Tinmore

for his money so Genna and her sister Tess and half-brother Edmund would not be plunged into poverty. So they, unlike Lorene, could make respectable marriages and marry for love.

Genna had not forgiven Lorene for doing such a thing— sacrificing her own happiness like that, chaining herself to that old, disagreeable man. And for what? Genna did not believe in her sister's romantic notions of love and happily ever after. Did not love ultimately wind up hurting oneself and others?

The wind picked up, rippling her painting.

Rossdale put his fingers on the edge of it to keep it from blowing away. His brow furrowed. 'You have captured the house, certainly, but the rest of it looks nothing like this day...'

She unfastened the paper from the easel and carefully placed a sheet of tissue over it. She slipped it in a leather envelope. 'I painted a memory, you might say.' Or the emotion of a memory.

The wind gusted again. She turned away from it and packed up hurriedly, folding the easel and her stool, closing her paints, pouring out her jug of water and wrapping her brushes in a rag. She placed them all in a huge canvas satchel.

'How far to your home?' Rossdale asked.

Her *home* was right below them, she wanted to say. 'To Tinmore Hall, you mean? No more than five miles.'

'Five miles!' He looked surprised. 'Are you here alone?'

She pinched her lips together. 'I require no chaperon on the land where I was born.'

He nodded in a conciliatory manner. 'I thought perhaps you had a companion, maybe someone with a carriage visiting the house. May I convey you to Tinmore Hall, then?' He glanced towards the clouds. 'The sky looks ominous and you have quite a walk ahead of you.'

She almost laughed. Did he not know what could happen if a Summerfield sister was caught in a storm with a man?

Although Genna would never let matters go so far, not like her sister Tess who'd wound up married to a man after being caught in a storm. Why not risk a ride with Rossdale?

She widened her smile. 'How kind of you. A ride would be most appreciated.'

Ross secured her satchel behind the saddle and mounted Spirit, his favourite gelding, raised from a pony at his father's breeding stables. He reached down for Miss Summerfield and pulled her up to sit side-saddle in front of him.

She turned and looked him full in the face. 'Thank you.'

She was lovely enough. Pale, flawless skin, eyes as blue as sea water, full pink lips, a peek of blonde hair from beneath her bonnet. Her only flaw was a nose slightly too large for her face. It made her face more interesting, though, a cut above merely being beautiful. She was not bold; neither was she bashful or flirtatious.

Unafraid described her better.

She spoke without apology about being one of the scandalous Summerfields. And certainly was not contrite about trespassing. He liked that she was comfortable with herself and took him as he was.

Possibly because she did not know who he was. People behaved differently when they knew. How refreshing to meet a young woman who had not memorised Debrett's.

'Which way?' he asked.

She pointed and they started off.

'How long have you been a guest of Lord Penford?' she asked.

'Two days. I'm to stay through Twelfth Night.' Which did not please his father overmuch.

'Is Lord Penford having guests for Christmas?' She sounded disapproving.

He laughed. 'One guest.'

'You?'

'Only me,' he responded.

She was quiet and still for a long time. 'How—how do you find the house?' she finally asked.

He did not know what she meant. 'It is comfortable,' he ventured.

She turned to look at him. 'I mean, has Lord Penford made many changes?'

Ah, it had been her home. She was curious about it, naturally.

'I cannot say,' he responded. 'I do know he plans repairs.'

She turned away again. 'Goodness knows it needed plenty of repairs.'

'Have you not seen the house since leaving it?' he asked.

She glanced back at him and shook her head.

The grey clouds rolled in quickly. He quickened Spirit's pace. 'I think it will snow.'

As if his words brought it on, the flakes began to fall, here and there, then faster and thicker until they could not see more than two feet ahead of them.

'Turn here,' she said. 'We can take shelter.'

Through a path overgrown with shrubbery they came to a folly built in the Classical style, though half covered with vines. Its floor was strewn with twigs and leaves.

'I see Lord Penford did not tend to all of the gardens,' Miss Summerfield said.

'Perhaps he did not know it was here.' Ross dismounted. 'It is well hidden.'

'Hidden now,' she said. 'It was not always so.'

He helped her down and led Spirit up the stairs into the shelter. There was plenty of room. She sat on a bench at the folly's centre and wrapped her cloak around her.

He sat next to her. 'Are you cold?'

Her cheeks were tinged a delightful shade of pink and her lashes glistened from melted snowflakes. 'Not very.'

He liked that she did not complain. He glanced around. 'This folly has seen better days?'

She nodded, a nostalgic look on her face. 'It was once one of our favourite places to play.'

'You have two sisters. Am I correct?'

She swung her feet below the bench, much like she must have done when a girl. 'And a half-brother.' She slid him a glance. 'My bastard brother, you know.'

Did she enjoy speaking aloud what others preferred to hide?

'He was raised with you, I think?' It was said Sir Hollis tried to flaunt his love child in front of his wife.

'Yes. We all got on famously.'

She seemed to anticipate unspoken questions and answered them defiantly.

'Where is your brother now?' he asked.

'Would you believe he is a sheep farmer in the Lake District?' she scoffed.

'Why would I not believe it?' Almost everyone he knew could be considered a farmer when you got right down to it.

'Well, if you knew him you'd be shocked that he wound up raising sheep. He was an officer in the Twenty-Eighth Regiment. He was wounded at Waterloo.' She waved a hand. 'Oh, I am making him sound too grand. He was a mere lieutenant, but he *was* wounded.'

'He must have recovered?' Or he would not be raising sheep.

'Oh, yes.'

'And your other sister?' He might as well get the whole family story, since she seemed inclined to tell it.

'Tess?' She giggled but tried to stop herself.

'What amuses you?'

'Tess is married.' She strained not to laugh. 'But wait until I tell you how it was she came to be married! She and Marc Glenville were caught together in a storm. A rainstorm. Lord Tinmore forced them to marry.'

How ghastly. Nothing funny about a forced marriage. 'I am somehow missing the joke.'

She rolled her eyes. '*We* are caught in a storm. *You* could be trapped into marrying me.' She wagged a finger at him. 'So you had better hope we are not discovered.' Then an idea seemed to dawn on her face. 'Unless you are already married. In that case, only I suffer the scandal.' She made it sound as if suffering scandal was part of the joke.

'I am not married.'

She grinned. 'We had better hope Lord Tinmore or his minions do not come riding by, then.'

No one would find this place unless they already knew its location, even if they were foolish enough to venture out in a snowstorm. If they did find them, though, Ross had no worries about Lord Tinmore. Tinmore's power would be a trifle compared to what Ross could bring to bear.

She took a breath and sighed and seemed to have conquered her fit of giggles.

'I am acquainted with Glenville,' he remarked. 'A good man.'

'Glenville *is* a good man,' she agreed.

He could not speak of why he knew Glenville, though.

He'd sailed Glenville across the Channel in the family yacht several times during the war when Glenville pursued clandestine activities for the Crown. Braving the Channel's waters was about the only danger Ross could allow himself during the war, even if he made himself available to sail whenever needed. This service had been meagre in his eyes, certainly a trifle compared to what his friend Dell had accomplished. And what others had suffered. He'd seen what the war cost some of the soldiers. Limbs. Eyes. Sanity. Why should those worthy men have had to pay the price rather than he?

He forced his mind away from painful thoughts. 'I had not heard Glenville's marriage had been forced.'

'Had you not?' She glanced at him in surprise. 'Goodness. I thought everyone knew. I should say they seem very happy about it now, so it has all worked out. For the time being, that is.'

'For the time being?'

She shrugged. 'One never knows, does one?'

'You sound a bit cynical.' Indeed, she seemed to cycle emotions across her face with great rapidity.

Her expression sobered. 'Of course I am cynical. Marriage can bring terrible unhappiness. My parents' marriage certainly did.'

'One out of many,' he countered, although he knew several friends who were miserable and making their spouses even more so. His parents' marriage had been happy—until his mother died. In his father's present marriage happiness was not an issue. That marriage was a political partnership.

'My sister Lorene's marriage to Lord Tinmore is another example.' She glanced away and lowered her voice as if speaking to herself and not to him. 'She is wasting herself with him.'

'Has it been so bad? She brought him out of his hermitage, they say. He'd been a recluse, they say.'

'I am sure *he* thinks it a grand union.' She huffed. 'He now has people he can order about.'

'You?' Clearly she resented Tinmore. 'Does he order you about?'

'He tries. He thinks he can force me to—' She stopped herself. 'Never mind. My tongue runs away with me sometimes.'

She fell silent and stilled her legs and became lost in her own thoughts, which excluded him. He'd been enjoying their conversation. They'd been talking like equals, neither of them trying to impress or avoid.

He wanted more of it. 'Tell me about your painting.'

She looked at him suspiciously. 'What about it?'

'I did not understand it.'

She sat up straighter. 'You mean because the sky was

purple and pink and the grassy hills, blue, and it looked nothing like December in Lincolnshire?'

'Obviously you were not painting the landscape as it was today. You said you painted a memory, but surely you never saw the scene that way.' The painting was a riot of colour, an exaggeration of reality.

She turned away. 'It was a memory of those bright childhood days, when things could be what you imagined them to be, when you could create your own world in play and your world could be anything you wanted.'

'The sky and the grass could be anything you wanted, as well. I quite comprehend.' He smiled at her. 'I once spent an entire summer as a virtuous knight. You should have seen all the dragons I slew and all the damsels in distress I rescued.'

Her blue eyes sparkled. 'I was always Boadicea fighting the Romans.' She stood and raised an arm. *"When the British Warrior queen, Bleeding from the Roman rods..."* She sat down again. 'I was much influenced by Cowper.'

'My father had an old copy of Spencer's *The Faerie Queene*.' It had been over two hundred years old. 'I read it over and over. I sought to recreate it in my imagination.'

She sighed. 'Life seemed so simple then.'

They fell silent again.

'Do you miss this place?' he asked. 'I don't mean this folly. Do you miss Summerfield House where you grew up?'

Her expression turned wistful. 'I do miss it. All the familiar rooms. The familiar paintings and furniture. We could not take much with us.' Her chin set and her eyes hardened. 'I do not want you to think we blame Lord Penford. He was under no obligation to us. We knew he inherited many problems my father created.' She stood again and walked to the edge of the folly. Placing her hand on one of the columns, she leaned out. 'The snow seems to be abating.'

He was not happy to see the flakes stop. 'Shall we venture out in it again?'

'I think we must,' she said. 'I do not want to return late and cause any questions about where I've been.'

'Is that what happens?' he asked.

'Yes.' Her eyes changed from resentment to amusement. 'Although I do not always answer such questions truthfully.'

'I would wager you do not.'

Rossdale again pulled Genna up to sit in front of him on his beautiful horse. How ironic. It was the most intimate she had ever been with a man.

She liked him. She could not think of any other gentleman of her acquaintance who she liked so well and with whom she wanted to spend more time. Usually she was eager to leave a man's company, especially when the flattery started. Especially when she suspected they were more enamoured of the generous sum Lord Tinmore would provide for her dowry than they were of her. No such avaricious gleam reached Rossdale's eyes. She had the impression the subject of her dowry had not once crossed Rossdale's mind.

They rode without talking, except for Genna's directions. She led him through the fields, the shortest way to Tinmore Hall and also the way they were least likely to encounter any other person. The snow had turned the landscape a lovely white, as if it had been scrubbed clean. There was no sound but the crunch of the horse's hooves on the snow and the huff of the animal's breathing.

They came to the stream. The only way to cross was at the bridge, the bridge that had been flooded that fateful night Tess had been caught in the storm.

'Leave me at the bridge,' she said. No one was in sight, but if anyone would happen by, it would be on the road to the bridge. 'I'll walk the rest of the way.'

'So we are not seen together?' he correctly guessed.

She could not help but giggle. 'Unless you want a forced marriage.'

He raised his hands in mock horror. 'Anything but that.'

'Here is fine.' She slid from the saddle.

He unfastened her satchel and handed it to her. 'It has been a pleasure, Miss Summerfield.'

'I am indebted to you, sir,' she countered. 'But if you dare say so to anyone, I'll have to unfurl my wrath.'

He smiled down at her and again she had the sense that she liked him.

'It will be our secret,' he murmured.

She nodded a farewell and hurried across the bridge. When she reached the other side, she turned.

He was still there watching her.

She waved to him and turned away, and walked quickly. She was later than she'd planned to be.

She approached the house through the formal garden behind the Hall and entered through the garden door, removing her half-boots which were soaked through and caked with snow. One of the servants would take care of them. She did not dare clean them herself as she'd been accustomed to do at Summerfield. If Lord Tinmore heard of it, she'd have to endure yet another lecture on the proper behaviour of a lady, which did not include cleaning boots.

What an ungrateful wretch she was. Most young ladies would love having a servant clean her boots. Genna simply was used to doing for herself, since her father had cut back on the number of servants at Summerfield House.

She hung her damp cloak on a hook and carried her satchel up to her room. The maid assigned to her helped her change her clothes, but Genna waited until the girl left before unpacking her satchel. She left her painting on a table, unsure whether to work on it more or not.

She covered it with tissue again and put it in a drawer. She would not work on it now. Of that she was certain. Instead she hurried down to the library, opening the door cautiously and peeking in. No one was there, thank goodness, although it would have been quite easy to come up with a plausible excuse for coming to the library.

She searched the shelves until she found the volume she sought—*Debrett's Peerage & Baronetage*. She pulled it out and turned first to the title names, riffling the pages until she came to the Rs.

'Rossdale. Rossdale. Rossdale,' she murmured as she scanned the pages.

The title name was not there.

She turned to the front of the book again and found the pages listing second titles usually borne by the eldest sons of peers. She ran her finger down the list.

Rossdale.

There it was! And next to the name Rossdale was *Kessington d.* D for Duke.

She had been in the company of the eldest son of the Duke of Kessington. The heir of the Duke of Kessington. And she had been chatting with him as if he were a mere friend of her brother's. Worse, she had hung all the family's dirty laundry out to dry in front of him, her defiant defence over anticipated censure or sympathy. He'd seen her wild painting and witnessed her nonsense about Boadicea.

. She turned back to the listing of the Duke of Kessington. There were two pages of accolades and honours bestowed upon the Dukes of Kessington since the sixteen hundreds. She read that Rossdale's mother was deceased. Rossdale's given name was John and he had no brothers or sisters. He bore his father's second title by courtesy—the Marquess of Rossdale.

She groaned.

The heir of the Duke of Kessington.

Chapter Two

Ross sipped claret as he waited for Dell in the drawing room. The dinner hour had passed forty minutes ago, not that he'd worked up any great appetite or even that he was in any great need of company. He was quite content to contemplate his meeting with Miss Summerfield. He'd been charmed by her.

How long had it been since a young woman simply conversed with him, about herself and her family skeletons, no less? Whenever he attended a society entertainment these days all he saw was calculation in marriageable young ladies' eyes and those of their mamas. All he'd seen in Miss Summerfield's eyes was friendliness.

Would that change? Obviously she'd not known the name Rossdale or its significance, but he'd guess she'd soon learn it. Would she join the ranks of calculating females then?

He was curious to know.

The door opened.

'So sorry, Ross.' Dell came charging in. 'I had no idea this estate business would take so long. I've alerted the kitchen. Dinner should be ready in minutes.'

Ross lifted the decanter of claret. 'Do you care for some?'

Dell nodded. 'I've a great thirst.'

Ross poured him a glass and handed it to him.

'First there is the problem of dry rot. Next the cow barn, which seems to be crumbling, but the worst is the condition of the tenant cottages. One after the other have leaking roofs, damaged masonry, broken windows. I could go on.' He took a swig of his wine.

'Sounds expensive,' Ross remarked with genuine sympathy.

How many estates did Ross's family own? Five, at least, not counting the hunting lodges and the town house in Bath. There were problems enough simply maintaining them. Think of how it would be if any were allowed to go into disrepair. This was all new to Dell, as well. He'd just arrived in Brussels with his regiment when he'd been called back to claim the title. His parents, older brother and younger sister had been killed in a horrific fire. Ross had delivered the news to him and brought him home.

A few weeks later Dell's regiment fought at Waterloo.

'A drain on the finances, for certain,' Dell said. 'Curse Sir Hollis for neglecting his property.'

'Do you have sufficient funds?' Ross asked.

His friends never asked, but when Ross knew they were in need he was happy to offer a loan or a gift.

Dell lifted a hand. 'I can manage. It simply rankles to see how little has been maintained.' He shook his head. 'The poor tenants. They have put up with a great deal and more now with this nasty weather.'

The butler appeared at the door. 'Dinner is served, sir.'

Dell stood. 'At least food is plentiful. And I've no doubt Cook has made us a feast.'

They walked to the dining room, its long table set for two adjacent to each other to make it easier for conversing and passing food dishes. The cook indeed had not disappointed. There were partridges, squash and parsnips. Ross's appetite made a resurgence.

'I hope your day was not a bore,' Dell said. 'Did you find some way to amuse yourself?'

'I did remarkably well,' Ross answered, spearing a piece of buttered parsnips with his fork. 'I rode into the village and explored your property.'

'And that amused you?' Dell looked sceptical.

'The villagers were talkative.' He pointed his fork at Dell. 'You are considered a prime catch, you know.'

Dell laughed. 'I take it you did not say who *you* were.'

Not in the village, he hadn't. 'I introduced myself simply as John Gordon.'

'That explains why there are no matchmaking mamas parked on the entry stairs.'

Ross smiled. 'I do believe tactics were being discussed to contrive an introduction to you.'

Dell shrugged. 'They waste their time. How can I marry? These properties of mine are taking up all my time.'

How many did he have? Three?

'I'm not certain your actual presence was considered important.' To so many young women, marrying a title was more important than actually being a peer's wife. 'In any event, it would not hurt to socialise with some of your more important neighbours, you know.'

'Who?' he asked unenthusiastically.

Ross took a bite of food, chewed and swallowed it before he answered. 'They said in the village that Lord Tinmore was in the country.'

'That prosy old fellow?' Dell cried.

'He's influential in Parliament,' Ross reminded him. 'It won't hurt at all to entertain him a bit. He might be a help to you when you take your seat.'

'Your father will help me.'

'My father certainly will help you, but it will not hurt to be acquainted with Tinmore, as well.' Ross tore off some meat from his partridge. 'You are related to Tinmore's wife and her sisters, I was told.'

'They are my distant cousins, I believe,' Dell said. 'The ones who grew up in this house.'

'Perhaps they would like to visit the house again.' Ross knew Genna would desire it, at least.

Dell frowned. 'More likely they would resent the invitation. I learned today that, not only was the estate left in near shambles, but the daughters were left with virtually nothing. My father turned them out within months of their father's death. That is why the eldest daughter married Tinmore. For his money.'

'Seems you learned a great deal.' No wonder Genna Summerfield sounded bitter.

Dell gave a dry laugh. 'The estate manager was talkative, as well.'

'Perhaps it would be a good idea to make amends.' And it would not hurt for Dell to be in company a little.

Dell expelled a long breath. 'I suppose I must try.'

Ross swirled the wine in his glass. 'I would not recommend risking offending Lord Tinmore.'

Dell peered at him. 'For someone with an aversion to politics, you certainly are cognizant of its workings.'

'How could I not be? My father talks of nothing else.' Ross refilled Dell's glass. 'I would not say I have an aversion, though. I simply know it will eventually consume my life and I am in no hurry for that to happen.'

Dell gulped down his wine and spoke beneath his breath. 'I never wanted this title.'

Ross reached over and placed his hand on Dell's shoulder. 'I know.'

They finished the course in silence and were served small cakes for dessert.

When that too was taken away and the decanter of brandy set on the table, Dell filled both their glasses. 'Oh, very well,' he said. 'I will invite them to dinner.'

Ross lifted his glass and nodded approvingly.

Dell looked him in the eye. 'Be warned, though. The youngest sister is not yet married.'

Ross grinned. 'I am so warned.'

Two days later, Genna joined her sister and Lord Tinmore at breakfast. Sometimes if she showed up early enough to share the morning meal and acted cheerful, she could count on being left to her own devices until almost dinner time. Besides, she liked to see if Lorene needed her company. There were often houseguests or callers who came out of obligation to the Earl of Tinmore. Most were polite to Lorene, but Genna knew everyone thought her a fortune hunter. Genna often sat through these tedious meetings so Lorene would not be alone, even though it was entirely Lorene's fault she was in this predicament.

A footman entered the breakfast room with a folded piece of paper on a silver tray. 'A message arrived for you, sir.'

Tinmore acknowledged the servant with a nod. The footman bowed and left the room again.

Tinmore opened the folded paper and read. 'An invitation,' he said, although neither Lorene nor Genna had asked. He tossed the paper to Lorene. 'From your cousin.'

'My cousin?' Lorene picked up the paper. 'It is from Lord Penford, inviting us to dinner tomorrow night at Summerfield House.'

Genna's heart beat faster. Was she included?

'We must attend, of course,' Tinmore said officiously. 'He peered over his spectacles at Genna. 'You, too, young lady.' He never called her by her name.

'I would love a chance to see Summerfield House again!' she cried.

Lorene did not look as eager. 'I suppose we must attend.'

The next day Genna was determined not to agonise over what to wear to this dinner. After all, it would be more in the nature of a family meal than a formal dinner party. There would not be other guests, apparently, save his houseguest, perhaps. A small dinner party, the invitation said, to extend his hospitality to his neighbour and his cousins.

Genna chose her pale blue dress because it had the fewest embellishments. She allowed her maid to add only a matching blue ribbon to her hair, pulled up into a simple chignon. She wore tiny pearl earrings in her ears and a simple pearl necklace around her neck. She draped her paisley shawl over her arm, the one with shades of blue in it.

She met Lorene coming out of her bedchamber.

Lorene stopped and gazed at her. 'You look lovely, Genna. That dress does wonders for your eyes.'

Genna blinked. Truly? She'd aimed to show little fuss.

'Do I look all right?' Lorene asked. 'I was uncertain how to dress.'

Lorene also chose a plain gown, but one in deep green. Her earrings were emeralds, though, and her necklace, an emerald pendant. The dark hue made Lorene's complexion glow.

Lorene looked like a creature of the forest. If Lorene were the forest, then Genna must be—what? The sky? Genna was taller. Lorene, small. Genna had blonde hair and blue eyes; Lorene, mahogany-brown hair with eyes to match. No wonder people whispered that they must have been born of different fathers. They were opposites. One earthbound. The other…flighty.

Genna put her arm around Lorene and squeezed her. 'You look beautiful as always. Together we shall present such a pretty picture for our cousin he will wish he had been nicer to us.'

Lorene smiled wanly. 'You are speaking nonsense.'

Genna grinned. 'Perhaps. Not about you looking beautiful, though.' They walked through the corridor and started down the long staircase. 'What is he, anyway? Our fourth cousin?'

Lorene sighed. 'I can never puzzle it out. He shares a great-great-grandfather or a great-great-great one with our father. I can never keep it straight.'

Genna laughed. 'He got the fortunate side of the family, obviously.'

They walked arm in arm to the drawing room next to

the hall where Lord Tinmore would, no doubt, be waiting
for them. Before they crossed the threshold, though, they
separated and Lorene walked into the room first, Genna a
few steps behind her. Tinmore insisted on such formalities.

Lord Tinmore was seated in a chair, his neckcloth loosened. His valet, almost as ancient as the Earl himself, patted
his forehead with a cloth. Tinmore motioned the ladies in,
even though they were already approaching him.

Lorene frowned. 'What is amiss, sir? Are you unwell?'

He gestured to his throat. 'Damned throat is sore and I
am feverish. Came upon me an hour ago.'

Lorene put her cloak and reticule on the sofa and pulled
off a glove. She bent down and felt her husband's wrinkled,
brown-spotted forehead. 'You are feverish. Has the doctor
been summoned?'

'He has indeed, ma'am,' the valet said.

She straightened. 'We must send Lord Penford a message. We cannot attend this dinner.'

Not attend the dinner? Genna's spirits sank. She yearned
to see her home again.

'I cannot,' Tinmore stated. 'But you and your sister
must.'

Genna brightened.

'No,' Lorene protested. 'I will stay with you. I'll see
you get proper care.'

He waved her away. 'Wicky will tend me. I dare say he
knows better than you how to give me care.'

So typical of Tinmore. True, his valet had decades more
experience in caring for his lordship than Lorene, but it was
unkind to say so to her face.

'I think I should stay,' Lorene tried again in a more
forceful tone.

Tinmore raised his voice. 'You and your sister *will* attend this dinner and make my excuses. I do not wish to insult this man. I may need his good opinion some day.' He
ended with a fit of coughing.

A footman came to the door. 'The carriage is ready, my lord.'

'Go.' Tinmore flicked his fingers, brushing them away like gnats buzzing around his rheumy head. 'You mustn't keep the horses waiting. It is not good for them to stand still so long.'

Typical of Tinmore. Caring more for his horses' comfort than his wife's feelings.

Genna picked up Lorene's cloak and reticule and started for the door. Lorene caught up with her and draped the cloak around herself.

At least Lord Tinmore was too sick to admonish Lorene for not waiting for the footman to help her with her cloak.

'I really do not want to go,' Lorene whispered to Genna.

'Lord Tinmore will be well cared for. Do not fret.' Genna was more than glad Tinmore would not accompany them.

'It is not that,' Lorene said. 'I do not wish to go.'

'Why not?' Genna was eager to see their home again, no matter the elevated company they would be in.

Lorene murmured, 'It will make me feel sad.'

Goodness. Was not Lorene already sad? Could she not simply look forward to a visit home, free of Tinmore's talons? Sometimes Genna had no patience for her.

But she took her sister's hand and squeezed it in sympathy.

They spoke little on the carriage ride to Summerfield House. Who knew what Lorene's thoughts must be, but Genna was surprised to feel her own bout of nerves at the thought of seeing Rossdale again.

The Marquess of Rossdale.

If he expected her to be impressed by his title, he'd be well mistaken. *She* would not be one of those encroaching young ladies she'd seen during her Season in London, so eager to be pleasing to the highest-ranking bachelor in the room.

Heedless of the cold, she and Lorene nearly leaned out the windows as they entered the gate to Summerfield House, its honey-coloured stone so familiar, so beautiful. She'd seen the house only from afar. Up close it looked unchanged, except that the grounds seemed well tended. At least what she could see of them. A thin dusting of snow still blanketed the land.

When the carriage pulled up to the house, Genna saw a familiar face waiting to assist them from the carriage.

'Becker!' she cried, waving from the window.

Their old footman opened the door and put down the stairs.

'My lady,' he said to Lorene, somewhat reservedly. He helped her out.

'So good to see you, Becker,' Lorene said. 'How are you? In good health?'

'Good health, ma'am,' he replied.

He reached for Genna's hand next and grinned. 'Miss Genna.'

She jumped out and gave him a quick hug. Who cared if it was improper to hug a servant? She'd known him all her life.

'I have missed you!' she cried.

His eyes glistened with tears. 'The house is not the same without you.'

He collected himself and led Lorene and Genna through one of the archways and up the stairs to the main entrance. A guidebook had once described the house:

Summerfield House was built by John Carr, a contemporary of Robert Adam, in the Italianate style, with the entrance to the house on the first floor.

Genna loved that word. *Italianate.*

The door opened as they reached it.

'Jeffers!' Genna ran into the hall and hugged their old

butler, a man who had been more present in her life than her own father.

'Miss Genna, a treat to see you.' He hugged her back, but quickly released her and bowed to Lorene. 'My lady, how good to have you back.'

Lorene extended her hand and clasped Mr Jeffers's hand in a warm gesture. 'I am happy to see you, Jeffers. How are matters here? Is all well? Are you well?'

He nodded. 'The new master has had much needed work done, but it is quiet here without you girls.'

Genna supposed Jeffers still saw them in their pinafores. She touched his arm. 'We were never going to be able to stay, you know.'

Jeffers smiled sadly. 'That is true, but, still…' He blinked and turned towards the door. 'Are we not expecting Lord Tinmore?'

'He sends his regrets,' Lorene explained. 'He is ill.'

'I am sorry to hear it. Nothing serious, I hope?' he asked.

'Not serious.' Lorene glanced away. 'You should announce us to Lord Penford, I think.'

How very sad. Lorene acted as if Lord Tinmore was looking over her shoulder, ready to chastise her for performing below her station with servants. These were servants they'd known their whole lives, the people who had truly looked out for their welfare, and, even though Tinmore was nowhere near, Lorene could not feel free to converse with them.

Jeffers looked abashed. 'Certainly. They are in the octagon drawing room.'

He and Lorene started to cross the hall.

'Wait!' Genna cried.

She stood in the centre of the hall and gazed up at the plasterwork ceiling. There was the familiar pattern, the rosettes, the gold gilt, the griffins that hearkened back to her grandfather's days in India. Why had she never drawn the ceiling's design? Why had she not copied its pale cream, green and white?

'Come,' Lorene said impatiently. 'They are waiting for us.'

Genna took one more look, then joined her sister. As they walked to the drawing room, though, she fell back, memorising each detail. The matching marble stairs with their bright blue balustrades, the small tables and chairs still in the same places, the familiar paintings on the walls.

They reached the door to the drawing room. Would it be changed? she wondered.

Jeffers opened the door and announced. 'Lady Tinmore and Miss Summerfield.'

Two young gentlemen stood. One, of course, was Lord Rossdale, dressed in formal dinner attire, which made him look even more like a duke's heir. The other man was an inch or two shorter than Rossdale and fairer, with brown hair and blue eyes.

Jeffers continued the introductions. 'My lady, Miss Summerfield, allow me to present Lord Rossdale—'

The Marquess bowed.

'And Lord Penford.'

But Penford was so young!

He approached them. 'My cousins. How delightful to meet you at last.' His voice lacked any enthusiasm, however. He blinked at Lorene as if in surprise and stiffly offered his hand. 'Where is Lord Tinmore, ma'am?'

Lorene blushed, which was not like her. She might be reserved, but never sheepish. Unless Tinmore had cowed her into feeling insecure in company. Or perhaps she was as surprised as Genna that Penford was not their father's age.

'Lord Tinmore is ill.' Lorene put her hand in Penford's. 'A trifling illness, but he thought it best to remain at home.'

Penford quickly drew his hand away. 'I am delighted you accepted my invitation.' He glanced past Lorene and looked

at Genna with a distinct lack of interest. 'And your sister.'
He perfunctorily shook Genna's. 'Miss Summerfield.'

The stiff boor. Genna made certain to smile at him.
'Call me Genna. It seems silly to stand on ceremony when
we are family.'

'Genna,' he repeated automatically. He glanced back
to Lorene.

'You may address me as Lorene, if you wish,' she murmured.

'Lorene,' he murmured. 'My friends call me Dell.'

Which was not quite permission for Lorene and Genna
to do so.

Rossdale stepped forward.

'Oh.' Penford seemed to have forgotten him. 'My friend
Ross here is visiting with me over Christmas.'

'Ma'am.' Ross bowed to Lorene. When he turned to
Genna, he winked. 'Miss Summerfield.'

She felt like giggling.

'Come sit.' Penford offered Lorene his arm and led her
to a sitting area, with its pale pink brocade sofa and matching chairs that their mother had selected for this room. He
placed her in one of the chairs and he sat in the other.

The Marquess gestured to Genna to sit, as well.

She hesitated. 'May I look at the room first?'

'By all means,' Penford responded.

'You lived here, I believe,' Rossdale said, remaining
at her side.

'I did, sir,' she said too brightly.

So far he was not divulging the fact they'd met before.
He stood politely while she gazed at another familiar plasterwork ceiling, its design mimicked in the octagon carpet
below. Again, nothing was changed, not one stick of furniture out of place, not one vase moved to a different table,
nor any porcelain figurines rearranged. She gazed at her

grandmother's portrait above the fireplace, powdered hair and silk gown, seated in an idyllic garden.

Rossdale said, 'A magnificent painting.'

'Our grandmother.' Although neither she nor Lorene bore any resemblance to the lady. 'By Gainsborough.'

'Indeed?' He sounded impressed.

Genna had always loved the painting, but it was Gainsborough's depiction of the sky and greenery that fascinated her the most, so wild and windy.

'I am pouring claret. Would you like some, Genna?' Penford called over to her.

She felt summoned. 'Yes, thank you.'

She walked over and lowered herself on to the sofa. Rossdale sat next to her.

'Does the room pass your inspection?' Penford asked, a hint of sarcasm in his voice.

He handed her the glass of wine.

Was he censuring her for paying more attention to the room than the people in it? Well, how ill mannered of him! It was the most natural thing in the world to want to see the house where one grew up.

'It is as I remember it,' she responded as if it had been a genuine question. 'I confess to a great desire to see all the rooms again. We were in much turmoil when we left.' When he'd sent them packing, she meant.

Penford's face stiffened. He turned to Lorene, shutting Genna out. 'Do you also have a desire to see the house?'

Lorene stared into space. 'I have put it behind me.'

'I imagine Tinmore Hall is much grander than Summerfield,' he remarked.

Grander and colder, Genna thought.

'It is very grand, indeed,' Lorene responded.

Genna turned to Rossdale. 'I expect the house where you grew up would make both Summerfield House and Tinmore Hall look like tenants' cottages.'

His brows rose. Now *he* knew *she* knew his rank.

'Not so much different.' His eyes twinkled. 'Definitely grander, though.'

'Ross grew up at Kessington,' Penford explained to Lorene. 'You have heard of it?'

Her eyes grew wide. Now Lorene knew Rossdale's rank, as well. Wait until Lorene told Tinmore whom he'd missed meeting.

'Yes, of course.' Lorene turned to Rossdale. 'It is in Suffolk, is it not?'

'It is,' he replied. 'And it is a grand house.' He grinned. 'My father should commission someone to paint it some day.'

He leaned forward to pour himself more wine and brushed against Genna's leg.

Secretly joking with her, obviously. What fun to flaunt a secret and not reveal it.

'I paint, you know,' she piped up, feigning all innocence. 'I even paint houses sometimes.'

'Do you?' Penford said politely. 'How nice to be so accomplished.'

Genna waited for him to ask Lorene her accomplishments, which were primarily in taking excellent care of her younger siblings for most of their lives. He did not ask, though, and Lorene would never say.

Genna could boast on her sister's behalf, though. 'Lorene plays the pianoforte beautifully. And she sings very well, too.'

Lorene gazed at her hands clasped in her lap. 'I am not as skilled as Genna would have you believe.'

'Perhaps you will play for us tonight,' Penford said, still all politeness.

'After dinner, perhaps?' Genna suggested.

'Perhaps after dinner you would show me the house, Miss Summerfield,' Rossdale asked. 'It would kill two birds with one stone, so to speak. Ease my curiosity about the building and give you your nostalgic tour.'

How perfect, Genna thought. Lorene would simply spoil her enjoyment if she came along and Lord Penford's presence only reminded Genna that all her beloved rooms now belonged to him. With Rossdale, she could enjoy herself.

She smiled. 'An excellent plan.'

Chapter Three

Ross enjoyed the dinner more than any he could recall in recent memory. Genna regaled them with stories about the house and their childhood years. She made those days sound idyllic, although if one listened carefully, one could hear the loneliness of neglected children in the tales.

Still, she made him laugh and her sister, too, which was a surprise. Heretofore Lady Tinmore had lacked any animation whatsoever. Dell was worse, though. He'd turned sullen and quiet throughout the meal.

It had never been Dell's habit to be silent. He'd once been game for anything and as voluble as they come. He'd turned sombre, though. Ross could not blame him. He simply wished Dell happy again.

In any event, Ross was eager to take a tour of the house with the very entertaining Genna.

After the dessert, he spoke up. 'I propose we forgo our brandy and allow Miss Summerfield her house tour. Then we can gather for tea afterwards and listen to Lady Tinmore play the pianoforte.'

Dell would not object.

'Very well,' Dell responded. He turned to Lady Tinmore as if an afterthought. 'If you approve, ma'am?'

'Certainly.' Lady Tinmore lowered her lashes.

She'd never let on if she did object, Ross was sure.

'What a fine idea! Let us go now.' Genna sprang to her feet and started for the door.

Ross reached her just as the footman opened it for her. She flashed the man a grateful smile and fondly touched his arm. These servants were the people she grew up with. Ross liked that she showed her affection for them.

They walked out the dining room and into the centre of the house, a room off the hall where the great staircase led to the upper floors.

'Where shall we start?' Ross asked.

Genna's expression turned uncertain. 'Would you mind terribly if we started in the kitchen? I would so much like to see all the servants. They will most likely be there or in the servants' hall. You may wait here, if you do not wish to come with me.'

'Why would I object?'

She smiled. 'Follow me.'

She led him down a set of stairs to a corridor on the ground floor of the left wing of the house. They soon heard voices and the clatter of dishes.

She hurried ahead and entered the kitchen. 'Hello, everyone!'

He remained in the doorway and watched.

The cook and kitchen maids dropped what they were doing and flocked around her. Other maids and footmen came from the servants' hall and other rooms. She hugged or clasped hands with many of them, asking them all questions about their welfare and listening intently to their answers. She shared information about her sisters and her half-brother, but, unlike her cynical conversation with Ross about her siblings, all was sunny and bright when she talked to the servants. So they would have no cause to worry, perhaps?

'Lorene—' she went on '*Lady Tinmore*, I mean—asked me to convey her greetings and well wishes to all of you. She is stuck with our host, I'm afraid, but I am certain she will ply me with questions about all of you as soon as we are alone.'

Ross remembered no such exchange between the sisters,

but it was kind of Genna to make the servants believe Lady Tinmore thought about them.

Finally Genna seemed to remember him. She gestured towards him and laughed. 'Lord Rossdale! I do not need to present you, do I? I am certain everyone knows who you are.' She turned back to the servants. 'Lord Rossdale begged for a tour of the house, but really only so I could see all its beloved rooms again and make this quick visit to you. I am told little has changed.'

'Only the rooms that were your parents,' the house-keeper told her. 'Lord Penford asked for a few minor changes in your father's room, which he is using for his own. He asked for your mother's room to be made over for Lord Rossdale.'

Ross turned to the housekeeper. 'He needn't have put you to the trouble, but the room is quite comfortable. For that I thank you.'

Genna looked pleased at his words. 'We should be on our way, though. I am sure Lady Tinmore will wish to return to Tinmore Hall as soon as possible, so we do not overstay our welcome.' She grinned. 'I am less worried about that. I'm happy for our cousin to put up with us for as long as possible. I am so glad to be home for a little while.'

But, of course, it would never be her home again.

There were more hugs and promises that Genna would visit whenever she could.

Ross interrupted the farewells. 'Might we have a lamp? I suspect some of the rooms will be dark.'

A footman dashed off and soon returned with a lamp. Genna extricated herself and, with eyes sparkling with tears, let Ross lead her away.

When they were out of earshot, she murmured, 'I miss them all.' She shot him a defiant look. 'No doubt you dis-approve.'

'Of missing them?'

'Of such an attachment to servants,' she replied.

He lifted his hands in protest. 'That is unfair, Miss Summerfield. What have I said or done to deserve such an accusation?'

She sighed. 'You've done nothing, have you? Forgive me. I tend to jump to conclusions. It is a dreadful fault. After this past year mixing in society, I learned to expect such sentiments. Certainly Tinmore would have apoplexy if he knew I'd entered the servants' wing. No doubt that is why Lorene stayed away.'

'Does your sister disapprove of fraternising with servants as well?' He would not be surprised. She seemed the opposite of Genna in every way.

'Lorene?' Her voice cracked. 'Goodness, no. But she tries not to displease Tinmore.' She shrugged. 'Not even when he could not possibly know.'

'What shall we see next?' he asked, eager to change the subject and restore her good cheer.

'I should like to see my old room,' she responded. 'And the schoolroom.'

They climbed the two flights of stairs to the second floor and walked down a corridor to the children's wing.

She opened one of the doors. 'This was my room.'

It was a pleasant room with a large window, although the curtains were closed. She walked through the space, subdued and silent.

'Is it as you remember?' he asked.

She nodded. 'Everything is in the right place.'

'You are not happy to see it, though.'

She shook her head. 'There is nothing of me left here. It could be anyone's room now.' She continued to walk around it. 'Perhaps Lorene knew it would feel like this. Perhaps that is why she did not wish to come.'

He frowned. 'I am sorry it disappoints you.'

She turned to him with a sad smile. 'It is odd. I do feel disappointed, but I also like that I am seeing it again. It helps me remember what it once was, even if the remembering makes me sad.'

Ross had rooms in his father's various residences, rooms he would never have to vacate, except by choice. For him the rooms were more of a cage than a haven.

'Let us continue,' she said resolutely.

They entered every bedroom and Genna commented on whose room it had been and related some memory attached to it.

They came to the schoolroom. She ran her fingers over the surface of the table. 'We left everything here.' She opened a wooden chest. 'Here are our slates and some of the toys.' She pointed to a cabinet. 'Our books will be in there.' She sighed. 'It is as if we walked out of here as children, probably to run out of doors to play.'

'To become Boadicea?' Ross remembered.

She smiled. 'Yes! Out of doors the fun began.' She clasped her hands together and perused the room one more time. 'Let us proceed.'

They peeked in other guest bedchambers, but she hesitated when they neared the rooms that had been her parents'. 'I certainly will not explore Penford's room.' She said the name with some disdain.

'You seem inclined to dislike my friend,' he remarked.

'Well, he might have let us stay here a while longer.' She frowned.

'Dell only inherited the title last summer. I believe your resentment belongs to his father.'

Her eyes widened. 'Oh. I did not know.'

Dell might not desire him to say more. Ross changed the subject. 'I have no objection to your seeing your mother's bedchamber,'

She recovered from her embarrassment and blinked up at him with feigned innocence. 'Me? Enter a gentleman's bedchamber accompanied by the gentleman himself? What would Lord Tinmore say?'

'This will be one of those instances where Lord Tinmore will never know.' He grinned. 'Besides, for propriety's sake we will leave the door open and I dare say my valet will be inside—'

Her eyes widened in mock horror. 'A witness? He might tell Lord Tinmore! We would be married post-haste, I assure you.'

She mocked the idea of being married, so unlike the other young women thrown at him.

Her expression turned conspiratorial. 'Although I am pining to show you something about the house, so we might step inside the room just for a moment.'

With no one else would Ross risk such a thing, for the very reason of which she'd joked.

He opened the door and, as he expected, his valet was in the room, tending to his clothes.

'Do not be alarmed, Coogan,' he said to his man. 'We will be only a moment.'

'Yes, Coogan.' Genna giggled. 'Only a moment.'

'Do you require something, m'lord?' Coogan asked. 'I was about to join the servants for dinner, but I can delay—'

'We are touring the house and Miss Summerfield wishes to show me something about the room,' Ross replied. 'Stay until we leave.'

Ross was glad to have a witness, just in case.

She stepped just inside the doorway and faced a wall papered in pale blue. She pressed on a spot and a door opened, a door that heretofore had been unnoticed by Ross.

'We'll be leaving now,' she said to his valet and gestured for Ross to follow her.

They could not have been more than a fraction of a minute.

As soon as he stepped over this secret threshold, she pushed the door closed. Their lamp illuminated a secret hallway that disappeared into the darkness.

'My grandfather built this house so that he would never

have to encounter his servants in the house unless they were performing some service for him. He had secret doors put in all the rooms and connected them all with hidden passages. The servants had to scurry through these narrow spaces. We can get to any part of the house from here.' She headed towards the darkness. 'Come. I'll show you.'

Dell remained in the dining room with Lorene until they'd both finished the cakes that Cook had made for dessert. Their conversation was sparse and awkward.

He'd never met his Lincolnshire cousins, knew them only by the scandal and gossip that followed the family and had no reason to give them a further thought. He'd not been prepared for the likes of Lorene.

Lovely, demure, sad.

When he and Lorene retired to the drawing room, he was even more aware of the intimacy of their situation. What had he been thinking to allow Ross and the all-too-lively Genna to go off into the recesses of the house? Why the devil had Tinmore not simply refused the invitation? Why send his wife and her sister alone?

He realised they were standing in the drawing room.

She gestured to the pianoforte. 'Shall I play for you?'

'If you wish.' It would save him from attempting conversation with her, something that seemed to fail him of late.

She sat at the pianoforte and started to play. After the first few hesitant notes, she seemed to lose her self-consciousness and her playing became more assured and fluid. He recognised the piece she chose. It was one his sister used to play—Mozart's *Andante Grazioso*. The memory stabbed at his heart.

Lorene played the piece with skill and feeling. When she came to the end and looked up at him, he immediately said, 'Play another.'

This time she began confidently—*Pathétique* by

Beethoven—and he fancied she showed in the music that sadness he sensed in her. It touched his own.

And drew him to her in a manner that was not to be advised.

She was married to a man who wielded much influence in the House of Lords. Dell would be new to the body. Ross was right. He needed to tread carefully if he wished to do any good.

When Lorene finished this piece, she automatically went on to another, then another, each one filled with melancholy. With yearning.

The music moved him.

She moved him.

When she finally placed her hands in her lap, they were trembling. 'That is all I know by heart.'

'Surely there is sheet music here.' He looked around the pianoforte.

She rose and opened a nearby cabinet. 'It is in here.' She removed the top sheet and looked at it. 'Oh. It is a song I used to play.'

'Play it if you like.' After all, what could he say to her if she stopped playing? His insides were already shredded.

She placed the sheet on the music rack, played the first notes and, to his surprise, began to sing.

I have a silent sorrow here,
A grief I'll ne'er impart;
It breathes no sigh, it sheds no tear,
But it consumes my heart.
This cherished woe, this loved despair,
My lot for ever be,
So my soul's lord, the pangs to bear
Be never known by thee.

Her voice was clear and pure and the feeling behind the lyrics suggested this was a song that had meaning for her.

What was her *'cherished woe'*, her *'loved despair'*? He knew what his grief was.

She finished the song and lifted her eyes to his.

'Lorene,' he murmured.

There was a knock on the door, breaking his reverie.

The butler appeared. 'Beg pardon, sir, my lady.'

'What is it, Jeffers?' Dell asked, his voice unsteady.

'The weather, sir,' Jeffers said. 'A storm. It has begun to snow and sleet.'

Lorene paled and stood. Dell stepped towards the window. She brushed against him as he opened the curtains with his hand. They both looked out on to ground already tinged with white. The hiss of sleet, now so clear, must have been obscured by the music.

She spun around. 'We must leave! Where is Genna?'

'I sent Becker to find her,' Jeffers said.

'Well done, Jeffers. Alert the stables to ready the carriage.' Dell turned towards Lorene. 'You might still make it home if you can leave immediately.'

Lorene placed her hands on her cheeks. 'We did not expect bad weather.'

Dell touched her arm, concerned by her distress. 'Try not to worry.'

'Where is Genna?' she cried, rushing from the room. 'Why did she have to tour the house?'

Genna led Ross through dark narrow corridors, stopping at doors that opened into the other bedchambers. On the other side, the doors to the secret passageways were nearly invisible to the eye. While they navigated this labyrinth, sometimes they heard music.

'Lorene must be playing the pianoforte,' Genna said.

The music wafting through the air merely made their excursion seem more fanciful.

It was like a game. Ross tried to guess what room they'd come upon next with the floor plan of the house fixed in his mind, but he was often wrong. Genna navigated the spaces with ease, though, and he could imagine her as a little girl running through these same spaces.

She opened a door on to the schoolroom. 'Is it not bizarre? The passageways even lead here. Why would my great-grandfather care if servants were seen in the nursery?'

'I wonder why he built the whole thing,' Ross said.

She grinned. 'It made for wonderful games of hide and seek.'

He could picture it in his mind's eye. The neglected children running through the secret parts of the house as if the passages had been created for their amusement.

'It even leads to the attic!' They came upon some stairs and she climbed to the top, opening a door into a huge room filled with boxes, chests and old furniture. Their little lamp illuminated only a small part of it.

Ross's shoe kicked something. He leaned down and picked up what looked like a large bound book.

'What is that?' she asked, turning to see.

He handed it to her and she opened it.

'Oh! It is my sketchbook.' Heedless of the dust, she sat cross-legged on the floor and placed the lamp nearby. She leafed through the pages. 'Oh, my goodness. I thought this was gone for ever!'

'What is it doing up here?' he asked.

'I hid it for safekeeping and then I could not remember where it was.' She closed it and hugged it to her. 'I cannot believe you found it!'

'Tripped over it, you mean.' He made light of it, but her voice had cracked with emotion.

When had he ever met a woman who wore her emotions so plainly on her sleeve? And yet…there was more she kept hidden. From everyone, he suspected. With luck the Christmas season would afford him the opportunity to see more of her.

She opened the book again and turned the pages. Illumi-nated by the lamp, her face glowed, looking even lovelier than she'd appeared before. Her hair glittered like threads of gold and her blue eyes were like sapphires, shadowed by long lashes. What might it be like to comb his fingers through those golden locks and to have her eyes darken with desire?

He stepped back.

For all the scandal in her family she was still a respect-able young woman. A dalliance with her would only dis-honour her and neither she nor he wished for something more honourable—like marriage.

The time was nearing when he would be forced to pick among the daughters of the *ton* for a wife worthy of be-coming a duchess. Not yet, though. Not yet.

She looked up at him. 'What should I do with it?'

'Take it, if you wish. It is yours.'

Her brow creased. 'Would Lord Penford mind, do you think? He might not like knowing I was poking through the attic.'

He shrugged. 'I cannot think he would care.'

She stood and, clutching her sketchbook in one hand, brushed off her skirt with the other. 'We were not supposed to take anything but personal items.'

He pointed to the book. 'This is a personal item.'

She stroked it. 'I suppose.'

He crouched down to pick up the lamp. 'In any event, we should probably make our way back to the drawing room.'

She nodded.

He helped her through the door and down the stairs. She led him through the secret corridor down more stairs to the main floor where they heard their names called.

'Genna! Where are you?' her sister cried.

'Ross! We need you!' Dell's voice followed.

Genna giggled. 'They must think we have disappeared into thin air.'

'Does your sister not know of the secret passageway?'

'She knows of it, but we really stopped using it years ago.' She paused. 'At least Lorene and Tess did.' She seized his hand. 'Come. We'll walk out somewhere where we will not be seen emerging from the secret passageway.'

They entered another hallway, and Ross had no idea where they were.

'This is the laundry wing.' She led him to a door that opened on to the stairway hall, but before stepping into the hall, she placed her sketchbook just inside the secret passage.

'Genna!' her sister called again, her voice coming from the floor above.

'We are here!' Genna replied, closing the door which looked nearly invisible from this side. 'At the bottom of the stairs.'

Her sister hurried down the stairs, Dell at her heels. 'Where have you been? We have been searching for you this half-hour!'

Genna sounded all innocence. 'I was showing Lord Rossdale the house. We just finished touring the laundry wing.'

'The laundry wing!' Lady Tinmore cried. 'What nostalgia did you have for the laundry wing?'

'None at all,' Genna retorted. 'I merely thought it would interest Lord Rossdale.'

'I assure you, it did interest me,' Ross replied as smoothly as his companion. 'I am always interested in how other houses are run.'

Dell tossed him a puzzled look and Ross shook his head to warn his friend not to ask what the devil he was about.

'Never mind.' Genna's sister swiped the air impatiently. 'The weather has turned dreadful. Jeffers has called for the carriage. We must leave immediately.'

Genna sobered and nodded her head. 'Of course.'

Jeffers appeared with their cloaks and Ross hurriedly

helped Genna into hers. As they rushed to the front door and opened it, a footman, his shoulders and hat covered with snow, was climbing the stairs.

'The coachman says he cannot risk the trip,' the footman said, his breath making clouds at his mouth. 'The weather prevents it.'

They looked out, but there was nothing to see but white.

'Oh, no!' Lady Tinmore cried.

Genna put her hands on her sister's shoulders and steered her back inside. 'Do not worry, Lorene. This could not have been helped.'

'We should have left earlier,' she cried.

'And you would have been caught on the road in this,' Dell said. 'And perhaps stranded all night. We will make you comfortable here. I will send a messenger to Lord Tinmore as soon as it is safe to do so.'

'We will have to spend the night?' Lorene asked.

'It cannot be helped,' Genna said to her. 'We will have to spend the night.'

Chapter Four

The lovely evening was over.

Although Lord Penford had tea brought into the drawing room, Lorene's nerves and Penford's coolness spoiled Genna's mood. Lorene was worried, obviously, about what Lord Tinmore would say when they finally returned and who knew why Penford acted so distantly to them? Why had he invited them if he did not want their company? Had he done so out of some sense of obligation? Even so, it was Lord Tinmore who'd compelled them to accept the invitation and she and Lorene certainly had not caused it to snow.

Not that it mattered. If Tinmore wished to ring a peal over their heads, reason would not stop him.

All the enjoyment had gone out of the evening, though.

Lord Penford poured brandy for himself and Rossdale and sat sullenly sipping from his glass while Rossdale and Genna made an effort to keep up conversation. With no warning Penford stood and announced he was retiring for the night. Rossdale was kind enough to keep Genna and Lorene company until the housekeeper announced that their bedchambers were ready. At that point they also felt they must say goodnight.

The housekeeper led them upstairs. 'We thought you might like to spend the night in your old rooms, so those are what we prepared for you.'

'Thank you,' Lorene said.

Genna gave the woman whom she'd known her whole life a hug. 'Yes, thank you. You are too good to us.'

The older woman hugged her back. 'We've found clean

nightclothes for you, as well. Nellie and Anna will help you.' Nellie and Anna had served as their ladies' maids before they'd moved.

They bade the housekeeper goodnight and Genna entered her bedchamber for the second time that night. At least now there was a fire in the grill and a smiling old friend waiting for her.

'How nice it is that you can stay the night,' Anna said. 'In your old room. Like old times.'

'It is grand!' Genna responded.

Anna helped her out of her dress and into a nightgown.

'Come sit and I'll comb out your hair,' Anna said.

Genna sat at her old familiar dressing table and gazed in her old familiar mirror. 'Tell me,' she said after a time. 'What are the servants saying about Lord Penford?'

Anna untied the ribbon in her hair. 'We are grateful to him. He kept most of us on and we did not expect that. He does seem angry when he learns of some new repair to the house, but his anger is never directed at the servants.'

'He must be angry at my father, then,' Genna said. Did his anger extend to the daughters, too? That might explain why he was so unfriendly.

'I suppose you are right.' She pulled out Genna's hairpins and started combing out the tangles. 'He paid us our back wages, you know.'

Genna glanced at her in the mirror. 'Did he? How good of him.'

Paying their back wages was certainly something Lord Penford could have avoided if he'd chosen to. What could the servants do if he'd refused to pay them?

Anna gave her a sly grin. 'Why are you not asking about Lord Rossdale?'

Genna felt her cheeks grow hot. Why would that happen? 'Lord Rossdale? Whatever for?'

She stopped combing. 'Is he sweet on you? We were wondering.'

'He's not sweet on me!' Genna protested. 'Goodness. He's far beyond my touch. Besides, you know that I'm not full of romantic notions like Lorene and Tess. He knew I wanted to see the house so he asked for a tour.'

'So he said in the kitchen.' Anna resumed combing. 'I am still saying he's sweet on you.'

Genna stilled her hand and met Anna's gaze in the mirror. 'Please do not say so. At least not to anyone else. I admit Lord Rossdale and I do seem to enjoy each other's company, but it is nothing more than that and I do not want any rumours to start. It would not be fair when he has merely been kind to me.'

Anna shrugged. 'If you say so.'

As soon as Anna left, Genna started missing her. She missed all these dear people. Now she would have to get used to not seeing them all over again. It was so very depressing.

She stared at the bed, not sleepy one bit. All she'd do was toss and turn and remember when her room looked like *her* room. She spun around and strode to the door.

Like she'd done so many times when she was younger, she crossed the hallway to Lorene's room and knocked on her door.

'Come in,' Lorene said.

Genna opened the door. 'I came to see how you are faring. You were so upset about the weather and our having to spend the night.' How the tables had turned. Genna used to run to Lorene for comfort, now it was the other way around.

Lorene lowered herself into a chair. 'I confess I am distressed. What will he think?' She did not need to explain who *he* was. 'Knowing we are spending the night with two unmarried gentlemen without any sort of chaperon.'

Genna sat on the floor at her feet and took Lorene's wringing hands in hers. 'We are home. Among our own servants. And Lord Penford and Lord Rossdale are gentlemen. There is nothing to worry over.'

Lorene gave her a pained look.

Genna felt a knot of anger inside. 'Will Tinmore…give you a tongue lashing over this?' Or worse, he might couch his cruelty in oh-so-reasonable words.

Lorene leaned forward and squeezed Genna's fingers. 'Do not worry over that! Good heavens, he is so good to us.'

Only when it suited him, though. He liked to be in charge of them.

Well, he might be in charge of Lorene, but Genna refused to give him power over her—even if she reaped the advantages of his money. She could not escape admitting that.

She smiled at Lorene. 'Let us enjoy our time back in our old rooms, then. Back *home*. Does it not feel lovely to be here?'

Lorene pulled her hands away and swept a lock of hair away from her face. 'I cannot enjoy it as you do, now that it is no longer our home.'

Genna secretly agreed. She did not enjoy seeing the rooms empty of any signs of her sisters or brother or herself, but she'd never admit it to Lorene. The best part of the house tour had been showing Rossdale the secret passages; the rest merely made her sad, just as Lorene had anticipated.

Genna stood. 'I love being back. I'm glad we can stay. I'll sleep in my old bed. I'll wake to sun shining in *my* windows. Cook will make us our breakfast again. It will be delightful.'

Lorene rose, too, and walked to the window. 'We had better hope the sun shines tomorrow.' She peeked out. 'It is still snowing.'

Genna gazed out on to the familiar grounds, all white now. 'We must not worry about tomorrow until it comes.' She turned to Lorene. 'How did you and Lord Penford fare while we toured the house?'

Lorene averted her face. 'I played the pianoforte.'

'We heard,' Genna said. 'You learned to play on that piano. How nice you were able to play on it again.'

'Yes,' Lorene replied unconvincingly. 'Nice.'

Cheering up Lorene was not working at all. It was merely making Genna feel wretched. 'Well, I believe I will go back to my room and snuggle up in my old bed. You've no idea how I've yearned to do so.'

Even if she feared she'd merely toss and turn.

She bussed her sister on the cheek and walked back to the room where she'd slept for years, ever since she'd left the nursery.

But once in the room, she found it intolerable. She paced for a few minutes, trying to decide what to do. Finally she made up her mind. She picked up a candle from the table next to her bed and carried it to the hidden door. She opened the door and entered the passageway.

She made her way downstairs and to the space where she'd left her sketchbook. As she picked it up and turned to go back to her room, the light from another candle approached. Her heart pounded.

'Miss Summerfield.' It was Lord Rossdale.

He came closer and smiled. 'I came to pick up your sketchbook. I see you had the same notion. I am glad you decided to keep it.'

She clutched it to her chest. 'I have not decided to keep it. I just wished to look at it in my room. I cannot take it back with me. It is too big to conceal and I do not wish to cause any problems.'

'I am certain Dell would wish you to have it,' he said.

She could not believe that. Even so, Lorene would probably worry about her taking it out of the house. 'I do not wish to ask him or to have my sister know. She would not like him bothered.' Genna was certain Lorene would not wish her to ask anything of Lord Penford.

Rossdale did not move, though, and the corridor was too narrow for Genna to get past him.

'Enjoy the book tonight, then,' he said finally. 'Come, I'll walk you back to your room.'

She laughed softly. 'More like you want me to show you the way so you do not become lost.'

He grinned. 'I am found out.'

He flattened himself against the wall so she could get by, but she still brushed against him and her senses heightened when they touched.

How strange it was to react so to such a touch. She did not understand it at all.

And she dared not think about it too much.

The next morning did indeed begin with the sun pouring in Genna's bedroom window. For a moment it seemed as if the last year had never happened. That was, until her gaze scanned the room.

Still, she refused to succumb to the blue devils. Instead she bounded from the bed and went to the window. Her beloved garden was still covered in snow, not only sparkling white, but also showing shades of blue and lavender in the shadows. The sky was an intense cerulean, as if it had been scrubbed clean of clouds during the night, leaving only an intense blue.

Genna opened the window and leaned out, gulping in the fresh, chilled air, relishing the breeze through her hair, billowing under her nightdress to tingle her skin.

'It is a lovely day!' she cried.

On a rise behind the house, a man riding a horse appeared. A grey horse and a grey-coated man.

Lord Rossdale.

He took off his hat and waved to her.

Imagine that he should see her doing such a silly thing. In her nightdress, no less! Perhaps he had heard her nonsense, as well.

She laughed and waved back before drawing back inside and shutting the window. She sat at her small table and turned the pages of her old sketchbook, remembering when life was more pleasant here.

Unfortunately, some of her drawings also reminded her of unhappy times. Hearing her father bellow about how much his daughters cost him, or rail against her mother who'd deserted them when Genna was small. Then there were the times when he'd consumed too many bottles from the wine cellar and she'd hidden from him. Her drawings during those times were sombre, rendered in charcoal and pencil, all shadowy and fearful.

Most of the pages, though, were filled with watercolours. Playful scenes that included her sisters and brother. Sunny skies, green grasses, flowers in all colours of the rainbow.

Her technique had been hopelessly childish, but, even so, her emotions had found their way on to the paper. The charcoal ones, obviously sad. The watercolours, happy and carefree.

A soft knock sounded at the door. Before Genna could respond, Anna opened the door and poked her head in.

She paused in surprise. 'Good morning, miss. I thought you would still be sleeping.'

Genna smiled. 'The sun woke me.' She closed the sketchbook and gestured to the window. 'Is it not a beautiful day?'

'It is, indeed, miss.' Anna entered the room and placed a fresh towel by the pitcher and basin Genna had used since a child. 'Mr Jeffers sent one of the stable boys with a message to Tinmore Hall.'

'That should relieve Lorene's mind.' Genna swung back to the window. 'How I would like it if I had my half-boots with me. I would love to be outside.' Even if she had her watercolours and brushes with her, she could paint the scene below and include all the colours she found in the white snow. That would bring equal pleasure.

She gazed out of the window again, wishing she were

galloping across the snow-filled fields. On a grey horse, perhaps. Held by a grey-coated gentleman.

She turned away with a sigh. 'I suppose I might as well wash up. Then you can help me dress.'

Anna also arranged her hair in a simple knot atop her head.

When she was done, Genna stood. 'I might see if Lorene is awake yet.' She turned to Anna and filled with emotion again. 'I do not know when I will see you again.' She hugged Anna. 'I shall miss you!'

Anna had tears in her eyes when Genna released her. 'I shall miss you, too, miss. We all miss you.'

Genna swallowed tears of her own. 'I will contrive to visit if I can.'

She left the room, knowing she was unlikely to see it again, ever, and knocked on Lorene's door.

Lorene was alone in the room seated in one of the chairs. Doing nothing but thinking, Genna supposed.

'How did you sleep?' Genna asked.

'Quite well,' Lorene responded. Of course, Lorene would respond that way no matter what.

'Anna told me a messenger was sent to Tinmore Hall,' Genna assured her.

Lorene merely nodded.

Genna wanted to shake her, shake some reaction, some emotion from her, something besides worry over what Lord Tinmore would think, say, or do. She wanted her sister the way she used to be.

'Shall we go down to breakfast?' Genna asked.

Lorene rose from her chair. 'If you like.'

They made their way to the green drawing room where breakfast was to be served. Lord Penford sat at the table, reading a newspaper. He looked startled at their entrance and hastily stood.

'Good morning,' he said stiffly. 'I did not expect you awake so early.'

'We are anxious to return to Tinmore Hall,' Lorene said.

'Yes,' Penford said. 'I imagine you are.'

'*I* am not so eager to return,' Genna corrected. 'I have enjoyed my visit to our old home immensely.' She looked over the sideboard where the food was displayed. 'Oh, look, Lorene. Cook has made porridge! It has been ages and ages since I've tasted Cook's porridge!

Becker, one of the footmen, attended the sideboard. Lorene made her selections, including porridge, and was seated next to Lord Penford at the small round breakfast table.

Becker waited upon Genna next, placing a ladle of oatmeal into a bowl for her. She added some cheeses, bread and jam.

'Thank you, Becker.' She smiled at him as he carried her plate to the table and seated her opposite her sister.

Penford sat as well although he did not look at either of them. 'I trust you slept well.'

Lorene hesitated for a moment before answering, 'Very well, sir.'

'Fabulously well!' added Genna. 'Like being at home.'

Lorene shot her a disapproving look, before turning to Penford. 'It was a kindness to put us in our old rooms.'

He glanced down at his newspaper. 'The housekeeper's decision, I am sure.'

Goodness! Could he be more sullen? 'I hope you did not disapprove.'

He shot her a surprised look. 'Why would I disapprove?'

She merely answered with a smile.

Why had he invited them if he seemed to take no pleasure in the visit? Unless his main purpose was to curry favour with Tinmore. If so, Genna was glad Tinmore had not accompanied them. Well, she was glad Tinmore had not accompanied them, no matter what Penford thought. Perhaps if Penford had been a more generous man, he might have left his cousins in the house to manage it in his absence.

He might have come to their rescue instead of tossing them out of the only home they'd ever known and forcing Lorene to make that horrible marriage.

Lorene broke in. 'The porridge is lovely. Just as I remembered it.'

Penford's voice deepened. 'I am glad it pleases you.' He put down his paper and darted Lorene a glance. 'I sent a man to Tinmore Hall early this morning. The roads are passable. You may order your coach at any time.'

He was in a hurry to be rid of them, no doubt.

'Might we have the carriage in an hour?' Lorene asked this so tentatively one would think she was asking for the moon instead of what Penford was eager to provide.

'Certainly.' Penford nodded towards Becker, who bowed in reply and left the room to accomplish the task.

Genna sighed and dipped her spoon into the porridge. She'd hoped to see Lord Rossdale one more time, but likely he was still galloping over the fields.

The rest of the breakfast transpired in near silence, except for the rattle of Lord Penford's newspaper and the bits of conversation exchanged between Genna and Lorene. Genna used the time to think about the house. Her time away had seemed to erase it as her home. Leave the place to the dour Lord Penford. Her life here was gone for ever. More of its memories had been captured in her sketchbook, but she had no confidence that it would ever return to her possession. Likely she would not even see Rossdale again.

When it came time for them to leave, the servants gathered in the hall to bid them goodbye, just as they had done when Genna and her sisters first removed to Tinmore Hall. This time the tears did not fall freely, although many bid them farewell with a damp eye. Lorene shook their hands. Genna hugged each of them. Lord Penford stood to the side and Genna wondered if he felt impatient for them to depart.

When the coach pulled up to the front, Penford walked

outside with them, without greatcoat, hat, or gloves. One of the coachmen helped Genna climb into the coach.

Lord Penford took Lorene's hand to assist her.

Lorene turned to him, but lowered her lashes. 'Thank you, sir, for inviting us and for putting us up for the night.' She lifted her eyes to him.

For a moment Penford seemed to hold her in place. He finally spoke. 'My pleasure.' He'd never seemed to experience pleasure from their visit. 'I shall remember your music.'

Lorene pulled away and climbed into the coach.

'Safe journey,' Penford said through the window.

As the coachman was mounting his seat, a horse's hooves sounded near. A beautiful silver-grey steed appeared beside the coach.

Rossdale leaned down from his saddle to look inside the coach. 'You are leaving already!'

Genna leaned out the window. 'We must get back.'

'Forgive me for not being here to say a proper goodbye.' His horse danced restlessly beside them.

Genna spoke in a false tone. 'I do not believe I shall forgive you.' She smiled. 'But thank you for allowing me to give you a tour of the house. It was most kind.'

He grinned. 'It certainly was more than I ever thought it would be.'

The coach started to move.

'Goodbye!' Genna sat back, but turned to look out the back window as the coach pulled away.

Rossdale dismounted from his horse and stood with Penford watching the coach leave.

They watched until the coach travelled out of their sight.

Chapter Five

Lorene fretted on the road back to Tinmore Hall. 'I wish we had not gone. He will have been frantic with worry when we did not return last night.'

Did she fear the effect of Tinmore's worry on his health or that he would blame her for their absence?

'He wanted us to go,' Genna reminded her. 'He ordered us to go.'

Lorene curled up in the corner of the carriage, making herself even smaller. 'Still, we should not have gone.'

Genna tried to change the subject. 'What did you think of our cousin, then? *Lord Penford.* Did you know he just inherited the title this summer?'

Lorene did not answer right away. 'I did not know that,' she finally said. 'Perhaps that was why he was so sad.'

'Sad?' Genna had not considered that. Perhaps he had not been disagreeable and rude. Perhaps he'd still been grieving. His father would have died only a few months before. She felt a pang of guilt.

'He's taking care of the house,' Genna said, trying to make amends, at least in her own mind. 'Anna said he paid the servants their back wages.'

'Did he?' Lorene glanced back at her. 'How very kind of him.'

Genna might have continued the conversation by asking what Lorene thought of Rossdale, but she didn't. She felt Lorene really wished to be quiet. Instead Genna recounted their tour of the house, intending to fix in her memory the details of each room they'd visited. More vivid, though, were Rossdale's reactions to those details. She'd enjoyed showing him the rooms more than she'd enjoyed visiting them.

Their carriage crossed over the bridge and the cupolas of Tinmore Hall came into view. The snow-covered lawn only set off the house more, its yellow stone gleaming gold in the morning sun. Genna's spirits sank.

She hated the huge mausoleum. The house hadn't seen a change in over fifty years. At least her mother had kept Summerfield House filled with the latest fashion in furnishings—at least until she ran off with her lover.

The carriage passed through the wrought-iron gate and drove up to the main entrance. Two footmen emerged from the house, ready to attend them. Moments later they were in the great hall, its mahogany wainscoting such a contrast to the light, airy plasterwork of Summerfield House.

Dixon, the butler, greeted Lorene. 'It is good you are back, m'lady.'

'How is Lord Tinmore?' she asked.

'His fever is worse, I fear, m'lady,' he responded. 'He spent a fitful night.'

Oh, dear. This would only increase Lorene's guilt.

'Did the doctor see him yesterday?' Lorene handed one of the footmen her cloak and gloves.

Dixon nodded. 'The doctor spent the night, caught in the storm as you were. He is here now.'

The doctor's presence should give Lorene some comfort.

'I must go to him.' Lorene started for the stairway. 'I ought to have been at his side last night.'

'He would not have known it if you were,' Dixon said.

Lorene halted and turned her head. 'He was that ill?'

'Insensible with fever, Wicky told us.'

'That is good, Lorene,' Genna broke in. 'He cannot be angry at you if he does not know you were gone.'

Lorene swung around. 'It is not good!' she snapped. 'He is ill.'

Genna felt her face grow hot. 'I am so sorry. It was a thoughtless thing to say.'

'And very unkind,' Lorene added.

'Yes,' Genna admitted, filled with shame. 'Very unkind. I am so sorry.'

Lorene turned her back on Genna and ran up the stairs.

Why could she not still her tongue at moments like these? She must admit she cared more about Lorene's welfare than Tinmore's health, but she did not precisely wish him to be seriously ill, did she?

She took a breath and glanced at Dixon. 'Is Lord Tinmore so very ill?'

His expression was disapproving. 'I gather so from Wicky's report.'

Genna deserved his disdain. By day's end the other servants would hear of her uncharitable comment and would call her an ungrateful wretch.

Which she was.

Over the next three days Genna hardly saw Lorene, who devoted all of her time to her husband's care. Genna would have happily assisted in some way—for Lorene's sake, not Tinmore's—but no one required anything of her and anything she offered was refused. She kept to her room, mostly, and amused herself by drawing galloping horses with tall, long-coated riders. She could never quite capture that sense of fluid movement she'd seen that day when she'd gone to make a painting of Summerfield House.

She had just finished another attempt and was contemplating ripping it up when there was a knock at her door. Her maid, probably. 'Come in,' she called, placing the drawing face down on her table.

'Genna—' It was Lorene.

Genna turned and rose from her chair. 'How is—?' she began.

Lorene did not let her finish. 'He is better. The fever

broke during the night and now he is resting more comfortably.'

'I am glad for you,' Genna said.

Lorene waved her words away.

Genna walked over to her. 'You look as if you need rest, too. Might you not lie down now?'

Lorene nodded. 'I believe I will. I just wanted you to know.'

'Thank you.' Genna felt careful, as if talking to a stranger. 'I am glad to know it.'

Lorene turned to leave, but a footman appeared in the corridor.

'My lady, two gentlemen have called to enquire after his lordship's health,' he said. 'Lord Rossdale and Lord Penford.'

Genna's heart fluttered. She would be excited for any company, would she not? Of course, they had not come to call upon her.

Lorene put a hand to her hair. 'Oh, dear. I am not presentable.' She turned to Genna. 'Would you entertain them until I can make myself fit for company?'

'Certainly. Anything to help.' Genna turned to the footman. 'Where are they?' There were so very many rooms in this house where visitors might be received.

'I put them in the Mount Olympus room,' he replied.

The room with the ceiling and walls covered with scenes from mythology, cavorting, nearly naked gods, all painted over a century before.

'Very good,' Lorene told him. 'Have Cook prepare some tea and biscuits.'

'Tea?' Genna said. 'Offer them wine. Claret or sherry or something.'

Lorene pursed her lips. 'Very well. Some wine, then, as well as tea and biscuits.'

The footman bowed and rushed off.

Lorene glanced at Genna.

'I can go down directly.' Genna took off the apron she wore to cover her dress and hurried to wash the charcoal off her fingers. She dried her hands. 'I'm off!'

Ross craned his neck and stared in wonder at the ceiling. It looked as if the mighty Zeus and all the lesser gods surrounding him might tumble down on to his head.

'This is quite a room,' he remarked. 'I am reminded of our Grand Tour—the palaces of Rome and Venice. Remember the murals? On every ceiling it seemed.'

'A man cannot think. The room fills the mind too much,' Dell responded.

Ross grinned. 'We did not do much thinking in those days, did we?'

Dell nodded, his face still grim. 'None at all, I recall.'

Ross perused the ceiling and walls again. 'In those days we would have been riveted by the naked ladies.' He stopped in front of one such figure, a goddess who appeared as if she would step out from the wall and join them.

Dell paced. 'Remind me again why we were compelled to come here?'

Ross had already explained. 'You wanted to become acquainted with Lord Tinmore, so calling to enquire after his health is only polite, especially after his illness kept him away from your dinner.'

The door opened and both men turned. Ross smiled. It was Genna, the one person he'd hoped to see when he concocted this scheme to call at Tinmore Hall.

Genna strode over to them. 'Rossdale. Penford. How good of you to call. My sister will be here in a few minutes. She has ordered refreshment for you, as well.'

Dell frowned. 'Lord Tinmore is still ill, then?'

'Lorene can better answer your questions.' She gave Dell a cordial smile. 'But, yes, Tinmore remains unwell.'

She gestured to the gilt stools cushioned in green damask that lined the walls of the room. 'Do sit.'

The room was in sore need of a rearrangement of furniture more conducive to conversation, Ross thought. A style more in tune with the present.

'Tell me, how is the weather?' Genna asked politely. 'I see our snow still covers the fields. Was it not terribly cold to ride this distance?'

'Not so terribly cold.' Ross kept his expression bland. 'I suspect some people would consider walking this far even when it is cold outside.' He darted a glance her way and saw she understood his joke.

'We felt it our duty to enquire into Lord Tinmore's health,' Dell said solemnly.

'How very good of you,' she responded, her voice kind.

Ross gave her an approving look.

'How were the roads?' she asked.

Dell shrugged. 'Slippery in places, but the horses kept their footing.'

'I think they relished the exercise,' Rossdale added. He'd relished it, as well.

She looked at a loss for what else to say. He fished around to find a topic and rescue her from having to make conversation.

She beat him to it. 'Tell me, do you plan to stay at Summerfield House for Christmastide?'

'At present that is our plan,' Dell responded.

Genna looked surprised. 'Do you not travel to visit your families?'

Dell averted his gaze and Rossdale answered. 'We decided to avoid all that.'

He hoped his tone warned her not to ask more about that. Dell's grief at the loss of his entire family was still raw. It was why Ross had elected to pass up a Christmas visit to his father at Kessington Hall. So he could be with his friend at such a time.

That and because he preferred his friend's company

to the politically advantageous guests his father always invited.

'What are your plans?' Ross asked her.

She sighed. 'Lord Tinmore plans a house party. Several of his friends will come to stay.' She did not seem to look forward to this. 'Guests should arrive next week.'

'No, they will not.' Her sister entered the room. Genna and the gentlemen stood. 'How do you do, sirs? It is kind of you to call.'

Dell's voice turned raspy. 'How—how fares Lord Tinmore?'

Lady Tinmore glanced up at him, then gazed away. 'He is better. The fever broke, but he remains too weak to receive callers.'

'We do understand,' Dell said stiffly. 'Please send our best wishes for his recovery.'

Lady Tinmore darted another glance at him. 'I will. Thank you, sir.'

Dell seemed uncomfortable around these sisters. Not ready for even this relatively benign social call?

Genna turned to her sister. 'What did you mean the guests will not arrive next week?'

Her sister replied, 'Tinmore has asked that the house party be cancelled. His secretary is to write to the guests today.'

The refreshments arrived. Ross and Dell accepted glasses of wine and offers of biscuits.

Ross stepped away while Lady Tinmore poured for Dell. To his delight, Genna joined him.

He wanted a chance to speak to her. 'Are you disappointed about the house party?' he asked.

She laughed. 'Not at all. I do not rub well with Lord Tinmore's friends.'

Her sister heard her and snapped, 'It is cancelled because Lord Tinmore needs the time to recover. He has been very sick, Genna.'

'I know that, Lorene,' Genna said softly.

Ross felt for her. No one liked being reprimanded in front of others.

He took a sip of his wine. 'Tell me about this room, Lady Tinmore. It is quite unusual.'

'It is called the Mount Olympus room,' Lady Tinmore responded, sounding glad to change the subject. 'Depicting the Greek gods. My husband said it was painted over one hundred years ago by the Italian muralist, Verrio. He painted a similar scene even more elaborate at Burghley House. And one at Chatsworth, as well. My husband prefers this one, though.'

Ross noticed Genna gazing at the walls and ceiling as if seeing them for the first time.

'It is hard to imagine one even more elaborate,' he said diplomatically. 'Although it does remind me of rooms we saw in Rome and Florence and Venice.'

'You've visited Rome and Florence and Venice?' Genna's eyes grew wide.

'We did indeed,' Ross replied. 'On our Grand Tour. You would have appreciated the fine art there.'

'Lord Tinmore's grandfather and great-grandfather collected many fine pieces of Italian art. They are hung in almost every room of this house,' Lady Tinmore said almost dutifully.

'They are?' Genna looked surprised.

Dell drained the contents of his wineglass and placed it on the table. 'We must take our leave.' He spoke to Lady Tinmore, but did not quite meet her eye. 'I do hope Lord Tinmore continues to improve.'

'Thank you,' she murmured.

Ross bowed to her. 'It was a pleasure seeing you again, ma'am.' He turned to Genna. 'And you, Miss Summerfield. I hope we meet again.'

'Yes.' Genna smiled. 'I would enjoy that.'

Perhaps he could convince Dell to call upon Lord Tinmore again. Or he could call upon the gentleman himself, although he had less reason to do so and no interest in meeting the man. He merely wanted to see Genna again.

And he still must devise a way to deliver her sketchbook to her as he had promised.

Before Ross could say another word, Dell strode out of the room as if in a hurry. Ross was compelled to follow, although he did so at a more appropriate pace.

He also turned back to the ladies when he reached the door. 'Good day, ma'am. Miss Summerfield.'

When he caught up to Dell in the hall, Dell had already sent the footman for their greatcoats, hats and gloves.

'What the devil was the rush?' Ross asked him.

'We were intruding.' Dell did not meet his eye. 'Tinmore is still ill. Sick enough for him to cancel his house party. The last thing Lady Tinmore needs are callers.'

'She did not seem to mind,' Ross insisted.

The footman brought their coats and assisted in putting them on. 'Your horses are being brought from the stable.'

They waited in uncomfortable silence until the horses were outside the door.

They were on the main road from the estate before Ross spoke. 'What is amiss, Dell?'

'Amiss?' he shot back. 'I told you. We were intruding. I should not have allowed you to talk me into this visit.'

Ross spoke in a milder tone. 'I did not see any indication that we were not welcome. Lady Tinmore seemed very gracious. I think she appreciated our concern for her husband.'

'She was gracious,' Dell admitted, sounding calmer. 'She was—' He cleared his throat. 'Perhaps we might call again. In a week or so, when we are certain of Tinmore's recovery.'

Genna and Lorene waited at the window until they saw Rossdale and Penford ride away.

Lorene then turned to tidy up the wineglasses and plate of biscuits, putting them back on the tray, something for which her husband would chastise her if he knew of it.

Acting like a servant, he would say.

Genna liked those old habits of Lorene's—her tendency to take care of things and save others the trouble.

Genna put her hands on her hips and stared at the Mount Olympus mural. 'I had not noticed before, but this really is a remarkable painting.' Verrio had painted the perspective so skilfully the figures in the painting appeared to be stepping into the room. Remarkable.

A footman had stepped into the room, ready to take the tea tray away.

Genna walked out of the room with Lorene. 'How serious is Lord Tinmore's illness?' she asked. 'I confess, I was surprised he cancelled the house party.'

'He is very weak, but his breathing is less laboured.'

The footman opened the door for them and Genna wondered what he thought about her ladyship tidying the room.

Lorene continued talking. 'If he had not cancelled it today, there would not have been enough time for letters to reach everyone. He did not want guests arriving with him lying abed. He said I should have known to cancel the house party two days ago.'

'Did he?'

And if Lorene had cancelled it, he would have been angry at her for interfering with his plans. But Genna would not say so to Lorene, who was still too sensitive on the subject of her husband. Genna missed being able to speak her mind to Lorene, but even more she wished she could ease Lorene's hurt feelings. Lorene would never complain to her, though.

They entered the hall and started up the stairway.

'How did you find Lord Penford?' Genna asked instead. That seemed like a safe subject.

Lorene avoided looking at her. 'What do you mean?' Her voice was sharp.

That took Genna by surprise. 'No special reason. You thought him sad before. I wondered if that was why he seemed so uncomfortable.'

'I think he realised it was not a good day to call,' Lorene said, as if defending him.

Genna had not intended any criticism of the man. 'Perhaps.' Better to agree than risk an argument. 'I suspect you are right.'

They reached the first floor where Lorene's set of rooms were located. And Lord Tinmore's.

'Is there anything I can do for you, Lorene?' Genna asked.

'Nothing,' her sister said.

'You will rest this afternoon, then?' Lorene still looked very fatigued.

'I will.' Lorene smiled wanly. 'I believe I will have dinner sent up to my room. May I tell Cook you will not expect to be served at the table?'

'Of course you may!' Genna assured her. 'A simple plate will do very nicely for me. Whatever is on hand.'

She was not the servants' favourite at any time, even though she tried never to put them to too much trouble for her. Like expecting a full meal prepared and served to her alone.

She reached over to buss Lorene's cheek. 'Promise you will rest.'

Lorene nodded.

Genna walked up another flight of stairs to her bedchamber. As she entered the room, a wave of loneliness washed over her. She had never felt lonely at Summerfield House—well, almost never. But here she felt so very alone.

She hadn't felt lonely with Rossdale. In fact, she'd felt happy, as if she'd found a real friend.

Right now, he felt like her only friend.

Chapter Six

Having dinner in the dining room was no pleasure. Lord Tinmore recovered well over the next few days, well enough to dress for dinner and to expect his wife and her sister to do the same. Genna complied, of course, and placed herself on her best behaviour. She was well capable of being agreeable at mealtime, especially when Lord Tinmore expected an audience rather than conversation.

They dined in the formal dining room, but at one end of the table. Lord Tinmore sat at the table's head. Lorene sat to her husband's right and Genna to his left. He was a little deaf in his left ear so there was little need for Genna to speak. Mr Filkins, his secretary, who was nearly as old as he, also dined with them. Filkins was seated next to Lorene, the side of the table upon which Tinmore focused most of his attention.

By the time the main course was served Tinmore had exhausted a recitation of the frequency of his cough, the colour of his phlegm and the irregularities of his bowels, to which Mr Filkins made appropriately sympathetic comments.

He went on to lament his decision to cancel the house party.

'I now see I will be quite well enough,' he said. 'I should have known I would recover swiftly. I have a strong constitution.'

'That you do, sir,' agreed Mr Filkins. 'But you had to decide quickly and I believe you made the most prudent of choices.'

'Yes,' Tinmore readily agreed with him. 'Besides, what is done cannot be undone.' He pointed his fork at Genna. 'Although I had high hopes for you, young lady. There was many a good catch invited to that party.'

Yes. Eligible men of Tinmore's age looking for a young wife to take care of them and their sons and grandsons looking for a dowry big enough to tempt them.

'A lost opportunity,' Genna said.

'What?' Tinmore cupped his ear.

'A lost opportunity,' she said louder.

Tinmore stabbed a piece of meat with his fork and lifted it to his mouth. After he chewed and swallowed it, he glanced at Lorene. 'You never told me about the dinner with Lord Penford.'

How like Tinmore to accuse rather than merely ask.

'You were so ill, I put it entirely out of my mind,' Lorene said.

'Put it out of your mind? Something as important as all that? Where is your head, my dear?' He took another bite of meat and waved his fork at her. 'Well, how was it? Were you treated well?'

Lorene responded as if she'd been asked with some kindness. 'We were treated very well, I assure you. Were we not, Genna?'

Genna nodded. 'Very well.'

Lorene went on, 'Although Lord Penford was disappointed you were unable to attend.'

Tinmore looked pleased at that. 'What did he serve?'

Goodness. Genna hardly remembered. Lorene, though, provided a rather thorough list of the courses. Genna wondered if she made up some of them.

'Was he a reasonable fellow, this Penford?' he went on to ask. 'I knew his father.' He would have seen the late Lord Penford in the House of Lords last Season. 'I have great hopes of turning the son to my views. Get them while they are new, you know.'

Mr Filkins laughed appreciatively.

'He was very amiable,' Lorene said. 'Although he and his friend did not talk politics with us at all, did they, Genna?'

'Not at all,' Genna agreed.

Tinmore straightened. 'His friend? Who was this friend?'

'Lord Rossdale,' Lorene responded.

Tinmore half-rose from his seat. 'Rossdale? Rossdale? The Duke of Kessington's son?'

'Yes, that is who he was,' Lorene responded. 'He was very nice, as well.'

'The Duke's son?' He pounded his knife down on the table. 'You should have told me you dined with the Duke's son.'

'Well, you were ill,' Genna said.

Tinmore turned to her. 'What, girl? Speak up. Do not mumble.'

She raised her voice. 'You were ill!'

He ignored her response. 'Kessington is the last man I would wish to offend. We must do something about this immediately!'

'I do not believe Lord Rossdale was offended,' Lorene assured him. 'He offered kind condolences over your illness when they called here the other day.'

'The Duke's son called here the other day?' Tinmore's face was turning red.

Lorene reached over and patted his arm. 'Do not make yourself ill over this. I am sure they understood completely that you were too ill to receive them. Perhaps we can invite them for dinner one night when you are a little stronger.'

'Dinner. Excellent idea,' Tinmore said.

'Excellent idea,' Mr Filkins agreed.

Tinmore pointed the knife towards him. 'But we must not wait. Must do something immediately.'

'Might I suggest a letter?' Mr Filkins offered. 'I will

pen something this very night and if it meets with your approval it can be delivered to Lord Rossdale in the morning.'

'A letter. Yes. A letter is the thing.' Tinmore popped a piece of potato into his mouth. 'But address it to Penford. He was the host. Make certain you mention Rossdale in it.'

'I quite comprehend, sir,' the secretary said. 'An excellent point.'

Genna smiled to herself. At least she would see Rossdale again.

'In fact,' Tinmore went on, 'invite them for Christmas Day.' He turned to his wife. 'Do you know if they are staying through Christmastide?'

Lorene nodded. 'That is what they told us. Through to Twelfth Night, at least.'

'Ha!' Tinmore laughed. 'We shall have a house party after all. At least Christmas dinner with elevated company.' He tossed a scathing look at Genna. 'Rossdale is not married. But you come with too much baggage to tempt him.'

Baggage?

The sins of her mother and father, she supposed. As well as her sisters and brother. She'd not done anything to deserve society's censure.

At least not yet.

On Christmas Day Ross and Dell made an appearance at the parish church for morning services and later in the day rode over to Tinmore Hall in Dell's carriage. The invitation to Christmas dinner had been somewhat of a surprise, albeit a welcome one for Ross. He was eager to call upon Genna again and curious to meet the formidable Lord Tinmore. Dell seemed less enthusiastic. Less enthusiastic than he'd been when first he'd invited Tinmore to dinner. Then he'd thought it prudent to ingratiate himself to the old lord, but now he seemed to relish meeting the man as much as one might look forward to having a tooth pulled.

The nearer the carriage brought them to Tinmore Hall, the bigger Dell's frown seemed to grow.

'Are you certain it will not be thought presumptuous to bring presents?' Dell asked.

Gifts had been Ross's idea. 'Presumptuous? Guests always brought my father gifts for his Christmas parties.'

Dell shot him a glance. 'Then if Tinmore seems offended, you must tell him that it was your father's custom.'

'I will.' Ross grinned. 'I dare say that will make the practice quite appreciated.'

The roof line of Tinmore Hall came into view in all its Elizabethan glory. As they passed through the gate, a herd of deer bounded across the park, their hooves kicking up clods of snow from the patches that still dotted the grass.

'At least it is merely a dinner and not a house party,' Dell said. 'I would detest having to spend the night.'

That would not have brought pleasure, would it? Ross agreed silently. No secret passages to explore. No surprise meetings when others were abed. Still, a conversation with Genna would prove stimulating. The closer Christmas Day came, the more withdrawn Dell had become. Ross supposed his friend remembered what his Christmases used to be like.

The carriage drew up to the entrance and four footmen emerged, forming a line to the carriage door. They were ushered into the hall, their cloaks taken and packages carried behind them as the butler led them to the Mount Olympus room and announced them.

The room was fragrant with greenery and spice. Garlands of evergreen were draped around the windows, holly, red with berries, lined the mantelpiece. Bowls of apples sat on the tables. Ross glanced up. Mistletoe hung in the doorway.

Seated in the huge room were Lord Tinmore and his wife, an incongruous pair. Tinmore, who must have been in his seventies at least, had the pallor and loose skin typical of an aged man who'd lost whatever looks he might have once possessed. He was thin, with rounded posture, but still his presence seemed to dominate the room. His wife, on the other hand, was a beauty in her prime. Flawless skin, rich dark hair, clear eyes and pink lips. A figure any man would admire, but she seemed a mere shadow in the wake of her husband's commanding presence.

Ross preferred her sister, who sparkled with life.

Tinmore, using a cane, rose from his chair. 'Good to see you. Good to see you. Happy Christmas to you.'

Ross and Dell crossed the room to him.

Lady Tinmore stood at her husband's side and made a more personal introduction. 'May I present my cousin, Lord Penford, and his friend, Lord Rossdale?'

Dell bowed. 'A pleasure, sir, to meet you.'

'And you, sir,' Tinmore said to Dell. He turned to Ross. 'Knew your grandfather. A decent man.'

'I have always heard so.' Ross hardly remembered his grandfather. The only image he could conjure up was of a remote figure, always busy, too busy to bother with an inquisitive, energetic boy. Rather like his father became after Grandfather died.

'Please, do sit,' Lady Tinmore said. 'We have refreshments.' She turned towards the fireplace where a bowl sat on the grate. 'Wassail, for you.'

A footman in attendance ladled wassail into a glass, which Ross took gratefully. The carriage ride had given him a thirst.

Tinmore asked about the carriage ride. The conditions of the road were discussed and the weather, of course, and the fine quality of the drink. The church services and sermons were compared, a devious way for Tinmore to discover whether they had attended the services at their parish.

Tinmore had not attended church, but his wife and her sister had.

And where was her sister?

He took the first opportunity to ask. 'Will we have the pleasure of Miss Summerfield's company today?'

Lady Tinmore frowned slightly. 'She should be here. I dare say something has detained her.'

'I am here!' Genna burst into the room, her arms laden with packages wrapped in brown paper and string. 'I was wrapping gifts.'

'Gifts?' Tinmore said disparagingly.

Ross rose from his chair. 'We also brought gifts. My father always insisted on gifts on Christmas Day.' He looked around. 'Although I am not quite sure what has become of them.'

Tinmore gestured to a footman, who bowed and left the room.

Genna placed her packages on a table and walked up to Dell and Ross. 'How delightful you could be with us today.' She smiled. 'Happy Christmas!'

Ross shook her hand. 'Happy Christmas, Miss Summerfield.'

Tinmore had not stood at her entrance. 'You are late, girl.'

Her smile stiffened. 'I do apologise, sir. I fear the wrapping took longer than I had anticipated.'

She sat on the sofa next to her sister, which placed her next to Ross's chair. She glanced at him as she sat and her smile softened again.

'I hope you have not been extravagant, girl,' Tinmore said. 'I do not provide you an allowance for frivolities.'

How ungentlemanly of Tinmore to make it a point that her allowance came from him.

She lowered her voice. 'I assure you. I was not extravagant.'

The footman handed her a glass of wassail and she took a sip.

Dell asked a question about the next session of Parliament and Ross was grateful to him for deflecting Tinmore's attention from Genna.

Not wanting to spend the holiday discussing politics, Ross turned to the ladies. 'The room smells and looks like Christmas.'

'It was Lorene's doing,' Genna said. 'I think it turned out lovely.'

'Lovely, indeed.'

Lady Tinmore's cheeks turned pink at the compliment. 'Genna helped.'

Genna grimaced. 'She means I supervised the gathering of the greens. The decoration was completely up to Lorene.'

'You did well, ma'am,' he said.

Genna gazed around the room and looked as if she was trying to stifle a laugh. 'It is a bit incongruous, though, do you not think? All these Roman gods amidst greenery meant to celebrate the Christian holiday.'

'The gods appear to be joining in the revelry,' he responded.

It was amusing that this room in particular was used to entertain guests on this special day, especially because this house must have several other drawing rooms that would be suitable. Was this chosen as the most impressive?

Lady Tinmore's brows knitted and Ross suspected she did not see the humour so evident to her sister.

Lady Tinmore changed the subject. 'We will eat dinner early. In a few minutes, perhaps. I hope that will be to your liking?'

Ross took a sip of his wassail. 'I am usually ready to eat at any moment of the day, so whatever you have planned will suit me very well.' He glanced at Genna. 'Perhaps after dinner there will be time for you to give me a tour of this house.'

She smiled. 'I would be pleased to do so.'

* * *

They'd had time enough to finish the wassail when Dixon announced dinner.

Mr Filkins, Tinmore's secretary, had not been included in the meal. Genna supposed the poor man was eating in his room alone on this day, which did not seem at all right to her.

The conversation was not as lively or amusing as it had been when she and Lorene had shared a meal with Rossdale and Penford at Summerfield House. It was dominated by Lord Tinmore and, as such, did not include Genna. She was seated across from Rossdale, but unable to speak with him. If only he'd been seated at her side they might have been able to have a little private conversation.

'Your father is Whig, is he not, Rossdale?' Tinmore asked.

'Very,' Rossdale responded.

'And yourself?' Tinmore went on.

'Me?' Rossdale responded. 'I am not in politics.'

'But you must have a party, a set of beliefs?' Tinmore took a bite of roast goose.

'Must I?' he answered. 'I can see no reason at the moment. When my father dies, I will choose, but I am in no hurry to do so.'

'Odd thing, not declaring your party.' Tinmore turned to Penford. 'And you, sir? Do not say you are Whig.'

The Whigs advocated reform, to give more power to the people and Parliament and less to the monarchy.

Penford nodded. 'I must say so, at least in desiring to ease the suffering of our people. There is more suffering to come, I fear, now that the war is over.'

'Now that the war is over, we must protect our property and the prices of our crops. That is what the Corn Laws are all about.' Tinmore landed a fist on the table for emphasis.

The Corn Laws fixed the prices of grain and imposed

tariffs to prevent imported grain from undercutting those prices.

'I do understand, sir,' Penford replied. 'But I fear the high prices will cause many to go hungry.'

Tinmore turned to Rossdale. 'I suppose you were against the Corn Laws. Your father certainly held out until the last, but we won him to our side.'

'I did not have to make the choice,' Rossdale said. 'But it would be hard to vote for a hardship for so many.'

Tinmore jabbed a finger in Rossdale's direction. 'If our farms fail, we all go hungry.'

Had Rossdale's father voted against his beliefs? 'It must be very difficult to choose,' Genna said. 'Especially when one does not know what the future will bring.'

'Humph!' Tinmore said. 'What do you know of such things?'

She had forgotten for a moment. Tinmore did not expect her to have opinions.

Rossdale spoke up. 'I quite agree with Miss Summerfield. Those in Parliament must live with many difficult decisions. It can be a great burden.'

Rossdale stood up for her? When was the last time anyone had done that for her?

Tinmore straightened in his chair. 'It is a great privilege! And one's duty!'

'I agree it is both of those things, as well,' Rossdale responded.

Tinmore seemed unexpectedly at a loss for words.

Ross rescued him, as well. 'Sir, I must tell you I am intrigued by this house. I have heard there is much to admire here.'

Tinmore swelled with pride. 'The first Earl of Tinmore was in the service of Queen Elizabeth. In her honour, the house was designed like the letter E, which might not be apparent to you. One can see it is shaped like an E if one climbs to the roof, though.'

'I should like to see that,' Rossdale said.

'I'll have Dixon take you around after dinner.'

'We do not need to trouble your butler. Miss Summerfield gave me a tour of Summerfield House. I am certain she will do a fine job of showing me Tinmore Hall.'

Genna felt herself go all warm. First he stood up for her; now he complimented her.

Tinmore waved his fork. 'Dixon will do it. The girl knows nothing of this house.'

Genna tensed, but tried to keep her voice composed. 'Then I should like to go along, if I may. To learn what Dixon can teach me.'

'Suit yourself,' Tinmore said, swallowing another bite of goose and smiling ingratiatingly towards Rossdale. 'I'll have Dixon take you around after tea.' He signalled to the butler who then had the footmen remove the main course. 'Time for the pudding,' Tinmore said.

Chapter Seven

After the pudding, Genna and Lorene left the gentlemen to their brandy and retired to the drawing room again.

'Do be careful, Genna,' Lorene warned as they walked to the Mount Olympus room. 'You know how he is. And I do not believe he is as recovered as he makes us believe. His temper is easily piqued, I fear.'

How did Lorene know? Had he lost his temper with her? 'I am being careful. I forgot myself for one moment, that is all.'

'Being late did not help matters either,' Lorene added.

'Yes, I realise it.' Genna doubted Tinmore cared whether she'd been present or not. 'I do wonder, though, why he is not throwing me at these two *eligible* gentlemen. He is so eager for me to make a match and here they both are.'

She meant it as a joke, but Lorene answered her in all seriousness. 'He thinks they are too high for you, Genna. Marrying you would not give either of them any advantage.'

Lorene's words stung. 'I was not being serious. Do you not think I know they are too high for me?'

They entered the room and sat on the sofa where they had been before dinner. Genna's back was stiff and with effort she kept her hands still in her lap. She could not think of a word she wished to say to her sister, at the moment.

Or rather, she could not think of a civil word she wished to say.

Once upon a time she would have shared with her sister that she had no plans to marry, that she intended to make her own way in the world unshackled by any man.

But Lorene's decision to marry Tinmore had altered matters. Lorene and she did not look upon the world with the same eyes.

'What are these gifts you are giving?' Lorene asked, breaking the silence.

'They are gifts,' Genna said. 'You discover the gift when you open it, not before.'

Lorene's brow furrowed. 'You have gifts for Lord Rossdale and Lord Penford?'

'For our guests, you mean? Yes, that was rather the point of it all.' Although she would have given Lorene her gift before the day was over, even if there had been no guests.

Lorene bit her lip. 'I do hope Lord Tinmore finds them appropriate.'

What were the chances of that? 'Do not worry, Lorene. They are mere trifles.'

The footman brought in tea and they lapsed into silence again. Genna occupied herself by staring at the paintings that covered the walls of the room, studying Verrio's use of colour, of movement and illusion. Whatever room she had found herself in these last few days she'd examined the paintings. How had she not allowed herself to see them before?

Ross felt as if he was sitting at his father's table with all Tinmore's talk of the politics of the day. Ross was not oblivious to the issues facing the country now that the war was over and he was not indifferent, but while his father was still alive he had no role to play in deciding such matters as what should be taxed, what prices should be fixed and what tariffs imposed. He also did not have to consider the consequences of whether he voted aye or nay. His day would come for all this, but now it was in the hands of others.

Tinmore slapped the table with the palm of his hand. 'The power must remain with the King and the aristocracy! We shall never go the way of France!'

His words became lost in a paroxysm of coughing. His butler quickly poured more brandy for him.

He downed the drink in one gulp. 'Shall we join the ladies?' His voice still choked.

'Excellent idea.' Ross tried not to sound too eager—or sarcastic.

Tinmore leaned heavily on his cane as he led them back to the drawing room. His butler followed rather solicitously.

The ladies looked up at their entrance.

'Would you like tea, gentlemen?' Lady Tinmore asked as they approached.

Lawd, no, thought Ross. More tea, more conversation.

'They don't want tea,' Lord Tinmore snapped. He signalled to the butler. 'Bring more brandy.'

The butler bowed and left the room.

In Ross's mind, the Earl had imbibed quite enough brandy already. He glanced at Lady Tinmore, who looked both chastened and concerned. Genna merely looked furious. Even Dell looked displeased.

Such a disagreeable man, especially to his wife and her sister.

The brandy was brought quickly and poured by the butler.

Ross detested the pall brought on by Tinmore's ill humour. He'd be damned if he let the evening go on like this. 'Shall we open the presents?' Tinmore would not dare contradict him.

Few men contradicted the son of a duke.

'If you desire it,' Tinmore agreed, sipping his brandy.

Genna turned to Ross. 'Do you mind if we open my gifts first? They really are mere trinkets.'

Ross smiled at her. 'If it pleases you, Miss Summerfield.'

She jumped out of her seat. 'It does, indeed!' She rushed over to the table where she'd placed her packages and brought them over. Handing them out, one to her sister, one to Dell, one to Ross. Even one to Tinmore, who, after all, provided her with lovely clothes, a roof over her head and an allowance.

'Please, do open them.' Her eyes sparkled in anticipation.

Dell was the first to open his. 'It is Summerfield House!'

The gift was a small framed watercolour of Summerfield House, obviously painted by Genna. It was not the one with the wild colours that she'd made the day he'd met her, though. This one showed snow on the ground and candlelight shining from the windows.

'It shows the night of your dinner party,' Genna said.

'So it does.' Dell looked up at her.

'I painted it for you,' she said.

He gazed at it appreciatively. 'It is a fine remembrance of that evening.'

Genna beamed with pleasure.

Ross opened his next. Another watercolour of a similar size, this one of a man on a galloping horse, his greatcoat billowing behind him. It was meant to be him, he realised, riding Spirit. He caught her eye to show he knew.

'I surmised that any gentleman would like a picture of a horse,' Genna explained.

So it was to be just between them that she'd drawn him?

He grinned. 'I like it very much.'

She smiled back, her face radiant.

Lord Tinmore tore open his gift next. His was smaller. He looked at it without comment.

'It is a miniature of Lorene,' Genna said.

She'd made a very small ink-and-watercolour painting of her sister and placed it in a frame small enough to be carried in the pocket of a coat.

Tinmore turned to his wife. 'It does you no justice, my dear. Amateur work.' He tossed it aside and it fell on the carpet by Dell's feet. 'When we go to London I will commission a proper portrait of you from the finest miniature artist in town. Perhaps Cosway or Engleheart are still painting. If not, someone quite as renowned.'

Genna's cheeks turned red, as if she'd been slapped in the face. She might as well have been.

Ross was too outraged to speak. How unspeakably rude and cruel to both women.

Dell picked up the small painting and looked at it. 'I disagree, Tinmore.' He turned to Genna. 'Well done, Miss Summerfield. This is a charming likeness of your sister.' He placed it carefully on the table, catching Lady Tinmore's eye as he did so.

She immediately glanced away. 'Let—let me open mine,' she said, her voice shaking and her fingers tremulous. 'Oh, Genna!' Lady Tinmore turned her small painting around for the others to see.

It showed four children, a boy and three little girls, playing at a folly, the folly where Ross and Genna had taken refuge from the weather.

'It is us,' whispered Genna.

Her sister looked up at her with glistening eyes. 'Look how happy we were.'

Tinmore tapped his cane on the carpet. 'We should allow our guests to present their gifts, since they have gone to the trouble.' He glanced at the butler who gestured to a footman to bring the gifts to them.

'I fear our gifts will pale in comparison to such thoughtfulness on Miss Summerfield's part,' Ross said. 'As you shall see.'

Ross took the gifts from the footman and handed one to each of them. Even in the wrapping, it was pretty obvious what he and Dell had brought for Lord Tinmore.

The man opened it eagerly. 'Cognac. Remy Martin 1780!'

'From my father's cellar,' Ross said.

Tinmore gushed. 'This is a fine gift indeed. A very fine gift. Even finer that it came from the Duke's cellar.'

'Open yours, Lady Tinmore,' Dell said.

It was a large and heavy box that she balanced on her knees. When she opened the box, she gasped, 'The music!'

Dell spoke, 'I am merely returning what is yours.'

She lifted each sheet of music as if it were as precious as jewels. 'I did not think to bring the music with me when we left Summerfield House. You have restored it to me.'

'Look,' Genna said, 'some are the pieces from which we first learned to play.'

'Lovely memories,' Lorene murmured.

Genna looked up. 'It is my turn, I suppose.' She untied the string and opened her box. 'My sketchbook!'

'Again, we merely return what is yours,' Dell said.

Ross had talked Dell into bringing Genna's sketchbook and presenting it as a gift. He had, after all, promised to return it to her. It was Dell who thought of the piano music, though.

Genna opened the book and glanced at some of the pages before closing it again and clasping it to her breast. 'I am so happy to have it. I thought it lost for ever.' She faced Ross and her smile widened. *Thank you*, she mouthed.

Ross turned to Lord Tinmore. 'See, sir, nothing precious.'

Tinmore looked affronted. 'I assure you, the cognac is quite precious!'

Ross had brought it for Dell and rather wished the two of them had made short work of it instead of leaving it with this disagreeable man who did not even have the courtesy to offer to share it with them.

Ross suddenly could not stand to be in this man's presence another second.

He stood. 'I desire to prevail upon your butler for the house tour now. I have a great need to stretch my legs.'

Tinmore was still examining his bottle of cognac, turning it around in his hands. He looked up and smirked at Ross. 'I am certain Dixon would be delighted to start the tour.' He snapped his hand to his butler. 'Dixon, show Lord Rossdale the important rooms of the house, the state rooms.'

Dixon bowed. 'Very good, sir.'

Ross glanced at Dell. 'Do you come, too, Dell?' Perhaps Dell needed a break from this disagreeable man, as well.

Dell darted a glance at Lady Tinmore and shook his head. 'I am content to stay.'

Genna rose from her chair. 'I will go.' She faltered and turned to Tinmore. 'You gave your permission, sir.'

Tinmore waved her away. 'Go, then.'

'This way, m'lord,' Dixon said, leading the way.

When they crossed the threshold, Ross glanced up at the mistletoe, but this would certainly not be an opportune time to take advantage.

Besides, it would send the wrong message to her.

Instead he whispered to her, 'Tinmore is unpleasant and cruel. I am sorry for you and your sister.'

'I am able to bear it,' she whispered back, 'but I worry about Lorene.'

'We will begin at the hall,' the butler said, cutting off more conversation.

Genna inclined her head towards the butler. 'Dixon will repeat anything we say to each other.'

Ross took the warning and stepped away from her.

The hall, the first room seen when one entered the house from the main entrance, was wainscoted in dark mahogany and its walls were adorned in armament of early times, when it was important that a lord show his military strength. Though the swords, battleaxes, lances, rapiers and pikes were arranged in decorative patterns, the sheer numbers were a warning.

'You can see,' the butler intoned, 'the power that has always been a part of the Earls of Tinmore.'

Rossdale Hall had an armament room with twice as

many weapons on display and countless more stored away in an attic somewhere, but Ross did not mention that fact.

'Depressing, is it not?' murmured Genna just loud enough for Ross to hear.

Dixon gestured to a huge portrait of a gentleman on the left wall. 'This is the first Earl of Tinmore, a favourite of Queen Elizabeth and one of her trusted advisors. He was given this land and title as a reward for his faithful service to the Queen.'

The first Earl had the pointed beard, ruff and rich velvets of his era.

'And on the right is his Countess.'

The portrait matched the size of the first Earl of Tinmore's. His Countess wore a black gown with an even wider white ruff and huge puffed sleeves.

'The house has over one hundred rooms…' Dixon said.

He led them from salon to dining room to gallery and Ross made no more attempt to talk with Genna. This house tour had none of the delight of her tour of Summerfield House. His only consolation was that they were free of Tinmore's company.

And he could watch Genna.

In each room, Genna paid close attention to the paintings. The house contained an impressive array of them. Most were Italian, as Tinmore had suggested. Ross recognised the style from the Grand Tour he and Dell had taken in their youth, but there was also an impressive number of Dutch paintings, classical sculpture, and later portraits by Lawrence and Reynolds.

What was she thinking as she examined the artwork? Ross wondered. Her mind was alive, he could tell, but he did not have an inkling what was passing through it.

He rather liked that.

Tinmore waved a hand towards the pianoforte. 'Play for our guest,' he demanded of his wife.

Dell steeled himself. He'd managed to act as if he was not affected by Lorene, but he did not know how long he could tolerate Tinmore's company. He would have fled the room with Ross and Genna, but he could not bear to leave Lorene alone with him.

Foolish. She was his wife. She would be alone with him the moment they left for Summerfield House.

She rose from her sofa and gracefully moved to the pianoforte in one corner of the room. The pianoforte was a work of art unto itself, like the walls of the room with their Roman gods spilling over each other. Trimmed in ebony and gold, the pianoforte sparkled in the candlelight, as dreamlike as the Mount Olympus scene.

Dell held his breath as her hands touched the keys. Since the night she had played for him at Summerfield House, he could not get her music out of his head—or the vision of her playing it. It came back to him during moments of solitude when he could not keep himself busy enough to stop thinking.

She began with the Beethoven piece she had played for him before, the one that revealed to him all her sadness and loneliness and so reminded him of his sister. It took a few bars of the music to transport her and then her lovely face glowed as if the music had lit her from within. He had to close his eyes from the sheer beauty of her.

'No. No,' her husband interrupted. 'Do not play your gloomy nonsense!'

She stopped with a discordant note and her back stiffened.

Tinmore had downed another glass of brandy. How many had he consumed? Dell and Ross prided themselves on being able to empty a few bottles at night, but where they'd restrained themselves, Tinmore had indulged.

'Our guest does not want to hear this.' He pounded on the carpet with his cane.

'I assure you I do wish to hear whatever your wife chooses,' Dell said through clenched teeth.

Tinmore smirked at him. 'You need not be polite, Penford. She can play something cheerful. Something fitting for Christmas Day.'

She paused for a moment, as if collecting herself, before she played the first notes of *Here We Come A-wassailing*.

Lord Tinmore started to sing, *'"Here we come a-wassailing among the leaves so green—"'*

Another fit of coughing overtook him.

Lorene rose and hurried over to him. 'My lord, you are ill again.'

Dell poured him a cup of tea, tepid now. Better tea than more brandy. He handed it to Tinmore without milk or sugar. Tinmore gulped it down and the coughing eased, but his breathing was laboured.

'You are wheezing.' Lorene placed a hand on Tinmore's forehead. 'Let me help you to your room.'

Tinmore pushed her hand away. 'Stop fussing. Think of your duty, woman. We have a guest. You stay and entertain our guest. Wicky will take care of me.' He motioned for the footman attending the room to approach. 'Help me to my room and get Wicky for me.'

'His valet,' Lady Tinmore explained.

Dell did not care who tended to Tinmore.

The old Earl hobbled out of the room with the footman bearing his weight. His coughing came back, echoing behind him.

This damned man. How could he be so churlish towards his wife, even while she showed him great solicitude? How did she bear moments like this, being callously dismissed and rebuffed?

She still faced the door from which her husband exited. Dell indulged in his desire to gaze at her, so graceful, so perfect.

Lawd! Why should this woman be married to such a man?

He raised his arm, wanting to comfort her, but he had no right. He had no right to even speak to her about her husband.

But he could not help it. 'Does he always speak to you so?'

She turned and lifted her eyes to his. 'Quite often.'

'He should not,' he answered in a low voice. 'You do not deserve it.'

She lowered her lashes. 'It is kind of you to say so.'

There was so much more he wished to say. He wanted Tinmore to go to the devil and never do her feelings an injury again.

Instead the two of them stood there, less than an arm's length apart. Too close. Much too close.

He could not help but reach out and touch her arm. 'Would you play the Beethoven piece for me?' he murmured. 'I would very much like to hear it again.'

She nodded. 'Of course.'

She returned to the pianoforte and began *Pathétique* and the notes of the music transformed into sheer emotion. He could not quiet the storm inside him. As she played he walked back to the chair where he had been sitting, spying on the table the miniature Genna had painted of her. Lorene's back was to him and, for the moment, there was no one else in the room. He picked up the miniature and placed it in his coat pocket.

When she finished *Pathétique*, she turned to him. 'Do you mind if I play some of the music you brought to me?'

'Not at all,' he responded. He picked up the box and brought the sheet music to her. She set it on the piano bench and started to look through it.

'Some of this is so frivolous,' she said. 'Some too simple.'

'Like what?' he asked.

'King William's March,' she responded. 'This is one of the first pieces I learned to play.'

She put the sheet of music on the stand and played the crisp lively notes. He stood behind her and watched the confident movement of her fingers on the keys and was glad that the music had led her to something more cheerful. When the piece was done her mood seemed to have lifted.

She looked through her box again. 'Let us look for a nice song!'

'The wassail song?' he asked.

She laughed. 'No, not that one.' She continued to riffle through the pages. 'This one.' She handed him a sheet.

'Barbara Allen?' He placed it on the stand. 'Even I know that one.'

She placed the box on the floor and moved over on her bench. 'Then sit and sing it with me.'

They sang the old song together, her voice high and crystalline; his deeper.

> *In Scarlet town where I was born*
> *There was a fair maid dwelling...*

The song was a tragedy, two lovers dying.

She played other pieces of music from her box, all songs of thwarted love, it seemed. He remained at her side, watching her, joining in on the songs when he knew them. Time seemed suspended as her music went on.

'You select one,' she said, handing him the box.

He picked out *The Turtle Dove*. She played and he sang.

> *Fare you well, my dear, I must be gone,*
> *And leave you for a while,*
> *If I roam away I'll come back again,*
> *Though I roam ten thousand miles...*

He sang to the end of the song:

O yonder doth sit that little turtle dove,
He doth sit on yonder high tree,
A-making a moan for the loss of his love,
As I will do for thee, my dear.

When he finished, she placed her hands on the bench at her sides, but continued to stare at the piano keys. The room turned very quiet.

He touched her hand, a bare touch with only two fingers entwined with hers. He was merely feeling sympathy for her, was he not? She was a relation of sorts so it stood to reason he would care about her.

Very slowly she faced him and met his gaze.

Dell stopped thinking.

She leaned towards him, still holding his eyes.

The door opened and Genna's laughter reached their ears.

Genna and Ross entered the room.

'We are finished with the tour!' Genna said.

Dell stood up and moved away from the pianoforte. 'And we must take our leave,' he said.

'Now?' Ross looked surprised.

'Yes—now—' Dell sputtered. 'Lord Tinmore took ill again. We should leave. Now.'

Chapter Eight

London—February 1816

Six weeks later Genna sat behind her sister in the recesses of Lord Tinmore's box at the Royal Opera House. Onstage was *Don Giovanni* and all the *ton* were keen to see it—and to be seen seeing it. Thus, the boxes were packed with ladies in silks and gentlemen in impeccably tailored formal dress. Those in the orchestra were not so fashionably dressed, but those people mattered very little to the fashionable world.

Genna loved to see the fashionable clothes the London ladies wore. Genna, though, considered it important to set herself off from the latest fashion, with a twist on whatever was the rage. She and Lorene used a modiste who used to be their sister Tess's maid. Nancy was a particularly creative collaborator in Genna's quest to express herself in her dress.

Her wardrobe, of course, was possible only through the benevolence of Lord Tinmore, a fact which niggled at Genna's conscience a little, even though he considered her dress mere pretty packaging to attract suitors. Tinmore's intention was to marry her off this Season. Genna was just as determined to resist.

If she could only hold out this Season. In the autumn she would turn twenty-one and then she intended to do as she pleased.

In the meantime she would enjoy the Season's entertainments, like this lovely opera, so filled with humour and drama. The Season was hardly at its height, but more of the fashionable elite arrived every day and more and more were hosting balls, breakfasts, or musical soirées.

Not that Genna expected to be invited to many of them. Tinmore was a generation or two too old to be on everyone's guest list and Genna was certain many hostesses seized on any excuse to keep from inviting the scandalous Summerfield sisters.

'Look! Look there!' Tinmore cried above Leporello's solo. 'I do believe that is the Duke of Kessington.' He lifted his mother-of-pearl opera glasses to his eyes. 'Yes. Yes. It is. Rossdale and Penford are in his company.'

Rossdale. Her heart skittered.

She knew there was a chance she would see Rossdale during the Season. It was unlikely they would attend the same entertainments, but it was possible that their paths would cross somewhere like this. She hardly knew what greeting to expect from him, if he deigned to greet her at all. He and Penford had left so abruptly on Christmas Day. They quit Lincolnshire entirely within that same week, she'd heard, even though they'd said they would stay past Twelfth Night.

Something must have offended them. What other explanation could there be? Something must have happened while she and Rossdale were touring the house. Lorene professed to know nothing, but Genna did not know whether to believe her or not.

She'd missed Rossdale. She fancied him her friend and Genna had enjoyed his company more than anyone she could remember.

Although perhaps he'd merely been kind to a silly chit with scandalous parents and siblings.

'Who is Tinmore talking about?' her sister Tess leaned over to ask.

Another of the delights of London was the opportunity to see Tess, who now stayed in town most of the time with her husband and his parents, Viscount and Viscountess Northdon.

Genna answered her. 'He is talking about our cousin, Lord Penford, and his friend. They sit in the Duke of Kessington's box.'

'Our cousin attends the opera with a duke?' Tess's brows rose. 'Impressive.'

'His friend is the Duke's son,' Genna explained.

The Duke's box was positioned almost as advantageously as the King's box, which seemed a great distance from Genna at the moment.

Once she would have told Tess about every moment with a man like Rossdale, but since Lorene married and turned their world on its ears, Genna had become too used to keeping secrets.

Tess glanced at the Duke's box again. 'Lorene told me you had dined with our cousin, but I did not know about his friend.'

Genna joked, 'I suppose Lorene and I are so accustomed to lofty acquaintances that it quite slipped our minds to tell you.'

Tess laughed. 'Who would ever have thought any Summerfield sister would be acquainted with a person of such high rank?'

'Indeed.' Though he might pretend not to know her now.

Ross saw Tinmore gazing at his father's box through opera glasses. Whether Dell saw Tinmore, too, Ross could not tell. He didn't dare ask either. Ever since Christmas night Dell had acted very strange. First he'd insisted they leave Tinmore Hall abruptly, then he'd decided to quit Lincolnshire entirely. Ross thought he would have left on Boxing Day if he could have, but it took a little longer than that to complete his business there.

Ross asked once what had happened to make Dell so adamant about leaving. Dell told him he did not want to risk having to be in Tinmore's company again. Neither he nor Ross could abide the man, but Ross had been disappointed that their visit was cut so short. He'd have risked a few moments in Tinmore's company if it meant spending more time with Genna. He'd at least hoped they would have had a chance to discuss the house tour or the artwork she'd examined that night.

Now every time he saw a painting, even the familiar ones in his father's town house, he thought of her. Would she see the painting as he did? Would she learn something from the artist's technique?

He must confess, he'd never given artistic technique a thought until meeting her, until seeing her wild use of colour in that watercolour of Summerfield House.

Was she in Tinmore's box? he wondered. He could not see her and he certainly did not wish to call upon Tinmore during the intermission if she were not present.

Could he renew his friendship with Genna here in London? He did not see how. Eligible men and marriageable women could not simply enjoy one another's company without wagging tongues putting them both in parson's mousetrap.

On stage Don Giovanni attempted to seduce Zerlina. *'This life is nought but pleasure,'* he sang in Italian.

But life was not all pleasure, Ross thought. For many there was nothing but suffering. He and Dell had visited some of the Waterloo wounded who'd been in Dell's regiment, men merely hanging on to life by a thread. He'd brought them bottles of brandy, but what they'd really wanted was food for their families. He'd seen to that later. Those families would never go hungry again.

If his father the Duke knew of his charity, he'd scoff and insist that the real solutions lay in Parliament. To his father, Parliament and its politics were everything. Even the guests the Duke had selected to share his box were chosen to bring some political advantage. Ross was not even sure his father and his wife paid any attention to the marvel of this opera.

What about merely inviting friends because you enjoyed their company? And why not help suffering individuals now? What was wrong with doing things his own way, not like his father?

Ross and Genna were alike in that way. They both wanted to choose their own way.

Ross stared at Giovanni, so determined to do as he wished, as reprehensible as his wishes were. Ross's desires were not reprehensible. He wished to do good for people. But the important thing to him was to assist by his own choice, not someone else's, not what the politics of the situation would require of him.

He shifted his gaze to Tinmore's box. Somehow he'd cross paths with Miss Genna Summerfield again. Why not?

When the opera was over the crowds spilled on to the street where the carriages were lined up to gather them. A fine mist of rain dampened the air and kept most of the crowd waiting in the shelter behind the Opera House's columns.

Genna stood with Tess and her husband, Marc Glenville, a few feet from Tinmore and Lorene, who remained under the portico. The rain was too thin to be of much concern and, after the close air and crowds inside the theatre, Genna relished the night air. The lamplight shone on the wet pavement and cobbles, making a play of light and dark that captivated her. How did artists paint such reflections?

Something else to try. There was always something about art that she discovered she did not know. Thanks to Rossdale, she'd begun to look at the paintings around her more carefully to try to answer some of these questions.

She took a breath.

Rossdale. Where was he? Somewhere in the crowd?

Odd to know he was so close. It made her skin tingle with excitement.

'What is the delay?' she heard Tinmore complain. 'I distinctly told the coachman to be at the head of the line. I detest waiting.'

Next to her, Tess gave an exasperated sigh. 'At least it is not pouring rain.' She clasped her husband's arm. 'It feels rather refreshing out here.'

Marc smiled and held her even closer. 'It does look as if we are in for a bit of a wait.'

'We could walk back faster,' Genna said.

'I would not mind,' Tess said.

Most of those from the orchestra seats seemed to be doing just that, filling the streets and blocking the carriages.

Tess hummed. 'Do you not have the music still in your head? I do.'

'It was good music,' her husband agreed.

Genna held on to the costumes, the stage designs and the colours and patterns of the theatre itself.

'Miss Summerfield?' A low masculine voice sounded behind her.

She turned. 'Lord Rossdale!' Her insides skittered with something like joy.

He tipped his hat and bowed. 'I thought that was you.'

'Rossdale! Rossdale!' Tinmore called out. 'Saw you in the theatre. You and your father. Give him my regards.'

Rossdale turned slowly and merely nodded to Tinmore before turning back to Genna. 'I hope you are well, Miss Summerfield.'

She smiled. 'I am always well, sir!' Her voice dropped. 'It is good to see you.'

She caught his gaze for a moment, when Tess, standing right beside her, said, 'Genna?'

'Oh.' She gestured from Tess to Rossdale. 'Tess, may I

present Lord Rossdale, with whom we became acquainted when he visited Lincolnshire. My sister, Mrs Glenville.'

Tess smiled at him. 'Lord Rossdale.'

Tess's husband spoke up. 'Rossdale. Good to see you again.'

'And you, Glenville.' He shook Marc's hand. 'Under better circumstances, yes?'

Marc glanced at his wife. 'Much better circumstances.'

'There it is!' Tinmore shouted. 'There is our carriage. Do not tarry!' He walked quickly, his cane tapping loudly on the pavement.

Genna exchanged a glance with Rossdale.

He stepped back. 'Goodnight, Miss Summerfield.' He nodded to Tess and Marc. 'Goodnight.'

'Make haste!' Tinmore called from the carriage door. 'I do not wish to remain here all night.'

They had no choice but to rush to the carriage.

Genna took a glance back as she was assisted into the carriage, but Rossdale seemed to have melted into the crowd.

Shortly after Lord Tinmore's carriage pulled away, Ross climbed into his father's carriage.

'Is Dell with you?' his father asked. They had all been invited to a supper after the opera.

'He is making his own way,' Ross replied.

Dell had left him right after the performance. Rather abruptly, Ross thought.

'I wanted to talk to him about this income-tax business,' the Duke said. 'We must settle this question. It is vital.'

Income taxes had been high during the war with Napoleon and now, with the peace, the citizens were eager for some relief.

'I heard much discussion among the others who called upon our box during the intermission,' the Duchess said.

Ross's father's second wife was perhaps even more serious about politics than was his father.

The carriage started to move.

Ross, though, had heard his father's discussion of the income tax—and the Duchess's—many times since joining them in London. He'd contributed all his thoughts on the subject already. Not that his father credited his opinion.

He turned his thoughts instead to Genna. To devising some way to see her again soon.

It was possible that eventually they would be invited to the same social affair, but that was leaving too much to chance. He needed to figure out a way to see her soon and he knew just how to arrange that.

'I heard something as well,' he began. 'Well, not so much heard, but noticed.'

'Something of importance?' his father asked sceptically.

His father believed Ross was merely pleasure-seeking, but, then, his father never knew Ross to do anything of importance. He never knew of Ross's voyages across the channel during the war, transporting spies like Glenville, Genna's brother-in-law, and of bringing exiles to safety. He certainly did not know of his assistance to Waterloo veterans and their families.

'Do you recall that Dell and I had some acquaintance with Lord Tinmore when we were in Lincolnshire?' Ross asked.

'That unpalatable fossil?' his father spat.

Ross suppressed a smile. His father did have a way with words. 'The very one. I ran into him tonight right before the carriage came. He asked me to give you his regards.'

His father peered at him. 'Ross, Tinmore's regards are of no importance to me.'

'I think they are,' Ross countered. 'The thing is, Tinmore is dazzled by you. He acted the complete toad-eater when Dell and I saw him in Lincolnshire. I believe he fancies being one of your set. I think he'd be easily swayed to

vote with you if he had the impression you favoured him.'
This was half-true at least. Tinmore was enamoured of
being in the company of a duke—or even his son. Whether
he'd change his vote was total speculation.

Ross's father nodded thoughtfully. 'You might be correct. And if I secure his vote, those old cronies of his might
follow suit.' He shook his head. 'No. If I befriend him now
he'll think I am merely seeking votes.'

Which was precisely what his father wished to do.

'Be subtle,' Ross urged. 'Do not approach him directly.
Invite him to some of your entertainments.'

The Duchess, who had been listening with keen interest,
spoke up. 'Invite him...I believe it could work, although I
hesitate to include that fortune-hunter wife of his.'

'I can ease your concern on that score,' Ross said
quickly. 'Lady Tinmore is actually a mild-mannered, well-
meaning woman. I think you might actually take a liking
to her.'

'Is she?' The Duchess's brows rose. 'Difficult to believe. Everyone knows her mother was as wanton as they
come even before she ran away with a foreign count.' She
leaned forward. 'You know people say each of the Summerfield daughters were fathered by different lovers. And
there is that bastard son. And Summerfield lost his fortune, of course.'

Leave it to the Duchess to know all the gossip there
was to know.

'I also heard the bastard son married Lord Northdon's
daughter,' she went on. 'A patched-up affair that was, I
am certain. Northdon packed them off to some farm in
the Lake District.'

How did she retain all this information?

'I do not dispute the sins of the parents,' Ross said.
'And I have never met the son. But the daughters are not
cut from the same cloth.' Genna was an original, that was

certain, but he saw nothing wanton in her. 'They would not embarrass you.'

She leaned back on the seat. 'I confess I am curious about them.'

'Invite them to your musicale next week,' he suggested.

Her mouth turned up in a calculating grin. She turned to the Duke. 'Shall we?'

He returned her expression. 'By all means.'

Chapter Nine

The invitation to the Duchess of Kessington's musicale was quite unexpected, but it put Lord Tinmore in raptures. He became nearly intolerable. From the moment he'd opened the gold-edged invitation bearing the Kessington crest his warnings and instructions had been incessant. He was convinced that Lorene or Genna would behave improperly and would prove to be an embarrassment to him.

Genna had no fears that she and Lorene would offend anyone. Tinmore's capacity to be objectionable, though, was another story altogether.

Along with a litany of dos and don'ts in the society of dukes and duchesses, Tinmore desired to select what gowns they were to wear and how they ought to style their hair. Goodness! He would probably have put them in stomachers and powdered wigs.

Somehow Lorene had been able to prevent that ghastly idea. It was a good thing, because Genna would have refused to wear whatever Tinmore selected, even if it had been her finest dress.

On the night of the musicale, with the assistance of Nancy, their modiste, they managed to look presentable, but that hardly eased Tinmore's nerves. When their carriage pulled through the wrought-iron gates of Kessington House on Piccadilly, he was nearly beside himself.

'Now remember to curtsy to the Duchess and, whatever you do, do not open your mouths. The less you say the less chance you will utter some drivel.'

They entered the hall, a semicircular room all white and

gold with marble floors and cream walls with gilded plasterwork. The curve of the room was repeated in the double-marble staircase, as was the gold. Its wrought-iron banister was gilded, the curves appearing again in its design.

A footman in fine livery took their cloaks and another led them toward the sounds of people talking and soft violin music playing.

The butler announced them, 'Lord and Lady Tinmore. Miss Summerfield.

Genna noticed heads turn towards them. Because of Tinmore or because two of the scandalous Summerfield sisters had arrived? She lifted her chin and allowed her gaze to sweep the room. Its walls were covered with huge paintings and mirrors, its ceiling a marvel of plasterwork design. Hanging from the ceiling was the largest crystal chandelier she had ever seen. The room was all pattern and opulence.

Tinmore impatiently tugged at her arm to follow him to where His and Her Graces greeted other guests who had arrived just before them. Rossdale stood next to them and caught Genna's eye as they approached.

He smiled and she knew the smile was just for her.

Tinmore effusively greeted the Duke and thanked the Duchess for including them. He made a big show of presenting Lorene to them before mumbling, 'My wife's sister, Miss Summerfield.'

'Very good of you to come,' the Duke said. 'I trust we will have some time to talk before the night is through.'

'It would be my honour.' Tinmore bowed.

The Duchess smiled graciously at Lorene and Genna. 'I must learn who your modiste is. Your appearance is charming. Charming.'

Rossdale stepped forward, extending his hand to Tinmore. 'Good of you to come, sir.'

'Rossdale.' Tinmore shook his hand eagerly. 'Good to see you again. Looking forward to this evening.'

Rossdale also took Lorene's hand. 'Welcome, ma'am. I dare say there should be some people you know here. Your cousin is here somewhere.'

'Lord Penford?' she said. 'Yes, I already glimpsed him.'

Finally he clasped Genna's hand and even through her glove she could feel his warmth and strength. 'Miss Summerfield. I hope you will allow me to show you the art work in this house. We have a considerable collection.'

She was so happy to see him, but feared it would show. She glanced at the paintings gracing the walls instead. 'I can see that already! There are so many wonderful paintings here.'

He released her. 'I took time to learn of them so you will be impressed with me.'

She laughed.

Tinmore took her arm and pulled her away. 'Do not waste the gentleman's time.'

'She is not—' Rossdale started, but other guests arrived and he had to turn away.

Tinmore led Genna and Lorene through the throngs of people and deposited them in a corner before insinuating himself into a group of other lords probably discussing their political matters.

'Do you suppose anyone will speak to us?' Lorene asked. 'I cannot help but feel this company is too high for us. Why were we invited, I wonder?'

'I wonder, too.' Did Rossdale have anything to do with it?

Two of the ladies seated nearby gave them curious looks. Did they disapprove of their being invited?

Lorene nodded to them and smiled sweetly. How could anyone not adore her sister?

Genna turned her attention to the painting on the wall behind them, a portrait of an old man in a turban. This was not an Italian artist, she would guess by the clothing and the style of painting. The colours were dark and the figure seemed to blend into the background, although his face seemed bathed in light.

'Lady Tinmore.' A male voice came from behind.

Genna turned. It was Lord Penford.

'How do you do, sir,' Lorene said, her voice barely audible.

'Penford!' Genna said lightly. 'Are you going to speak to us? No one else has dared!'

'I thought I might take you around and introduce you,' he said.

It was what Tinmore ought to have done.

'How very nice of you, Cousin.' Out of the corner of her eye Genna saw Rossdale working his way through the crowd. 'Take Lorene around. I wish to study these paintings a little longer.'

Neither he nor Lorene acted as if she'd said something odd. They left her. A footman brought her a glass of champagne which delighted Genna, who had only tasted the bubbly light wine two or three times during the last Season.

The two ladies seated nearby glanced at her again. They were of an age with her parents, Genna guessed. Perhaps they knew Genna's mother and father. If so, no wonder they stared.

Genna used Lorene's response and smiled at them. They smiled back. Did they wish her to speak with them? Genna could not tell.

No matter. Rossdale was coming closer.

'You are here alone,' he said when he reached her.

She turned to the wall. 'I was studying this painting. It is not Italian, is it?'

He grinned. 'Good girl. It is Dutch. Rembrandt.'

She looked at it again, more closely. 'I have never seen a Rembrandt. Look how he paints the black cloak of the man. It blends into the background, but it is still clear it is a coat if you look closely.'

He nodded. 'Do you wish a tour of the other paintings in the room?' he asked.

She glanced at the ladies nearby who looked her way again. 'I am afraid it would look odd with all your guests here.' She leaned closer to him. 'Tinmore might have apoplexy if I do anything to draw attention to myself. He has a great fear that Lorene and I will do something to mortify him.' She huffed. 'Of course, as soon as he could, he left us in this corner. I suppose he thought we would stand here like statues.'

He inclined his head. 'I saw Dell introducing your sister to other guests. Would you like me to introduce you?'

She giggled. 'Let Tinmore worry that I'll do something objectionable in your company.'

He started with the two ladies who had made her and Lorene an object of interest. 'May I present Miss Summerfield, sister-in-law to Lord Tinmore? Miss Summerfield, the Duchess of Archester and the Duchess of Mannerton.'

Genna executed a perfect curtsy. 'Your Graces. I am honoured to meet you.'

The Duchess of Archester peered at her. 'I knew your mother, Miss Summerfield.'

And she probably knew about all her mother's lovers and how her mother had left her children with a father who cared nothing for them and ran off with a foreign count.

'Did you, ma'am?' Genna smiled and held her gaze steady.

'I knew her quite well,' the Duchess said. 'How is she faring? I hope she is in good health.'

Genna managed to keep her composure. 'I have not seen her for many years.' Since she was three years old. 'But my sister, Mrs Glenville, met her in Brussels last summer. By her report my mother is in good health and prospering.'

'Is she still with Count von Osten?' asked the Duchess of Mannerton.

Was this any of their concern?

'Yes, she is.' Genna still smiled. 'My sister reports they are quite happy together.'

She was not about to give them the satisfaction of imagining her mother going to rack and ruin by leaving a loveless, desolate marriage for a man who loved her and could give her everything she desired.

Except her children.

To her surprise, though, the Duchesses looked pleased. 'I am delighted to hear it,' the Duchess of Mannerton said. 'A bad business it was, but she found her way in the end.'

Rossdale asked if the Duchesses needed anything and if they were enjoying themselves while Genna still reeled from this reaction to her mother.

'I cannot believe it,' she said as Rossdale escorted her away. 'I think they actually liked my mother. I thought they were looking at Lorene and me because they disapproved of us.'

'Perhaps they knew your mother well enough to realise she did the right thing,' he said.

She stiffened. 'Right for her, perhaps.'

He walked her around the room and introduced her to guests who were not deep in conversation. It seemed as if most of the guests were high in rank or important in government and all were quite uninterested in her.

'Ah, Vespery is here,' Rossdale said. 'Now, he is someone you must meet.'

He brought her over to a rather eccentrically attired gentleman, his neckcloth loosely tied, his waistcoat a bright blue. His black hair was longer than fashionable, very thick and unruly. As were his eyebrows.

The gentleman's eyes lit up upon seeing Rossdale.

'Rossdale, my lad,' he said. 'Are you in good health?'

'Very good, Vespery.' Rossdale turned to Genna. 'Miss Summerfield, allow me to present Mr Vespery to you.'

'How do you do?' Genna extended her hand, over which Vespery blew a kiss.

'Charmed,' the man said.

'Vespery is a friend of the Duchess's,' Rossdale explained. 'He is painting portraits of her and my father.'

'You are an artist!' The first true artist she'd ever met.

His eyes assessed her. 'Are you in need of an artist? Please tell me you wish to have your portrait painted. I would be more than delighted to immortalise you on canvas.'

She laughed. 'I am not important enough to be immortalised.'

'Miss Summerfield is an artist herself,' Rossdale told him.

'Are you?' Vespery's rather remarkable brows rose.

Genna rolled her eyes. 'An *aspiring* artist is more precise. But I am very serious about it.'

Vespery leaned forward. 'Do tell me. What is your medium?'

'Watercolours,' she replied. 'But only because I've never been taught how to use anything else.'

At that moment the Duchess of Kessington came up to Rossdale. 'I need you Rossdale. I must take you away.'

The Duchess took him out of earshot. 'What are you about, Ross? Spending all your time with the Summerfield girl? We have other guests.'

'Is that why you took me away?' Ross frowned.

'You know how it will look if you favour one young lady.' She kept her smile on her face. 'Especially a Summerfield.'

'Both Lord Tinmore and her sister left her standing alone,' he said. 'There is no one of her acquaintance here. Would it not be rude to leave any guest in that circumstance?'

'Well, be careful,' the Duchess said. 'You would do well to join some of the conversations among the peers tonight.

These are very important times, you know. You will learn much from the experience of these gentlemen.'

'Constance.' He looked her directly in the eye. 'Do not tell me what I must do.'

She released his arm. 'I speak for your father.'

Ross doubted that. Although her father and she were perfect partners, both working hard to further his political power and influence, Ross was reasonably certain his father was motivated by duty to the country and its people. Ross feared the Duchess merely liked power and influence for its own sake.

Ross's father married Constance when Ross was in school. Her connection was to his father and his role in society, not to Ross. It was fortunate that she had no interest in mothering Ross, because no one could replace the mother he had adored. The duty in which Constance revelled was what had killed his mother.

Ross scanned the room and found his father deep in conversation with his cronies. Tinmore, who looked very gratified, was included.

'I dare say the Duke has not given me a thought since the party began,' Ross told her. 'So do not tell me he has spoken of me to you.'

'You are impossible.' She swept away.

Ross glanced towards Genna, who seemed to be delighted to be in conversation with Vespery. As much as he hated to admit it, the Duchess was correct that people would notice if he spent the whole of the evening in Genna's company. He must make the rounds of the room and speak with other guests before returning to her. That should keep his father's wife satisfied.

He approached Dell, who still remained at Lady Tinmore's side, obviously not feeling the same obligation to limit his time with any one person.

'Is Dell taking good care of you?' he asked Lady Tinmore.

She blushed, although why she should blush at such a statement he could not guess.

'He has been very kind,' she said.

Ross glanced over at her husband, who was listening intently to something Ross's father was saying. 'Lord Tinmore seems quite preoccupied.'

'Indeed,' she said. 'I fear Lord Penford took pity on me. I am grateful to him.'

Dell looked like a storm ready to spew lightning and thunder.

'I know some ladies who might be very interested to speak with you.' Ross meant the Duchesses Archester and Mannerton.

'Would you like that?' Dell asked her.

'Of course.' She lowered her lashes. 'And it would free you from having to act my escort.'

Dell nodded, but Ross could not tell if he wanted to be rid of Lady Tinmore or not. Nor could he tell what Lady Tinmore really wished.

Lady Tinmore took Ross's arm and Dell followed.

Ross presented Lady Tinmore to the Duchess of Archester and the Duchess of Mannerton. 'The Duchesses told your sister that they knew your mother,' he told Lady Tinmore.

'Come sit with us, dear.' The Duchess of Archester patted the space next to her on a sofa.

Ross bowed and he and Dell walked away.

'Tinmore appears to have forgotten his wife,' Ross remarked.

'Yes.' Dell's voice was low. 'I thought it my duty to step in.' He took two glasses of champagne off a tray offered by a passing footman and handed one to Ross. 'Cousin and all. Why ever did your stepmother invite them?'

'Do not call her my stepmother.' Ross had told him this many times. She was his father's wife, but not any sort of mother to him. 'She invited them at my suggestion.'

'Your suggestion?' Dell gaped at him.

Ross shrugged. 'I had a desire to see Miss Summerfield again.'

'Miss Summerfield?' Dell took a sip of champagne. 'I am surprised.'

'Are you?' Ross responded. 'She is refreshing.'

Dell's brows knit. 'Your father will not approve, you know.'

'There really is nothing for him to approve or disapprove,' Ross said. 'I merely enjoy her company.'

'Will you court her?' Dell asked.

'I do not intend to court anyone,' Ross replied. 'You know that. I am in no hurry to be leg-shackled or to be shackled to a title. Time for that later.' His father was in good health. The need to produce an heir and be about the business of a duke was some years away yet.

Dell put a stilling hand on Ross's arm. 'Take care not to trifle with that young woman. She's got enough of a trial merely living with Tinmore. Besides, she's barely out of the schoolroom.'

'She's not as young as all that. She'll reach her majority within a year.' A friendship with Genna was sounding more and more impossible.

But it should not be. They should be free to be friends if they wished to.

'Take care, Ross,' Dell said. 'Tinmore means for her to be married. And he is just the sort to force the deed, if you give him any reason.'

Genna could not help but keep one eye on Rossdale. She fancied she could tell precisely where he stood in the room at any time. It made her heart glad merely to be in the same room with him, knowing he would eventually speak to her again. In the meantime what could be more delightful than to be in the company of a true artist, a man who made his living by painting! There was so much she wanted to ask Vespery, so much of his knowledge and skill she wished to absorb.

She asked him about the paintings.

'What of this one?' She pointed to a nearby landscape, a pastoral scene with a cottage, a stream, horses and a wagon, cattle, men working.

He pulled out spectacles and perched them on his nose. 'This painting? This painting is Flemish, of course.'

She wondered how one could tell a Flemish painting from a Dutch one. Although even she had been able to tell the Dutch painting was not Italian.

'It is a Brueghel, I believe,' he went on. 'Jan the Younger, if I am not mistaken. There were several generations of Brueghels. Some of them painted fruit.'

'How old is it?' she asked.

'Oh, possibly two hundred years old. Seventeenth century.'

She looked at it again.

Vespery moved closer to the painting. 'Notice the composition. All the triangles.'

She stared at it. 'Yes! The roof of the cottage. The shape of the stream. Even the tree trunks.' Patterns. Like the pattern of curves in the hall of this house. 'It makes it pleasing to look at.'

She wished she could find Rossdale and tell him what Vespery had taught her.

She glanced around the room and saw Rossdale speaking to an older woman and a younger one, possibly the older woman's daughter. The excitement in her breast turned into a sharp pain.

Why should she ache? Rossdale was merely speaking to a young woman who was his social equal. Genna could not aspire to be anything but a friend to him, not that they could manage a friendship in London during the Season when everyone and everything centred on marriageable young ladies finding eligible gentlemen to marry.

Chapter Ten

The musicale was announced and the guests filed out of the drawing room.

Genna excused herself from Vespery. 'I should find my sister.' No doubt Tinmore would leave her to walk into the music room alone.

She found Lorene near where Tinmore had first deposited them.

'I have had the most remarkable conversation with two duchesses,' Lorene said when Genna reached her. 'You spoke with them, too, Rossdale said. They knew our mother.'

The Duchesses of Archester and Mannerton. 'Yes. I did.'

'They knew her when she eloped with Count von Osten. I must tell you all about it later.' Lorene glanced around the room.

Tinmore had attached himself to another grey-haired gentleman and was leaving the room, but Lorene did not remark on it. Genna walked with Lorene as if it was the most natural thing in the world to be left without an escort.

Except Lord Penford appeared. 'I will escort you ladies to the music room.'

They followed the other guests to another huge room, this one painted green with cream accents and more gold gilt at the border of the ceiling and along the chair railing on the walls. Chairs upholstered in a brocade the same shade as the walls were lined up facing an alcove whose entrance was flanked by two Corinthian columns, their elaborate ornamentation painted gold.

'This is a lovely room,' Lorene exclaimed.

'Let me find you seats,' Penford said.

Tinmore hobbled up to them. 'There you are!' he said peevishly. 'Come. Come. Let us sit.'

Penford stepped back and when Genna next glanced his way, he'd disappeared.

'Here. Sit here.' Tinmore gestured with his cane.

They were near the centre of the room, several gentlemen having chosen seats in the back and Tinmore knew better than to take the front seats that more properly went to those of higher rank. On each chair was a printed card edged in gold like the invitation had been. It listed the program.

When everyone was seated, the butler stood at the front of the alcove and announced the program. 'Mozart's Quintets in D Major and G Minor.'

He backed away and five musicians entered the alcove through a door hidden in the wall, two violins, two violas and a cello. They sat and spent a few minutes tuning their instruments before beginning the first piece.

Lorene gasped and leaned forward, her colour high and the hint of a smile on her face. Genna silently celebrated. Her dear sister was awash in pleasure from the beautiful music. It was a joy to see her so happy. Genna glanced around the room, looking for Rossdale.

He stood in the back of the room, his arms folded across his chest, looking perfectly comfortable—and slightly bored. And very handsome. How lovely to have a handsome friend.

But she must not be caught staring at him.

She turned her attention instead to the lovely array of colours of the ladies' gowns, like so many flowers scattered about. She looked for patterns and shapes, but, unlike the symmetry of the room's decor, the guests were a mishmash. How would one put a pleasing order on a painting of this event?

Feeling like a hopeless amateur, she gave up and closed her eyes.

To her surprise she heard a pattern of sounds in the music, a repeated melody, but as soon as she identified it, the music changed and the pattern was lost. Sometimes it came back; sometimes a new pattern of notes emerged. Frustrating.

After talking with Vespery she'd entertained the idea that all art used pattern. Hearing it in the music expanded the idea. But then Mozart broke the pattern and her idea seemed suddenly foolish.

She opened her eyes again and looked around her.

Lord Tinmore leaned on his cane, his eyes closed and his breathing even. The music had put him to sleep. Goodness! She hoped he would not snore.

Rustling in the back suggested that other guests were restless. Lorene, though, was rapt and that was enough for Genna.

She wanted to glance behind her to see Rossdale's reaction to the music, but she feared it would be noticed.

When the first piece finished there was a short intermission during which the musicians left the room and the footmen served more champagne.

Some guests rose from their seats, but Lorene and Genna remained seated. Tinmore woke, but his eyes remained heavy.

'What did you think of the music?' Genna asked her sister.

'I thought it marvellous.' Lorene said. 'I wonder if there is sheet music for piano. I should love to learn it.'

'Perhaps we can visit the music shops and find out.' The shopping was another of the delights of London. There was a shop selling anything one could imagine.

After a few minutes the glasses were collected and the musicians returned to the alcove.

They began to play.

This piece was not as light-hearted as the first. It was melancholic. Sorrowful.

It reminded Genna of all she had lost. The home in which she'd grown up. Her mother.

And now her sisters and brother whose lives really did not involve her any more.

She blinked rapidly. She would not give in to the blue devils. She would not. No matter how dismal her life became. She was in London, a city of many enjoyments. She would enjoy as many as she could and would take it as a challenge to thwart any of Tinmore's plans for her to marry.

She would do just as she pleased.

The last movement began, a slow cavatina. It was a veritable dirge, pulling Genna's spirits low again. Then the music paused and Genna braced herself against a further onslaught of depression.

Instead, the music turned ebullient. Genna almost laughed aloud in relief as the notes danced cheerfully along, brushing away all that darkness.

That was what she would do. She'd brush away the darkness, make her own happy life and leave the rest behind.

She smiled and dared to glance back at Rossdale.

Ross scanned the supper room, although he knew precisely where Genna sat. Lord Tinmore had brought his wife and her sister into the supper room, but Ross's father had called him over to his table and Tinmore never looked back. The ladies were again left alone. Ross had been ready to cross the room to them, but both Dell and Vespery approached their table and sat with them. So he made the rounds again, but kept his eye on her, determined to spend a little more time with her before the night was over.

He moved through the room and finally stopped at their table.

Genna smiled up at him. 'Might you sit with us a little while?'

'I would be pleased to,' Ross answered truthfully. 'I do not believe I have sat down since the evening began.'

'Not even during the Quintet,' she stated.

'I stood in the back.' He turned to Lady Tinmore. 'Did you enjoy the performance?'

Lady Tinmore certainly had appeared as if she had. Of all the guests, she was the one whose attention to the music did not waver.

Her face lit up. 'Oh, yes! I do not know when I have so enjoyed music.'

He was baffled. The music had been competently played by the musicians and the pieces were pleasant enough. 'Why do you say so?'

'The first piece. In D major. It lightened my heart. There were so many musical ideas in it that I could not see how Mozart would be able to make it into a coherent whole.' She smiled. 'But, of course, he did.' She looked at the others. 'Did you not think so?'

'I listened for patterns of melody,' Genna said. 'But as soon as I heard one, the music changed to something else.'

'That is what I mean! So many ideas,' her sister cried. 'Please someone say they heard what I heard.'

Vespery threw up his hands. 'I do not analyse. I merely listen.'

Dell's chair had been pulled back as if he were not quite a part of this table. He stared into his glass of wine. 'I thought it complex. And beautiful.'

Lady Tinmore nodded. 'Yes,' she whispered. She looked shyly at Ross. 'What did you think?'

'I agree it was pleasant to listen to.' Music had never captured his interest. Neither had art of any sort, really. He liked what he saw or not, liked what he heard. Or not.

'What of the second piece?' Genna asked. 'That was not pleasant.'

'Beautiful.' Vespery raised a finger. 'But not pleasant.'

'But there were so many surprises in it!' Lady Tinmore cried. 'Like those harsh chords in the minuet.'

One thing Ross could say. Lady Tinmore had suddenly come to life. She had a personality after all. And emotion. Hidden, he supposed, because of her overbearing yet neglectful husband.

Genna spoke up. 'I thought I should be driven to a fit of weeping by those movements. Right when I was beginning to completely despair, that happy ending came.'

'Yes!' her sister cried. 'Was that not marvellous?'

Ross liked both the Summerfield sisters, he decided.

Lord Tinmore appeared at the table, but he spoke only to Ross. 'Rossdale, I was just telling your father, the Duke, that this was a most competently played musical evening. I am honoured to have been in the audience.'

Ross saw Genna cover her mouth, but her eyes danced. Tinmore did not notice. His attention was only on Ross. He also did not see Dell pull his chair further back and slip away.

'Kindly said, Tinmore,' Ross responded.

'I fear, sir, that I must bid you goodnight,' Tinmore went on. 'I already bade goodnight to your father and the Duchess. I hope that my years will excuse me to you and your family. Fatigue plagues me.'

They were leaving? He'd hardly had time to speak to Genna.

'Come!' Tinmore snapped to his wife and Genna. 'We must leave now.'

Lady Tinmore rose. 'I must thank the Duke and Duchess first.'

'They do not want to be bothered, I assure you,' Tinmore said. 'I said all that was required.'

All the life glimpsed a moment ago seemed drained from Lady Tinmore now. Genna looked red-faced with anger.

This boor.

Ross put on a smile he did not feel. 'I must agree with your wife, sir. My father and the Duchess take great offence when guests do not bother to thank them. I will accompany your wife and her sister to bid their farewells. You rest here.'

As Ross offered his arms to each of the ladies, Tinmore looked at Vespery and demanded, 'Who are you?'

Ross did not wait to hear Vespery's reply.

When they stepped away from the table, Genna murmured, 'It was nonsense.'

'What was?' Ross asked.

'He fell asleep during the whole concert,' she said. 'He did not hear it competently played at all.'

Ross inclined his head to her. 'I noticed. I could see from the back.'

She giggled.

'Want to hear more nonsense, ladies?' Ross asked.

'Indeed!' Genna said.

Her sister remained subdued.

He stopped and looked from one to the other. 'My father and the Duchess do not care a fig if you bid them goodnight.'

Genna's eyes sparkled. 'Oh, you are trying to make me laugh out loud!'

Yes. He definitely wanted to see more of Genna Summerfield.

Because she made him want to laugh out loud, too.

The next morning Ross strode down Bond Street and entered a shop he had never set foot in before. Mori and Leverne's Music Shop. He'd passed it countless times on his way to Gentleman Jackson's Boxing Salon, but he'd never had a reason to enter it before.

He had a whim to purchase sheet music to the Mozart pieces performed at the Duchess's musicale to give to Lady

Tinmore. It seemed the one thing that made her happy. He'd present it to Lord Tinmore for his wife and no one would think anything of that, not that any member of the *ton* would know of it. Tinmore would take it as a compliment to him, Lady Tinmore would receive some pleasure from it and perhaps Genna would also be pleased with him.

He stood inside the door without a clue how to find the piece he desired. The music seemed to be arranged in aisles, filed in some order that escaped him.

The clerk stood behind a counter at the far end of the shop, speaking to two ladies.

As Ross approached one of the ladies turned and broke into a smile. 'Rossdale!'

Genna. And her sister.

'What a surprise to see you!' Genna said. 'We came looking for the music from last night's musicale, but the last copy was sold just this morning.'

'I am terribly sorry,' the clerk said. 'The gentleman came early when the shop opened. You might try Birchall's down the street.'

'We did try there,' Lady Tinmore said.

So much for his idea of giving the music to her.

'What are you here for, Rossdale?' Genna asked. 'Do not tell me you were searching for the same music.'

Very well. He would not tell her. 'I was considering a gift,' he said.

Her smile faltered. 'Oh.' She seemed to recover, though. 'Perhaps we can help you. What sort of music did you have in mind?'

He shrugged. 'Perhaps something by Mozart. For the piano.'

'Ah!' said the clerk. 'I have some over here.'

'Help him, Lorene,' Genna said. 'You will be able to tell him what music is best.'

Lady Tinmore acted as reserved as usual. 'If you like.' She lowered her lashes.

'I would be grateful,' Ross said.

She riffled through the sheets of music the clerk indicated. 'Here is one.' She pulled out the sheet and studied it. 'A piano sonata. Number eleven.'

She handed it to him and he glanced at the page. He could follow almost none of it. 'Do you have this music?' he asked her.

'No,' she replied. 'I merely think it would be a pretty one to play.'

He handed the sheets to the clerk. 'I will purchase this one.' He gave his information to the clerk.

Upon learning where the bill was to be directed, the clerk became even more solicitous. 'Allow me to place this in an envelope for you, my lord.'

'Did you want to look for something else?' Genna asked her sister.

Lady Tinmore shook her head.

Ross, music in hand, walked with the ladies to the door. At the door, though, he stopped and handed the envelope to Lady Tinmore. 'This is for you, ma'am,' he said.

'For me?' Some expression entered her face.

'Lorene!' Genna broke into a smile.

'But, why?' Lady Tinmore asked.

'For being the guest last night who most enjoyed the concert,' he replied.

And to give her some happiness since she certainly did not have that in her marriage.

Ross opened the door and held it. Lady Tinmore walked out first.

Genna paused and looked up at Ross. 'Take care, Lord Rossdale. You might make me like you very much.'

He grinned. 'There must be worse fates than that.'

Although what good would it do them to like each other? Unless they could spend time together.

He was determined to figure out a way, but unless he made a formal gesture, he could not even call upon her.

All he could do was wait until they saw each other by accident, like this, or were invited to the same parties. And who knew when that would be?

Chapter Eleven

What was he thinking? They were together now. Ross could contrive to spend more time with Genna, even if her sister was also present.

'Where are you ladies bound after this?' he asked when they were out on the pavement.

'I believe we will go home,' Lady Tinmore said.

Genna looked disappointed. Perhaps she wanted more time together, as well. He was not surprised they were of one mind.

'May I escort you?' he asked.

Genna's eyes pleaded with her sister. The walk back to Curzon Street and Tinmore's town house would be a short one, but to accompany them would be more enjoyable than if he simply left them here.

Lady Tinmore lowered her lashes. 'If you like.'

Genna smiled.

As did Ross.

He offered his arm to Lorene, who, as a countess, had precedence. Genna walked next to her.

They strolled past the shops on Bond Street and turned on Bruton Street.

'Are you enjoying your Season in London?' Ross asked in a polite tone.

'Yes, quite,' Lorene answered agreeably.

He leaned over and directed his gaze at Genna. 'And you, Miss Summerfield?'

Genna appeared for a moment to be doing battle with

herself. Trying not to say something she really wanted
to say.

Her words burst forth. 'To own the truth, I am feeling
a bit restrained.' Apparently what she wanted to say won
out. 'There is so much to do and see here in town and, as I
cannot go out alone, I am confined to the house.'

'Genna!' her sister chided.

'Well, it is true,' Genna protested hotly.

They had reached Berkeley Square.

Ross deflected the impending sisterly spat. 'Shall we do
and see something right now?' he asked. 'Here is Gunter's.
Shall we stop and have an ice?'

Lady Tinmore's brows knit. 'I do not know if we should.'

'It would be respectable,' Ross said. 'I would not have
asked otherwise.'

'Oh, let's do, Lorene.' Genna pleaded. 'It will be fun.'

Lady Tinmore looked as if she were being dragged to a
dungeon instead of the most fashionable tea shop and con-
fectioner in Mayfair.

'Very well,' she finally said.

Genna skipped in apparent delight.

'The day is overcast, though, as well as being chilly,'
Ross said. 'Let us not eat in the square under the trees. We
should go inside.'

They entered the shop and sat at a table.

A waiter stepped up to serve them. 'Sir? Ladies?'

'What would you like?' Ross asked Genna and her sister.

'Not an ice,' Lorene said. 'Not on such a cold day. I
shall have tea.'

Genna huffed. 'I do not care how cold it may be, I am
having an ice!'

The waiter handed them cards that had the flavours
printed on them. 'Your choice, miss.'

Genna read part of the list aloud. 'Barberry, elderflower,
jasmine, muscadine, pistachio and rye bread...' She handed

the card back to the waiter. 'I shall be adventuresome. I will try the rye-bread ice.'

'Rye-bread ice,' repeated the waiter in a voice that showed her exotic choice was commonplace for him. 'And you, sir?'

'Pineapple,' Ross said.

The waiter bowed and left.

'Pineapple?' Genna looked at him in mock disapproval. 'That is not very daring.'

'It is what I like,' he explained.

'But how do you know that you will not like another flavour better unless you try it?' she asked.

'Genna fancies whatever is new and different,' her sister said.

'You make me sound frivolous,' Genna complained, but she turned to Ross and laughed. 'What am I saying? Lorene is correct! That is me! Liking whatever is new and different.'

Therein was her charm. 'And you are eager to see new and different sights while you are here?' he asked.

'I am eager. Not very hopeful, though.' She frowned and her face tightened in frustration. 'I think I might be content to do anything but stay in the house.'

'Genna!' her sister again chided. 'You must not say such things. They can be misinterpreted. You'll sound fast.'

'Oh, I think Lord Rossdale knows what I mean,' she said with confidence. 'I just want to *do* things. The places I see do not even have to be new. Something I've liked before and wish to do or see again would be fine.'

'Like what?' he asked.

'Well.' Her mouth widened into an impish smile. 'Like having an ice at Gunter's.'

He liked her humour. 'What else?'

Lady Tinmore answered for her. 'Genna wishes to see Napoleon's carriage at the Egyptian Hall.'

Ross laughed inwardly. He wanted to see Napoleon's carriage, as well.

'I do wish to see it!' she protested. 'Who would not?'

'It has created quite a stir,' he admitted.

Genna gave Lorene a smug look. 'See, Lorene, I am not the only one.' Lorene folded her arms across her chest and glanced away.

He had no idea what to do with sisterly disputes. He had no brothers or sisters. It was one of the reasons his father was so eager for him to marry and produce an heir.

Perhaps if his mother had lived it would have been different. Perhaps there would have been little sisters or brothers for him to spat with.

Genna went on. 'I would love to see everything in the Egyptian Museum. I also want to see Astley's Amphitheatre, the menagerie at the Tower, and—' She paused and looked away. 'I want to see the Elgin Marbles.'

She was game for everything.

Like his mother had been.

Until his father inherited the title and the burden of that responsibility fell upon him. And her.

'You cannot see the Elgin Marbles,' Lady Tinmore said. 'No one can. They are stored away until Parliament decides whether or not to purchase them for the British Museum.'

They were stored at Montagu House.

Their ices and Lady Tinmore's cup of tea were brought to them.

Genna dipped into hers eagerly. And made a face, but she took another spoonful and another.

Ross's spoon was poised to taste his. 'How is it?'

She put on a brave smile. 'It is—it is—it is…' She faltered. She finally laughed. 'It is quite dreadful, actually.'

Her sister murmured, 'Of course it is.'

Ross pushed his untouched pineapple ice towards her. 'Here. Have mine. I only ordered it so you would not have to eat alone.'

She looked at it longingly, then pulled it the rest of the way towards her. 'Oh, thank you! I love pineapple ices.'

Her sister stood and Ross quickly stood, as well.

'I believe I will choose some confections to bring to Lord Tinmore,' she said.

'Shall I assist you?' he asked.

'Not at all. The clerk will help me.'

There was a clerk behind a counter who had just assisted someone else.

Ross sat again as Lady Tinmore walked away.

'She is purchasing confections for Lord Tinmore,' he repeated, finding it difficult to believe.

Genna's countenance turned serious. 'She tries very hard to please him. An impossible goal, I believe.'

He thought he ought to be careful what he said. 'Tinmore is very…critical…of her.'

She swallowed a spoonful. 'He is an awful man, but do not say so in front of her. She will defend him.'

He was puzzled. 'She has a regard for him?'

She shook her head. 'Not in the way you mean. She is grateful to him for marrying her. She married him so that my sister Tess, my brother and I would have a chance to make good matches and not be required to be governesses or ladies' companions, or, in my brother's case, to stay in the army and be sent some place terrible like the West Indies.'

'She married him for you and your sister and brother?' Marrying for money took on a different meaning in that case.

She nodded and glanced over at her sister. 'Although I never wanted any of it. I won't use his dowry, no matter what Tinmore thinks.'

'Surely you wish to marry, though,' he said.

She scoffed. 'With no dowry, I cannot expect to marry, but that does not trouble me. I do not wish to marry.'

'How would you live, then?' he asked.

Young ladies of good birth had few choices in life except to marry. The few they had were dismal. Ladies' companions or governesses, as she'd said.

'Well, if you must know, I wish to make my living as an artist. Like your Mr Vespery.' She took another spoonful.

'You wish to paint portraits?' That was how Vespery made his living.

'I would prefer to paint landscapes, but I doubt that will bring me enough money.' She shrugged.

He smiled. 'Ones with purple skies and blue grass?'

She laughed. 'I doubt that sort of landscape would bring me any income at all!' She glanced down at her almost finished ice. 'I have so much more to learn, though. I do not even know how to paint in oils.'

Maybe Vespery could be persuaded to give her lessons, Ross thought. But would Tinmore allow such a thing?

She smiled and took the last bite. 'I can always become a lady's companion. I would make a good one, do you not think?'

He grinned. 'You would keep some lady on her toes, that is true.'

Lady Tinmore walked back to the table, a small package in hand. Ross stood.

'I believe we should go, Genna,' she said.

Genna rose. 'Thank you, Lord Rossdale. That was a lovely interlude.'

'My pleasure.'

It was his pleasure, a pleasure to have a candid conversation with an intelligent young woman who enjoyed new experiences as much as he did. He was not going to leave their next meeting to chance. After he delivered Genna and her sister to the town house on Curzon Street, he would make another call nearby. The Duchess of Archester was planning a ball in two weeks' time. He would wager she could be persuaded to invite the daughters of her old friend, Lady Summerfield.

* * *

After Rossdale left Genna and Lorene at their door and the footman carried away their cloaks, Lorene turned to Genna. 'Do you not think you are acting a bit too free with Lord Rossdale?'

She should have known Lorene would have something to say about her behaviour. Too often her husband's words seemed to be coming out of Lorene's mouth.

'Too free? I do not take your meaning.'

They started up the stairs.

'You say too much. About wanting to go to the Egyptian Museum, and Astley's and all. Might he not take it you want an invitation from him?'

She made herself laugh. 'Perhaps I did! How else am I going to do things unless someone invites me?'

'Not the son of a duke!' Lorene cried. 'You must not mistake his father's interest in Lord Tinmore for the son's intention to court you.'

Sometimes Lorene could sound every bit as dispiriting as her husband.

She continued up the stairs, a few steps ahead of her sister. 'I like Lord Rossdale. And I think he likes me. But he is not going to court me. It is not like that.'

No one would court her if she had anything to do with it. Tinmore could not force her to marry. She just needed a little more time to be ready to forge her own way.

Lorene went on. 'You must not speak so familiarly to gentlemen. It is not the thing to do. You must be careful. The last thing we want is to be the objects of gossip.'

Of scandal.

Genna did not have the horror of gossip and scandal that her two sisters did. She did not care what others thought of her.

Had her mother been like her?

If she should ever again be in the company of the Duchesses of Archester and of Mannerton, she would ask them.

They were met on the first floor by the butler. 'A package arrived for you, my lady.'

'For me?' Lorene sounded surprised.

'It is in your sitting room.' He bowed.

Lorene had a parlour near to her bedchamber where she could receive callers—if anyone called on her, that was.

'Let us go see what it is!' Genna cried, the sharp words between them forgotten.

They rushed to the sitting room. On the tea table was an envelope very similar to the one Lorene held in her hand, the music Rossdale had purchased for her. She placed that envelope on the table and picked up the other. It was tied with a ribbon like a gift. A card was stuck underneath the ribbon.

Lorene pulled the card out and read it. She handed it to Genna.

'"*For your enjoyment*",' Genna read. She looked up at Lorene. 'It is not signed.'

Lorene opened the envelope and pulled out sheets of music. She gasped. 'The Mozart pieces from the musicale last night!'

'Oh, my goodness,' Genna exclaimed. 'It must have been purchased by that gentleman the clerk mentioned. Who could it be?'

Lorene traced her fingers along the lines of music, a strange, soft expression on her face. 'I do not know.'

Not Tinmore, that was for certain.

Two weeks later Lord Tinmore, Lorene and Genna were invited to the Duchess of Archester's ball, the first important ball of the Season. It was a coup Tinmore credited to his new alliance with the Duke of Kessington, Rossdale's father. He was more certain than ever that Lorene or Genna would embarrass him completely, so every dinner for over a week had been consumed with his incessant instructions.

He insisted both Genna and Lorene have new ball

gowns, as if they would not want a new gown themselves. Their modiste made certain their dresses were beautifully fashionable. Genna's was a pale blue silk with an over-dress and long sleeves of white net. The hem of the skirt was trimmed in white lace as were the neckline and cuffs.

Tinmore insisted that a hairdresser be hired as well, but Genna disliked what the man did. She had her own maid take down her hair and rearrange it to a style less fussy and more comfortable for her. She wound up with curls around her face and the rest pulled high on her head. A long string of tiny pearls was wrapped around her head and up through the crown of curls.

Lorene's gown was white muslin embellished with gold embroidery that shimmered in the candlelight. She wore a gold-and-diamond band in her hair and diamonds around her neck. Her usually straight hair had been transformed into a mass of curls. How anyone could look at another lady there, Genna did not know. Her sister took her breath away.

When they were announced at the ball, Genna felt secure in their appearance—and totally mismatched with the grey-haired, wrinkled man who escorted them. They first waited in a line to greet the Duke and Duchess of Archester. When it was finally Genna's turn, the Duchess greeted her warmly.

The Duke held on to Genna's hand for a moment. 'You are the image of your mother, young lady,' he said with feeling.

Genna felt a stab of pain. She could not remember what her mother looked like.

She curtsied. 'Thank you, your Grace.' What else could she say?

Tinmore quickly whisked them away from the Duke and Duchess.

As they crossed the ballroom floor, Tinmore whispered, 'There will be some eligible men here, girl. I expect you to be on good behaviour. Make a good impression. I have already spoken to some gentlemen on your behalf, so you will have some dance partners.'

Genna forced a smile. 'I never want for dance partners, sir.'

She had no intention of encouraging his matchmaking. She was perfectly capable of having a good time all on her own.

'Now, do not come bothering me if I am in conversation,' he whispered to Lorene. 'It will likely be about a matter of importance. There will be other ladies for you to speak to. Make certain you are agreeable.'

Lorene was always agreeable, Genna wanted to say, but Tinmore left them before she could open her mouth.

'There are so many people here!' Lorene looked around nervously.

Genna scoured the room. 'Good! Perhaps Tinmore's gentlemen will not be able to find me. If I spy them coming, I'll hide behind a jardinière of flowers.'

'He merely wants to see you settled,' Lorene said defensively.

'He wants me out of his house so he can have you all to himself,' Genna retorted in good humour, although she really meant it.

She caught sight of two men walking towards them. 'Here are two gentlemen we know.'

Rossdale and Penford.

Rossdale smiled. 'Good evening, ladies.'

Lord Penford merely nodded and asked, 'May I get you some refreshment?'

Genna saw liveried servants carrying glasses with what she hoped was champagne. 'Yes, Penford. Thank you.'

Was he Lorene's secret admirer?

Impossible. Genna could not tell whether or not Penford even liked Lorene. He was all obligation, Genna feared.

'Are you available for the first set?' Rossdale asked Genna.

Her heart danced in her chest. 'I am.' There was no one she would rather dance with.

He turned to Lorene. 'Will you be dancing, ma'am? Perhaps you will favour me with a set?'

Now Genna's heart melted. He'd included her sister who desperately deserved to enjoy herself.

Lorene's eyes darted towards where her husband was conversing with other men. 'I am not certain if I should.'

'Of course you should,' cried Genna. 'It is a ball and you look so lovely many gentlemen will want to dance with you.'

Penford came up and handed her and Genna a glass of champagne.

'Dance the second set with me,' Rossdale said. 'Then you may retire if you wish.'

'Oh, say yes, Lorene!' Genna said impatiently.

She lowered her eyes. 'Very well.'

By the time they finished the champagne, couples were lining up for the first dance. Rossdale took Genna's hand to lead her on to the dance floor. Genna turned back to smile at her sister. She felt a little guilty for leaving Lorene, but Penford, taciturn as he was wont to be, stood by her side and was some company, at least.

Genna filled with excitement. To see Rossdale again. To be dancing with him. To have a friend.

Ross smiled as they faced each other in the line, waiting for others to join.

The music started and the couples at the head of the line began dancing their steps and figures. Each couple would repeat the figures, couple by couple, down the line.

'Do you enjoy dancing?' Ross asked Genna, although it was clear she did.

Her colour was high and her eyes sparkled.

'I do indeed.' she responded. 'It is so lively. And I love

how pretty it is when all the couples perform the figures together.'

Ross mostly considered dancing a social obligation, but it was impossible not to catch Genna's excitement and enjoy himself along with her. There was a rhythm to it, a pattern, he found pleasant, especially if he forgot anything but the dance.

And Genna.

He noticed that Dell and Lady Tinmore had joined the line. When he and Genna came together in the figures, he said to her, 'Your sister dances.'

'I noticed,' she replied as the dance separated them.

It brought them together again.

'Do you suppose Penford felt an obligation?' she asked.

His answer had to wait until they came together again. 'That is what he says.'

'I am delighted she is allowing herself some fun,' Genna said. 'I wonder if Tinmore even notices.' They parted and came together once more, turning in a circle. 'I hope she thinks of nothing but the dancing.'

He decided to offer Genna what she wanted for her sister—a chance to think of nothing but the dancing. He did not attempt more than a comment or two after that.

The sets often lasted a half-hour or more and this one was no exception. Ross usually succumbed to boredom after the first ten minutes, but this time he was not even aware of how much time had passed.

When the music stopped, he stood facing Genna again. They both stared at each other as if shocked the dance had ended. Finally she curtsied, he bowed, and he took her hand to return her to where she had stood with her sister.

Her step quickened when they neared her. 'Was that not lovely?' she asked.

Lady Tinmore darted a glance at Dell, who quickly looked away. 'Lovely. Yes.'

A footman bore a tray with champagne and they each took a glass.

It made perfect sense for Ross to remain with Genna and her sister. He would be dancing with her sister the next set, but after that he must leave them and dance with others. He could swing back for a second dance. Two dances were the limit unless he wished for there to be speculation about a betrothal between them.

He glanced around the room and saw his father's wife standing with the Duchess of Mannerton. His father was deep in conversation with the Duke of Mannerton and Lord Tinmore was hovering around the edges of these higher-ranking men. His father's wife, on the other hand, kept tossing disapproving looks Ross's way.

Another reason why he must leave Genna and seek out other partners. The Duchess could be a formidable enemy if she so chose and he certainly did not wish her to choose Genna as an enemy.

A young gentleman with whom Ross had a passing acquaintance, approached them.

He bowed to Genna. 'Miss Summerfield, how good to see you.'

She smiled at him. 'Why, good evening, Mr Holdsworth.'

Holdsworth was the younger son of Baron Holdsworth. He could not be more than twenty-one, more of an age with Genna than Ross, who was nearing thirty.

Holdsworth nodded nervously to Ross and Dell, who easily outranked him.

His attention returned to Genna. 'Are you engaged for the next set? If not, would you do me the honour of dancing with me?'

'Yes, of course, Mr Holdsworth,' she responded right away. 'I remember dancing with you last Season. I enjoyed it very much.'

The young man beamed with pleasure. He bowed and withdrew.

Ross's mood turned sour.

'Do you know Mr Holdsworth?' she asked Ross. 'I should have introduced you, shouldn't I?'

'I am acquainted with him,' Ross answered.

'He is quite fun to dance with, as you will see.' She laughed. 'Very energetic.' She leaned closer to his ear. 'And he is not one of Lord Tinmore's choices.'

Ross frowned. 'Tinmore has chosen who will dance with you?'

'Widowers with a dozen children to manage or younger sons needing the dowry Tinmore offers.' She glanced around the room. 'I shall avoid them if I am able.'

Lorene glared at her. 'Genna, may I speak with you for a moment?'

Her sister drew Genna aside. 'What are you saying to Rossdale about Lord Tinmore—?'

Ross could not hear the rest.

He turned to Dell, who looked preoccupied. 'How are you faring, Dell?'

'Well enough, I suppose.' Dell composed his features, but only briefly. His eyes shone with pain. 'Actually, not well at all. I need some respite.'

'Is there anything I can do?' Ross asked. He'd been surprised that Dell had danced at all. In fact, he was surprised Dell had agreed to come. These social events were not easy for him.

'No. Nothing.' Dell glanced towards Genna and her sister. 'Please make my excuses to the ladies.' He turned and walked away without waiting for Ross's agreement.

Both sisters, looking somewhat heated, returned to where Ross stood. Neither looked very happy.

'Dell had to excuse himself,' he told them. 'He bids you goodnight.'

'Oh?' Genna glanced at her sister. 'I do hope he comes back.'

'Was there anything amiss?' Lady Tinmore asked. 'He appeared upset.'

'He is not yet completely recovered from the loss of his family,' Ross replied. 'It strikes him unawares at times.'

'What happened to them?' Genna's face looked pinched.

'They were killed in a fire. All of them,' he said in a low voice.

Lady Tinmore gasped.

'You and your sisters and brother, Lady Tinmore, are all the relations he has left,' he added.

The musicians signalled the next set and couples began to line up on the dance floor. Mr Holdsworth strode over eagerly and extended his hand to Genna, who seemed to have lost her sparkle.

He ought not to have spoken. Both ladies immediately grasped the enormity of Dell's loss and were affected by the news.

Ross turned to Lady Tinmore. 'This is our set, I believe.'

She glanced up at him and for a moment he thought she would start weeping. 'You do not have to dance with me, Lord Rossdale. I—I feel it is almost unseemly to dance after hearing…' Her voice trailed off.

'Forgive me,' he said. 'This was not the proper time to tell you of Dell's loss. He would be vexed with me if he found out I ruined this ball for you. Please dance with me.'

She nodded.

They took their place in the line not far from Genna and Mr Holdsworth.

Lady Tinmore noticed him looking Genna's way.

He changed the subject. 'I hope you and your sister settled your quarrel.'

'Quarrel?' She could not quite meet his eye. 'She has such lively spirits. Sometimes she is too forward and her tongue runs away with her.'

Ross responded, 'I admire your sister's forthrightness. It is a refreshing change from those who only say what is expected.'

'Then do understand. She is not trying to get you to court her.'

The music had begun and the first figures were starting down the line of dancers.

He knew that. Even from his first meeting with Genna, he knew she was not trying to trap him into marriage. But it depressed him to hear her sister say it aloud.

It was Genna's and Mr Holdsworth's turn to dance. They were quite well matched in lively steps and grace, which somehow did not please him. Genna seemed to regain some of her former enthusiasm, though.

At the end of the set, Lady Tinmore thanked him and added, 'I do hope Lord Penford returns to the ballroom.'

He bowed to her. 'I hope so, as well.'

He escorted her back to the place they'd been standing and she lowered herself into a nearby chair. 'I believe I will sit for a while.'

'Shall I bring you some refreshment?' he asked, although he also watched Genna and Mr Holdsworth still on the dance floor talking together.

'I would love something to drink.' Lady Tinmore fanned herself.

He brought her a glass of champagne and noticed Genna leaving the dance floor.

'I see your sister is returning to you,' he said to Lady Tinmore. 'I must take my leave.'

She thanked him again for the dance and said goodbye.

He made himself walk through the ballroom and converse with various people he knew. His father was doing the same, as was his father's wife, but they had an agenda—to turn as many members of Parliament as possible to their way of thinking. Important work, but when did his father ever simply enjoy himself? His father used to smile and laugh and be willing to do things just for the doing of them.

Ross spied Genna conversing with yet another young man. A man who looked to be in his forties—one of Lord Tinmore's choices, perhaps?—hung around her for a bit, but gave up trying to get her attention away from the young buck. A quadrille was called and the young man escorted her to the dance floor.

Ross asked the daughter of one of his father's closest allies to dance the quadrille with him, which certainly would meet with the Duchess's approval. The young lady was in want of a partner and Ross did not wish to leave her a wallflower.

But he intended to get a second dance with Genna before the night was through.

Unless another gentleman claimed her first, that was.

Chapter Twelve

After the quadrille, Ross noticed Genna leave the ballroom. She disappeared into the ladies' retiring room and he waited in the corridor to catch her when she came out.

The door opened and Genna peeked carefully around before stepping into the corridor. She seemed in no hurry to return to the dancing.

He approached her from behind. 'Genna?'

She jumped and put her hand on her chest when she saw it was him. 'Oh, Rossdale! You startled me. I thought you were someone else.'

'Who?' One of the young men who occupied her time?

She waved a hand. 'Oh, one of Tinmore's widowers. I am eager to avoid him.'

He took her arm. 'Then let's not return to the ballroom.'

He led her outside on to a veranda. The Duke of Archester's town house was one of the few in Mayfair to have a garden of any size behind it. They were not the only ones to seek a quieter, more secluded place. Other couples stood close together on the veranda or on benches in the garden. After the close, warm air of the ballroom, the chilly March air felt welcome, although Ross doubted that all the couples outside were merely seeking fresh air.

Genna inhaled deeply. 'Oh, how nice. I can breathe out here.'

It occurred to him that she smiled at him the way she smiled at her other dance partners. He didn't like that thought, though. 'You appeared to be having a good time dancing.'

She sobered. 'I am having a good time, although I cannot help thinking about Lord Penford. Has he returned to the ballroom?'

'Not that I've seen.' It pleased him that she felt concern for his friend.

Her lovely forehead knitted.

'Do not let it spoil your enjoyment, though. He would not wish that and I should feel quite regretful that I spoke of his family.'

She nodded. 'I have enjoyed the dancing.' She slid him a sly smile. 'So far I have not had to dance with any of the men Tinmore picked to court me.'

'Is he so determined to get you married?' he asked.

She nodded. 'But I only have to get through this Season. I will be twenty-one soon and I can go my own way.'

He thought about her desire to become an artist. It was a daring choice. Women artists were rare, but some had made a good living with their art.

She shivered and he led them to a corner more protected from the cool air.

She gazed at him with curiosity. 'But what of you? There seem to be several young ladies with whom to dance. Are you not looking to make a match?'

He stiffened. 'I am in no hurry to take on that responsibility.'

She peered at him. 'You do not seem the sort to wish to shirk responsibility.'

'Perhaps responsibility is not the proper word.' How could he explain? 'My station dictates that a match should be a carefully considered one. Advantageous to both parties.'

Her expression turned sympathetic. 'How dreadful.'

He was not ready to explain it all, though. 'I know I must marry and produce an heir. It is my duty. I know I will have to bear the mantle of the title eventually, but my father is in excellent health. There is no reason for me to rush. There is so much more I wish to do.'

Her face relaxed. 'Like what?'

What did he wish to do? Since the war's end, he hadn't been sure, although there certainly was plenty to do for the returning soldiers. With the war's end, several regiments would disband and the soldiers would return home without a pension and many without a trade to support them.

He'd already cast Genna and her sister into the dismals by talking of Dell's loss; he certainly did not wish to depress her further with the plight of the soldiers.

'I'd like to travel, perhaps,' he said instead. Who would not wish to travel? 'Visit Paris, for one thing. The rest of the Continent. Maybe return to Rome and Venice.'

Her eyes lit up. 'And see the works of art there! Would that not be wonderful?'

Lately, because of Genna, he'd been noticing the artwork wherever he went. He'd like to learn more, appreciate it more.

She laughed. 'Here I am, pining merely to see the sights of London. You are thinking of the world!'

He smiled. 'Not the world, perhaps.' Although he was intensely curious about the Colonies. 'But certainly the Continent. Do a Grand Tour all over again, but widen my horizons.'

She sighed. 'You did a Grand Tour?'

'With Dell,' he said. 'We have been friends since we were boys.'

'How lovely!'

A footman came to the veranda door. 'Supper is being served.'

'We missed the supper dance,' she said, sounding relieved.

'You wanted to miss it?' he asked.

She grinned. 'One of Tinmore's widowers was searching for me. That is why I left the ballroom. Imagine being trapped with him through supper.'

'You know this gentleman?'

She nodded. 'Tinmore introduced us last Season, but he was not out of mourning yet, so he's been encouraged to court me now.' She glanced away and back again. 'He is a perfectly nice man. I do not mean to make a jest of him. I merely do not want him to court me. There are so many ladies who would love to marry him, but I would feel imprisoned.'

Other couples crossed the veranda and re-entered the house.

'Would you consider it undesirable to be trapped with me through supper?' he asked.

Her gaze rose to meet his. 'I can think of no one else I would rather be trapped with.'

Sitting with Rossdale for supper was a delight. With anyone else she would have restrained herself and taken care what she said, but with Rossdale she felt free to say anything. Even better, she was not beneath the watchful eye of her sister, who she finally spied in a group of other ladies and gentlemen. And Lord Penford.

She was relieved to see Lord Penford back.

After supper some of the young gentlemen with whom she became acquainted the previous Season engaged her to dance. Lord Rossdale asked her for the last dance.

A waltz.

It was exciting that the Duchess of Archester allowed the waltz, still considered scandalous by some. Genna usually did not relish the less lively dances, but she did love to dance the waltz. She liked being free of the lines of the country dances or the squares of the quadrilles. You stayed with your partner throughout the whole dance. With the right partner, the waltz was heaven.

And Rossdale was the right partner.

When the music began, they walked on to the dance floor with hands entwined and, finding a place, faced each other. She curtsied. He bowed. She put her hands on his shoulders. He placed his hands at her waist. Her heart fluttered.

Why did her body react so when he touched her? She could only think that it was because they liked each other so well and were as alike as two peas in a pod.

He led her in the dance, moving in a circle together.

Usually in the waltz, Genna relished the sight of the couples all turning on the dance floor, the ladies' dresses like spinning flowers. This time, though, she could not take her eyes off Rossdale. She was taller than fashionable, but it hardly mattered when dancing with him. She had to tilt her head to see his face and she much preferred that to staring at the top of some gentleman's head.

Especially because Rossdale's lovely eyes and smiling mouth made her feel happy inside.

Staring only at him made the rest of the room a blur. Genna felt as if they were alone in the room, moving to the music, like one unit. She was tired from the dancing and giddy from a bit too much champagne and it all felt like a lovely dream, one she did not want to end.

But end it did. The music stopped and it took a moment longer for Genna to tear her eyes from his.

'What a lovely way to end a ball,' she murmured.

He nodded.

He took her hand and they walked through the guests, looking for her sister. Or Tinmore. How lucky Genna had not seen Tinmore during the whole ball. That in itself had contributed to the night's enjoyment.

Lorene had returned to where Tinmore had originally left them and she stood with poor Lord Penford, although they were not speaking to each other. Lorene had danced many of the dances, Genna had been glad to see.

'There you are,' Genna cried. 'Did you dance the waltz?'

Lorene glanced at Penford. 'Yes. We did.'

Goodness. Penford even asked her to dance the waltz.

'I would have been without a partner otherwise,' Lorene added.

'We have had such a nice time,' Genna said, squeezing Rossdale's hand before he released hers. 'I must find the Duchess and thank her for including us.'

'I had an opportunity to speak with her,' Lorene said. 'I did convey our thanks.'

Genna laughed. 'I was too busy dancing.'

Penford inclined his head towards the door of the ballroom. 'Lord Tinmore is bidding you to come.'

Tinmore was leaning on his cane with one hand and waving the other. He looked very impatient.

'I wonder where he was all this night,' Genna said.

Lorene pulled her arm. 'Come, Genna.'

She turned and smiled at Rossdale and Penford. 'Goodnight!'

Ross and Dell watched the Summerfield sisters rush to where Lord Tinmore was beckoning.

'You spent a great deal of time with Miss Summerfield,' Dell said.

'As much as possible.' Ross slid him a sideways glance. 'And you with Lady Tinmore, I might add.'

Dell frowned. 'By happenstance.'

Ross clapped his friend on the shoulder. 'I am glad you came back.'

Dell nodded.

Dell was living with him in Ross's father's house while the shell of his burned London town house was restored.

'The thing is, I like them. I like both of them,' Ross said.

'They are not what I expected,' Dell said. 'I will agree to that.'

The two men followed the crowd out of the ballroom, taking their time, having no reason to hurry. They caught up with his father and the Duchess. His father's wife had remained in the ballroom the whole time, making her rounds and keeping an eye on Ross's activities. His father spent most of the time in the card room, where Ross imagined Tinmore stayed, as well.

His father and the Duchess joined them and they all stood waiting for the carriage.

Ross's father pointed to him. 'Brackton's daughter.' His father spoke as if their conversation had begun earlier than this moment. 'She'd be a good match for you. Marquess's daughter. A step up for her. Good family, too.'

Obviously the Duchess had reported to his father that he'd danced with Lady Alice.

'I danced with her, sir,' Ross said. 'I did not make an offer.'

'You should,' his father responded. 'You are not getting any younger and neither am I.'

Ross glanced towards Dell, who averted his gaze. Both had heard this conversation before. 'I am not ready to consider marriage,' Ross said. 'Not yet.'

'What are you waiting for?' his father snapped.

'There are things yet I wish to do.' He never discussed his activities with his father and certainly not with the Duchess. They both assumed he merely caroused.

His father sliced the air with his hand. 'Marry. Beget an heir. Then do as you wish until the title is yours.'

Ross gave him a scathing look. 'Do you hear yourself? What sort of marriage would that be for the woman?'

'If the woman is a proper partner, she will understand,' the Duchess said. 'She will have her duty, as well.'

'Do not spout any romantic nonsense,' his father said.

'I was not planning to.' Ross's anger rose.

Once his father had engaged in romantic nonsense. When Ross's mother had been alive. When it had been just the three of them. His father had loosened his reserve and expressed the love and affection he had for both his wife and son. When Ross's grandfather died and his father inherited the title, everything had changed. His father grew distant, always busy, too busy. Too busy to notice when Ross's mother became ill.

'No romantic nonsense,' his father repeated more softly. To Ross's surprise what looked like pain etched the corners of his father's eyes. His father gave him a fleeting bleak look that told him his father, indeed, remembered those halcyon days when he and Ross's mother engaged in romantic nonsense.

The Duchess did not see. She was too busy looking smugly at Ross. 'You need a wife who will understand that being a duchess is not play. It is serious business.'

Ross understood, though. A duchess needed to be more like her, more in love with the title than the man, because she had to run her own enterprise, something for which his gentle mother with her freedom of spirit had not been suited.

His father's countenance hardened again. 'You have waited long enough, Ross. This is the Season. No more tarrying.'

The carriage arrived and they all climbed in.

The next day Lorene and Genna called upon the Duchess of Archester to thank her for the ball. They stayed only fifteen minutes. Tinmore had made such a fuss about how they should behave with decorum that Genna said very little during the visit. Several other ladies and gentlemen had also called, including Mr Holdsworth, who left at the same time as Genna and Lorene.

'May I walk with you?' the young man asked.

Lorene nodded and walked a little ahead of them.

'It is a lovely day, is it not?' Mr Holdsworth said.

He continued to utter the sort of polite conversation that contained very little of interest to Genna. He was also visibly nervous, which puzzled her. They were acquainted. What was there to be nervous about?

She found herself comparing him to Rossdale, which was rather unfair. Rossdale had years on him and the experience with it. Rossdale made her laugh. Rossdale listened. He talked to her about art. Did Mr Holdsworth even know she painted watercolours?

They reached the corner of Curzon Street.

'May—may I call upon you, Miss Summerfield?' His voice shook.

Ah! She understood now. He wanted to court her.

Why on earth would he want to court her? There was so much more he could see and do before settling down to marry. So many more young ladies to meet who would suit him better.

She slowed her pace. 'Oh, Mr Holdsworth!' She spoke in exaggerated tones. 'If it were up to me, I would say yes, because we have such fun dancing together. But Lord Tinmore would never allow it. He is looking for someone much grander for me.'

Holdsworth looked wounded, as well he should. She'd just told him he was not good enough because of something he could do nothing about—the status of his birth. Better that, though, than telling him he simply did not interest her.

'Do tell me you understand, Mr Holdsworth,' she said pleadingly. 'I should not like Tinmore to ruin our friendship.'

He brightened a little. 'I do understand.'

They reached the door of the town house.

His brow furrowed. 'You do not think Lord Tinmore will change his mind? I will have money.'

She shook her head. 'It is status with him, you see.'

'I value your candour.' He bowed. 'And I must bid you good day.'

'Good day, Mr Holdsworth.'

He walked away with shoulders stooped.

Lorene glared at her. 'What are you about, Genna? Lord Tinmore would find Mr Holdsworth perfectly acceptable, I am certain.'

'But I do not find him acceptable, Lorene,' she said.

'Why not? He's the son of a baron. And he's a very nice young man.'

Maybe that was it. Genna felt years older than Mr Holdsworth. 'You know I would run rings around him. Why make him miserable being stuck with the likes of me? And what happened to all your romantic notions? Were you not the one who wanted Tess and Edmund and me to marry for love?'

'Of course I did,' Lorene shot back. 'I still do, but—'

Tess and Edmund did not marry for love. They married to escape scandal. It was just by sheer luck they found happiness and who knew how long it would last?

'Then do me the honour of allowing me my own choice of a husband.' Or no husband at all.

'Well.' Lorene huffed. 'Do not say it is Lord Tinmore who must approve your choice.'

'I had to say something,' she said. 'Would you have me wound the poor fellow? Say I simply do not fancy him?'

'It would be more honest,' Lorene countered. 'But let us not debate this at the door to the town house. We can continue inside.'

Where the servants would hear and report whatever they said to Lord Tinmore.

A footman attended the door and took their things. 'A gentleman to see you, Miss Summerfield. He is waiting in the drawing room.'

'To see me?' Her spirits plummeted. One of Tinmore's widowers, no doubt. 'Who is it?'

'Lord Rossdale,' the footman said.

She smiled. 'How delightful!' She started to climb the stairs to the drawing room.

Lorene hurried to catch up with her. 'I should come with you.'

To chaperon? She'd been alone with Rossdale more than once.

But she would not argue. 'Of course.'

When they entered the room, he was standing and gazing at one of the paintings on the wall. He turned at their entrance.

'Why, hello, Rossdale,' Genna said. 'How nice of you to call.'

He bowed. 'Lady Tinmore. Miss Summerfield.'

'Would you care to sit, sir?' Lorene said. 'Shall I send for tea?'

He held up a hand. 'No, please do not go to that trouble. I will only stay a minute.' He turned to Genna. 'I merely stopped by to ask if you would care to take a turn in the park with me this afternoon.'

She grinned at him, but looked askance. 'I do not know, sir. It depends upon your vehicle...'

He smiled in return. 'A curricle. Nothing too fancy, though. It will have a matched pair, however.'

She pretended to think. 'A matched pair, you say?'

'Matched chestnuts.'

She sighed. 'Oh, very well.' Then her grin broke out again. 'I would be honoured to. Really.'

He nodded. 'Three o'clock?'

Four was the fashionable hour.

'Yes.' Her voice turned a bit breathless. 'I will be ready.'

'Then I must take my leave.' He bowed again.

When he left, Lorene shook her head. 'I do not understand you. The way you talk.'

'Oh, Lorene.' Genna groaned. 'It is all in fun. Rossdale knows that.'

Her sister gave her an exasperated look. 'If you wish to gain his interest, it is no way to talk to him, though.'

'I am not trying to gain his interest,' Genna retorted. 'As you have said many times, he is too far above me.'

Besides, she knew Rossdale's desire was to avoid marriage.

Lorene's brows rose. 'Then why would he ask you to take a ride in the park?'

'I think he is taking pity on me.' Why else? 'I did moan to him about wanting to go places and see things.'

'Well…' Lorene turned to leave the room '…do heed your behaviour on this outing. Lord Tinmore's new connection to the Duke of Kessington is important to him.'

After Lorene left the room, Genna said, 'Oh, yes. Lord Tinmore's well-being is of the utmost importance to us all.'

Chapter Thirteen

Ross pulled up to the Tinmores' town house in his curricle with its matched chestnuts. Gone were his days of driving high flyers and racing down country roads. Those had been exhilarating times, but, once experienced, he'd no need to repeat them. His curricle was the latest in comfort and speed, though he'd not tested how fast he could push it.

He suspected Genna would not care if he pulled up in a mere gig.

His tiger jumped off and held the horses while he knocked on the door.

As the footman let him inside, Genna was coming down the stairs, putting on her gloves. 'I saw you drive up.'

She wore a pelisse of dark blue and a bonnet that matched, nothing too fussy.

'Shall we go, then?' he asked.

'Absolutely!' she cried. 'I am ready.'

He helped her into the carriage. She pretended to examine it. 'I suppose this will have to do.' She sighed.

He took the ribbons from his tiger and climbed in next to her. 'It must do, because it is the only one I possess.'

She blinked at him. 'Truly? A duke's son with only one carriage?'

He smiled. 'All the others belong to my father.'

She laughed. 'All the others! At Summerfield House we had one pony cart and one coach.' Her smile fled. 'My father had a curricle.'

He'd prefer her laughing. 'Shall we take a turn in Hyde Park?'

She smiled again. 'By all means.'

The park was mere steps away from Curzon Street. They entered through the Stanhope Gate. Right inside the gate, he stopped the curricle and the tiger jumped off. He'd pick him up again on their way out. He drove the curricle towards the Serpentine. The weather was overcast and a bit chilly, not the best, but at least it was not raining.

'There is a rug beneath the seat,' he told her. 'Let me know if you feel cold.'

'I like it,' she said. 'It feels so good to be out of doors.'

He turned to her. 'And you are one to set up your paints while the snow is falling.'

She protested, 'Not fair! I packed up when it began to snow.'

'That you did.'

He'd guessed correctly that the Park would be thin of other vehicles at this hour. He'd wanted to be as private with her as possible. He waited until they'd passed the Serpentine, where some children were playing under the watchful eyes of their nannies and others were feeding the ducks.

'You probably wondered why I asked you for this ride—' he began.

'No.' She looked surprised. 'I didn't wonder.'

'I have a proposition for you.'

'A proposition?' She pretended to look shocked.

'It will indeed be shocking,' he said. 'But hear me out.'

The carriage path was edged with shrubbery and there were no other vehicles in sight. He slowed their pace.

Her expression conveyed curiosity, nothing more. This was why he could ask what he planned to ask. She would not take advantage, nor would she assume more than he intended.

He continued. 'I have a plan that will get us both through the Season without feeling like commodities in the marriage mart.'

Her interest kindled. 'Indeed?'

'It will also give you the freedom you desire, freedom to explore London, and it will satisfy my father who has begun to pressure me into marriage.' He glanced to the horses who were plodding along.

'What is this plan?' she asked.

'We become betrothed.'

She stared at him, but did not speak.

He quickly added. 'Betrothed. Think of it. If we are betrothed, I could escort you all around London. We could see the sights you wish to see. Do the things you wish to do. The cost of doing so would be no object.'

Her brows knitted. 'But a betrothal means becoming married. You just implied you do not wish to marry.'

'Not any more than you,' he responded. 'I said *betrothed*, not married. We would not have to marry. You could cry off, but not until you turn twenty-one and are free to do as you wish.'

And he had the funds to be certain she could do as she wished, but now was not the time to offer her money, not when she might misconstrue his intent. He meant merely to help her become the artist she wished to be. At least one of them would be free to do as they wished.

'No one would know it was not a real betrothal,' he added. 'It would be our secret.'

She stared at him again.

He actually began to feel nervous inside. 'Tinmore would see it as a feather in his cap if you were betrothed to a duke's son. He would stop sending you suitors.' Had he misread how daring she might be? 'There might be a little scandal. I fear you might receive some criticism for ultimately refusing me, but it is also likely that it will be assumed I was at fault.'

'What would your father say?' Her voice lacked enthusiasm.

He shrugged. 'What could my father say? He has been

pressuring me to marry and it would seem as though I was doing what he asked of me.'

'But surely he has someone else in mind besides me. My father was a mere baronet.'

'That is the beauty of it,' he explained. 'He cannot complain that I've become betrothed, but he is likely not to complain when you cry off.'

'Because I am not suitable for you.' She turned away and he feared he might have offended her.

'Betrothed,' she murmured.

He gazed at the horses and gripped the ribbons. 'I will understand if you do not wish this.'

She swivelled back to him, seizing his arm as she did so. 'Betrothed?'

He dared look at her again.

Her eyes were sparkling. 'A pretend betrothal.'

'Yes. To free us both.'

A smile lit up her face. 'It is a capital idea! We can go anywhere, do anything and no one will wonder over it.'

'That is the idea. We can enjoy this Season in a way that would have been impossible before.'

At their social engagements they would be free to be together the whole time. They could dance more than two dances. No greedy suitors would bother her; no matchmaking mamas would throw their frightened or eager daughters at him.

She frowned. 'I do not like the idea of keeping secrets from my sisters.' She paused and broke into a smile again. 'Why do I worry? They both kept secrets from me.'

He tilted his head. 'Then you say yes?'

She took a breath and he thought she would say yes. Instead she said, 'Let me think about it a little.'

'Take all the time you need,' he responded, disappointed. A delay usually meant no.

He flicked the ribbons and the horses moved faster. They

continued to circle the park, turning at the Cumberland Gate and proceeding along the perimeter of the park.

She finally spoke again. 'Would—would you take me to see places like the Egyptian Museum and Astley's Amphitheatre?'

He glanced at her. 'It would be my pleasure to do so.'

She fell silent again for so long Ross felt like fidgeting.

'You do realise, I could make you honour your promise to marry me,' she said in a serious tone. 'You would be taking a great risk.'

He turned to her again. 'But you won't. You are not the sort to break your word.'

Her eyes glowed as if satisfied by his response.

'You realise *I* might make you honour your promise,' he countered.

Her eyes danced in amusement. 'But you won't. You are not the sort to break your word. Besides, I have the right to cry off.'

They rode on, nearing the Serpentine again.

She bit her lip. 'Do you think that we can stretch it out until I am twenty-one?'

'When is your birthday?'

'October.'

He nodded. 'We can stretch it out that long.'

She shifted in her seat, as if setting her resolve. 'Then let us do it, Rossdale! Let us have this false betrothal. We'll fool everyone and have a lovely time of it!'

He turned to her and grinned and, to his surprise, had an impulse to embrace her. He resisted it.

'Then you had better call me Ross, if we are to be betrothed,' he said instead.

She laughed. 'Ross. And you'll call me Genna.'

He wouldn't tell her he'd been thinking of her as Genna since that first meeting.

Genna threaded her arm through Ross's and squeezed her cheek against his shoulder. 'I already feel as if I am set free. No longer can Tinmore dictate to me. I can simply direct him to you.'

'I should speak to him first,' Ross said. 'Ask his permission.'

She bristled. 'He is not my guardian. He has no say in who I marry, no matter what he thinks.'

'No,' he agreed. 'But let us use his arrogance. Appeal to his vanity. Let him think he has some say. If he believes he has given his permission, he is less apt to question the validity of the betrothal. He'll be less apt to exert control over your activities.'

She nodded. 'I see your point, though it rankles with me.' It was really no different than the way she'd always handled Tinmore, though. Make him think she would do as he desired, but really do what she pleased. 'Promise me one thing, though.'

He turned his head to glance at her. 'What?'

'Promise me you will refuse the dowry he has offered me.' She did not want Tinmore to think his money had any influence, even on this pretend-betrothal.

'Genna.' He looked her straight in the eye. 'We are not really to be married. The dowry makes no difference, because I will never receive it.'

'It makes a difference to me.' Her voice rose. 'I want Tinmore to know that I do not need his dowry money, that it had nothing to do with you proposing to me. It is bad enough I must accept his money for my dresses and such.'

She had to admit that Tinmore's money had given her a rather comfortable life these last two years. She had as many dresses as she could want, food aplenty and enough spending money to keep her in paints and paper. It was the cost to Lorene that ate at Genna's insides.

Ross nodded. 'I promise you that if the subject of the dowry comes up, I will refuse it.'

'The subject will come up. Tinmore will want you to know what a huge sacrifice he has made for me.'

He glanced at her and back at the road. 'Then I will make a very convincing refusal.'

While he was attending to the road and the horses, Genna had a chance to study him in detail. His was a strong profile, high forehead, gracefully sloping masculine nose, strong jaw and lovely thick brows and lashes. She loved that his face was expressive when he wished it to be and devoid of all expression when he did not.

She was so lucky, so fortunate that he would do her this great favour. Certainly she would receive more benefit from it than he. Tinmore's dictates that she marry would be silenced now, because Tinmore would think she was marrying Rossdale.

Ross.

The mere thought of his name brought flutters inside her. These sensations, all so new to her, were a puzzle and one she did not wish to examine too closely. She just wanted to enjoy his friendship.

This plan of his made it so they could be friends.

'So you will call upon Lord Tinmore tomorrow.' She had to keep talking or the flutters would take over.

'Correct.'

She did not mind keeping this secret from Tinmore and the rest of the world, but this was another huge secret to keep from Lorene and Tess. She'd told them nothing of her intent to be an artist or her determination to refuse marriage to anyone. This would distance them from her even further.

'Will you tell Lord Penford the truth?' she asked.

He thinned his lips and took his time to answer her. 'I would like to tell Dell,' he said finally.

She frowned. Since learning he'd lost his family in a fire, Genna's heart went out to him, but she still was not certain how he felt about her and Lorene. Sometimes Penford looked at them as if he wished they were in Calcutta, but at other times he behaved in a most thoughtful and attentive manner.

'Surely he will not approve of our scheme,' she said. 'Who would?'

'Even if he does not approve, we can trust him to keep the secret.' Ross met her eye. 'I would trust him with my life. In any event,' he added, 'we may need an ally.'

But if Penford disapproved, would he be an ally?

She examined Ross's face.

If she embarked on this plan of theirs, she must trust Ross. 'Very well. You may tell Lord Penford.'

'Do you wish to confide in your sisters?' he asked.

She shook her head. 'I shall wait to announce this betrothal to Lorene, though,' she said. 'And to Tess and Marc.'

They fell into silence again until they neared the Stanhope Gate. Ross signalled to his tiger to get on the back and in what seemed like the blink of the eye, they pulled up to the town house.

The tiger jumped down again and held the horses while Ross helped Genna out of the curricle and walked her up to the door. When the footman opened the door, Ross bid her good day and she skipped inside, wanting to dance through the hall and up the stairs. How could she be expected to contain her exuberance?

Once in her room, she gave in to her impulse and spun around in joy.

Until there was a knock at her door. 'Come in,' she said tentatively.

Lorene entered. 'I saw Lord Rossdale pull up. How was your outing?' Her voice was filled with expectation.

Genna felt a great pang of guilt. She was about to lie about the lie they were going to tell everyone. 'It was lovely. We do get along famously, so there was a great deal to talk about.'

'Did you get any notion of why he asked you?' Lorene persisted.

'None except companionship.' This was not precisely a lie. Companionship was what they'd agreed upon, was it not?

The next day Ross called upon Lord Tinmore. When the butler announced him to Lord Tinmore in his study, Tinmore's head was bowed. It snapped up at the footman's voice. The old man had fallen asleep.

When Ross approached the desk, Tinmore fussed with the papers there as if he had been busy with them. He tried to stand.

Ross gestured with his hand. 'Do not stand, sir. No need of ceremony with me.'

'Kind of you, Rossdale. Kind of you,' Tinmore muttered. 'And how is your father? And the Duchess? In good health, I hope?'

'In excellent health,' Ross replied. 'And you, sir?'

'Excellent!' he repeated. 'Could not be better.' Tinmore sat back in his chair.

Ross wasted no time. 'I know you are a busy man, sir, so I will not waste your time with prattle. I have come to talk with you about Miss Summerfield.'

'What?' Tinmore straightened. 'What has the girl done now?'

Tinmore's automatic disapproval chafed. 'You assume she has done something of which you would disapprove?'

Tinmore's expression turned smug. 'Why else would you come here?'

'To ask your permission to marry her.'

Tinmore recoiled as if Ross had struck him in the chest. 'Marry her!'

Genna would like that reaction. Sheer surprise.

'Yes,' Ross stated. 'Marry her. Assuming she will accept me, that is.'

'Accept you?' Tinmore continued to look dumbfounded. 'She's naught but the daughter of a baronet. She's not fit—'

Ross's anger flared. 'I assure you, she is my choice.' He glared at the man. 'I might remind you that you married the daughter of a mere baronet.'

'An entirely different matter, sir!' Tinmore said indignantly. 'An entirely different situation.'

Ross inclined his head. 'In any event, I wish to become betrothed to Miss Summerfield and I would like your permission to ask her to marry me.'

'I would not refuse you.' Tinmore shook his head. 'But I feel an obligation to your father to advise you against this idea.'

This man was intolerable. He ought to be looking after Genna's best interests, not the best interests of a duke's son.

'Then I will be obliged to explain your reticence to my father, sir. I thought you would be pleased to unite our families.' Let him ponder that. 'What will he conclude but that you do not desire to be so closely connected?'

Tinmore's eyes bulged. 'No. No. No. I do not mean that. I would not offend— Mustn't think so. Mustn't think so.'

'Then I have your permission?'

The Earl still looked reluctant, but he finally nodded his head. 'Yes. Yes, my boy. If that is what you want.'

'I want her,' Ross said. Hearing his words, he could almost believe it himself, that he wanted Genna, to marry her.

'She comes with a handsome dowry, my boy. Very respectable amount. I made certain of that.'

Ross rubbed his chin. 'About the dowry, sir.'

'Is it not enough?' Tinmore looked anxious. 'We can negotiate the amount. Might be fitting for me to increase it for marrying the heir to a dukedom.'

'I do not wish an increase,' Ross said. 'I do not want it at all.'

'Do not want it?' Tinmore's voice rose.

'I have no need for it,' Ross responded. 'I am wealthy in my own right and my wealth will increase when I inherit the title. Make some other use of the dowry. Gift it to the poor. God knows there are plenty of hungry people in England with these Corn Laws.' Very likely Tinmore voted for the Corn Laws that made bread so expensive that many people could no longer afford it. 'I can advise you on where the money might do the most good.'

'If you insist,' Tinmore said, like air leaking from a bellows. 'Give it to the poor.'

Ross raised his eyebrows. 'May I see Miss Summerfield now?'

'You want to speak with her?' Tinmore seemed completely rattled.

Ross straightened and looked down his nose as his father did when his father wanted to intimidate someone. 'It is my wish to speak with her now.' He made it sound like a command.

'Yes. Yes.' Tinmore's head bobbed up and down. 'I will make certain she sees you.'

Ross felt quite certain Genna would need no pressure from Tinmore to receive him.

'Now, if you please,' Ross mimicked his father.

Tinmore popped up from his chair so fast he needed to hop to get his balance. 'Dixon!' he cried. 'Dixon!'

The butler opened the door. 'My lord?'

Tinmore waved one hand. 'Escort Lord Rossdale to the drawing room, then find my wife's sister and send her to him.'

The butler bowed.

'Now, Dixon! Now,' Tinmore cried.

Ross followed the butler to the drawing room, but he wound up cooling his heels for several minutes before Genna entered the room.

She grinned at him. 'I waited ten minutes so I would not look too eager.' She took his hands and led him to the sofa. 'How was it? Did he faint away in shock?'

'He was gratifyingly surprised.' Ross would not tell her how Tinmore tried to talk him out of proposing to her.

'Did he bring up the dowry?' she asked eagerly.

He nodded. 'As you predicted.'

'And did you refuse it?' she pressed.

'I refused it and told him to give the money to the poor.'

Her eyes sparkled. 'Oh, that is famous! He won't do it, of course. It is not in his nature. Why waste good money on poor people?'

'Are you ready for me to propose to you now?' he asked.

Her fingers fluttered. 'You already did so yesterday.'

'I think I must repeat the event.' Ross glanced towards the door. 'Is there a crack between the door and the door-jamb?'

She looked startled. 'I have no idea. What does it matter?'

'Just in case there are curious eyes watching, I will do this right.' He slid to the floor on one knee. 'Will you become betrothed to me, Miss Summerfield?' He lowered his voice. 'Now you must act surprised. Slap your hands on your face. Cry out. Act as if you are being proposed to by a duke's son.'

She giggled. 'I *am* being proposed to by a duke's son.' But she slapped her cheeks and squealed with pleasure. 'Oh, Lord Rossdale,' she said louder. 'This is so sudden.'

'Do not keep me in suspense.' He put his fist to his heart. 'Let me know if I will be the happiest man in all of May-fair, or cast me down into the depths of despair.'

'What should I do?' she cried, playing along with his joke. 'I cannot decide.'

'Why, say yes, of course.'

Her smile softened. 'I will accept your proposal, Lord Rossdale. I will become betrothed to you.'

Chapter Fourteen

After Ross left, Genna danced around the drawing room, the way she'd danced in her bedchamber the day before. No one would guess that her happiness was not in anticipation of marriage to a duke's heir. It was because he'd set her free to be herself for the whole Season and more.

It would be impossible to keep her happiness a secret. It burst from her every pore. The source of it might need to be kept secret, but the emotion could not be held in. Still, it felt so precious to her she wanted to keep it to herself a little while longer, savour it alone in all its aspects. Unfortunately Tinmore would tell Lorene soon enough. Genna would rather her sister hear the news from her.

She smoothed her skirt and tidied her hair and took a deep breath. She could pretend to be composed, at least for a little while. She left the room with her head held high and her step unhurried, when she really felt like skipping and taking the stairs two at a time.

Lorene would probably be in her sitting room where she spent a great deal of her time practising on the pianoforte there. It was not as grand as the pianoforte in the drawing room, but it was the one she preferred.

As she neared the room's door, though, she did not hear music—except the joyous refrain inside her.

Genna knocked anyway and heard Lorene say, 'Come in.'

Genna opened the door.

Lorene stood. 'Genna, I was just about to send for you. Look who is here.'

Her sister Tess came up to her and bussed her cheek. 'I thought I would call upon my sisters. I have not seen you since the opera. Lorene has been telling me all about the musicale you attended and the Duchess of Archester's ball. Did you enjoy yourself?'

Ross had engineered those invitations, Genna was sure. 'I did.'

She could hardly keep from hopping from one foot to the other. How fortunate that both of her sisters were here. She could tell them both at once.

'I am glad you are here, Tess,' she said, 'because I have some news.'

'That Lord Rossdale called upon Tinmore?' Lorene broke in. 'I told her of it.'

Genna hesitated. Had Lorene been told why he called? Did they already know?

Lorene turned to Tess. 'Tinmore has lately become better acquainted with Rossdale's father, the Duke of Kessington.'

'Did you tell Tess that Rossdale took me for a ride in Hyde Park yesterday?' she asked instead.

Tess looked surprised. 'He did?'

'That is not all,' Genna said. 'He called upon me today after seeing Tinmore.'

'He has been attentive to Genna, that is true.' Lorene made it sound as if she'd forgotten such an unimportant event.

'He had a reason for calling upon me,' she said.

Genna looked from one sister to the other. 'I am betrothed to him.' The words sounded awkward to her ears, but she could not make herself say he'd asked her to marry him. He had not done that. The proposal was for a betrothal, not marriage.

'What?' Lorene cried.

Tess gave a surprised laugh, but immediately seized

Genna's hands. 'Do not say so! He asked you to marry him? Just now?'

Genna nodded. 'First he spoke to Lord Tinmore and then to me.' She glanced at Lorene. 'Yesterday he spoke to me about it a little. To see if I might be willing.'

Lorene looked dazed. 'I did not expect this—I—I feared his intentions were dishonourable.'

'Dishonourable?' Genna retorted. 'Rossdale is an honourable man.'

If you did not count his willingness to engage in a scandalous secret, that was.

Tess pulled back and peered at Genna. 'One moment—was this another of Tinmore's machinations? Did he put pressure on Rossdale?'

Tinmore had forced Tess and Marc to marry. Marc rescued Tess from a storm and the two were forced to take refuge overnight in a deserted cabin. Tinmore insisted Marc had compromised Tess.

'No,' Genna told her. 'Rossdale really asked me. There was no pressure or any such thing. I believe he merely sought Tinmore's approval before asking me.'

'Not that you would want Tinmore's approval,' Lorene said sarcastically.

Genna met her gaze. 'You have the right of it, Lorene. I do not care a fig whether your husband approves or not, but it was a respectful thing for Rossdale to do.'

Tess sat down on a sofa near Lorene. Genna was too excited to sit.

'A duke's son,' Tess said breathlessly. Her voice changed to shock. 'Oh, my stars. He is the heir, is he not? You will be a duchess some day!'

No, I will not, Genna said to herself. But her sisters could not know that. Genna felt her insides squirm with guilt.

'It makes no sense, does it?' Lorene said. 'A duke's son and a penniless baronet's daughter.'

'We get on well together,' Genna said defensively.

'Of course you do,' Tess said soothingly.

'We must do something for a formal announcement.' Lorene frowned. 'A ball or something.'

'I do not know—' Genna plopped down next to Tess. This was becoming too big. A formal announcement seemed wrong when the betrothal was not real.

'Of course you must do something,' Tess agreed. 'If not a ball, *something.* You will be marrying a man who will be a duke. You cannot go higher than that unless you married one of the royal princes.'

Genna was as likely to marry one of them as to marry Ross.

A small pang of disappointment struck her at that thought, but she pushed it away immediately. She did not wish to marry a duke. She did not wish to marry anyone and be trapped the way Lorene was trapped.

'A ball.' Lorene sounded stressed. 'I do not know how to host a ball.'

Genna had not thought that she would distress her sister. She felt as small as a bug. 'A ball is too much fuss! I do not see why you should even think of it.'

'Oh, it must be done,' Tess said with decision. 'It would cause more talk not to have some sort of event to announce your engagement.' She laughed. 'Do you realise this will be the only wedding in the family that adheres to propriety?'

'The wedding,' Lorene groaned. 'What is proper for a future duke's wedding?'

This was all going too far. Genna felt miserable. 'Do not talk of wedding plans. It will not be before next autumn at the earliest.'

'So long a wait?' Tess looked surprised. 'Whatever for?'

How could she explain? 'Because that is what we've decided.'

'Oh, but never mind that.' Tess took Genna's hands in hers again. 'Tell us about Rossdale! He is very handsome, is he not?'

Genna had to agree. 'He is handsome.' But that was not the half of it. They could laugh together. But he did not laugh at her plans or her ambitions.

Lorene and Tess would never understand how important both those things were to her.

Lorene leaned towards her. 'Genna, do you have a genuine regard for him? Or do you feel obligated to marry him? Because you do not have to accept the first offer you receive. I will support you in waiting for a love match. It is all I've ever wanted for you.'

Now Genna felt even worse. Lorene wanted her to be happy so much she'd defy her husband for it. And all Genna was doing was deceiving her.

Genna softened her tone. 'I do have a great regard for Rossdale. What is more, I believe he feels the same towards me.'

They *liked* each other and that was the truth.

'Oh!' Tess had tears streaming down her cheeks. She hugged Genna. 'You have found the dream! A husband you love who loves you!'

Genna stiffened. 'You found it as well, Tess.'

'Yes, but mine was hard won. Luck was a big factor in it, too.' She shuddered. 'If I had been rescued by some wretched man my life would be a misery.'

Like Lorene's, Genna thought.

'I care only that my sisters are happy,' Lorene said, her voice catching.

Tess gestured for her to join them on the sofa and the three sisters wrapped their arms around each other. Genna was filled with love for them.

And consumed with guilt for deceiving them.

Dell sat at a desk in the bedchamber he used in the Kessington town house. He tried to make sense of a line of figures representing crop yields and estimates of the effect of allowing foreign grain and produce to undercut prices.

He tried to make his own calculations based on the figures provided, but his results did not match the author of the material he'd been studying.

He sat back and pinched his nose.

A knock sounded at the door and a familiar face peeked in. 'Do you need an interruption?'

Dell glanced up and smiled. 'Ross! An interruption would be most welcome.'

Ross approached the desk and sat in a nearby chair. 'What are you reading?'

'Writings about grain prices. This author seems to have fabricated his results, however. I don't know how one ever knows who to believe.' Dell set the papers aside. 'What do you wish to see me about?'

Ross looked defensive. 'What? I cannot simply knock on your door?'

'I think you have a reason,' Dell said. It was written all over Ross's face.

Ross stood again and paced. 'I do have a reason. Something I want to talk over with you. Something I want to tell you.'

Dell watched him and waited.

Ross finally faced him. 'I've become betrothed to Genna Summerfield.'

Dell could not believe his ears. 'What? You don't want to marry. You've always said.'

'I don't want to marry,' Ross agreed. 'At least, not yet.'

Dell felt alarmed. 'Do not tell me you are being forced into this.'

Ross held up his hand. 'No. Not at all. Hear me out. I'll explain the whole thing.'

Dell crossed his arms over his chest.

'It is not a real betrothal—' Ross looked uncomfortable. 'Genna does not wish to be married any more than I do. We are merely pretending to be betrothed so that my father will take the pressure off me and Tinmore will no longer plague her. I'll take her all the places she wishes to go, to see what she wishes to see. We will have an enjoyable Season instead of one spent dodging suitors or matchmaking mamas.'

Dell looked sceptical. 'You never had difficulty resisting your father's pressure before or dodging matchmaking mamas. Why take such an extreme step? It makes no sense.'

Ross sat again. 'You are correct. It is not for me, but for her. I want to help her.'

'Help her resist pressure from Tinmore?' Dell scoffed. 'Genna seems strong-willed and self-assured. I'd wager she knows just how to resist whatever Tinmore wants her to do.'

'That may be so, Dell.' Ross rose again. 'But why should we have to fight everyone when there is enjoyment to be had instead?'

Dell frowned. 'Enjoyment?' Surely Ross did not intend to trifle with the young woman?

'Nothing untoward, I assure you,' Ross said.

'You've told me over and over that you find no pleasure in a frivolous life any more. So do not tell me you do this for enjoyment.'

'I like her company, Dell.' He paced. 'There are places to show her here in London that I could not show her unless we are betrothed.'

Dell peered at him. 'You will pretend to be betrothed so she can see the sights of London?'

'It is more than that,' Ross insisted. 'I cannot explain. I cannot see the harm.'

Dell raised his brows. 'Can you not? I can think of all kinds of harm. People will be hurt over this; you mark my words.'

'It is only for a few months,' Ross added. 'Next autumn she'll cry off and that will be the end of it.'

'Oh, yes.' Dell spoke with sarcasm. 'That will not cause harm. Nor gossip. Nor scandal.'

Ross leaned across Dell's desk. 'It will not be that bad.'

'I disagree,' Dell said. 'This is a mistake.'

'I'll prove you wrong,' Ross challenged.

'We'll see,' Dell said.

They glared at each other, as they had done when they were boys and argued about something or another.

Ross backed away. 'No matter. It is done. I simply wanted you to know the truth of it all.'

So he was burdened with the secret as well? He wouldn't mention that bit to Ross, though.

'Just take care,' Dell said. 'I'd not like to see either of you hurt.'

Ross met Dell's eyes again. 'May I have your word you will keep this in confidence?'

Dell nodded. 'You have my word. I will keep your secret.'

'Even if you believe it is a mistake?' Ross pressed.

'Even so,' Dell said.

Ross left Dell's bedchamber with some of his high spirits dampened. He supposed he harboured the hope that Dell would understand his reasons for this betrothal, not that he could tell him the whole of it.

He had an idea of how to make certain Genna's plans worked out just as she wished, even though he had more to work on how to make that happen. To help her live the life of her own choosing was all he desired. He might be destined for duty, but he'd make certain Genna could be free, like he, his mother and father had been free in the days before duty took over.

Ross's next task was to inform his father and the Duchess. He dreaded it.

It was nearing time to dress for dinner. With luck he'd catch his father and the Duchess alone for a few minutes before guests arrived. There were always guests for dinner, it seemed. Dinner was one of the venues where his father could influence others to agree with his views.

He had his valet dress him hurriedly and he was the first to enter the drawing room where they would wait for dinner to be announced. A decanter of claret was on the table. Ross poured himself a glass and sipped it while he waited for his father and the Duchess.

They walked in the room, discussing the impending marriage of the Princess Charlotte to Prince Leopold of Saxe-Coburg-Saalfeld and the various monies and property Parliament would vote to bestow upon the young woman who might some day become Queen.

'Ross!' his father exclaimed upon seeing him there.

Ross was rarely early.

'Do you stay for dinner, Ross?' the Duchess asked. 'I do hope so. It will even out our numbers. I already told the butler you would dine with us.'

'I will stay, then,' he said. 'When do the guests arrive?'

'Not for a half-hour,' she said. 'Unless they are late, which they usually are.'

He poured them each a glass of claret. His father took a long sip of his.

No reason to delay, Ross thought. 'There is something I wish to tell you.'

Interest was lacking in both their eyes. His father considered most of what Ross talked about to be of no consequence, usually about some poverty or injustice he'd discovered. His father thought only in terms of the fate of the country, not individuals. The Duchess merely regarded Ross as the heir and not as a person who could further the Duke's influence and power.

'I have done something you have begged me to do—' he began.

They both glanced at him then.

'I have become betrothed.'

'What?' cried the Duchess.

'This is excellent!' His father's face lit with excitement. 'Who is the lady?'

'As long as she is suitable,' the Duchess said warily.

Ross met her eyes. 'She suits me very well.'

The Duchess blanched. 'Please do not say it is that woman—'

Ross knew that his father and the Duchess would not approve. That was part of what would make the scheme work, but it angered him, nonetheless.

'Miss Summerfield, do you mean?' He did not want the Duchess to say her name first. 'Yes. I have made Miss Summerfield an offer and she has accepted.' Which was the truth.

'Summerfield?' His father raised his voice. 'That chit connected to Tinmore?'

'Ross, she is a nobody,' the Duchess said quickly. 'Worse than that, look at her family. There is not a one of them who has not been the subject of gossip. Her mother and father—bad blood, indeed.'

'Has Miss Summerfield done anything objectionable?' Ross challenged.

The Duchess's lips thinned. 'Not as yet.'

In that she was correct. In a few months, Genna would cry off and that would certainly cause gossip. Not to mention what people would say when she became an artist and lived as an independent woman.

'Will you not reconsider?' his father pleaded. 'I'll never get Tinmore off my neck if you are married to his wife's sister.'

Of course, his father would think of himself. 'Miss Summerfield will have no difficulty distancing herself from Lord Tinmore, if that is your only objection.'

'Not my only objection,' his father snapped. 'She's not spent any time in town. She knows nobody of importance. What does she know of entertaining? Of managing houses as grand as our family's?'

'She has a quick intelligence,' Ross said. 'These matters can be learned.'

His father's eyes turned pained. 'Some women cannot learn.'

Like Ross's mother. She'd never adapted to the strains of being a duchess.

Ross's anger at his father melted a little.

'You are in your prime, Father,' he said softly. 'There will be time for Genna to learn how to be a duchess.'

But it would never get that far. He'd forgotten that for a moment.

His father's wife broke in. 'Why could you not court Lady Alice? She is a sweet girl. And her father is a marquess. It would be much wiser for you to court the daughter of a marquess and bring some advantage to the union.'

'It is done, Constance.' There was no use arguing over what would never come to pass. 'I am betrothed to Miss Summerfield.'

'But we could induce her to cry off even before word gets out,' she persisted. 'It is not too late.'

'I do not want to break this engagement. I have a high regard for Miss Summerfield.' Which was very true. 'And I intend to honour my promise to her.'

Both the Duchess and his father's faces were pinched in disappointment.

For no reason. The marriage would never take place.

'Regard this,' he told them. 'I have done as you wished, as you have begged me to do for years now. I have become betrothed. We will marry in the autumn, probably.'

The Duchess lifted a shoulder as if to say that was not concession enough.

'Well, if you say it is done, it is done and we will have to devise the best way to approach this.' His father poured himself another glass of claret. 'I beg you not to speak of it at dinner. Let us think upon how to have this announcement made.'

'As you wish.' Ross finished his claret.

Chapter Fifteen

For the next week Ross called upon Genna every day, taking her to all the places she'd desired. They'd battled the crowds to see Napoleon's carriage at the Egyptian Museum, gaped at the beasts kept at the Tower, and sat in choice seats at Astley's Amphitheatre. Every day brought new delights and new ideas and Genna could not have been happier.

She had almost been able to forget that Lord Tinmore had invited the Duke and Duchess of Kessington and Ross to dinner to discuss the announcement of the betrothal.

She wished the announcement could be made in the newspapers, rather than for her to face the stares and whispers of those who wouldn't think a duke's son would actually wish to marry her. It made it worse knowing she and Ross were deceiving everyone about their true intent.

The dinner with the Duke and Duchess was the only entertainment for Tinmore and Lorene this week. It had taken that many days to find an evening the Duke and Duchess could attend. Ross requested that Lord Penford be invited, to which Tinmore readily agreed, but about whom Genna and Lorene heard Tinmore's endless complaints that the table would be uneven.

Lorene had little to do with the planning of the dinner. Nothing would do but for Tinmore to see to every detail, in consultation with Mr Filkins, his secretary, and Dixon, the butler. She knew nothing of planning important dinners, Tinmore had said, so Lorene spent long hours practising her new music instead. Genna regretted leaving her for the pleasures Ross's outings provided, but she shoved her feelings aside. She must learn to see to her own well-being and leave Lorene to cope with the life she'd chosen.

Even though Lorene had chosen this dismal life for Genna's sake.

When the evening of the dinner came, Genna's mood darkened. She did not need Ross to tell her that the Duke and Duchess would disapprove of the betrothal. No one would approve such an unbalanced pairing. Besides facing them, she would also be seeing Lord Penford for the first time since he'd learned the truth of the betrothal. And she would have to endure Lord Tinmore, who took credit for the match.

In a way, Tinmore deserved credit. If he were the least bit tolerable, she might never have decided to pursue a career as an artist. Truth be told, she was nowhere near being able to do that. She'd solved one problem by agreeing to this pretend betrothal, but she still needed to learn so much more before she could begin to support herself with painting and she'd not painted for days.

Before her maid came in to help her dress, she sat down with her crayon and sketched some of the images she'd seen over the week. A lion from the African continent. Dancing horses from Astley's. The crowd gaping at Napoleon's carriage. She forgot everything else and lost herself in her drawings.

When the maid entered the room carrying her dress, Genna jumped in surprise.

'Is it time already?' She closed her sketchbook and walked over to her pitcher and basin and washed the chalk from her fingers.

'I'll dress your hair first,' the maid said.

Genna missed the camaraderie she'd had with Anna, her maid at Summerfield House. She did not dare confide in this woman even in simple ways. Tinmore's servants had a habit of reporting back to Tinmore everything Genna or

Lorene said or did. So she merely told her how she wished to wear her hair and what dress she desired.

This night she was donning a pale rose dinner dress, a nice complement to the deeper red Lorene had chosen. She wanted to take some care with her appearance for Ross's sake, so the Duke and Duchess would not find fault with her looks.

The maid seemed to be moving particularly slowly this evening. Genna feared she would be late in presenting herself in the drawing room where they would all have a drink of wine before dinner.

Before the line of buttons down the back of her dress were fastened, Genna heard a carriage arrive. 'Please hurry, Hallie. I believe they have arrived.'

'Yes, miss,' the maid said, but she went no faster.

When the maid finally finished, Genna dashed down the stairs to the drawing room. She forced herself to stop at the door and compose herself. Why did she worry? The more the Duke and Duchess disliked her, the less dust they would kick up when she broke the sham betrothal.

She lifted her chin, put a smile on her face and walked in.

'About time, girl,' Tinmore snapped.

He stood near the fireplace with the Duke and Ross. The Duchess sat on the sofa with Lorene and Penford stood apart from them all.

Ross was the only one to smile at her entrance. 'Genna!' He walked up to her and took her hand.

She curtsied to the Duke. 'Good evening, Your Grace.' And to the Duchess. 'Your Grace. Forgive my tardiness.' She decided to give no excuse.

'We have been discussing how to make an announcement of this betrothal,' the Duchess said, making it sound like it was something loathsome. 'We have decided that it should be done at the ball we are already scheduled to give in two weeks' time.'

Tinmore spoke up. 'I would be honoured to host the entertainment where the announcement is made. I think it only appropriate—'

The Duchess held up a hand. 'No. We've settled it. It will be at our ball.'

Genna glanced at Lorene, but her face was blank and she could not tell how Lorene felt about this.

'I should most like to do what my sister wishes to do,' Genna said. 'If you have her approval, then I am happy to have the announcement at your ball. I do wish for my whole family to be included. Our brother will not come, of course. He and his wife are too far away, but I insist my sister Tess and her husband be included. And his parents, of course.'

'Lord and Lady Northdon?' the Duchess said through a sneer.

Lord and Lady Northdon were practically shunned by the *ton*, because Lady Northdon was a French commoner by birth and the daughter of French Jacobins.

'Yes.' Genna kept her gaze steady. 'I consider them part of my family.'

The Duchess glanced away. 'If we must.'

'Certainly we must,' added Ross. He turned to Genna. 'Would you like some Madeira?'

'I would.' Lots of it, in fact.

It was Penford who poured her the wine and handed it to her.

'How are you, sir?' she asked him.

He met her eyes. 'Very well.'

His expression was as blank as Lorene's, but not hostile. Genna supposed she must be content with that.

He turned to Lorene. 'More wine?'

'Thank you,' she murmured, handing him her glass.

The dinner was a stilted affair. What troubled Genna the most was her sister, who seemed even more unassuming than usual. It was as if all the life had been sucked out of her. Genna had caused it, she knew, and it ate at her. But what could she do about it now? She could not blurt out to them all that the betrothal was a sham and they should not take it all so seriously.

Her saving grace was having Ross seated across from her. When Lord Tinmore and the Duke's conversation became particularly tedious, Ross needed only to look at her and she could smile inside.

After dinner when the ladies left the gentlemen to their brandy, the Duchess spent the time lecturing Genna and Lorene in proper behaviour at this upcoming ball, as if they did not know how to behave. She also discussed the politics of the day, to which Lorene and Genna agreed to her every word merely to be polite.

When the men returned to the drawing room, Ross rolled his eyes at Genna, making her smile again. Dell looked bleak. Lord Tinmore and the Duke continued to discuss Princess Charlotte's impending wedding and the Duchess joined in.

Dell looked down on Lorene. 'Do you play for us this evening, ma'am?'

Her gaze rose to his. 'If you wish it.'

Dell extended his hand to Lorene to help her rise. She sat at the pianoforte in the corner of the room and played softly the Mozart piece that had been performed at the musicale.

While Tinmore, the Duke and Duchess discussed politics and Lorene played Mozart, Ross gestured for Genna to come with him. They sneaked out of the room and into the hallway. Genna pulled him into the library, which was dark. She could hardly see his face.

'Has it been too ghastly for you?' he asked.

She smiled. 'Perhaps a bit more than dinners here usually are.'

He stood close. 'The Duchess is intent on having her own way. I apologise for that.'

She felt the warmth of his body even though they were

not touching, such an odd but pleasant sensation. 'I wish we did not have to make a formal announcement.'

'Do not put too much on it,' he responded. 'No one else will. We will be stared at for a while, whispered about and then they will forget us. They will be talking of Princess Charlotte and no one else.'

The wedding of the Princess was a welcome distraction. As the only child of the Prince Regent, she would be Queen one day.

'I hope you are right,' she said.

He held her hands. 'I will call upon you early tomorrow. Are you able to spend the day with me?'

She smiled. 'I would be delighted.'

He gave her a kiss on the cheek, then stepped away. 'We should go back.'

She put her fingers where his lips had touched and where she still felt the sensation of the kiss. 'Yes. Let us go back.'

The next day Genna stopped by Lorene's sitting room before leaving for her outing with Ross.

Lorene was playing the pianoforte when Genna knocked and entered the room. 'I'm off with Ross in a few minutes. I just wanted to let you know.'

Lorene made an attempt at a smile. 'Where do you go this time?'

Genna sat in a chair near the pianoforte. 'I do not know. It is to be a surprise.'

'A surprise? How nice.'

Genna had not had a chance to speak with Lorene after the Duke and Duchess left after dinner. 'I wanted to see if you are all right.'

'All right?' Lorene blinked. 'Of course I am. Why ever would I not be all right?'

'You—you seemed different last night,' Genna said. 'So very subdued. I worried about you.'

Lorene turned back to the keyboard. 'Oh, there is nothing to worry about. I—I merely had little to say. The Duke and Duchess and Tinmore had so many strong opinions on what should be done, I merely let them sort it out.'

Genna rose and leaned over to give her sister a hug from behind. 'I am certain I would have been happier with whatever plan you could come up with.'

Lorene covered Genna's hand with her own and squeezed it. 'A very small dinner party with family and close friends?'

'Perfect!' Genna said. Especially if the betrothal were real.

Lorene turned to her again. 'I cannot tell you how delighted I am that you are going to marry Rossdale. The two of you are so fond of each other. Your happiness shows.' She still held Genna's hand and squeezed it again. 'It is what I dreamed of for you.'

Genna felt her guilt like a dagger twisting in her chest. How shameful to deceive such a loving sister! Still, she had to steel herself. She needed to find her own way.

'I am happy,' she said and realised there was truth in those words. When she was with Ross, she could push aside all the other feelings that swirled around inside her.

A footman came to the door. 'Lord Rossdale has arrived, miss.'

She hugged Lorene again. 'I'll stop in when I return and let you know where it is he has taken me.'

'Yes,' Lorene gave her that forced smile again. 'Do enjoy yourself.'

Genna always enjoyed herself when in Ross's company.

She raced to her room and had the maid help her into her pale pink pelisse and bright blue bonnet. She hung her reticule over her arm and pulled on her gloves as she hurried down the stairs.

When she entered the drawing room, Ross stood with another man.

'Look who will accompany us today,' Ross said, gesturing to the man standing next to him.

'Mr Vespery!' She smiled at the artist who'd been so kind to her at the Duchess of Archester's ball. 'How lovely to see you.'

The artist blew a kiss over her hand. 'Miss Summerfield, it is my pleasure to be in your company.'

She turned to Ross, even more excited than before. 'Where are we going?'

Instead of answering her directly, he said, 'Somewhere you will like. But first I have a gift.'

He handed her a package wrapped in brown paper. She looked at him, puzzled.

'Open it,' he said.

She removed the paper. It was a beautifully bound book. She opened it and found the title page. '*A Treatise on Painting* by Leonardo da Vinci,' she read aloud, then words failed her.

'It is the only book on art I could find,' he said apologetically.

'It is wonderful,' she finally managed, leafing through the book and glancing at da Vinci's words.

'A classic work,' Vespery added.

'And a hint about where we are bound today,' Ross said. 'We are going to look at art.'

Genna looked up and grinned. To be with Ross gazing at art and learning from Vespery. This day was going to be wonderful.

Ross had come with one of the Duke's carriages so they all sat comfortably for the short ride to their destination. When the carriage stopped and Ross helped her out, she was even more puzzled. They were in front of Carlton House, the residence of the Prince Regent.

'Here we are,' Ross said.

'But this is—'

He threaded her arm through his. 'This is our destination.'

The palace of the Prince Regent.

As they walked through the portico and up to the door, he explained, 'With His Royal Highness's permission, we will meet one of his art advisors, Sir Charles Long, who will take us on a tour of His Royal Highness's collection.'

Before Genna could form a coherent thought, the door opened and they were greeted by a line of four footmen and a nattily dressed gentleman.

'Ah, you must be Lord Rossdale. Welcome.' He bowed to Ross and turned to Vespery. 'Good to see you again, sir.'

Vespery bowed.

The gentleman then regarded Genna. 'And you must be the young lady who Rossdale insisted be shown the collection.'

Ross stepped forward. 'Miss Summerfield, may I present Sir Charles Long, one of His Royal Highness's art advisors.'

Genna curtsied. 'Sir Charles, I am in awe already!'

They stood in the entrance hall, which was as bright as daylight with its white marble floors, white walls and domed ceiling accented with yellow-gold columns and statues in alcoves.

The footmen took their coats.

'His Royal Highness is quite a collector of fine art. There are one hundred thirty-six paintings in the principal rooms and another sixty-seven in the attics and bedrooms. We will not see those, of course. We will not intrude on His Royal Highness's private rooms,' Sir Charles said. He gestured for them to follow him. 'Come.'

Genna lost track of time as they walked from one spectacular room to another. The architecture and decor rivalled the paintings on the walls. So opulent. So beautiful. So much like pieces of art in themselves. The grand staircase deserved its name as it rose in graceful, symmetrical curves. Gilt was prominent in almost every room. Light from the candles and the fireplaces reflected in the gold, making them seem to glow from within. There were rooms of all colours and styles. Round rooms. Blue rooms. French rooms. Gothic rooms. She wished she had a sketchbook with her to record the unique beauty of each.

Then there was the art. Almost every wall displayed a painting or several. Vespery and Sir Charles pointed out the different styles and time periods and artists. There were old paintings, many of them by the Dutch masters—Rembrandt, Rubens, Van Dyck, Jan Steen. And newer ones like Reynolds, Gainsborough and Stubbs. And countless others. Genna tried to keep everything they said in memory, but she knew she would forget half of it. She listened as intently as her excitement allowed her.

When it was possible, Vespery had Genna look closely at the brushwork of the paintings. He explained how the artists created the effects, some of which were so real looking that Genna thought the people would come alive and join them on the tour. Sir Charles spoke of how the Prince Regent was able to purchase so many paintings so quickly. In the aftermath of the French Revolution, a glut of paintings came on the market, paintings once owned by aristocrats.

Genna gasped. 'The owners must have died on the guillotine!'

'Indeed,' agreed Sir Charles, his expression sombre. 'Or drowned at Nantes.'

'At least the Prince Regent rescued the art,' Vespery said.

'Because one could not save the people,' added Ross.

Snatches of memory came back to Ross, memories of the Terror—or what he'd heard of it from his parents or other adults who seemed to have spoken of little else during that time. What he remembered was mostly feeling their fear and anguish. His mother had known some of the aristocrats who'd been executed. A cousin had been killed.

That whole time was fraught with upheaval and tension. His grandfather had just died and his father disappeared into his new role as Duke. His mother, so carefree and gay, turned fearful of an uprising in England such as had happened in France. She feared she, his father and even Ross would be targets if the people rose against aristocrats, high aristocrats especially, like dukes and duchesses.

His mother never recovered from that time, Ross realised later. She tried to fulfil her duties as duchess, but without any pleasure whatever. His father did not help, always too busy with Parliament and running the estates. Ross had been sent to school by that time. On holidays, his mother seemed even more anxious and withdrawn.

When she became ill, she simply gave up.

He was at school, his father in town and she in the country at Kessington Hall when the last fever took her away for ever.

He'd vowed then to live as his mother had once lived, for adventure and enjoyment, like his family used to do. He'd succeeded, too, until he realised men like Dell and other friends were putting their lives at risk fighting in Spain. Then he tried to do his part, meagre as it was, transporting men across the Channel.

He'd been thinking more about his mother lately. Since meeting Genna, actually. Like his mother, Genna embraced new experiences and was not afraid to let her enjoyment of them show. He liked that about her.

Genna, though, was brave. She was unafraid of a very uncertain future.

He was perhaps a bit more realistic about what she would face trying to support herself as an artist, but he was determined to help her succeed.

Vespery, Genna and Sir Charles continued to discuss the paintings in these rooms while Ross stood nearby. Afterward Sir Charles returned them to the entrance hall where the footmen were waiting with their things.

'I do not know how to thank you, Sir Charles,' Genna said, her voice still ebullient. 'And please convey my thanks to His Royal Highness. Tell him you have made a lady artist very happy.'

'I will do so at my first opportunity,' Sir Charles said.

Vespery also bade him goodbye.

Ross extended his hand to Sir Charles. 'Thank you, sir, and convey my regards to His Royal Highness.'

When they went out the door, their carriage was waiting for them.

Genna clasped Ross's arm as they walked to the carriage through the portico with its Corinthian columns. 'I do not know how to thank you, Ross. Nothing could duplicate that experience!' She reached one arm out to touch Mr Vespery's hand. 'And to you, sir. I learned so much by listening to you.'

When they were seated in the carriage, Ross said, 'There is more planned, Genna. Not for today, though.'

'Good.' She sighed. 'I do not think I could endure any more today. I am already bursting with new knowledge.'

The carriage first took Mr Vespery to his rooms in Covent Garden.

When he left the carriage, Genna said, 'Thank you again, Mr Vespery.'

His eyes twinkled. 'I will see you again soon, my dear.'

'I hope so, sir.'

When the carriage pulled away she turned to Ross. 'What did he mean by "I will see you soon"? Do you have another outing planned?'

He grinned. 'Perhaps.'

She leaned against his shoulder. 'You could not possibly please me more than you have done today.'

He could try, though. He could try.

Chapter Sixteen

The next day, Genna eagerly watched out the window for Ross's arrival. This time he drove up in his curricle with his tiger seated on the back. She rushed down the stairs and was in hat and gloves by the time he was admitted to the hall.

'I am ready!' she cried.

His ready smile cheered her. 'Then we shall be off.'

The footman held open the door as Ross escorted her out of the house. He helped her on to the curricle and climbed up beside her. The tiger jumped into his seat.

When they pulled away, Genna could not resist asking, 'Where are we bound?'

Ross grinned at her. 'Do you actually think I would tell you?'

She pretended to be petulant. 'I had hoped you would not be so cruel as to leave me in suspense.'

'But that is my delight,' he countered.

She spent the rest of the time guessing where they might be bound.

He turned down Park Lane to Piccadilly. 'Are we to visit the shops?'

'No.' He looked smug.

'Westminster Abbey!' she cried. 'Are we headed there? I've always wanted to see Westminster Abbey.'

'Another time, perhaps,' he said.

He turned on Haymarket.

She had a sudden thought, one that made her heart beat faster. 'Somerset House?'

Somerset House was the home of the Royal Academy of Art.

'Not today,' he said.

She gave up and felt guilty for being disappointed, but her hopes grew again when they turned down Vespery's street. 'Will Vespery accompany us again?' If so, where would he sit? This curricle sat two comfortably; three would be a crush.

'No,' he said.

He pulled up in front of the building where Vespery had his rooms. The tiger jumped down and held the horses. Ross climbed down and reached up to help Genna. He held her by her waist and she put her hands on his shoulders. She felt the strength of his arms as he lifted her from the curricle. When her feet hit the ground she lurched forward, winding up into his arms. Her senses flared at being embraced by him and she did not wish to move away. Ever.

It was he who released her. 'We are calling upon Mr Vespery.'

That was the surprise? She'd enjoy spending time with Vespery, especially because he was so filled with helpful information, but her mind had created something grander. How nonsensical was that? To be disappointed in whatever nice thing Ross created for her. What an ungrateful wretch she was.

'Calling upon Vespery will top Carlton House?' she said in good humour.

'Oh, indeed it will,' he assured her in a serious tone.

He must be making a jest. What could top Carlton House?

The housekeeper answered the door. 'He is in his studio.' She turned and started walking. 'This way.'

Genna's interest was piqued. 'I've never been in an artist's studio before.'

His studio was in the back of the building with a wall of large windows facing a small garden patch. As they entered, he turned from his canvas to greet them. 'Ah, Miss Summerfield. Lord Rossdale. Welcome to my studio.'

The housekeeper left.

In the corner of the room was a chair behind which was draped red velvet fabric. Obviously this was where his clients sat for him. Facing that area was a large wooden easel with a canvas on it large enough for a life-sized figure to be painted upon it. The painting in progress, Genna noticed right away, was of the Duchess of Kessington.

She approached the painting. 'Oh! Am I to have the honour of watching you work?'

Next to the easel was a table stained with paint of all colours. Vespery's palette was equally as colourful. Several brushes of all sizes stood in a large jug.

'You will watch me work, my dear,' Vespery said. 'And you will paint, as well. Lord Rossdale has asked me to give you lessons in oil painting.'

She swivelled around to Ross. 'Painting lessons?'

'As many as you need,' Ross said. 'You said you had much to learn.'

She ran to him and clasped his hand, lifting it to her lips. 'Ross! How can I thank you?'

He covered her hand with his. 'When you are ready, paint my portrait.'

She stood on tiptoe and kissed his cheek. 'It will be my honour.'

'Come,' Vespery said. 'I have a smock to cover your dress. Let us begin.'

Ross found a wooden chair in the studio and sat in it, stretching out his legs in front of him. He watched as Vespery showed Genna the easel, palette, brushes, paints, canvas, and other necessities Ross had purchased for her at Vespery's direction.

Vespery started by teaching Genna about the paint. How the colours were made. How they could be mixed to create any colour she wished. She seemed to pick up the concepts quickly from her knowledge of watercolours and Ross learned more than he'd ever known before about this basic element of oil painting. She practised mixing the colours and then she practised putting them on a canvas stretched on a wooden frame. Vespery showed her how to draw on the canvas, either with paint or with a pencil. It seemed that artists did not make detailed drawings on the canvas, but rather bare outlines.

Next Vespery taught her about the different brushes and the effects produced by each and she practised with each one.

'You are quick enough to begin a painting,' Vespery told her. He wiped the paint off her canvas, though an imprint of the colours remained. 'With the oil paints, you are able to paint over them. You can scrape off your mistakes and start again. You can change what you don't like in the painting.' He set a plain bowl on a table covered with a dark cloth. 'Try painting this.'

Ross watched her with pride. She painted a credible likeness of the bowl, although she was not satisfied with it. She scraped it off with a palette knife and started over.

The time passed with impressive speed. From a distant room, Ross heard a clock chime. 'By God, we've been at this for three hours. I believe I must return you to your home and leave Vespery to finish the Duchess's portrait.'

'Oh!' She dipped her brush in the turpentine and cleaned it off with a nearby rag. 'I had no idea we were here that long! I hope I did not take you too long from your work, Mr Vespery.'

'The light is always better in the morning,' the artist said. 'That makes the afternoon perfect for your lessons.' He took her palette and covered it with a cloth. 'That should keep your paint moist until tomorrow. Let me show you how to clean your brushes.'

When Vespery finished instructing her how to clean up at the end of a session, they retrieved their hats and gloves and overcoats. Vespery walked them to the door.

'Thank you, Mr Vespery,' Genna said, shaking the man's hand.

'My pleasure, Miss Summerfield,' he responded.

Ross said his goodbyes, as well.

When he and Genna stepped outside, the curricle was not there.

'We are at least a half-hour later than when Jem was told to bring the carriage here,' Ross explained. 'He will be walking the horses around the streets, I expect.'

'I do not mind waiting,' She met his gaze. 'That was—' She paused as if searching for words. 'That was—marvellous.'

'I am glad you thought so,' he responded. 'You will have as many lessons as you need.'

She blinked. 'I should not accept this. I am certain it is costing you dear.'

'I have wealth enough to afford it.' He wanted to spend it on her. 'Think of it as a betrothal gift.'

She gave a nervous laugh. 'But we are not really betrothed.'

'Then think of me as being a patron of the arts. That is a long tradition, is it not?'

She smiled up at him. 'Then I accept.'

His tiger appeared at the end of the street. 'Ah, here is Jem now.'

During the drive back to Mayfair, Genna kept hold of his arm and sat close to him. He found it a very comfortable way to ride.

'Where do you go after you drop me off?' she asked.

He paused, uncertain of what to say. 'Somewhere I cannot take a lady.'

'Oh.' She let go of his arm.

He glanced at her, but she turned her head away.

'I am sorry.' Her voice was strained. 'I did not mean to pry into your—your affairs.'

Did she think he was going carousing? He certainly did not wish to give her that impression. 'I—I do not make a habit of speaking of this,' he began. 'I am driving to a workhouse. There are some soldiers there. I am paying their debts so they can be released.'

She turned back to him. 'You are paying their debts?'

He glanced away. 'It is a trifle to me, but will mean a great deal to them and to their families.'

She took his arm again. 'How did you find out they were in the workhouse? Did they tell you? Or did someone else tell you.'

He turned the curricle on to the next street. 'Someone told me. One of the other soldiers I help.'

'Other soldiers? What other soldiers?'

The soldiers should thank Dell for this. If Dell had not taken Ross to the hospital to see those wounded men from his regiment, he never would have sent baskets of food to their families. He never would have created a system where several needy families received food from him on a regular basis. Enough to keep them, their wives and children in good health.

'There are several soldiers and their families who I help.'

He lifted a shoulder. 'I simply went to the workhouse and asked if there were any soldiers there. I gathered their names and the amounts of their debts and today I return to pay them and secure their release.'

She lay her head against his shoulder. 'How good of you, Ross. How very good of you.'

After Ross brought her home, Genna could not get out of her mind how wonderful this man was. To her and to others. He was giving her the best chance for her to achieve her desire to support herself with her art. How could she ever repay him?

'Lady Tinmore wishes to see you,' the footman attending the hall told her.

How could she repay her sister? Look what Lorene had done for her, misguided as it was. She must become a success. What other choice did she have than to give them what they desired for her?

'Will I find her in her sitting room?' she asked him.

'I believe so, miss.'

Genna hurried up to her bedchamber where she removed her hat, gloves and redingote. She looked at her fingers. All the paint had not washed off them. She scrubbed them some more at her basin without complete success, gave up and hurried to Lorene's sitting room.

She knocked and entered without waiting for an invitation. 'I am back. You wanted to see me?'

Lorene sat at her pianoforte, but Genna had not heard her playing. She looked up at Genna with an expression of disapproval. 'We had a fitting scheduled this afternoon. Did you not remember?'

Genna placed her hand over her mouth. 'I completely forgot.' She had been so enthralled with painting that everything else dropped out of her mind. 'Lorene, I am so sorry.'

The fitting was for their new ball gowns, the ones they were to wear to the Duke and Duchess of Kessington's ball.

'I sent word that we would come tomorrow.'

'What time?' Genna asked.

'Morning.'

Excellent! She would not have to miss her art lesson.

She did not want to tell Lorene about her lessons, afraid Lorene would somehow stop them.

'I promise I will be ready tomorrow,' she said. 'Will Tess come?'

'Tess and Lady Northdon,' Lorene responded.

Nancy, Tess's former maid turned modiste, had come up with an idea for their gowns to complement one another, so when they stood together, they would make one pretty picture.

'I will not fail you tomorrow,' Genna vowed.

She turned to go, but Lorene stopped her.

'Will you attend the rout with me tonight?' There was an edge to Lorene's voice that made Genna pause.

'Is Tess not going?' Genna asked over her shoulder.

'No,' Lorene said. 'They did not receive an invitation.'

It was shameful how often Tess's husband's family was shunned by the *ton*. If Tess was not attending this rout, then who would Lorene talk to? Tinmore would leave her for the card room.

Genna turned back to her sister and gave her a reassuring smile. 'Of course I will attend with you. It should be very enjoyable.'

Dell walked through the crush of guests at the rout and kicked himself for attending. Why had he come?

He knew why. He suspected Lord Tinmore would receive an invitation and Dell wanted a moment with Lorene to see how she was faring.

The last time he'd seen her—at that ghastly dinner party with the Duke and Duchess—she'd looked even more beaten down than usual. Not that he'd believed Tinmore beat her—God knew what he would do if he discovered her husband was beating her. It was bad enough to witness Tinmore slashing at her spirit.

He was concerned because they were cousins—was that not so? Distant cousins, though. They shared a great-great-grandfather. That made them family and he had no one else but the Summerfield sisters.

If only he'd known their plight perhaps he could have convinced his father to allow them to stay at Summerfield House. Then Lorene would not have needed to marry Tinmore for his money. His father might have helped them instead.

Foolish notion. His father would never have listened to his younger son. Had his brother Reginald spoken it would have been a different matter, but Dell could not see either his father or his brother taking pity on the scandalous Summerfield sisters.

He heard a grating voice. 'Duke! How good to see you!' It was Tinmore greeting Ross's father. 'Do you play cards tonight?'

Tinmore was abandoning her again. Did the man not realise he left her adrift like a ship without a rudder? Someone must guide her, protect her from those pirates who delighted in attacking the vulnerable.

He found her in the crowd. Standing with her was her sister, a young woman made of sterner stuff than Lorene.

'Good evening, ladies.' Dell bowed.

Lorene lowered her gaze. 'Good evening, sir.'

'Lord Penford!' Genna responded. 'At last we see a friendly face. I was beginning to think that no one would know us here.'

Though he suspected several of the guests had been introduced to these two ladies before. 'I am happy to be of service. Would you like some refreshment?'

'Would you get us whatever is in those wine glasses we keep seeing the servants carry?' she asked.

'My pleasure.' He bowed and went in search of a footman carrying a tray.

When he returned, Lorene was conversing with the Duchess of Archester, but she accepted the wine with a fleeting smile. He bowed to her again.

Genna stood close to him. 'I hope you are speaking to me, Lord Penford.'

'Why should I not?' he asked.

She gave him a knowing look. 'Because of the betrothal.'

He met her gaze. 'I am not fond of keeping secrets. No good comes of it.'

She lowered her gaze for a moment, then raised her chin. 'Have you no secrets?' she asked.

He resisted the impulse to glance at her sister. 'I have your secret,' he said. 'I gave my word to keep it.'

She placed her hand on his wrist. 'I thank you for it, I really do. I know you do not approve.'

He lifted one shoulder. 'It is between you and Ross, ultimately.'

She glanced over to her sister. 'I know it will affect others, but Ross will make certain everything concludes well.'

'I hope so.' But he could not keep the scepticism from his voice.

She glanced around the room. 'I never know what to do in these entertainments. Everyone seems to stand around and talk and take some refreshment.'

'One is supposed to mingle,' he said.

She laughed. 'You make it sound very easy, but there are few people who wish to mingle with Lorene and me. That is why I am here. To be certain she is not alone.'

Lorene was one of the most alone people Dell had ever known. 'That is kind of you.'

She sighed and tapped her foot. 'She will never know what a sacrifice it is! I have yet to devise a way to make a rout enjoyable.' She watched a young man approach. 'But I shall try.'

It was Baron Holdsworth's younger son. 'Good evening, Lord Penford.' He tossed a shy glance to Genna. 'Miss Summerfield.'

She gave the young man a big smile. 'Hello, Mr Holdsworth! How good to see you. I was just trying to make Lord Penford explain to me how one should act at a rout. Do you know?'

He looked stricken. 'Why—why—you merely talk to people.'

'Ah.' She shot a mischievous glance to Dell. 'How lucky I am, then. I will talk to you.'

Dell took a step back, intending to leave Genna with Holdsworth, an obvious admirer. He slid a glance to Lorene, who was still conversing with the Duchess of Archester. He slipped away.

Better not to be seen paying too much attention to the Summerfield sisters. All he needed—all *Lorene* needed—was to be talked about because he paid too much attention to her.

He had just found another footman with a tray of wine, when the Duchess of Kessington, Ross's stepmother, sidled up to him.

'I see *she* is here with her sister,' the Duchess said in scathing tones.

Dell knew precisely whom she was talking about. 'Who with what sister?'

'You know who I mean. Those odious Summerfields.' She glanced towards Genna.

Dell took a sip of his wine. 'You forget, Duchess, that I am a Summerfield.'

'But you are not one of *those* Summerfields,' she protested. 'You have a title and property.'

He'd trade it all to have his family back.

She leaned towards his ear. 'What are we to do about this betrothal?'

'What can be done of it?' he countered. 'Ross made his decision.'

'He cannot marry her!' she said in an agitated whisper. 'She is entirely unsuitable. Why, her mother is still living in Brussels with the man she ran away with years ago. And her father—'

He held up a hand. 'I have heard the gossip.'

'Even Lord Tinmore cannot put enough shine on her,' the Duchess went on. 'Why, the girl received no offers last Season. She was not even admitted to Almack's, you know.'

'Many young ladies have Seasons without offers. Many do not attend Almack's.'

She sniffed. 'Obviously she was waiting for a duke's son.' She placed a hand on his arm. 'I hope I can rely on you to do what you can.'

He faced her. 'Duchess, recall the lady you are discussing is my relation.'

She lifted her nose. 'A distant relation. You cannot credit it.'

But he did credit it. He held on to that distant family connection much more firmly than he would have imagined he could. 'In any event, the matter is between Ross and Miss Summerfield. I will not interfere.'

Her eyes flashed. 'I see I cannot rely on you. I must act alone to prevent this ghastly mistake.'

She turned with a swish of her skirts and strode away, joining another group with a cordial smile and ingratiating manners.

Chapter Seventeen

During the next week, Genna had lessons with Vespery almost every day and when she was not at the easel in Vespery's studio, she snatched time to read the da Vinci book Ross gave her. Vespery said she was progressing very quickly, but not quickly enough for her. She had only half a year to prepare to be a working artist. Painting still life— vases of flowers, food, cloth of various textures—like Vespery had her doing was not going to earn her money. She needed to paint portraits and she needed to be good at it.

She sighed. Patience was not one of her virtues!

Genna paced the floor of her bedchamber. There would be no lesson today, no outing with Ross. She sat at the desk in her room and pulled out her latest sketchbook from the drawer.

If she could not paint, she could at least draw.

The pencil in her hand made some sweeping curves on the page, but, before she knew it, she was making a sketch of Ross, how he appeared when his face was in repose. For practice, she told herself. For when she would paint his portrait.

She had to admit, she missed Ross as much as the painting lessons. He stayed during most of her lessons, always ready to assist, to bring them food, to shop for supplies. He professed to find the process interesting, but he must become bored some of the time. When Vespery left her to paint, Ross talked with her. Or rather she talked with him, telling him all the inconsequential details of her unvaried life at Summerfield House. She told him about the governess who'd taught her to draw and paint in watercolours. What a talented woman that governess was, nurturing Lorene's love of piano, as well.

Until their father, who'd stopped paying the woman, forced her to find employment elsewhere. She was their last governess. After that, Tess and Lorene took over teaching Genna mathematics, and French and history and such. Genna and Lorene tended to their talents on their own.

Ross listened to her tell all this nonsense. She wished he would tell more about himself, but he did not. There was so much she wished to know about him.

Tonight was the night of the Kessington ball, the night their betrothal would be announced and more people deceived by the secret they kept. The announcement would not be applauded, she suspected. Who would think it a good idea for a duke's heir to marry one of the scandalous Summerfields?

Tinmore had insisted she stay home this day, to be rested and ready for the ball. Her maid would be coming in at any time to help her dress. She'd refused a hairdresser this time, setting off a tirade from Tinmore, but his tirades had become a mere annoyance now that he had no power over her.

Her maid Hallie entered the room, carrying her ball gown. 'Are you ready to dress, miss?'

'I am indeed.' She closed her sketchbook and put it away.

She promised herself she would not worry about her appearance. She would wear her hair in her favourite way, high on her head with curls cascading. Her dress was lovely, a blush so pale it was almost white. It matched Lorene's and Tess's and even Lady Northdon's, Tess's mother-in-law. Genna's was designed to shine the brightest. She was eager for the scandalous Summerfield sisters and the notorious Lady Northdon to be seen together as the very height of fashion.

While Hattie was putting the last pins in her hair, there was a knock at the door.

A footman handed Hattie a package. She brought it to Genna. 'This came for you.'

First she read the card. 'It is from Lord Rossdale.'

Genna unwrapped the paper to discover a velvet-covered box. She opened it.

'Oh, my!' she exclaimed.

It was a pendant and earrings. The pendant was a lovely opal surrounded by diamonds set in gold and on a gold chain. The earrings were matching opals.

It would go perfectly with her gown.

'But how did he know?' she said aloud.

'Do you wear them tonight?' Hattie asked without enthusiasm.

'Of course I will!' Genna cried.

With a gift such as this, who could ever guess their betrothal was a sham? She must remember, though, that such a gift must be returned when their charade was over.

When Lord Tinmore's carriage pulled up to the Kessington town house, Tess, her husband and his parents were waiting for them on the pavement.

Tess hurried up to Genna and Lorene as they were assisted from the carriage. 'We saw you coming and Lady Northdon said we should wait. We can be announced at the same time and walk in together!'

Genna gave her sister a buss on the cheek. She said hello to Lady Northdon. 'It is a wonderful idea.'

'Let us give them a spectacle, no?' Lady Northdon said in her French accent.

Lord Tinmore grimaced when he greeted Lord Northdon, who looked no happier, but Lord Northdon's expression changed to completely besotted when his wife took his arm. Lord and Lady Northdon might defy Genna's disbelief in happy marriages, except for the fact that the Northdons had been miserable together until very recently. Who knew how long this period of marital bliss would last?

They all walked into the house and were attended by footmen in the magnificent marbled hall whose vaulted ceiling rose over two floors high. Other guests were queued on the double stairway of white marble with its gilt-and-crystal bannisters. It struck Genna that the design of this stairway mimicked the one at Carlton House. Or was it the other way around? Surely this house had been built first. It was a majestic sight, one Genna tried to commit to memory. What a lovely painting it would make with all the ladies in their colourful finery gracing the stairs like scattered jewels.

'Come. Hurry,' Tinmore snapped. 'There are enough people ahead of us as it is.'

They hurried to their place on the stairs. Genna looked down and noticed that each step was made of one complete piece of marble.

Her sister Tess stood beside her. 'Do you realise that all this will be yours some day?'

'I cannot think that,' Genna said honestly.

A quarter of an hour later they reached the ballroom door.

The butler announced, 'Lord and Lady Tinmore and Miss Summerfield.'

Tinmore marched ahead, but Genna and Lorene held back until Lord and Lady Northdon and Mr and Mrs Glenville were announced. The four ladies crossed over the wide threshold together as heads turned towards them and a murmur went through the crowd already assembled in the ball room, a room even bigger than the ones they had been before.

A *frisson* of excitement rushed up Genna's spine. They presented a lovely picture, each dressed in a shade of pink, Genna's the palest, Lady Northdon's the richest. Their gowns were not identically styled, but the fabric was the same, net over fine muslin so that their skirts floated around them.

Genna leaned to Tess. 'Tell Nancy her styles have triumphed.'

'How gratifying it is,' Tess responded. 'Because you know half these guests were certain we would not come off so well.'

Genna glanced at the receiving line, where Lorene had hurried to catch up with Lord Tinmore. Ross shook the hand of the gentleman who'd been announced before them, but when the man moved on, Ross glanced up and smiled at Genna.

Suddenly all that mattered was that he like her gown.

She touched the opal pendant and stepped forward to greet the Duke and Duchess.

The Duchess greeted her with a fixed smile. 'Don't you look sweet, my dear.'

She curtsied to the Duke.

'Good. Good. You are here.' He made it sound as if he wished she wasn't.

'I am honoured to be here, Your Grace,' she responded.

Then she came to Ross who clasped her hand and leaned close to her ear. 'You look beautiful.'

Her spirits soared.

She touched her opal. 'Thank you, Ross. It is lovely.'

'Save me the first dance,' he added.

She smiled at him. 'With pleasure.'

Lady Northdon waited behind her. 'There are guests behind us,' she reminded Genna.

Genna stepped away from Ross, but waited for Lady Northdon and Tess to be finished. Together they walked across the ball room to where Lorene stood with Tinmore.

As soon as they reached her, Tinmore glanced from Lorene to Tess. 'I am off to the game room, but I will return for the announcement. In the meantime, behave with decorum. I'll not have the Tinmore title besmirched by hoydenish antics.'

As if Lorene could ever be hoydenish. Genna felt like creating a fuss just to upset him.

'Look at this room!' Tess said in awed tones.

The walls were papered in red damask, but were covered with huge paintings depicting scenes from Greek mythology. Genna wished she could get up close to examine the brushwork, the use of colour. She knew so much more now than when she first met Vespery.

'Look at the ceiling!' Tess said.

The ceiling had intricate plasterwork dividing the ceiling into octagons and squares, each of which were painted. It made the ceiling of the drawing room where they had been the night of the musicale look plain in comparison.

Her husband came to her side. 'This is a magnificent room, is it not?'

Lorene said, 'There is Lord Penford standing alone. I believe I will walk over to him and say hello.'

Ross joined Genna as soon as he could leave the receiving line. He danced with her, with each of her sisters and even with Lady Northdon, whom he'd never met before but liked immediately. He noticed plenty of disapproving stares, which angered him. Why should the Summerfields and Lord and Lady Northdon be judged so negatively? Nothing they had done deserved this denigration. Except maybe for Lady Tinmore, who did marry for money, but after five minutes seeing her with Lord Tinmore, one could feel nothing but pity for her.

One of the footmen approached him. 'Her Grace says you should come now.'

Time for the announcement. 'Thank you, Stocker.' Ross turned to Genna, who was laughing at something Lady Northdon said. 'It is time,' he told her.

Her face fell, but she nodded and said to her sisters, 'I think they are ready for the announcement.'

'Oh,' cried Tess. 'Let us all go up front where we can see you better.'

Ross and Genna led the way and the rest of their party followed. In their wake were audible murmurs from the other guests.

Ross's father and the Duchess stood at the far end of the ballroom where, on an elevated platform, the orchestra still played quietly. The Duchess looked crestfallen; his father, grim.

'Are you ready?' his father asked.

Ross smiled down on Genna. 'Indeed we are.'

She straightened her back, lifted her chin and smiled back at him. Brave girl.

His father and the Duchess, all smiles now, climbed on to the orchestra's platform. The musicians sounded a loud chord and went silent.

Ross's father raised his hands. 'May I have your attention? Attention!'

The guests turned towards him and fell silent.

'We have an announcement to make,' his father said. 'A happy announcement.' He gestured to Ross. 'As you know, the Duchess and I have long desired to see my son Rossdale settled and tonight I am delighted to report that he has done as we wished.'

The crowd murmured.

Ross's father went on. 'My son, the Marquess of Rossdale, has proposed marriage to Miss Summerfield, daughter of the late Sir Hollis Summerfield of Yardney and ward of Lord Tinmore—'

Tinmore waved and bobbed from nearby.

The Duke continued, 'And I am happy to report that Miss Summerfield has accepted him.'

'No!' a lone female voice cried from the back of the

room amidst other shocked sounds from other guests. The Duchess's smile faltered.

Ross stepped on to the platform and helped Genna up to stand beside the Duke and Duchess. 'Thank you, Father.' He turned to the crowd. 'Miss Summerfield is not well known to many of you, but I am confident you will soon see all the fine qualities she possesses. I could not be a happier man.'

He put his arm around Genna, who smiled at him with much admiration in her face. Her family beamed from below them, but only a few others in the crowd looked pleased.

Ross knew this world, where birth and titles and wealth mattered more than character. He and Genna knew the disapproval they would face. So why should he feel so angry at these people and so protective of Genna?

He lifted her off the platform. 'There. It is done.'

She grinned at him. 'And I am still standing!'

Her sisters, Glenville and his parents clustered around her with hugs and happy tears of congratulations. Lord Tinmore disappeared into the card room again. Several others offered congratulations, a few genuinely meant, others so as not to offend the Duke of Kessington.

Dell approached them just as the music for the supper dance began. 'I thought I should congratulate you as well, or it might look odd.'

'I appreciate it.' Ross kept a smile on his face as he shook Dell's hand. 'I'm glad this part is over. Now we can simply enjoy the rest of the Season.'

Dell turned to Genna. 'How are you faring?'

She smiled, too, as if accepting good wishes. 'I am actually surprised that some people with whom I have no connection seemed happy for me.'

It had surprised Ross, too. He planned to make a note of those people.

'Are you dancing the supper dance?' Genna asked Dell.

'With your sister,' he responded. 'As it is likely Lord Tinmore will not escort her in to supper.'

'So good of you,' Genna said.

His face turned stony. 'My duty to my cousin.' Dell bowed and presumably went in search of Lady Tinmore.

Ross took Genna's hand. 'Let us skip the supper dance. There is someone here I should like you to meet.'

'As you wish,' Genna said in exaggerated tones. 'I am a biddable fiancée.'

He laughed. 'Biddable?'

He brought her to a pleasant-looking woman in her forties who sat among other ladies not dancing.

'Lady Long.' He bowed. 'Allow me to present to you my fiancée—'

'Your very biddable fiancée,' Genna broke in.

'My *biddable* fiancée,' he corrected. 'Miss Summerfield.'

'How do you do, ma'am.' Genna curtsied.

'Not as well as you, young lady,' the woman said in good humour. 'Landing yourself a future duke.'

Genna made a nervous laugh.

Ross quickly spoke. 'Your husband was gracious enough to give Miss Summerfield and me a tour of the artwork at Carlton House.'

'You are Sir Charles's wife?' Genna exclaimed. 'I am so delighted to meet you. Your husband was too generous to take the time for that wonderful tour. I learned so much!'

Ross continued. 'Lady Long is an accomplished artist, Genna. She has exhibited at the Royal Academy.'

Genna's eyes grew wide. 'You have?'

Ross turned to Lady Long. 'Miss Summerfield is also an artist.'

'It is my abiding passion,' Genna said. 'What do you paint? Portraits?'

'Landscapes,' Lady Long responded. 'I suppose you could say that gardens and landscapes are my abiding passion.'

'Landscapes,' Genna repeated in awed tones.

'And what do you paint, my dear?' Mrs Long asked.

'I am hoping to learn to paint portraits, but most of what I've done before are landscapes.'

Like the one she'd painted of Summerfield House with the purple and pink sky and blue grass.

'What medium do you use?' Genna asked.

'Watercolours,' the lady said.

'I love to paint landscapes in watercolours.' Genna sighed. 'Tell me, Lady Long, do your watercolours sell for a good price?'

'Sell?' Mrs Long scoffed. 'Goodness me, no. I do not *sell* my paintings, my dear. I enjoy painting and am lucky enough to have my skill recognised, but I enjoy many pastimes. I adore designing my garden, but I would never hire myself out to design anyone else's.'

Ross saw disappointment in Genna's eyes, but she kept a pleasant expression on her face for the older woman. 'Do you design your own garden, then?'

Ross suspected Genna was not very interested in moving trees and shrubbery about.

'Sir Charles and I are creating our garden. We've been inspired by Repton and Capability Brown, but the ideas are our very own,' she answered proudly.

'That is an art as well, is it not?' Genna added diplomatically.

The lady smiled. 'It is, indeed, my dear. You must call upon me some time and I will show you my garden—in my sketchbook, that is. Our house is some distance away. We are staying in town while Parliament sits.'

'That would be lovely,' Genna said. 'I would love to see your sketchbook.'

Genna curtsied and Ross bowed and they walked away.

'I am ever so much more interested in the sketchbook than actually seeing the gardens,' she told him in a conspiratorial tone.

'I would have surmised that,' he responded.

She drew closer to him. 'Thank you for introducing me to her. Imagine. She has exhibited at the Royal Academy!'

'I thought you would like to meet a fellow lady artist,' he said.

'I should like to meet one who earns enough to live on from her art. Someone like Vigée-LeBrun.'

'Who?'

'Madame Vigée-LeBrun. She was Marie Antoinette's portraitist.' She peered at him. 'You really know very little about art, do you not?'

'Only what I have learned from you, Sir Charles and Vespery,' he told her. 'Before that I either liked a work of art, disliked it, or noticed it not at all.'

Her eyes looked puzzled. 'Then why become an artist's patron?'

He raised his brows. 'Because of you, of course.'

She gave him a puzzled look. 'I do not understand.'

The music was loud and the guests who were not dancing tried to talk above it. He did not fancy shouting at her to be heard.

'Let us go somewhere quiet.' He escorted her out the ballroom door and down a hallway to a small parlour.

The room was lit by a crystal chandelier. Most of the rooms were lit in case the guests should wander in. The Duke refused to appear as if he needed to economise about such things as the cost of candles.

As soon as they entered, though, Genna was distracted by the decor. 'Oh, more plasterwork and gilt. Is every room in the house so beautiful?'

Her attention was caught by a painting in the room, a long painting depicting some Classical battle scene, with overturned chariots, rearing horses and fighting soldiers in gleaming helmets, swords and shields.

'Who painted this?' she asked.

'I have no idea,' he responded. 'I grew up with these

paintings, but I knew nothing of them. I liked this one when I was a boy, because it was a battle scene—not that I saw it often when my grandfather was alive. He would not allow children in the public rooms, in most of the rooms, actually, but sometimes my mother would sneak me out of the nursery and take me on a tour of the house.'

She turned from the painting to him. 'I think I would have liked your mother.'

He gestured to a sofa in a part of the room set up as a seating area.

She sat on the sofa and he sat next to her.

'I think I understand why you are helping me,' she said. 'It is like your soldiers, is it not? When you discover someone in need, you help them.'

His reasons for helping her were a great deal more personal than that. 'Genna—' he began.

From the hallway they heard a loud voice making an announcement.

She grimaced. 'It must be time for supper.'

He extended his hand to help her up, but pulled too hard. She wound up in his arms, her body flush against his.

She laughed and looked up into his eyes. 'If anyone saw us now, they would think we truly were betrothed.'

The blood surged through his veins, as powerful an arousal of his senses as he could remember experiencing.

'Let us convince them even more.' He lowered his head and took possession of her lips, suddenly ravenous for her.

An eager sound escaped her lips. She put her arms around his neck and pressed her mouth against his. Her lips parted, giving his tongue access. He backed her up until she was against the wall and he could hold her tighter against him. His lips left hers and tasted the tender skin of her neck. She writhed beneath him, her hands holding his head as if she feared he would stop kissing her.

From the hallway, the butler's voice rose again.

Ross froze. Good God. 'We must stop,' he managed, releasing her and stepping away.

Her chest rose and fell, her breath rapid. 'Oh, my!'

He filled with shame. 'Genna, I—'

She expelled one more deep breath before smiling up at him. 'That was quite wonderful, Ross! Last Season a fellow or two pecked at my cheek, but now I feel I have been truly kissed!'

He'd resisted such impulses so many times when they'd been together. Why had he weakened now? 'It was poorly done of me.'

She laughed and threw her arms around his neck again, giving his mouth a quick kiss. 'I would say your kiss was rather skilfully done.'

He held her cheeks in his palms. 'You are outrageous, Genna Summerfield.' He released her again. With difficulty.

She straightened the bodice of her dress and smoothed her skirt. 'Me? You are the one who kissed me.'

He checked his own clothing and made certain he was together. With any luck the visible evidence of his arousal would disappear by the time they reached the dining room.

Chapter Eighteen

Genna hardly knew what to think as Ross escorted her to the dining room. Such a kiss! She'd never imagined a kiss could be so sublime. Could leave one so…wanting.

She should have been furious at Ross. She should have slapped his face.

Instead, when he'd pulled away from her, she'd wanted to pull him back and start the kiss all over again. Was this the sort of physical thing that made men and women desire to marry? Or, like her unhappily married mother and father, was this what made them seek other lovers?

If a mere kiss could be so powerful, what, then, would marital coupling be like? For the first time, she wanted to know. If Ross's kiss could bring such breathless pleasure, what could his lovemaking bring?

The supper was set out in three separate rooms, the dining room and two others set up with tables and chairs. Unlike the musicale, the food would be served at the table. She and Ross were expected in the dining room where the guests of highest rank were to be seated. When they entered the dining room, most of the guests had already taken their seats. The Duke at the head of the table, the Duchess at the other end, but, beyond that, precedence was abandoned. One supped with one's recent dance partner.

From across the room, the Duke stood and called, 'Ross!' He gestured for them to come to him. Two empty chairs next to the Duke had obviously been intended for them.

A footman held Genna's chair for her. To her dismay,

Lord Tinmore procured a place almost directly across from her. She glanced down the table and spied Lorene seated with Lord Penford.

The room was another grand exhibition of opulence. Walls of green damask, two marble pillars at each end of the room, another intricate plasterwork ceiling, its designs outlined in gilt. The paintings on the walls were huge and awe-inspiring, depicting scenes from ancient history.

'You are late,' the Duke chastised.

'A bit late,' Ross responded without a hint of apology.

'You disappeared from the ballroom.' The Duke's tone did not change.

'Only briefly,' Ross said.

A gentleman on the Duke's other side asked him a question and he turned away.

The white soup was served, but the guests selected other fare from the dishes set before them on the table. Because a hot meal would never have stayed hot for so many guests, the dinner consisted of cold meats and fish, jellies, pastries, sweetmeats and ices, among a myriad of other dishes. The room was soon filled with the noise of conversation, and silver knives and forks clanking against dinner plates of fine porcelain china.

The Duke and the other gentleman began a heated exchange about the rash of violence occurring lately, of several break-ins, thefts and murders by gangs of men.

The Duke half-stood, his face red. 'We cannot ignore that people are hungry, sir!'

Genna wanted to tell him that Ross fed hungry people. Perhaps the others should do the same. But she did not dare.

The Duke sat down again, drained the contents of his wineglass and suddenly clasped his hand to his chest, with a cry of pain. He collapsed on to the table, scattering dishes and food and spilling wine.

One of the guests screamed in alarm.

'Father!' Ross was first to his feet and first to reach his

father. He sat his father back in the chair. 'Wake up, wake up,' he cried.

His father moaned.

Ross turned to the butler. 'Fetch the doctor immediately.'

The butler rushed from the room.

Penford ran up from where he had been sitting. 'Shall we carry him to his bedchamber?'

'Yes,' Ross immediately agreed.

The two men picked up the Duke and carried him out of the room.

The Duchess stood and tried to make herself heard above the rumblings of the guests. 'He's merely had a spell. He will recover soon. Please let us continue with supper.'

Finish supper? Genna could not finish supper. She left the room to see if she could help in some way. Out in the hallway, she looked for Ross and Dell, but they were out of sight.

She found a footman. 'Show me where Rossdale took his father.'

There was no reason the footman should do what she demanded, but he did. She caught up with them right as they reached the Duke's bedchamber door.

'May I help?' she asked.

Both men looked surprised to see her.

At that moment, though, the Duke made a sound and struggled to get out of Ross's and Penford's arms. 'What? What happened?'

'You lost consciousness, Papa,' Ross told him. 'We're bringing you to your room.'

'Nonsense. Must be—we are giving a ball. Perfectly fine.' He stumbled and Ross caught him before he lost his balance.

Genna spoke up. 'Your butler has sent for your physician. You should lie down until he comes.'

The Duke peered at her as if never having seen her before, then the puzzlement on his face cleared. 'Oh, I remember you.'

'See?' She smiled at the Duke. 'That is a good sign. You remember me. But you continue to be unsteady on your feet. Best to wait for your physician.

'Come on.' She stepped forward and took his arm. 'If you feel dizzy you may simply hang on to me.'

'I do feel dizzy,' he murmured.

He was inside the door of his room when his valet appeared. 'They said below stairs that His Grace took ill.'

'A little spell, that is all,' His Grace said.

The valet lost no time in getting him in the room and over to his bed. Ross remained with him.

Genna walked back to the hall.

'I was amazed he would follow your orders,' Penford said.

She slid him a smile. 'So was I. Sometimes people do, though.' She peeked in the room where the valet and Ross were convincing his father to lie down. 'I hope he is not seriously ill.'

'Indeed.' Penford closed the door all but a crack. His voice turned low. 'We should not like to lose him.'

Another death for Penford to endure? How hard for him. 'You must know the Duke well.'

He shrugged. 'I know Ross well. The Duke is too busy and too steeped in politics to be known well. I do not believe he ever spoke to me until I inherited my title.'

'Ross is so unlike that,' she said.

He nodded in agreement. 'According to Ross, his father was never like that.'

'What do you mean?' she asked.

He peeked through the crack in the door. 'They are dressing him for bed,' he said before answering her question. 'According to Ross, his father was light-hearted before he inherited the title. He and Ross's mother were always taking Ross to some new place for some new adventure. His father was game for anything, apparently. His mother, too.'

'Did you know Ross's mother?' she asked.

Penford shook his head. 'I met her once, but by then she was ill and much altered, Ross said.'

She glanced away. She had no memory of her own mother and her father had never bothered with her at all.

'Let us hope he does not lose his father as well,' she murmured.

Penford's face was grim.

Ross came out the door. 'He is in bed resting. His valet will stay until the physician arrives. I should return to the guests. Apprise them of his condition.'

'And the Duchess. She will be worried,' Genna said.

Ross frowned.

'What does that frown mean?' she asked.

'She should be here,' he said bitterly. 'Not trying to salvage her social event.'

Another less-than-ideal marriage? Genna was not surprised.

'Everyone will still be at supper,' she said. 'While you go to the Duchess, shall I tell the guests in the other rooms what occurred and of your father's present status?'

Ross did not answer right away.

'I'll do it,' Penford said.

Ross threaded her arm though his. 'Come with me. Stay by my side.'

At this moment, if they were truly betrothed, she would be expected to stay by his side. Oddly enough, at this moment, it was also where she most wanted to be.

Although the Duchess had wanted the ball to go on in spite of her husband's sudden malaise, no one wished to dance and pretend to enjoy themselves while the host of the party had taken to his bed.

So Ross stood where his father would have stood, at the

Duchess's side, while one after the other, the guests approached to say goodbye and to extend their good wishes to the Duke.

In the midst of all this, the doctor arrived and, since the Duchess showed no inclination to accompany the physician to her husband's room, Ross accepted that duty, as well. He managed only the briefest goodnight to Genna, a mere glance as he hurried behind the doctor.

After examining him, the doctor told his father, 'It is your heart. We have talked of this before. You must curtail your activity. Now it is imperative that you rest. For at least a month.'

'A month!' the Duke cried. 'I cannot rest. There is much to do in Parliament. And my duties to the wedding of Princess Charlotte—I will be expected to participate.'

The doctor was unfazed by these excuses. 'If you fail to rest, another episode like this one could put a period to your existence.'

Ross's father crossed his arms over his chest and pursed his lips like a sulking child.

The doctor stepped away from the bed. 'I will stop in to see how you are faring tomorrow, but now I am very desirous of returning to my bed.'

'We are grateful you came,' Ross said, extending his hand.

The doctor shook it. 'I'll see myself out.'

Ross walked him to the door. Ross was also eager to get some sleep.

His father called to him. 'Ross?'

He turned. 'Yes, Father?'

'You must take over for me.'

Ross knew this even before the doctor gave his diagnosis. 'Yes, whatever you require, but sleep now. I'll come in the morning. Tell me then what you need me to do.'

The next day instead of Ross coming to pick up Genna for her painting lesson, he sent a message and a carriage, explaining why he could not go with her. She understood. Goodness! His father was ill; what else could he do? He promised to call upon her in the afternoon.

When she arrived at the studio, Vespery was disappointed that Ross was not there. 'I was going to have him pose for you. You are ready to try a portrait.'

The portrait seemed suddenly much less important to her than before.

'I could paint you,' she said.

'No, *you*. Paint you.' He brought over a mirror and set it up where she could look at herself and her canvas.

Genna began as he'd taught her to begin on other paintings. Make a few lines as a guide, a rough idea of the shape of her head, where to place her eyes, nose and mouth. At each step, he stopped his own work and taught her what she needed to know next. What colours to mix for skin pigment, what colours for shadow and highlights. How to block in the colours, then how to refine them. By the end of the day she had a portrait of herself in a rough, unpolished form.

'This is a very good effort,' Vespery said. 'A very good effort, indeed.'

She wondered if Ross would be pleased.

'I am becoming used to the paints,' she said to Vespery.

When the carriage came to take her home that day, all she could think of was seeing Ross that afternoon.

She entered Tinmore's town house more subdued than at any other time when returning from her art lessons. She'd barely stepped into the hall when Lorene came down the stairs.

'Where were you?' Lorene's voice was angry. 'You were not with Rossdale. I saw you leave. You were alone.'

'He sent a carriage for me,' she stalled.

'You did not meet him, though, did you?' Lorene accused. 'Lord Tinmore said it was Rossdale, not the Duke, who met with some of the other lords to discuss the changes in coinage.'

Parliament would vote on changing the currency to a fixed gold standard. She'd heard gentlemen talking about it at the ball last night.

Lorene glared at her. 'If Rossdale was there, he was not with you.'

'No, he was not with me,' Genna admitted. Her art lessons were another secret she kept from her sister.

'Then where did you go alone in Rossdale's carriage?' Lorene demanded.

Genna glanced around her. The footman who had opened the door for her was standing stony-faced, but in hearing distance. 'May we go up to your sitting room? I will explain everything there.'

Lorene answered her by simply turning and climbing the stairs again. When they reached the sitting room, Lorene remained standing.

'Explain, then,' Lorene said.

'I have been taking lessons in oil painting,' Genna said.

Lorene's brows rose. 'Oil painting?'

'From Mr Vespery. Do you remember him? He was at Her Grace's musicale. He is painting portraits of the Duke and Duchess.'

Lorene shook her head in disbelief. 'Lessons? With a man? Unchaperoned?'

'Well, Ross was with me until today, but, I assure you, Mr Vespery is merely my art teacher, not my paramour.'

Lorene's eyes scolded. 'Genna! Honestly! You are much too free-speaking.'

Genna lowered her gaze. 'I am sorry, Lorene. I should not have been so sharp.'

Lorene waved a hand. 'Never mind that. Whatever possessed you?'

'To get art lessons?' How much could she explain without telling all of it? 'We've been surrounded by astounding paintings in this house, at Tinmore Hall, in every house we've visited. I want to paint like that.'

'Genna, those paintings were done by masters. You cannot expect to paint like them.'

Lorene's words stung, but Genna wanted her to understand. She took her sister's hand and pulled her over to the chairs. 'I love it, Lorene. And I am progressing very quickly at it. Please do not make it so I cannot continue.' In other words, tell Lord Tinmore.

'But why? How did you even start it?' Lorene asked.

'One day I mentioned to Ross that I would like to learn to paint in oils and the next day he took me to Mr Vespery's studio. Ross bought me all the supplies and paid for the lessons.'

Lorene looked shocked. 'You cannot accept that!'

'Why not?' Genna countered. 'He is my fiancé. If he gave me a diamond bracelet, you would think that a fine thing.' If he were really her fiancé, she should say.

Lorene's eyebrows knitted. 'I do not know. In some ways Lord Rossdale seems the perfect husband for you, but it is difficult to see you as a duchess.'

On that Genna could agree. She would make a horrible duchess.

Genna leaned forward. 'Please do not spoil this for me, Lorene. I am doing no harm and I do love it so.'

Lorene glanced away. 'I suppose…'

Genna sprang from her chair and kissed her sister on the cheek. 'You do understand! It is like your music.'

'Like my music,' Lorene said wistfully. 'Like if I could take lessons…'

'You could!' Genna seized her sister's hands. 'London is the perfect place to find a wonderful piano master. We can ask if anyone knows of one. I'll ask Ross. Or Lord Penford.'

'No!' Lorene said sharply. 'It is a lovely idea, but I cannot do it.'

'You could.' Genna sat again, but kept hold of Lorene's

hands. 'Ask Lord Tinmore. He likes to do things for you.' But not for anyone else. She shook her sister's hands. 'Think of it! You already play beautifully, but you were mostly self-taught. There might be all sorts of things you could learn.'

'Perhaps...' Lorene glanced away.

When Ross called that afternoon Genna met him in the drawing room. Seeing him standing, waiting for her, she had an impulse to rush into his arms. It stunned her. The events of the previous night, seeing Ross so distressed, it had changed something in her.

'Ross,' she managed.

He walked towards her and took her hand. 'Forgive the message this morning. I hope you got to your lesson with no difficulties.'

'None at all.' She led him to the sofa and they sat. 'But, tell me, how is your father?'

His brow furrowed. 'Weaker than he will admit. The doctor said he must rest for at least a month. The only way I could get him to agree to do that was to take over whatever of his duties I am able to perform.'

'Of course you must.' But she felt sad for him. It must be a great deal of responsibility thrust upon him so suddenly.

'I must renege on my promise to take you wherever you wished to go,' he said.

She put her hand on his. 'Do not fret over that.'

'Tell me.' He gave a wan smile. 'What did you paint today?'

The stress on his face put all thoughts of painting out of her mind. She did not wish to cause him worry so she exclaimed, 'It was the very best day! Vespery started teaching me to paint portraits. At last!'

'Who did you paint?' he asked.

She'd not mention that he was supposed to have been her first model. 'I painted myself. Vespery gave me a mirror.'

'I would like to see that,' he said.

She laughed. 'No, you would not. It is rather awful at the moment, but I will improve it.' She took a breath. 'I can master this, Ross. I can paint portraits. Thanks to you, I will be able to earn moncy.'

'And that is what you desire more than anything,' he stated as if finishing her sentence.

She sobered. 'But how are you faring?'

He smiled sadly. 'I can manage. I suppose I absorbed more of my father's thinking than I guessed. I still hope to break away one of these days and come and visit Vespery's studio.'

'Whenever you are able,' she said. 'I would welcome you.'

Chapter Nineteen

Ross returned to the Kessington town house after calling upon Genna. The footman attending the hall told him his father wished him to come to his bedchamber.

Ross knocked and was admitted.

He walked to his father's bedside. 'How do you fare today, Father?'

His father, always so strong and commanding by nature, looked shrunken and pale against the bed linens. 'I'm tired, is all. Merely need a little rest.'

'The doctor listened to your heart. You need to heed him,' Ross countered.

His father made a dismissive gesture. 'I know. I know. I am doing as he says.'

His father's valet, who was in the room folding clothes, spoke up. 'Your Grace, I dare say the physician would not have approved of your getting up and working at your desk for over an hour.' His father's desk was in his study attached to the library on the floor below.

'You may leave us, Stone,' his father snapped.

The valet bowed and left the room.

'Gossips worse than an old woman,' Ross's father muttered.

'He is concerned about you.' Ross's brows knitted. 'You must rest, Father. It has only been a day since your spell.'

'Sitting at my desk did not seem such an exertion,' his father said.

'But walking there. Climbing stairs. Stay in this room.

Please. I can take care of what you cannot.' What other choice did Ross have?

'Very well. Very well,' His father gestured to a chair by his bedside. 'Sit, my son.'

Ross sat.

His father glanced away as if uncertain what he wished to say. Finally he spoke. 'This spell has alarmed me, if you must know. Your grandfather died of such a spell. He was about my age.'

Yes. Everything changed when his grandfather died.

'It is time for you to settle down, my son,' he said.

Ross's brows rose. 'I am. I am betrothed—'

His father interrupted. 'But you plan to marry in autumn! I may not be here in autumn. I do not know how long I will be here. I would like to know if there will be an heir to the title before I die.' He leaned forward in the bed. 'Get on with it! Get a special licence and marry right away. What is this waiting?'

This deception of his and Genna's suddenly felt like a foolish mistake.

His father's voice rose. 'It is nonsensical to wait. Are you wishing to get out of it? Believe me, Constance and I would be delighted to see you look elsewhere. But if it must be this Summerfield chit, marry her now, even though I doubt she is up to the rigours of becoming a duchess!'

Ross disagreed. Genna would make a duchess unlike any other. The problem was, if he truly wished to make her his wife, he would kill her dreams. His mother's dreams had been dashed; Ross would not see the same for Genna.

She'd become that important to him.

Ross answered the Duke defensively. 'Stop trying to control when I marry and what I do.' He rose from the chair. 'I will take over whatever duties you need me for. I will do that for your sake and for the sake of the title and all the people dependent upon us, but allow me my own choice of who to marry and when.'

'You are a disappointment to me!' his father shouted. He pressed a hand to his chest and sank back against the pillows.

'Calm yourself, Papa!' Ross cried in alarm. He softened his tone. 'Just rest. Trust me. You will get well. All will work out as it should.'

His father turned his face away.

Ross stepped back. Curse his idea of this false betrothal!

'Rest, Papa,' he said again. 'I'll come see you later.'

His father continued to ignore him. Ross turned and strode out of the bedchamber.

The Duchess stood right outside the door. She joined him as he walked away.

'I am not in favour of your marrying right away,' she said.

He did not look at her. 'Eavesdropping, Constance?'

She huffed. 'I was walking by. Your voices were raised. I could not help but hear.'

Ross did not believe her.

'You can change your mind about marrying Miss Summerfield,' the Duchess went on. 'I am certain she can be persuaded to cry off. She has not the vaguest notion of what it will take to be a duchess. She is entirely unsuitable.'

'It is none of your affair, ma'am,' he warned.

She continued anyway. 'Now that your father is ill, you can see how important it is to marry well, to have a dignified, capable woman for a wife, not a frivolous girl with a scandalous upbringing.'

What had his father ever seen in this woman? Ross wondered. She was all calculation and no heart.

He stopped and faced her. 'Take care, Constance. If my father's health fails completely—if he dies—you will want to be in my good graces. I will be Duke then.'

He left her and did not look behind.

For the next three weeks, Ross barely had time to think about his father's wishes and the Duchess's mean-spiritedness. He was too busy going from one task to another. There always seemed to be problems on the estates, decisions to make about finances, Parliamentary bills to advocate for, or Court functions to attend.

There were more Court functions than a typical Season. All to celebrate the upcoming wedding of Princess Charlotte. To these functions he was required to escort the Duchess. They were dreary affairs.

When he could Ross included Genna in his attendance to other parties, but those were infrequent. There were one or two functions which she attended with Lord Tinmore and her sister.

All in all, though, he saw very little of her.

He missed her.

He stopped in at Vespery's studio a few times. It was clear she was thriving there. Her portraiture was remarkably skilled, he thought. He coveted the self-portrait she painted. Perhaps he could own it, to remember her by.

He found himself dreading the day they must part. Too often he wished their betrothal to be real.

But it was time for him to face truth. She did not want to marry. Even if she did want it, marrying him would rob her of everything she desired—to be an artist. To answer to no one but herself. To live free of constraints.

Life with him would be nothing but constraints.

His father gained strength, enough that the doctor allowed him to participate in Princess Charlotte's wedding, but afterwards Ross must continue to assume the lion's share of his father's burdens.

On the day of the wedding, his father seemed his old robust self. Perhaps the excitement over this event would carry him through.

Ross had not been included in the wedding invitation, but ladies and gentlemen were allowed to stand in the entrance hall of Buckingham House to greet the Princess and other royal personages as they came out to their carriages.

Ross took the opportunity to escort Genna and Lady Tinmore to the event. Also in their party were their other sister, her husband and his parents. And Dell. To everyone's delight, Tinmore begged off, unable to bear the exertion of the event.

When the royals emerged, Genna's excitement burst from her and spilled over all of them.

'Look! There is the Queen! I never thought to see the Queen!' She jumped up and down.

Princess Charlotte appeared.

'Tess! Look!' Genna cried. 'Look at the Princess's gown. It shimmers!'

She commented on all of the Royal Princesses, as well. Ross was surprised she recognised them.

'I've seen engravings of their portraits in magazines,' she explained.

Afterwards they all walked to the Northdons' town house for a breakfast.

'It is said that Charlotte's choice of a husband is a love match,' Tess remarked over the meal.

'Yes, but what about Prince Leopold?' Genna retorted. 'Surely the prospect of becoming the Queen's consort had much to do with his agreeing to the marriage. Much higher status than the prospect of ruling a duchy.' Leopold was one of the German princes of a duchy that had been taken over by Napoleon. 'Did he fall in love with the Princess or with the idea of being the husband of an extremely wealthy queen?'

'One can fall in love even if a marriage has political advantages, can one not?' Tess asked. 'Look at you and Rossdale. People will say you marry him because of his rank.'

Genna reddened. 'I assure you, Ross's rank is of no consequence to me.'

Again, their deception reared its ugly head. These good people thought them to be in love, thought they would marry. Ross could now admit to himself that he loved Genna, but he would never marry her.

After leaving the Northdons' breakfast, Genna walked with Ross through the streets of Mayfair to Tinmore's town house on Curzon Street. Lorene had left earlier, escorted home by Lord Penford. It was already dusk and the streets were a lovely shade of lavender against a pink sky.

The exhilaration of the day had settled into melancholy and Genna fought an urge to simply burst into tears. To see the royal family had been thrilling, but now sadness swept over her. How could she explain it to Ross when she did not understand it herself?

She forced herself not to dwell on it. 'I rather hope they will be happy.'

'Who?' Ross asked.

She held his arm. 'Princess Charlotte and Prince Leopold. They have little chance, of course, but it would be nice if they could be happy. Goodness knows, Princess Charlotte's parents were not happy with each other.'

It was well known that the Prince Regent and his wife, Caroline of Brunswick, detested each other from first sight.

'You cannot judge every marriage after that of the Prince Regent. Think of the King and Queen. Theirs has been a long and, by all reports, a happy marriage.'

He was right, of course, but she resisted any evidence contrary to what she believed. 'Well, he turned insane. That can't be happy.'

'You won't hear of a happy marriage, will you?' His voice turned low.

'There are far more unhappy ones, you must agree,' she said. 'Better to be like my mother and take a lover.'

He said nothing for several steps. 'Is that what you plan to do? Take a lover?'

'I suppose,' she said without enthusiasm, although what

other man could she possibly want for a lover besides Ross? 'It seemed to be what made my mother happy.' Even at the expense of her children's happiness, but Genna would turn into a watering pot if she thought about that too much. 'What about your parents? Were they happy?'

He frowned. 'For a long time, very happy. Until my father inherited the title.' He paused. 'The revolution in France, becoming a duchess, it was all too much for my mother, not to mention my father's complete preoccupation with the role. It killed her.'

'Oh, Ross!' She leaned against him in sympathy. 'Could unhappiness truly kill her?'

He shrugged. 'She contracted a fever, but I believe she could have fought harder to live if she'd wanted to.'

'Both our mothers left us,' she murmured, blinking away tears, but it was not losing her mother that most pained her now. It was knowing she and Ross would have to part. In many ways, she'd already lost him.

Like his mother, she realised. She'd lost Ross to his new duties just as his mother had lost the Duke.

She continued to hold on to him tightly, as if that would keep him with her for ever.

They walked for half a street before he spoke again. 'We should talk—' he began.

That sounded ominous.

'My father's illness has changed things. He is pressing for us to marry right away. He wants to know the succession is secured in case his heart gives way completely. You might say he wants us to get on with it.'

With creating an heir, he meant.

He went on. 'Father doesn't know, of course, that we will not marry—'

'Do you want me to cry off sooner?' She tried to keep her voice from cracking.

He'd be free to marry someone else, then.

'No,' he said quickly. 'I tell you this only so you will be prepared if he speaks to you. I want us to continue as we planned. To make certain you are ready to become the artist you wish to be.'

To ultimately part in the autumn, when everyone expected they would marry. Would he marry someone else then? He must, she thought. What other choice did he have?

She made herself speak brightly. 'Yes! Let us enjoy the rest of the Season. You will have more time, will you not, now that your father is more recovered? You must let me paint you.'

'I would be honoured,' he said, but his eyes looked as sad as she felt inside.

The next morning Ross called upon Vespery before Genna was expected. His housekeeper sent him to Vespery's studio where the artist was at work on a portrait.

'Ross, my boy, how good to see you.' Vespery put down his brushes and palette and greeted him. 'To what do I owe the pleasure of this visit? Without Miss Summerfield?' He gestured to the seating area where Ross used to sit to watch Genna paint.

'I am here about Miss Summerfield,' Ross said, taking a chair. 'How is she faring?'

'She progresses very rapidly, Ross.' He motioned for Ross to rise again. 'Come. I'll show you.' He walked over to several canvases leaning against the wall. He turned one of them, Genna's self-portrait. 'Here is her first effort at portraiture. It is competent, is it not?'

Ross thought it looked very much like Genna. It even captured some of her irrepressible personality.

'I am no judge of competence,' Ross admitted. 'It is very like her, though.'

'Yes. And that was her first effort.' He walked over to another canvas still on an easel and removed the cloth covering it. 'Here is another.'

It was the housekeeper and even Ross could tell Genna had improved her technique.

'The woman's personality shows, does it not?' said Vespery.

'Indeed.'

'I believe there is nothing she could not paint if she wished to.' Vespery covered the painting again and walked back to the chairs.

Ross sat with him. 'Painting is what Miss Summerfield wishes to do and I want to make certain she can do it. So I have a proposition.'

Vespery's brows rose. 'Yes?'

'I will continue to pay you to take her on, but as an assistant, not a student.' He paused to gauge the artist's reaction. The man still looked interested. 'I will pay her salary, too, but she mustn't know it comes from me. It must seem as if you are paying her. I want this plan to continue until she has enough commissions to set up her own studio.'

Vespery looked puzzled. 'But you are to marry her, are you not?'

Ross stopped to think. Could he trust Vespery with the whole truth?

The artist's expression turned to alarm. 'Do not tell me you are planning to renege on your promise!'

'No,' Ross said. 'Not me. But lately I have thought perhaps—perhaps Miss Summerfield would like to cry off. The painting makes her much happier than being a duchess would do. I think that is beginning to dawn on her. When—if—she decides to end our engagement, I want her to have what she most desires—to support herself as an artist.'

'An artist's assistant makes a pittance,' Vespery cried. 'She cannot support herself on it!'

Ross lifted a stilling hand. 'You and I might know what an artist's assistant would make in salary, but she does not. I will pay enough for her to live comfortably.'

Vespery stared at him for a long time before answering.

'I will do it, of course. I would be a fool not to. I can double my output, be paid and have a skilled paid assistant at no cost to myself.' He leaned towards Ross. 'Are you certain, my lord, that Miss Summerfield would prefer art over marriage to you? I am not convinced.'

'I am certain,' Ross answered.

And he was also certain he wanted it for her.

Chapter Twenty

Three days later Genna put on her gloves, ready to be transported to Vespery's studio. It was time for the carriage to come and pick her up and she waited in the anteroom.

A knock sounded at the door. The footman announced, 'Your carriage, miss.'

She hurried out to the hall and was happily surprised. Ross stood there, hat in hand, looking magnificent in his perfectly tailored black coat, white neckcloth and buff-coloured pantaloons.

'Ross!' she cried, stilling an impulse to rush into his arms. Instead she approached him with her hands extended.

He clasped them and gave her a peck on the cheek. No doubt she would feel the sensation of his lips against her skin for the rest of the day.

'I was able to take the time.' There was only the hint of a smile on his face. 'Much has slowed down now that the Princess's wedding is over and my father is feeling better.'

'I'm glad.' She filled with hope. 'Will I see more of you, then?'

'As often as I can manage,' he responded, as she took his arm and they walked to the door.

The footman opened it and they stepped outside.

'You have your curricle!' she cried. 'It has been weeks since we were out in your curricle.'

He helped her up into the seat. 'I warn you, it is chilly today. I am regretting leaving my topcoat at home.'

'I do not care.' She cared about nothing else except that he was with her.

He took the ribbons and his tiger jumped on the back.

As soon as they started, Genna turned to him. 'Oh, Ross! I have some wonderful news!'

He glanced from the road to her. 'What is it?'

She could hardly get the words out. 'Vespery wishes to hire me to be his assistant. He will pay me a handsome amount, enough for me to live on.'

'That is wonderful news.' His voice did not sound as enthusiastic as she'd anticipated.

But, then, she did not feel as excited as she'd sounded.

She went on. 'I must tell him when I am ready, he said, but I am able to take as little or as much time as I wish.'

'That is good, is it not?' he responded.

'Yes. Very good.' She swallowed. 'It—it means we can break the betrothal whenever we wish.'

'I suppose it does.' His voice turned low. 'When do you wish it?'

'Never!' she cried, threading her arm through his and leaning her head against his shoulder. 'I wish everything could remain exactly as it is this minute.'

'Riding in a chilly curricle, you mean?' he quipped, but his throat was thick.

She tried to smile. 'You know what I mean.'

He turned on to Piccadilly. 'I was hoping you would want a break from the studio. A little outing. Two out-ings, actually.'

'Will you have that much time?' She hoped.

'I will.'

'I still want you to sit for a portrait for me,' she said.

He turned to gaze at her. 'I will make the time.'

When they reached Vespery's studio, Ross handed the ribbons to his tiger who would take the curricle back to the stable until it came time to pick them up again. Ross knocked at the door and the housekeeper admitted them.

The housekeeper broke into a smile when she saw

Genna. 'Good afternoon, miss,' the woman said brightly. 'And to you, sir.'

'Good afternoon, Mrs Shaw!' Genna turned to him. 'I painted a portrait of Mrs Shaw. She was my second one.'

'Did you?' He knew it, of course, having called upon Vespery the day he made his bargain with him. Ross glanced at Mrs Shaw. 'And have you seen it?'

'Oh, yes, my lord.' The housekeeper beamed. 'Miss Summerfield made me look so very nice.'

'I merely paint what I see,' Genna said. 'Lord Rossdale has agreed to sit for me next. Is that not brave of him?'

Brave because it would put them in each other's company for an extended period. They'd not been together so much since he'd kissed her, since he'd realised how much he wanted her.

The housekeeper patted Genna's arm. 'You will do a fine job of it, miss.'

They left Mrs Shaw to her duties and walked to the back of the house to the studio.

Genna burst into the light-filled room. 'Look who I have brought with me!'

Vespery put down his brush. 'Lord Rossdale. Good to see you,' he said, a bit stilted.

'Ross will be able to stay the afternoon, too,' Genna added. 'Is that not grand?'

Ross nodded to the artist and placed his hat and gloves on a table by the door. 'It seems I am to be Miss Summerfield's next model.'

He helped her off with her redingote.

'I can hardly wait to get started.' She glanced around the room. 'Do we have a canvas already stretched that I can use?'

Vespery pointed to several stacked against the wall. 'Pick whatever size you wish.'

He gave Ross a conspiratorial look while she selected her canvas and carried it to her easel.

'Ross knows of your kind offer, Mr Vespery,' she said.

Vespery jumped and his voice turned high. 'He does?'

She gestured for Ross to sit in the chair in the corner. 'I told Ross today.'

Genna looked at home in the studio, comfortable around the canvases and paints. More so, she looked relaxed and happy. He had no doubt she would ultimately be as big a success as Vespery himself, but, in the meantime, he would watch and make certain she wanted for nothing.

She positioned him, stepped back and surveyed him, then positioned him again. 'You must remember to sit this way tomorrow, too,' she said. 'You can come tomorrow, can you not?'

'I had planned one of those outings for tomorrow,' he said, trying to remain still.

'The next day, then.'

Vespery spoke up from his side of the room. 'As of tomorrow I will not be here. I will be away for a week on a commission out of town.'

'But we can come in, can we not?' she asked. 'Mrs Shaw can let us in.'

'Mrs Shaw will be away, too,' Vespery said. 'She will be visiting her sister.'

'Then might we have a key?' Genna pressed. 'If I am to be your assistant, surely you would trust me with a key.'

Vespery shrugged. 'I suppose.'

She ran over and gave him a hug. 'Thank you!'

The clock Vespery kept in the room chimed two o'clock.

'Two o'clock?' the artist said. 'I must be off. I am delivering the portraits to your father and the Duchess.'

'Would you prefer I take them?' Ross asked, though it would necessitate explaining to them why he'd been at Vespery's studio.

Vespery hurriedly cleaned his brushes. 'No. The Duchess will want me to bring them. I must ensure they are acceptable.' He wiped his hands and bid them good day.

Ross attempted to remain still.

'It has been a long time since you and I were alone together,' Genna remarked.

'Since the ball.' He remembered that moment. He'd kissed her.

And then everything changed.

She paused, brush in the air, and gazed at him. 'I liked being alone with you that night,' she murmured.

'As did I,' he responded.

She met his gaze.

It was a good thing he needed to remain in the chair, in that pose. Otherwise he might have crossed the room and kissed her again. God knew he wished to do so.

She turned back to her painting, making quick big strokes with the brush. Soon he could tell she was lost in the work, the concentration on her face enhancing her beauty. The pose he needed to keep gave him a great advantage. He needed to look in her direction. He could indulge in watching her all he liked.

The next day Ross picked up Genna earlier than the usual time. They would have nearly the whole day together, plenty of time for what he had planned for her.

When she sat next to him in his curricle, she smiled happily. 'It has been so long since we've had an outing. I cannot imagine where you are taking me.'

He felt happy, too, happier than he'd been since his father took ill. A whole day together, a day she was bound to enjoy. He turned on to Audley Street, heading north to turn right on Oxford Street.

As they left Mayfair, Genna looked around at everything. 'I have never been in this part of town,' she said, commenting on whatever caught her eye.

When they reached the end of Oxford Street, she asked, 'What part of town are we in now?'

'Bloomsbury.' He hated to give her too many hints.

'Oh.' She turned silent.

He pulled up to their destination, what once was the mansion of a wealthy duke who sold it to the British government when the Bloomsbury neighbourhood was no longer the fashionable place to live. The mansion had a large expanse of garden in the front so it took some time for the curricle to reach the doorway.

Genna finally spoke. 'I know where we are. I've seen this building in books. This is Montagu House, is it not?'

'That it is.'

Ross's tiger jumped off to hold the horses. Ross climbed down and turned to assist Genna.

'You've brought me to see the exhibits of the British Museum!' she cried in delight.

He held her by her waist as he helped her down. 'Even better,' he said.

She landed on her feet, but he did not immediately let go of her. She tipped her head up and looked directly in his eyes. Her eyes darkened and she leaned a little closer.

He released her then, before he forgot they were in a public place.

She took a breath and recovered her composure. 'What could be better than the British Museum?'

He knew this would please her. 'We will see the Elgin Marbles.'

Her eyes grew wide. 'Truly?'

He offered his arm. 'Truly.'

Genna's excitement grew as they approached the door of the museum. Ross knocked as if visiting someone's residence.

'The museum is closed?' Genna asked.

'Not to us,' he responded.

Obviously he had gone to some effort for this outing. For her.

The door was answered by a well-dressed gentleman. His brows rose. 'Lord Rossdale?'

Ross nodded. 'Mr Hutton, I presume.'

'Welcome to the British Museum.' Mr Hutton swept his arm in an arc and stepped aside for them to enter.

Ross turned to Genna. 'Miss Summerfield, may I present Mr Hutton, who has made this excursion possible.'

'My pleasure, Miss Summerfield.' Mr Hutton bowed.

'I am so grateful to you, sir.' And to Ross for making this possible.

Mr Hutton looked apologetic. 'You do understand you will not be able to tour the entire museum at this time. Let me escort you to the courtyard.'

They walked by a grand staircase and Genna spied huge giraffes at the top of the stairs, appearing as they might have been when alive. Other curiosities could be glimpsed as they made their way to the back of the mansion and out the door to the courtyard. Mr Hutton then led them to a huge wooden shed, which he unlocked, and opened the doors, filling the space inside with light.

'I will return in an hour,' Mr Hutton said. 'Obviously you may not move any of the sculptures, but I doubt you could. They are quite marvellous. I think you will agree.'

He left them in the doorway.

Huge slabs of marble lined the sides of the shed. Scattered around were ghostly figures. Headless. Armless. Standing. Reclining.

Genna stepped inside reverently. 'Oh, Ross!'

She walked along the perimeter gazing at the long slabs of marble that used to decorate the frieze of the Parthenon. The sculpted figures depicted all sorts of figures: men on horseback, on foot or racing chariots, women carrying items—for sacrifice to the gods, perhaps? Everything seemed in motion. Rearing horses, figures interacting, no two the same.

'It must tell a story,' Genna said. 'I wish I knew what it

was.' She dared to touch the sculpture, almost surprised the figures were not as warm as flesh they were so realistic.

'Here is a Centaur fighting a Lapith,' he said.

It was one segment, not a part of the long procession of figures that had been part of the frieze. Had there been more Centaurs? Did they tell a different story?

'Lord Tinmore criticises Elgin for removing these sculptures from the Parthenon,' Genna said. 'He likens it to theft.'

'I have heard that sentiment,' Ross responded. 'I have also heard Lord Elgin praised for saving the marbles. Apparently the Parthenon was a ruin and local builders thought nothing of using its sculptures as building blocks in their own buildings, some of which were ground down for cement.'

Genna shook her head. 'Can you imagine these magnificent carvings ground down into nothing? It would be an abomination!'

She walked the length of a section of the frieze. Many of the men were naked, some riding horses, some on foot. Genna was not such a green girl that she'd never seen a naked man before, although her knowledge of such was confined to seeing other statuary or spying her brother, a boy then, swimming naked. These figures, though, were all well-formed, muscular, powerful beings.

She glanced at Ross, who was examining one of the pieces. His shoulders were broad, like the Greek figures on the marbles, his legs well formed. She remembered the feel of his body pressing against hers when he'd kissed her the night of the ball. His muscles were as firm as marble.

Her skin flashed with heat.

She resisted the impulse to fan herself and turned away to examine the other marbles. One was a horse's head from what must have been a huge statue. She ran her hand down the horse's forehead to its muzzle, but it only made her wonder what it would be like to run her hand over Ross's skin.

She walked further away from him, over to three headless statues, all women attired in lavishly draped cloth. For all three, it was easy to see the bodies underneath, as evident as if they were real.

Then she came to a naked reclining male, exuding raw masculine strength.

Like Ross.

'Here is another Centaur,' called Ross from across the room.

She crossed the shed to him and her insides fluttered at being so near. She forced herself to gaze at the marble.

A mistake.

The Lapith in this fragment had the better of the Centaur, even though the Lapith's head and feet were missing. His body, though, splayed across the marble, displayed the muscles of his abdomen, his ribs, his masculine parts.

Her cheeks burned, not from embarrassment, but from a sudden desire to see Ross without his clothes, to again experience the warmth of his mouth against hers. She wanted to experience that kiss again. And more.

Sensible, independent Genna wanted a man's kiss—no, not a man's kiss—*Ross's kiss*. Ross's lovemaking.

She finally understood. The sensations she experienced in Ross's presence were carnal ones. She desired him, the way her mother had desired many men.

Was she like her mother? She must be. Like her mother, she felt willing to abandon all propriety to make carnal love with a man. *With Ross.* At this moment she desired Ross more than anything. More than respectability.

More than…art.

Why not? She had no intention of living a conventional life. Artists were allowed their passions, were they not?

Ross jarred her from her thoughts. 'I seem to remember a legend about Centaurs fighting Lapiths. Something we read in school.'

She turned to him, her whole body vibrating with wanting him. 'Did you read Greek?'

He groaned. 'Not well, but it was part of my studies.'

She crossed her arms around herself and forced herself to sound unaffected by desire. 'This is likely as close as I may get to studying a man's body. Vespery told me that the Royal Academy barred women from the classes with naked models.'

'You would want to take such a class?' He sounded surprised.

'Yes. I would.' She turned to him. 'I would like to study a man's naked body—' Ross's body. 'Does that shock you?'

His gaze seemed to smoulder. 'Nothing about you shocks me, Genna.'

Did she know she was arousing him? Ross wondered. Something was different.

A change had come over her, a change that made him think of how it would be to touch her naked skin, how it would feel to kiss her again. To make love to her.

He became more aware of her hint-of-jasmine scent, more aware of how she moved, of how her eyes slanted up when she smiled.

Good God. Was he going to be able to keep his hands off her?

She gazed up at him and he caught her chin between his finger and thumb. He tilted her face so he was looking straight down at her.

'Genna,' he murmured.

She rose on tiptoe, bringing her face just a little closer.

No. Not again. Not here. He released her and stepped away.

Mr Hutton appeared at the door of the shed. 'I fear it is time, my lord, miss.'

Genna turned towards him. 'I am ready.'

They walked through Montagu House again and out

the front door where Jem waited with the curricle, just as Ross had arranged.

'Where are we bound now?' Genna asked when they started off again.

'To Vespery's, if you like.'

'Yes,' she murmured. 'I would very much like that, if you are able to stay with me.' She paused. 'For the portrait, I mean.'

He also paused before responding. 'Yes. I am able to stay.'

Chapter Twenty-One

Ross and Genna entered Vespery's studio, which, Genna was acutely aware, they had all to themselves. She put on her smock and uncovered her palette. Ross sat in the chair and assumed the pose she'd placed him in before. They said little while she painted. She felt his eyes on her, though, and it made her hand tremble.

'I have another outing planned for you,' he told her after an hour had passed. 'Are you able to make a morning call with me tomorrow?'

'A morning call?' Her brows rose. 'To visit someone?'

'Precisely.'

'Am I to know to whom?' she asked, knowing he would not tell her, that he delighted in surprising her.

'No.' He smiled. She loved how his smile reached his eyes.

She turned back to her canvas. 'What time?'

'Eleven o'clock.'

She kept painting. 'Nothing grander than the Elgin Marbles, I am sure. Nothing could be.'

'Different' was all he said.

The marbles had been so magnificent, so detailed, so beautiful and real. If only she could bring those elements to her painting. Her portrait of Ross was flat. The statues gave the sensation of skin under drapes of clothing. Or muscles and veins under skin. Surely there was a way to convey the same impression in paint.

She closed her eyes and tried to imagine the naked statues.

It was not the same, though.

'Ross, unfold your arms' Maybe if he stood differently, she could see differently.

He unfolded his arm, stretching them as if to get the stiffness out.

Still they were covered with cloth—his coat, his waist-coat, his shirt.

She stepped away from the canvas and walked over to examine one of Vespery's nearly completed portraits set on his easel.

'What is amiss?' Ross asked her.

'Mine is too flat.' She pointed to Vespery's. 'See? His gentleman has shape to him. A sense of his physique.' She put her hands on her hips and stared at Vespery's painting. 'I begin to understand why artists take classes with naked models. For that sense of the body under the clothes.'

He gave a dry laugh. 'Do not tell me you wish me to take off my clothes.'

She turned to him. 'Would you? It would help so very much.'

'Genna, do not jest.'

She hurried over to him. 'I am not jesting. I need to know what you look like under your clothes. So—so the portrait is not flat.'

His return look was very sceptical.

'Please, Ross?'

'Do not be nonsensical,' he countered. 'You saw enough naked men in the Elgin Marbles. Think of those.'

'It is not the same. They were ideal images, not real men at all.' Although she suspected he might also be an ideal.

She faced him and stood so close she could touch him.

His eyes darkened as he held her gaze.

'It is for the art,' she protested. 'So I can paint a decent portrait of you.'

His gaze did not waver. 'You propose we act indecently so you might paint a decent portrait.'

Her face flushed. 'What harm would there be? No one would know.'

Still seated in the chair, he leaned forward. 'Do you know what I think?' His voice turned to silk.

It was difficult to take a breath. 'What?'

'I think this has nothing to do with art. You just wish to see me naked.'

Her heart pounded. How dare he say this wasn't for her art? 'What if I match you?'

His brows rose. 'Match me?'

She untied her smock. 'Tit for tat.'

She pulled it off and tossed it on to the floor.

It was a game. A dare.

Ross had no doubt at all that Genna wanted to see what a real man looked like beneath his clothes. No doubt she resented that women artists were barred from such experiences. But there was something more there as well, something she did not yet understand.

She did not know her powers of seduction, how easily she could draw men to her and how easily they could take advantage.

He ought to teach her. Arm her with that knowledge so she could protect herself when he could no longer be there keeping other gentlemen away.

'Tit for tat, then.' He unbuttoned his coat and removed it.

He thought he saw a flicker of anxiety in her eyes, but she quickly recovered and stared directly in his eyes.

She removed the fichu tucked into the neckline of her dress.

He untied his neckcloth and unwound it from his neck. 'Your turn.'

He had his waistcoat yet to take off and he'd still be covered by his shirt. For Genna, her dress would be next.

She flashed a grin and kicked off her shoes.

'Coward,' he said, unbuttoning his waistcoat and shrugging out of it. He lifted his chin in a silent challenge.

'I cannot do it myself.' She turned her back to him.

He had not accounted for touching her. He unbuttoned the buttons at the back of her dress, too aware of her slender neck and her smooth skin. She pulled off her sleeves and let the dress slip to the floor.

Only her chemise and corset remained. She spun around again. 'Now you.'

He could not help his eyes sweeping over her. Her corset showed her slender waist and pushed her breasts up to their voluptuous fullness.

She twirled a finger at him, indicating he should remove his shirt.

He undid the button at his neck and pulled his white linen shirt over his head.

Genna took in a sharp, audible breath.

She reached out and touched him, very softly, her fingers cool against his suddenly heated skin. She traced the contours of his bare chest, like he'd seen her touch the Elgin marbles.

'Oh, Ross,' she whispered.

He, unlike the statues, was not made of stone. Her touch, the awed look on her face, set his senses on fire. He forgot this was a game or a lesson he was going to teach her. He was alone with her, protected from everything outside, cocooned in a world existing only for the two of them.

'Genna,' he groaned, lifting her on to his lap so her legs straddled him.

She leaned into him, pressing against his arousal, and twined her arms around his neck. She dipped her head to him and he strained to meet her, capturing her mouth with his ravenous lips. The kiss was long and lingering. Like their one other kiss, she opened to him and his tongue touched hers, soft, warm and wet. She dug her fingers into his hair and matched his lips' demand.

When finally they broke apart long enough to take a breath, Genna murmured, 'Make love to me, Ross. Please. I want you to show me. No one else.'

He longed to show her. He wanted no other man to possess her like this.

He lifted her and rose from the chair. Her chemise was bunched about her waist and her stockinged legs wrapped around him. He carried her out of the studio into a small drawing room. He sat her on a couch and unlaced her corset, slipping it off entirely. He ran his hands over her body, still covered by her chemise. He freed her breasts from the thin fabric of the undergarment and relished their soft flesh and the nipples that hardened under his touch.

'Mmm…' she hummed. 'You were right. Not the art. This. I wanted this. From you, Ross. Only you.'

He lay next to her on the couch and kissed her again, still rubbing his palm against her nipples. It seemed so right for him to make love to Genna. He could not think of another time or another woman who felt this right. He wanted to show her pleasure, a fair exchange for the pleasure just being with her brought to him.

She placed her hands in his hair again and pulled him into another kiss. He felt her hunger, her yearning resonate within his whole body.

They were surely kindred spirits, two of a kind, and at this moment they were as free as ever they would be, without anyone nearby to see. Her kiss was eager and urgent and he knew he could satisfy her urges. Why not make love to her? Why not show her? Bring her pleasure?

His lips made a path down her neck to her breasts to her nipple. He relished the feel and taste of her against his tongue. She twisted and squirmed beneath him. He backed off for a moment and rubbed her in long, sweeping strokes. She calmed again.

His hand splayed over her abdomen. She seized his wrist and guided his hand downward over her bunched-up skirts.

Her arousal must tell her where the greatest pleasure lay. He obliged her by sliding his hand lower and gently touching the soft moist skin around her most womanly place.

'Ross!' she rasped. 'Yes. Yes.'

She moved beneath his fingers and he could feel her pleasure building, building. He wanted to give her the pleasure, to feel her pleasure beneath his hand.

He found her tender spot and her voice became more urgent. 'Yes. More. More,' she cried.

He gave her more, able to feel the passion rising in her, higher and higher until her back arched and she cried out, writhing with the explosion of pleasure he'd released in her.

'Ross,' she cried as her spasm eased. 'Ross.'

Genna basked in the sensations he had created in her. She'd never dreamed lovemaking could feel so—so pleasurable and unsettling. His touch was so acutely pleasurable it very nearly was pain. Not hurting, but agonising her with wanting what she had not known would come, that— that explosion of pleasure.

She pressed herself against him on the narrow couch. 'I—I never knew a touch could feel like that, but that was not all, was it, Ross? That was a mere taste of lovemaking, was it not?'

She was not so green a girl, even if she was a maiden. She knew the barest of elements of lovemaking. She simply had not guessed such pleasure and need could be built by a touch.

She loved it. And wanted to feel it again. She wanted to feel everything about lovemaking. She tried to remember every part of this. How his lips felt against hers. How warm his tongue was. How it tasted of tea. She wanted her body to remember the feel of his hands against her skin. And how different it felt for his hands to touch her breasts, how that sensation touched off a veritable riot in her feminine parts. If she could paint this, what colours would she use?

All of them, she thought.

The cool, smooth blues blended into purple and gradually built from red to orange to a bright yellow, as bright as the sun. How would she paint such a feeling?

Like a rainbow that burst and turned into sunshine.

This very sort of sensation must have been what tempted her mother away from her father, she realised, more powerful and compelling than the mothering of children. Genna understood it a little. Right before Ross created that explosion of pleasure, Genna would have given up everything else for it.

Was she like her mother?

It must be so.

'Show me the rest of it, Ross,' she murmured. 'I want to do this with you. Make love to me.'

He kissed her, a demanding kiss, one she was delighted to accept. Who knew a kiss could radiate throughout one's whole body? Or a touch could set off such pleasurable pain? Who knew a kiss and touch could lead to a rainbow bursting? She could hardly wait to experience what lay ahead.

She unbuttoned the fall of his pantaloons, her heart racing with excitement. She would join with Ross.

Only Ross.

She thought she'd never want this attachment to a man, like her mother's attachment to her lover, so imperative she'd leave her children for it.

She gazed down and saw his male member, swollen and long and so unlike the ones on the marble statues. She wavered. Would there be pain? How could he possibly fit inside her?

His hands, so gentle now, reassured her. Ross would never hurt her. Never.

His hand did not linger this time, but it tantalised, igniting her need for that bursting of colour.

'Now, Ross,' she begged. 'Now. Please.'

He groaned and positioned himself on top of her. She

felt his member touch the now-throbbing skin of her feminine parts. She parted her legs wider and he began to push in gently, gingerly.

She did not wish for him to be gentle. She wanted him to hurry. She wanted that pleasure to explode inside her again. Now.

'Please,' she begged, feeling that agonising need.

He pushed in a little more, and more, and pulled out again.

'Mmm…' she urged, ready for more, relishing the feel of him entering her. Joining with her.

He broke away and moved off her. Moved off the couch to stand a pace away.

'No, Genna,' he cried, raking a hand though his hair. He buttoned his pantaloons. 'I will not do this with you.' He sounded angry.

She felt bereft. Deserted. 'Why not, if I want it?' she asked.

'You did not think, did you? Of what could happen? We could make a child.' He strode out of the drawing room.

She sat up, stunned.

She'd not given one single thought to the idea that she might get with child from this. Even though she knew what had happened to her brother, why he had to hurry to get married. She'd acted as if this was only about feeling good.

She picked up her corset and put it on, tightening the laces as best she could. She returned to the studio.

He had already donned his shirt and waistcoat. He picked up his coat off the floor and glared at her.

She spoke. 'I thought only of you and me.'

'I could have ruined your life,' he said.

She lifted her chin. 'If I am to be an artist, it does not matter. I will not need to be proper.'

He wrapped his neckcloth around his neck and tied it in a terrible knot. 'And how many members of the *ton* will pay to have their portrait painted by a baronet's daughter who has a bastard child in tow? How many would let you paint their daughters?'

She turned away.

All the colour had been leached away. Only the black-and-white truth remained. She could not simply do as she wished. She could no longer act as if she and Ross were in their own fairy tale.

He moved closer to her, close enough to hand her her dress. 'Do not make me the one who will ruin you, Genna.'

He despised her now. Why not? She did not like herself very much.

She donned her dress.

'We should not be together,' he said as he buttoned it for her. 'Tidy your things. Jem will not be here with the curricle for another two hours. I'll get us a hackney cab now.' He walked out of the studio.

She did not want a hackney cab. She did not want to leave. She simply wanted to perish.

The brisk air did not do a great deal to cool Ross's senses. He was still burning with desire and blazing with anger at himself. He'd nearly ruined her! He'd taken far too many liberties with her even before this. What had he been thinking?

He wasn't thinking. Probably had not been thinking since he'd met her. He'd simply craved her—why pretend otherwise? He'd come up with the harebrained idea of a pretend betrothal so he could be with her. Had he thought of where that would lead? To seduction? Ruin? Risk?

He felt as if a fog had cleared and he suddenly could see around him.

He could have killed her dreams of being an artist. He could have got her with child. What then? He'd have to marry her. She did not want that. If he didn't marry her, he'd embroil her in a scandal that would affect the rest of her life.

Perhaps he already had ruined her life by encouraging her, by coming up with this misguided betrothal. What were the chances of her—a woman—becoming a success-ful artist? Successful women artists were rare.

He found the corner where the hackney cabs waited and hired one.

When it pulled up in front of Vespery's door, Genna emerged, locking the door behind her. Ross jumped out of the carriage to help her inside.

She did not look at him.

When the coach starting moving, she asked, 'What happens now?' Her voice was so tiny he hardly heard her.

'I take you home,' he said.

'And, then?'

He did not understand. 'And then—nothing.'

She averted her face, then suddenly squared her shoulders and lifted her chin. 'It was not such an abominable request, you know. To make love to me. Is it not how men and women are meant to be with each other?'

'If they are married,' he shot back. 'If they are safe from the kind of scandal that will wreck a lady's life. Widows can manage it. Married women sometimes manage it. But not you, Genna. Not you.'

She went on. 'I am not going to marry. I will not be in society. Are not the rules looser for women such as me?'

'If you came from Italy, perhaps. Or France. Or any-where besides the home of one of their own. You cannot fall from grace in the eyes of the *ton* and be acceptable to them. You know this, Genna.'

'I thought you would understand,' she accused. 'You, of all people. No one would know except you and me.'

'You and I have to face reality, Genna. Enough of these illusions.' He lowered his voice. 'Some things cannot be hidden, Genna.'

'It might not have happened,' she protested. 'I might not have got with child.'

He turned her face to him, like he had in the studio. 'What if we lost that gamble?'

She wrenched away.

They spent the last of the trip in silence.

When the coach pulled up to Tinmore's town house, Ross paid the driver and walked her to the door.

'This is goodbye, then?' she asked uncertainly.

'Yes. Goodbye,' he responded, sounding the knocker.

The door opened and she stepped over the threshold.

He called before the door closed again. 'Be ready tomorrow at eleven o'clock.'

She swivelled around to face him again. 'Tomorrow? You do not wish to cancel?'

'It is all arranged.'

She stared at him without speaking for several seconds. Finally she said, 'I will be ready.'

Chapter Twenty-Two

The next day Genna was ready early for Ross's outing. A bad idea. She had nothing to do while waiting except to think.

She'd deliberately sought to seduce him. That was the truth. She'd merely been deluding herself by saying she did it for her art. It had all been her fault and now he despised her for it.

Why he still wished to take her on this outing was a mystery to her. Their friendship was ruined now.

She had ruined it.

Consequences. The cost of keeping her head in the clouds. She'd liked him. More than liked him. He'd become the most important person in her life. Now she'd come crashing back to earth.

We should not be together, he'd said.

He'd leave her, too. After this outing, she supposed.

Her mother had left her. Her father never cared for her. Lorene and Tess and Edmund had left her, too, in their way when they married. She'd always known Ross would leave her. That was part of their secret plan. She'd cry off and they would part.

So why did it hurt so much?

She groaned in pain and rested her head on the table in front of her. She was making herself sick with all this self-pity.

The only person she could depend upon was herself. She'd known that since a child. She still had her painting.

She still would become Vespery's assistant. She could take care of herself.

Thanks to Ross. He'd given her the lessons with Vespery. He'd showed her so much more, as well.

A footman knocked at the door.

'Is Lord Rossdale here already?' she asked him. 'I'll be right down.'

'Not Lord Rossdale, miss.' He handed her a card.

The Duchess of Kessington, the card said. She glanced up at the footman. 'I will be down directly. Is she in the drawing room?'

'Yes, miss.' He bowed and left the room.

What on earth did the Duchess want with her?

She glanced in the mirror and smoothed her hair. She deliberately walked from the room at a normal pace. No good appearing before the Duchess out of breath from rushing.

When she entered the drawing room, the Duchess was examining a blue-and-white porcelain bowl. 'Chinese,' she stated.

'If you say so.' Genna did not smile. 'Good morning, Your Grace. Do have a seat. Shall I send for tea?'

'Do not bother.' The Duchess lowered herself into a chair. 'This will not take long.'

Genna sat nearby and folded her hands in her lap, trying to look calm. She certainly did not wish the Duchess to know her emotions were in turmoil.

She waited.

An annoyed look came over the Duchess's face, but she finally spoke. 'I came here to discuss something with you.'

Genna raised her brows.

The Duchess pressed her lips together before continuing. 'You cannot possibly marry Rossdale.'

'I cannot? I am betrothed to him.' Genna *would* not marry him, of course, but the Duchess did not know that.

'You are entirely unsuitable.' The Duchess leaned forward. 'I have learned that you spend your days unchaperoned, alone with a man. That is scandalous, young lady.'

Alone with Ross? No. That could not be what she meant.

'Alone with Mr Vespery? I am taking painting lessons from him, Your Grace.'

'I know that,' she snapped. 'But it is what else goes on when you are alone with him that concerns me.'

The inference was appalling. 'Ask his housekeeper. She is always nearby.'

'Hmmph!' The Duchess scowled. 'A servant doesn't matter. This has the appearance of scandal. That is all I need to know. It is not fitting for the wife of a future duke to be so shameless.'

Genna felt her cheeks heat. With anger. 'Rossdale knows of the painting lessons. He arranged them. He provides me transport to and from Vespery's studio. If he does not object to the lessons, why should I be concerned with what you or anyone else thinks of it?'

'Because of the title, Miss Summerfield! You must think of the title. Some day Rossdale will be the Duke of Kessington. For five generations that title has been unstained by scandal. I will not allow you to tarnish it.'

Genna straightened her spine. 'You insult me, Duchess.'

'I speak the truth!' the Duchess cried. 'I assure you, I am prepared to do anything possible to ensure that this marriage does not take place.'

'Does Ross know you have come to speak to me like this?' He would not have sent her. There would have been no need. He knew they would never marry.

'Ross is as foolish as you are,' the Duchess said. 'We thought he was coming to his senses and then he became betrothed to you. He needs a proper lady for a duchess, not the supposed daughter of an improvident baronet.'

Supposed daughter? How cruel to throw that particular rumour in her face.

'If the scandals in my family do not concern Rossdale, I see no reason they should concern you. You have no say in his affairs.'

She lifted her nose. 'I am the Duchess.'

'But no relation to Ross.' Genna stood. 'I will hear no more of your insults, though, Your Grace. Please leave.'

The Duchess rose. 'I have one more thing to say.'

Genna held the woman's gaze and waited.

'If you break your engagement to Ross, I will pay you handsomely for it.'

'Pay me?' Genna could not believe her ears.

'I am prepared to pay very well. *Very* well.'

Genna glanced away.

Money would provide her security. It was not as if she didn't intend to cry off anyway. The joke would be on the Duchess, then.

'Do you not wish to know how much money I offer?' the Duchess asked smugly.

Genna paused a moment before facing her. 'I assure you, Duchess, no amount of money would induce me to break my engagement to Lord Rossdale.'

Because it was already broken.

Genna walked briskly to the door. 'You must now have nothing more to say.'

The Duchess huffed and strode towards the door. 'You will change your mind. I am certain of it. You will change your mind or suffer the scandal I can spread.'

Genna held the latch of the door, blocking the woman's way. 'That is an empty bluff. Any scandal you cause me will bring shame on the precious title. That is precisely what you profess to avoid.'

She opened the door and the Duchess swept out.

Genna sank into the nearest chair and put her head in her hands. She'd defended herself as if the betrothal were real, but it had never been. She and Ross had fooled everyone, but, in so doing, they'd affected everyone. They'd certainly put the Duchess in a panic.

But it had all been lies.

Ross pulled up to Tinmore's town house and spied his father's carriage pulling away from its door. Through the carriage window he glimpsed the Duchess.

That did not bode well.

He jumped down from his curricle and handed the ribbons to Jem.

Ross was admitted by a footman at the same moment Genna appeared in the hall.

'You are here.' Her voice was stiff—and sad.

He nodded, wanting to ask her about the Duchess, but not in front of the footman.

'Are you ready?' he asked.

'I need to fetch my hat and shawl.' She climbed the stairs and disappeared from view.

The footman spoke. 'Would you care to wait in the drawing room, my lord?'

'No. I'll wait here,' he responded.

When she returned, they walked out the door to the curricle. He helped her into the seat and climbed up beside her. His tiger jumped on the back and they started off.

He could finally speak. 'I saw the Duchess driving away from the town house. What did she want?'

'She wanted me to cry off,' Genna said with little animation in her voice. 'I am too scandalous, apparently, because I take painting lessons from Mr Vespery and am, at times, alone with him. That and merely being a Summerfield with uncertain paternity.'

His anger flared. 'She said those things to you?'

'Think if she knew how scandalous I truly am,' she added sadly.

He did not know how to talk to her about that. 'I am sorry you had to endure her venom.'

She shrugged. 'Her threats were empty ones.'

He could not lay all blame for Genna's bleak mood on the Duchess. He was at fault.

He'd been foolish not to realise what could happen, what could ruin her friendship with him.

Their destination was not far. A mere street north of Cavendish Square, but she did not tease him to tell her where they were going. When he pulled up in front of the town house at 47 Queen Anne Street, she still asked nothing.

He needed to prepare her, though. 'This is the home of Mr Turner. He is an artist and also a lecturer at the Royal Academy. His work is quite renowned. It is said that Canova visited here last year and pronounced Turner a great genius.'

Canova was an Italian sculptor famous throughout Great Britain and the Continent.

'Canova,' she whispered, but without enthusiasm.

Ross knocked on the door. They were admitted by a housekeeper and joined Mr Turner in his sitting room.

'It is an honour to meet you, sir,' Ross said. 'And a very great privilege to be shown your gallery.' Ross introduced Genna. 'Miss Summerfield is an artist herself, sir,' he explained. 'A student of Mr Vespery, but I wanted her to see your paintings. She has been living in the country and has not had an opportunity to see the works of artists such as yourself.'

Genna managed, 'How do you do, sir.'

'A pleasure to meet a fellow artist,' Turner kindly said. 'Let us go straight to the gallery, shall we?' As he led the way, he asked, 'What is your medium, Miss Summerfield?'

'Watercolour, mostly, sir,' she replied. 'But I am lately a student of Mr Vespery, learning to paint in oils.'

'I have done both.' He chuckled. 'I often do both at the same time.'

He opened the door to a room built on to the back of his house. The room was bright from a skylight in the roof.

Genna stepped inside and gasped.

'Landscapes!' she exclaimed.

Hung on all four walls, or sitting on the floor, everywhere she looked, were landscapes. Large ones. Beautiful landscapes unlike anything she'd seen before.

Ross had known. He'd known she loved painting landscapes most of all.

'They are not all landscapes,' Mr Turner said. 'Some are history paintings.' He took her arm and walked her over to one painting on another wall. 'Like this one. This one is called *Hannibal and His Army Crossing the Alps.*'

History paintings depicted the people involved in some event in history, but in this painting, the landscape dominated and Genna had to strain to see the people. The painting depicted a huge black storm cloud, black paint that looked like it had been dabbed on by mistake, but, somehow, the canvas conveyed the feeling of the storm and of how inconsequential even a strong warrior like Hannibal was when faced with the forces of nature.

She walked over to a sea scene. There were several sea scenes. Ships or fishing boats or men fighting a stormy seas. Each conveyed the power of the ocean and its danger.

Turner painted how it felt, just as she had in that first fanciful painting Ross had seen that day overlooking Summerfield House. He'd remembered and brought her here.

Each of Turner's paintings were emotional, each done in ways she'd never seen a landscape painted.

One pulled at her artistic soul.

'This is *Dewy Morning,*' Turner said.

It was a lake scene, pretty ordinary in its composition, but, oh, the colour! The sky was orange and purple, its reflection in the water almost pink. It wasn't real. Ross had found a renowned artist who painted landscapes that were not real, just as she had done.

And he'd wanted her to see. It made her want to weep, especially because she'd ruined everything with him.

After they bid Mr Turner good day and returned to the waiting curricle, Genna spoke, even though she could not yet look directly at Ross, 'I know why you brought me here.'

Ross flicked the ribbons and the horses pulled away from the curb. 'To see the landscapes,' he said. 'It is what you first painted. I thought you would like to meet an artist who made his name painting landscapes not unlike the first painting I saw of yours, the one with the purple sky and blue grass.'

Her heart lurched.

He knew—no matter how much she went on about portrait painting—somehow he knew what she loved most to paint. Who else knew her that well? Who else would have cared?

'Shall I drive you to Vespery's studio?' he asked. 'I will not be able to stay with you, though. I'm required to do an errand for my father.'

She suspected he no longer wanted to stay with her. She felt a pang of pain, like a sabre slashing into her chest.

What she really wanted to do was return to her bedchamber and weep into her pillows.

'Take me to Vespery's,' she said instead. 'I want to paint.'

She wanted to finish his portrait even though it felt like she'd already run out of time to do so.

Ross drove her to Vespery's and escorted her inside, despite her protest that it was unnecessary. She did not wish to be in his presence at the place of her greatest pleasure and worst mistake, but he insisted and she endured it, watching his gaze wander to the couch in the drawing room and quickly look away.

'Will you be all right here alone?' he asked.

'I am used to being alone,' she replied, although, in truth, there were usually people around her.

He glanced around the room again. 'I'll pick you up at the usual time, then?'

'Yes. Thank you, Ross.' Her voice was tight.

He nodded. 'Goodbye, then, Genna.'

'Goodbye, Ross.'

He walked towards the door.

'Ross?'

He turned back to her.

'Thank you for taking me to call upon Mr Turner.'

He stared directly into her eyes. 'It was my pleasure, Genna.'

When he left, she dropped her shawl on a chair and removed her gloves and hat. She donned her smock and uncovered the painting and palette. When she stood in front of the painting, it was like standing in front of him. Only the eyes in the painting did not look upon her with strain, but with something warmer.

Something she'd lost.

Chapter Twenty-Three

Ross finished his father's errand and returned to pick up Genna at Vespery's studio.

He found her ready to go, but as distant as she'd been with him the whole day. This chasm between them seemed impassable.

She spoke to him only if he spoke to her first and he struggled to think of things to say. Their trip back to Tinmore's town house was a nearly silent one.

'How fares the portrait?' he asked her.

'I've done all I can do,' she answered. 'I need Vespery's opinion.' Several streets passed before she spoke again. 'So I do not need to go to the studio until he returns.'

Ross would have no reason to see her, then, unless he invited her to the opera or some other entertainment. If so, would she even attend with him?

He pulled up to the town house and helped her out of the curricle, holding her by the waist like he'd done before. He caught her gaze, fleetingly, and saw, not her usual sparkle, but pain and regret. It pierced him like a shaft to the heart.

He walked her to the door. 'I will not see you tomorrow, then?'

Those pained eyes looked up at him. 'There is no reason.'

Before Ross could knock at the door, it opened and the Tinmore butler stood in the doorway.

'Goodbye, Ross,' Genna said.

The butler stepped aside so she could enter. Ross turned

to go, but the butler called him back. 'Lord Tinmore wishes a moment with you, sir.'

Ross and Genna exchanged puzzled glances.

'Certainly,' Ross told the man. He called back to his tiger, 'I'll be a few minutes, Jem. Just walk the horses.'

Ross entered the house.

The butler said, 'Follow me, sir.' He led Ross to the library. 'I'll announce you.'

Tinmore dozed in a chair, but woke with a start when the butler spoke to him.

'Show him in, show him in,' Tinmore said.

Ross entered the room. The butler bowed and left.

'You wished to see me, Lord Tinmore?' Ross asked.

'Indeed. Indeed.' Tinmore gestured to a chair.

Ross sat.

'This betrothal,' Tinmore began. 'It won't do. Won't do at all.'

First the Duchess, now Tinmore?

'Sir?' Ross said in a gruff tone.

Tinmore leaned forward. 'The way the two of you are carrying on, you cannot afford a long engagement.'

Ross straightened. 'Carrying on?'

'Come now,' the old man said. 'The two of you meeting every day. At this rate the girl's belly will be swollen with child by the time you say the vows.'

'Lord Tinmore—' Ross's voice rose.

Tinmore went on as if Ross had not spoken. 'I'll not have it. I demand you marry the girl straight away. None of this waiting.'

'Tinmore!' he said more loudly. 'Enough! I'll not have you speak about Miss Summerfield in that manner.'

Tinmore pursed his lips.

'We are waiting until autumn.' But not to marry.

'Not good. Not good at all.' Tinmore coughed. 'I want the matter settled now before everyone knows you are carrying on. I won't have scandal. Won't have it.'

Ross spoke through gritted teeth. 'There is no carrying on. Miss Summerfield is taking painting lessons.'

Tinmore gave him a leering look. 'Is that what you call it?' He leaned towards Ross. 'I do not want anything to spoil this marriage. I want it settled now. The longer you wait, the more I think you are not going to come up to the mark. You asked for her hand in marriage and, by God, you need to take it.'

'Certainly not under pressure from you,' Ross said.

'I've already told your father that I will vote with him on every issue, every issue, if he makes you marry now. Get a special licence. You can be married within days.'

This man was mad. What a reason to make a vote.

Ross stood. 'We wait until autumn, Tinmore.'

Tinmore smirked. 'Then I will make the girl's life a misery. No more *painting* lessons. No more parties or balls. I'll banish her back to Lincolnshire. See how she likes that.'

Ross leaned close again. 'If you make her suffer, your life will be a misery.'

He turned and strode out.

Genna waited outside the door. 'What did he want?'

'For us to marry by special licence now.' He wouldn't tell her the rest of it, the part about *carrying on*. Why upset her even more?

She walked with him. 'What did you say?'

He wanted to say that he'd protected her dream, that she would be free to live the life she chose, that he wished more than life itself he could live it with her.

'I said no.'

Ross left her then. Again.

Genna hurried back to the library, but met Lorene along the way.

'Was that Rossdale?' her sister asked.

'Yes,' Genna replied. 'He has just talked to Tinmore.'

Lorene made a frustrated sound. 'I'd hoped to warn you. I could not convince Tinmore to leave you both alone.'

'You tried?' Genna was surprised.

'Yes, of course,' Lorene said. 'He would only make things worse for you and Rossdale to interfere like that.'

'I am going to speak with him,' Genna told her. 'You may come if you wish.'

She would stop this.

She entered the library without knocking. 'I would speak with you, sir!' she demanded.

'Not now, girl, I am busy.' He was seated in a chair, the same one, she suspected, where he'd sat with Ross. There were no papers or books around him.

'I'll not be put off,' Genna persisted. She stood in front of his chair. 'I want you to know where your attempts at manipulation and control have led me.'

'Now, see here——' he sputtered.

She did not stop. 'I am not going to marry Rossdale. Do you hear? I am going to cry off. Rossdale and I will not suit.'

'Cry off?' His brows shot up. 'Oh, no, you are not. He will be a duke. You will marry him now, without delay.'

'I tell you we will not suit.' The previous day had showed her how unsuitable she was. 'And I will not marry a man if we do not suit.'

'Genna! Do not be hasty,' her sister cried. 'Anyone can tell he loves you and you love him.'

He'd done so many loving things for her, but she'd ruined it. Now, at least, she could do something for him— get him out of this foolish plan they'd made.

She turned to Lorene. 'We will not suit, Ross and me,' she said. 'I am everything the Duchess and your husband think of me. Too inconsequential to be the wife of a duke's heir. Too scandalous.'

Tinmore rose from his chair and waved his cane at her.

'Now you listen to me, girl. You will marry that man. I do not give a fig whether he loves you or you love him. It is a better match than you deserve. If you cry off there will be no dowry. You will not get another chance.'

She stood her ground. 'I will not marry him.'

He hobbled closer to her. 'Then pack your things! I'll not see your face in this house, not with the fuss you are making. Crying off. A duke's heir, no less. I can hear the gossip now.'

'You cannot send her away!' Lorene cried. 'She has a right to cry off.'

'She's a fool. I do not suffer fools.' He shook his cane at Lorene. 'And I'll not have you contradicting me, Wife. Enough of that talk from you.'

Genna turned to leave, but Lorene stopped her. 'You could go to Tess. You should stay in town. Work things through with Rossdale. I am certain he will want to. You are not inconsequential to him, I am sure of it.'

She gave her sister a quick hug. 'You are a romantic, are you not? Do not fret, though, Lorene. I want to go.'

Lorene faced her husband again. 'You cannot simply toss her out. It—it will reflect poorly on you.'

He waved a hand and his cane pounded his way to the door. 'She can go to Tinmore Hall, but she needs to be out by the time we return there. I'm done with her.'

When he left the room, Lorene spoke again. 'Genna, do not do this. Give love a chance. It is all I've ever wanted for you.'

She touched her sister's arm. 'A person can have love and ruin it, Lorene. I must pen a letter and pack. It is better this way.'

The next morning at breakfast, a footman handed Ross a letter. 'This just came for you, sir,'

He opened it and read:

Dear Ross,

Recent events have convinced me it is better if we break the engagement now and that I leave town for a while. You deserve, at the very least, a peaceful Season without interference in your affairs. Who knows? Without me around, you might even meet a young lady worthy of you.

Please know that you have my sincerest gratitude. To you I owe my life and future livelihood, as well as treasured memories of all the wonderful places you took me. Carlton House. The Elgin Marbles. Mr Turner's gallery. Words cannot express what it meant to me to see those places. And to see them with you.

I realise we can never now be the friends we have been over these last several weeks. I am to blame, but please know you will always be my very best friend in my heart.

With fondest regards,

G.

He felt punched in the chest.

'What is it, Ross?' his father asked. 'Bad news? Nothing to interfere with our meeting today, I hope.'

The estate manager of their Kessington estate was in town expressly to meet with Ross, his father and his father's man of business. Overseeing the Kessington estate was one of the responsibilities Ross was assuming for his father.

'I'll be there,' he said.

With Genna gone, where else did he have to be?

Why did he feel as if a rug had been pulled out from under him? This was what he had planned, after all. He'd arranged it so she could become the artist she wished to be. He'd pay Vespery to make certain of it. He'd had a fine Season full of new experiences, shared with her. And finally she would cry off. He could search for what the Duchess would call a more suitable match.

Although that idea made him faintly ill.

Very ill, actually.

He'd made a terrible mistake with this scheme he'd talked her into. He'd been attracted to Genna right from the first meeting. It was not enough that he liked her; he'd also desired her. He thought he could keep that side of him in check. He had no illusions any more. She would have defied Tinmore's pressures, as she'd defied the Duchess's. She did not break the engagement because of Tinmore, she did it because he'd allowed his desire for her to go unchecked. He'd known the power of lovemaking; she had no way of knowing it. It was because of him she'd cried off.

Now he would likely never see her again.

That thought made it hard to breathe.

He fought to get it out of his head.

He glanced over at his father. 'Did you know the Duchess called upon Miss Summerfield yesterday?'

His father lowered the *Morning Post*. 'Did she? Glad she is coming around. We all have reservations about your choice of Miss Summerfield…'

By 'all' Ross assumed his father meant the Duchess and his cronies.

'But she is your choice, so we might as well become accustomed to her.'

Well, if that was not damning with faint praise, Ross did not know what was. 'Is that how Grandfather perceived my mother when you became betrothed to her?'

His father placed the newspaper on the table, a faraway look in his eyes. 'No, but, in those days, I would not have cared what he or anyone thought.' He picked up the newspaper again. 'I was a great deal younger than you, though. I must suppose yours is a more mature choice, even if I cannot see it.'

Ross had been living a fantasy, the fantasy that he and Genna could be together without consequences. To others. To Genna. To him. He'd made everything worse.

'Do you regret marrying my mother?' Ross asked.

'No,' his father said wistfully, but his expression hardened suddenly. 'Yes. Yes, I regret it. If I had not married her, she might still be alive.'

Ross stared at him.

His father lifted his newspaper again and spoke from behind it. 'Your Miss Summerfield is made of sterner stuff, I hope.'

Genna had been honed by living under an umbrella of scandal. She'd forgone all expected roles for herself to embrace one that fed her soul. Yes, that pointed to sterner stuff.

His father put down the *Morning Post* and stood. 'Well, I have much to do today before our meeting—'

His father listed several things he had to do, but, as Ross listened, he realised most were not important. What, really, would be different if his father chose to use that time, say, to visit the Elgin Marbles? Ross suspected the Duchess's duties were like that, as well. Optional.

His father left the room. Ross opened Genna's letter again and reread it.

Chapter Twenty-Four

A week later, Genna sat on the hill overlooking Summerfield House, her wide-brimmed straw hat shading her face from the warm sun. What a contrast to the chill and snow of the last time she'd been in this same place.

She glanced down at her sketchbook. Painting Summerfield House in a snow storm was a challenge in itself, especially on this fine May day with the hills dotted with white cow parsley, blue forget-me-nots, and, like an exotic accent, purple snakes' heads.

Perhaps she should give up painting memories and commit to what was presently before her eyes. Paint what you have, not what is gone.

She turned the page of her sketchbook and started again.

It was time to stop dreaming and to face life as it was. Not as vibrant and exciting as her fanciful drawing of Summerfield House with its impossible sky and grass, but lovely enough nonetheless.

She added the colour she saw before her and a peace descended upon her for the first time in days. There was beauty enough in the world as it was. Why had she not seen that?

She stepped back from the watercolour she'd produced and decided to add one more thing to finish it, something not really in the picture in front of her.

One tiny memory could not hurt, could it?

She added a grey horse and rider, galloping across the field. The horse's mane and tail were raised in the wind and the man's grey topcoat billowed out behind him, just like it had last December.

She'd been at this vantage point for over two hours and the sun was getting lower on the horizon. It was time to pack up, although returning to Tinmore Hall held no real appeal. She was barely tolerated by the servants there, who seemed to go out of their way to let her know they resented serving her. Perhaps she would write to Lord Penford and ask if she might stay the rest of the time at Summerfield Hall. She'd be content to use a room in the servants' quarters and she'd be happy to perform whatever useful service he might require.

As she rinsed her brushes in her jug of water, something caught her eye. A horse and rider galloping over the same space in the field where she'd painted them. A grey horse. Its rider wore no topcoat, though, and he was too far away to identify.

Could it be? It made no sense that it would be.

Hope could turn fanciful, apparently.

She dried her brushes with a clean cloth and poured the water on to the ground. Packing up her paints and her rags and placing them in her large satchel, she remembered the last time she'd done this very thing. It had started to snow and he had been watching her.

She heard a rustle behind her and the sound of a horse blowing air from its snout. She spun around.

'I did not nearly run you over this time,' he said.

The breath left her body. 'Ross.'

He smiled at her. 'I came to see if you needed assistance. A creature of habit, I suppose.' He dismounted and his horse, Spirit, contently found some grass to nibble. 'I see you are a creature of habit, as well, drawing the same scene.' He walked over to her easel and examined it. 'You've captured it,' he said. 'With the real colours this time.' He did not mention the horse and rider, though, but he touched them lightly with his gloved finger.

'I still do not understand why you are here,' she said.

A gust of wind blew over the easel. Ross caught the sketchbook before it tumbled to the ground.

He did not answer her. 'Are you returning to Tinmore Hall?' he asked. 'If so, may I convey you there? There is a place I would like to see on the way back. We could talk there.'

She nodded and he helped her pack the rest of her things into her satchel. He helped her on to Spirit and climbed on behind her. She knew where he was heading.

To the folly.

This part of the estate was as overgrown as ever. Apparently Lord Penford's improvements had not yet reached here. The white wood anemone covering the barely visible path reminded her of the snow that dotted this same area last time they rode here. They came to the folly, now canopied with trees bright green with new leaves. It looked even more fanciful than it had in the snow.

Ross slid off Spirit and reached up to help her down, their eyes catching as he held her waist. She climbed the three steps of the folly and sat on the bench, dangling her feet as she had done before.

She looked up at him. 'So?'

He leaned against one of the columns. 'I missed you.'

The words were like needles. She'd missed him, too. 'That cannot be why you are here.'

He paced. 'Not entirely.' He stopped and looked down at her. 'You once were willing to take a very big chance and I would not let you. Are you willing to take another?'

'Am I willing to seduce you again?' She shook her head. 'No.'

'Not that—although I might not object this time, provided you are willing to take this other gamble.' His eyes were warm on her face and filled her with so many memories.

'Just tell me what it is, Ross.'

He sat next to her and took her hands in his. 'Marry me.'

'Marry you?'

'Take a chance on me.' His voice was low and earnest. 'I know you do not believe in love, but I do. I have felt it since I met you and it did not leave even when you did.'

She pulled her hands away. 'No, Ross. I am unsuited. The Duchess was right in that regard. I would make a terrible duchess.'

'You would make an unconventional one,' he corrected. 'And I've no objection to that. I've watched my father plan his day and discuss his activities afterwards. It struck me that most of what he does is unnecessary. I do not have to play politics all the time. I can be a duke differently than the one he is, than who my grandfather was. You can be who you wish to be, as well. God knows I do not wish you to be like the Duchess. You can paint portraits or landscapes or whatever you wish. I have no desire to limit you—'

Think of the good she and Ross could do! Perhaps they could help all the hungry people, all the out-of-work soldiers—

No. Ross, perhaps, but not her. The *ton* would never accept one of the scandalous Summerfields as the Duchess of Kessington.

'I'm happy to use my rank to open doors for you,' he went on. 'And I will not require anything of you that you do not wish to do. All I ask of you is to take the chance to believe me. Believe that I love you and want you with me.'

He loved her now. Would he love her later? Or would he leave her like everyone else she loved?

'Would you answer me, Genna? Say something.' His voice sounded anxious.

She should stay safe and refuse him, but if she refused him now, it would guarantee losing him, would it not?

'I am too scandalous,' she said. Would he resent that some day? 'I have already caused scandal by breaking our engagement. I cried off. Surely the *ton* is abuzz with that news. Think what they will say if we wind up betrothed again.'

He stood and paced again. 'Do I care about that? Not a whit.' He turned and stood before her again. 'Besides, no one knows you cried off besides you and me. In the eyes of the *ton*, we are still betrothed.'

She looked up at him. 'Truly?'

He smiled. 'Truly.'

She glanced away again. 'I'm afraid, Ross. I'm afraid you will stop loving me, that I will do something odd or something scandalous, or something wrong and you will despise me for it.'

'I cannot promise to never be angry,' he said. 'Only to love you and be faithful to you.'

She thought of all the things he'd done for her. He'd known her better than anyone, even her sisters.

'Take a chance on me, Genna,' he murmured.

She rose and faced him. 'There is no one more important to me than you, Ross. No one. You have never failed me. Not once.' She took a deep breath. 'Very well, Ross. I will take a chance on you.'

He opened his arms and she bounded into them, holding him tight.

'I shall try to never fail you.' His lips caressed her ear.

'I love you, Ross.' Now she knew. Her feelings of friendship. The carnal desires. The wish for his well-being and happiness even over hers. What she felt was love.

'And I love you, Genna.' His head dipped down to hers. Before his lips touched hers, he added. 'For always.'

Epilogue

Summerfield House was fragrant with evergreen, with the turkey roasting in the kitchen and the flames licking around the yule log. The host and his guests burst into the hall, back from Christmas church services. Their cheeks were pink, and white flakes of snow on their hats, lashes and shoulders rapidly melted. They'd walked back from the village church, the one Genna and her sisters had attended all through their childhood. It was glorious to sit next to Tess again in the pew reserved for the Summerfields.

Almost all the Summerfields would be together to celebrate Christmas Day. Tess and Marc were staying at Summerfield House with Dell, Ross and Genna. Lorene and Tinmore were expected for dinner. No one was eager for Tinmore's company, but he was the price they would gladly pay to have Lorene with them.

Only Edmund could not be with them, which was a shame, but it was for a very happy reason. His wife, Marc's sister, was about to deliver a child in two or three months.

Other than Edmund being gone, it would almost be like it used to be.

Only better.

Because Genna was married to Ross.

People actually called her the Marchioness of Rossdale. It made her giggle.

In the hall of Summerfield House this Christmas Day, Genna hugged Lord Penford—Dell—the man responsible for this lovely day. 'Have I thanked you for inviting us all for Christmas, Cousin?'

'A dozen or so times, Genna.' Dell extricated himself from her grasp and turned to the others, who were all divesting themselves of topcoats, hats and gloves. 'I've asked the servants to have some wassail for us in the drawing room and something to eat.'

'Excellent!' Marc offered Tess his arm.

Before they had a chance to leave the hall, though, there was a knock on the door. The two footmen were already laden with coats and such, so Ross opened it.

'Lady Tinmore!' he exclaimed.

'Lorene,' she corrected, stepping inside. 'I did not expect to see you attending the door.'

He leaned his head outside before closing it.

'Lorene!' Genna ran over to her and gave her a buss on the cheek. 'Let us get those wet things off you. How did you get so full of snow?'

'I walked,' she said.

'Walked?'

'You are alone?' Ross asked. 'Where is Tinmore?'

Dell helped her off with her cloak.

'Tinmore refused to attend,' she said. 'I do not think he wished to be among my family. He tried to keep me from coming. Refused me the carriage, so I walked.'

'Goodness,' Tess said. 'Was he very angry that you defied him?'

Lorene shrugged. 'Quite. But I wanted to spend Christmas with my sisters. So I came anyway.'

'Good for you!' Genna said. 'You stood up to him.'

'We will see how good it is when I return home.' Lorene laughed.

'I do not know about the rest of you, but I am in great need of wassail,' Marc said.

'As am I,' Ross agreed.

* * *

The Summerfield sisters had a lovely afternoon together and a lovely dinner with the men most important to them. Afterwards, they all sat around the yule fire, exchanging gifts, Dell gave Lorene some piano music. He gave Tess and Genna trinkets from the house. Tess and Marc gave everyone books. Like the previous year, Genna gave them paintings she'd done. She'd painted scenes of Summerfield House, parts of the house or estate that had been special to each of her sisters. She gave a miniature of herself to Ross and one of Tess to Marc. She'd done one of Lorene for Tinmore, as well, as she had the year before. At least this one would not be thrown on the floor. Dell offered to hang it in Summerfield House instead. For Dell she framed an oil painting of the landscape around Summerfield House, showing the house in the distance.

'It is not a Turner,' Genna said, 'but I have improved since last year.'

'I do not know what the devil a Turner is,' Dell said, 'but this is quite good, I'd say.'

'It is very good,' Ross said. 'I may want to borrow it and get it accepted in the Royal Academy Exhibition.'

'I have a gift,' Tess spoke up excitedly. 'It is mostly a gift for Marc.' He took her hand and her gaze swept all of them. 'I am going to have a baby!'

'Another baby!' Genna cried. 'First Edmund, now you.'

'Lovely news,' Lorene said, rising to give her sister a kiss on the cheek.

Ross took a small wrapped box out of his pocket. 'I thought of giving Genna oil paints and watercolours, but those are her tools. She must always have what she needs. So I got this.'

He handed Genna the box and she opened it. It was a lovely diamond pendant. 'Oh, it is beautiful! I must wear it. Put it on me, Ross.'

He fastened the clasp. His fingers were warm against the tender skin of her neck and, as always, they made her body come alive. But she could wait, because she wanted to spend this precious time with her sisters and these wonderful men who had been so good to them. She could also wait, because she knew Ross would be there for her every night. She'd sleep in his arms tonight in the bed she'd slept in as a young girl vowing to make her own way in the world.

She could have done it, too. She could have made a living with her painting, but she'd found something she wanted even more.

Ross.

As it got later, Tess was yawning and Marc insisted on having her retire for the night. Dell ordered his carriage for Lorene and offered to accompany her back to Tinmore Hall. Genna and Ross were left alone in the drawing room.

'I suppose we ought to go to bed, too.' She fingered her pendant. 'I believe I shall sleep in my diamond. I do not wish to take it off.'

Ross put his arm around her and kissed the back of her neck. 'I am delighted it pleases you.'

She turned around and hugged him close. 'We should go.'

'One moment.' Ross stepped away and took a candle from one of the tables. He went to the hidden door and opened it. 'Let's take the hidden passage.'

She giggled. 'Of course.'

By the light of his sole candle she led him expertly to the hidden stairs and up to her bedchamber.

'The door is here.' She extended her hand to push the door open.

He seized her hand. 'Not so hasty.' He blew out the candle and the only light came through slits where the doors were. 'I want to do something I wished to do a year ago.'

'What did you wish to do?'

'This.' He pulled her into an embrace and placed his lips upon hers.

She could have stayed like this with him for ever.

* * * * *

COMPROMISED WITH HER FORBIDDEN VISCOUNT

To my friend Anne just because she deserves it!

Chapter One

Vauxhall Gardens,
June 1817

Viscount Willburgh wandered through throngs of shepherdesses, harlequins, Roman gods and goddesses, kings and queens of old, clergymen and devils, and dominos of every colour, all under a blaze of a thousand lamps hung in the trees of Vauxhall Gardens. Even if the revellers of the pleasure garden had not worn masks and half masks, it still would have been impossible to tell a servant from a lord from a pickpocket. Anyone could pay a shilling to be a part of Vauxhall Gardens' masquerade.

Unfortunately his companions, lacking imagination like Will and the majority of men in attendance, had seen fit to don black dominoes with white masks. The two of them had disappeared into the throng of dancers in the Grove and Will had given up searching for them.

Why the devil had he agreed to this escapade in the first place? Attending a raucous masquerade at Vauxhall Gardens did not suit Will's nature at all. Vauxhall was all illusion and decadence, but life's reality was hard work and weighty responsibility.

Even so, there was much he could see—The Cascade. The

rope walkers. The Chinese temple. He could even seek out the hermit in the farthest corner of the Gardens. None of it held much appeal. Affairs of state were plaguing his mind, especially after the Prince Regent's message to the Lords advising the continuance of the seditious practices.

Should Parliament approve suspension of habeas corpus? There was certainly unrest throughout the kingdom, but was that not to be expected? The price of bread was high. People were starving. Should not the Lords be doing something about feeding the people instead of taking their rights away?

The festive music of the orchestra and the crowd's gaiety did not sit well with such thoughts. Will edged his way to the relatively quieter Grand Walk, but a group of drunken carousers annoyed him even more.

Maybe a visit to the hermitage would do. At least it would be quieter down the Dark Walk, darker this night, because clouds covered the moon and stars, and the air carried the scent of impending rain.

The lamps in the trees that flanked the walk grew fewer in number, as did the promenaders, couples mostly, probably looking for a secluded nook for a private tryst. A wave of envy jolted Will. He'd never had much time for dalliances and, unlike his friends, had eventually concluded that amorous affairs of the temporary kind merely left him empty.

He ought to turn back. Find a boat to take him across the river. Avoid the rain.

He was about to do that very thing when he suddenly had the Walk to himself. Until some distance ahead of him a woman jumped from the trees. A man followed and seized her from behind. The woman cried out and struggled to get free, but the man covered her mouth and pulled her back into the darkness of the wood. Vauxhall was not all merriment; danger also lurked there.

Will sprang into action, entering the woods where he saw the man and woman disappear. The man was dragging her into a shelter, a private supper room designed for assignations.

Will charged the man, wrapping an arm around the man's neck, choking him. The man, dressed in a domino and mask like himself, released his prisoner. She fell to the ground. A fist to the man's face and a kick to his groin sent the fellow fleeing for his life. Will turned to extend his hand to help the woman to her feet.

'Are you injured?' he asked.

'Shaken a bit, is all.' She looked down at herself and gasped. 'Oh, dear!' The bodice of her dress was torn, revealing her shift and stays. Her hands flew to her chest.

'Come into the shelter,' Will said. 'We can put you back to rights.'

A lamp lit the shelter enough for Will to see she wore a red hooded cape and a plain blue cotton dress covered by a pinafore. Or it had once been covered by a pinafore. The pinafore and dress were torn at one shoulder and now were held in place by the woman's hand. Her eyes were a startling light brown, lighter than her hair, a warm brown shot through with gold where the lamplight caught it. She wore it down, as if she were a girl, not a woman. How old was she? Still masked she could be anything. A maid, a shopgirl, or even a harlot—although a harlot typically would not be struggling to free herself.

The shelter held a chaise-longue and a table upon which sat the lamp and a bottle of wine with two glasses, apparently arranged ahead of time.

The woman—girl?—turned away. 'I—I am remiss in not thanking you right away, sir. I cannot imagine what I would have done had you not assisted me.'

Will could well imagine what the man had planned for her.

But he focused on the practical. 'Do you have pins with you? To pin up your dress?'

'I do.' Still with her back to him she let go of the torn dress and lifted her skirt slightly to retrieve pins concealed in her petticoat. She set to pinning the bodice in place. 'If only I could see…'

'Turn this way,' Will said. 'I'll help you.'

She'd managed to cover herself. Will needed only to straighten the fabric to make it appear as if it had been stitched. He stood close to her, close enough to feel the warmth of her body and the scent of her—lavender and mint and sunny summer days. Of one thing he was certain—she was a woman, not a young girl. He had not been so close to a woman in a long time, certainly not in such an intimate situation.

'How do you know how to pin a dress?' Her words were breathless.

His breath accelerated, heating up the inside of his mask.

'I have a younger sister.'

The confounded mask. It made it difficult to breathe and even to see.

With an annoyed grunt, he pulled it off.

The woman jumped back. 'You!'

Will was puzzled. 'You know me?'

Her voice trembled. 'Oh, yes. I know you, Lord Willburgh.' She removed her own mask.

'The devil…' Will glared at her. No. Not the devil. 'A Dorman.' The name was poison on his lips. 'The Dorman whose father killed my father.'

She bristled. '*Your* father killed *my* father! It was your father who challenged my father to a duel!'

He countered. 'It was *your* father who seduced my mother!'

She lifted a brow. 'Was it?'

This animosity had not begun with Will's father's death. The Dormans had feuded with the Willburghs for generations, purportedly over ownership of disputed land. It had really started three generations ago, when Will's great-great-grandfather and that generation's Lord Dorman fought over a woman, the woman who became Will's great-great-grandmother. After that event the discord over the disputed land heated to a fever pitch. The fire was further fuelled by more romantic rivalry—Will's great-grandfather's affair with that generation's Lady Dorman, and most tragically for Will, the seduction of Will's mother by the current Baron Dorman's ne'er-do-well brother, who knew precisely what he was about. Will's father challenged that younger Dorman to the ill-fated duel.

They killed each other in that duel, a duel that changed everything for Will. At seventeen, he suddenly inherited a title, all its responsibility, and all the scandal that engulfed the family as a result. From then on—ten years now—Will's carefree life as a young man had ceased. Life became nothing more than Duty. Duty. Duty.

Staring at this Dorman woman brought it all back. All his grief. All his anger.

Her eyes lit with fear and she backed farther away.

He did not usually allow that part of him to show. 'Do not worry. I'm not going to kill you.'

Her voice turned low. 'What are you going to do?'

Will took a deep breath and slowly released it. 'I am going to finish pinning your dress and escort you back to wherever you should be.'

Will damped down his emotions and finished pinning the pinafore. She leaned as far away as possible as he did so. Even in his anger he experienced the allure of being so close to her.

He stepped back. 'That should pass, if no one looks too closely.'

Without another word he walked to the door and put his hand on the latch. She followed. As he opened the door, a bolt of lightning lit up the sky, followed by a crack of thunder.

And pouring rain.

Damnation.

He closed the door. 'We'll wait out the storm. With any luck it will pass quickly.' He inclined his head to the chaise-longue. 'You may as well sit.'

She hesitated, looking wary, but she had nothing to fear, even if she was undisputedly lovely. He wanted nothing but to be rid of her.

She perched on the edge of the chaise as if ready to escape at any moment.

He walked over to the table and poured himself a glass of wine. 'Would you like wine?'

Again she hesitated, but finally responded by holding out her hand.

He placed the glass in it and retreated to a corner to lean against the wall.

Will's emotions waged a war within him. Again he remembered galloping across the land to try to stop the duel, arriving just in time to hear the loud report of their shots and see the smoke from their pistol barrels before both men fell. He rushed to his father. Blood poured from his father's chest which heaved with every struggled breath.

'Your duty now,' his father gasped before his eyes turned sightless and his body went limp.

Will gulped down the whole glass of wine and poured himself another. His father had often warned Will he'd be

Viscount one day and his father must train him for it. But his father never had the time.

Never took the time.

Instead his father died foolishly and Will had to learn everything on his own at seventeen.

Rain battered the roof of the shelter and thunder continued to rumble. Will concentrated on the sound until the wine and the weather lulled him back to a semblance of calm.

He glanced at the Dorman woman, sipping her wine and patting her hair.

'Your hair stayed in place,' he said, breaking their silence and remembering how he'd admired it.

Her hand returned to her lap.

'Who are you supposed to be, anyway?' He gestured to her costume.

She glared at him. 'Red Riding Hood.'

He laughed. 'And you were almost caught by the wolf.'

She straightened. 'Or perhaps you are the wolf in disguise.'

'Not the wolf. Not your grandmother either.' He poured himself the last of the wine.

She pursed her lips, disapproving.

Disapproving his drink and accusing him of being the wolf? *Who does she think she is?*

Oh. Right. She was a *Dorman*.

He tossed back a defiant look. 'So what the devil were you doing alone at Vauxhall? That was flirting with danger surely.'

'I was not alone,' she countered. 'I was with my cousin and she met with—with—gentlemen of her acquaintance. Then we became separated.'

It was his turn to be disapproving. 'Two young ladies unchaperoned, then?'

She glanced away. 'I was the chaperone.'

Will laughed. 'That was a hare-brained plan, was it not? Like two sheep to the slaughter. I daresay there is more than one wolf prowling around Vauxhall.'

She gave him a direct look. 'I undoubtedly failed, did I not?'

'Undoubtedly,' he agreed, taking a sip of wine. 'Do you and your cousin often come to Vauxhall alone?'

'We were not alone. Lord and Lady Dorman and Lucius came, as well. They will wonder where I am. And I really must find Violet.'

He scoffed. 'Cannot the *gentlemen of her acquaintance* be trusted to keep her safe?'

Anna took another sip of wine.

She certainly was not going to tell *him* that Violet had tricked her into a meeting with Mr Raskin, the Season's most notorious rake, and his vile friend, the man who'd tried to carry her off.

Where was Violet? Was she in a shelter like this with Raskin? If so, Anna feared Violet needed no force to go with the man.

It had been Anna's responsibility to keep Violet from doing anything foolish. Lord and Lady Dorman counted on her for that and would blame her for Violet's behaviour.

Willburgh broke into her thoughts, his voice scathing. 'And where was your cousin Lucius while you two young ladies met gentlemen of your acquaintance at a Vauxhall masquerade?'

Lucius and Willburgh had been schoolmates at Eton, Anna knew, and briefly at Oxford. Until the duel. Lucius returned to Oxford then. Willburgh had not.

'I was not meeting any gentlemen!' she snapped. 'Lucius…' Wait. Why should she tell *him* what happened?

He made a derisive sound. 'Let me guess. Lucius abandoned you as soon as he was able.'

'He didn't *abandon* us,' Although Lucius had pretty much disappeared into the crowd as soon as they were out of sight of Lord and Lady Dorman.

Anna ought to have insisted they all stay together as Lord and Lady Dorman expected, but would Violet and Lucius have listened to her? They'd probably planned to abandon her all along without a thought about leaving her unprotected.

A familiar ache returned, the ache of being alone in the world, belonging nowhere to no one. She could almost hear the words of her father, Bertram Dorman, her beloved papa, after her mother died—'*It is just you and me now. And I'll never leave you.*'

Thanks to Willburgh's father, that was a promise her papa could not keep.

Anna's eyes stung with sudden tears. She'd loved him so.

And he was not even really her father, merely the only father she'd ever known. Her mother, on her deathbed, had confided that her real father had been an officer in the East India Company army, killed when she was a baby. Her mother married Bertram Dorman not even a year after and he was the only father Anna could remember. She'd adored him and he doted on her as if the sun rose and set upon her.

Anna blinked her tears away. She was lucky the Dormans became her guardians and allowed her to live with them. Otherwise she'd have been sent to an orphanage.

As they often reminded her.

She glanced at the man who was her rescuer. He leaned casually against the wall, his long legs crossed at the ankles, his arms across his chest. He was taller and more muscular than she'd thought, but then, she'd never before seen him up close. She caught the scent of bergamot and sandalwood that clung to him as she had done when he pinned up her dress. He'd been so gentle pinning her torn dress, although there was no doubt of his strength. He'd displayed it by easily dispatching her assailant. He'd frightened her only briefly when his anger flared.

The Dormans hated him and the other Willburghs because of that silly family feud, so Anna had never been this close to him. She'd spied him occasionally in the village and glimpsed him at some of the Season's society balls, but she'd given him a wide berth. Lucius had gone to school with him and perhaps something there made him particularly detest Willburgh, but Anna hated him because *his* father had killed her beloved papa.

This man was not responsible for that, of course. He'd been little more than a youth at the time. But his was the face her anger settled on.

At the moment Willburgh's head was bowed, as if he were pretending she was not even there. That certainly did not help appease her anger. To be thought of as being of no consequence to anybody only angered her more.

She'd make him see her. 'Where were you bound when my—my problem—detained you? Did I interrupt some important plans? Or were you merely wandering the Dark Walk in search of damsels in distress?' Or was he planning to meet some woman in a shelter like this?

He raised his head as if he had indeed forgotten her presence. 'I was on my way to see the hermit.'

'Alone?' She raised her brows.

He gave her a direct look. 'Like the hermit, I was seeking escape from the crowds and the noise.'

Anna hated the crowds and the noise, as well. Indeed,

she was not overly fond of London and all the delights of the Season. Ordinarily being caught inside during a rainstorm would have been a pleasantness.

'You—you do not like Vauxhall?' she asked him.

'I do not,' he responded.

'Then why come?'

He shrugged. 'I was talked into it.'

'Oh, really?' She let her voice drip with scepticism. As if a man like him truly could be talked into anything he did not wish to do.

Perhaps he'd been spurned by a lady companion—although somehow that idea did not fit him.

He shifted his position and took a step towards her. 'I was separated from my companions, as were you.'

She doubted he'd been left on purpose as she had been.

He laughed dryly. 'Perhaps it was fate. So I could rescue you and be stranded here.'

She lowered her lashes. 'I am grateful to you.'

When she raised her head again their eyes met and their gazes held.

Until he took a breath and walked over to the window and looked out. 'I think the rain has stopped. I'll escort you back.'

She rose and gathered her red cape around her. Neither of them bothered to put on their masks. They reached the door together, brushing against each other as Willburgh turned the latch and opened the door.

Only to see Lucius and Lord Dorman, also unmasked, standing right outside.

'Willburgh!' Lucius reeled back as if struck in the chest. He recovered, leaning forwards again to glare at Anna. 'You are with *him*? *Him?* How shameless can you be? With *him*!'

Chapter Two

Lucius's words slashed into Anna like knives.

'See here, Lucius—' Willburgh responded.

But Lord Dorman cut him off. 'Do you mock us, Anna? Disrespect all we have done for you? Of all men, you behave the trollop with this one?'

'She did not—' Willburgh began, only to be cut off again.

'Come, Lucius,' Lord Dorman demanded. 'Let us go back. I wash my hands of her.'

Anna stared in disbelief as they turned their backs on her and strode off.

'Make haste,' Willburgh said, but she was too stunned to move.

He seized her arm and pulled her through the door.

'It is not what it seems,' he called after Lucius and his father. 'You must hear me.'

Anna could hardly keep pace with Willburgh as he charged after Lucius and his father, their dominos billowing behind them in their haste. They did not even bother to turn around. She and Willburgh caught up with them at the Centre Cross Walk.

Willburgh released Anna and seized Lucius's arm. 'You will hear me!'

Lucius shrugged him off 'Hear you? We caught you in a

compromising position. What else is there to hear? Do you think we do not know what you were doing?' He laughed. 'Here I thought you were stiff-necked like your father. Obviously you take after your mother—'

'How horrid—' Anna broke in, appalled that Lucius would say such a thing out loud.

Other costumed people were in earshot and several stopped to observe the spectacle. They were easily recognised, having forgotten their masks.

Willburgh glanced at the observers and back to Lucius and his father. 'Have a care. Let us discuss this privately.'

'You may follow us to the supper box,' Lord Dorman said.

The way to the Dormans' supper box led them through the first Triumphal Arch and directly across from the Turkish Tent.

Lady Dorman, dressed in powdered wig and fashion from a century earlier, stood as they approached. 'You've found her, I see.' She sounded as outraged as her son and husband. Evidently the news has already reached her, even in those few minutes. She glared at Anna. 'An assignation with the enemy. How could you, Anna? After all we've done for you.'

'There was no—' Willburgh tried, only to be cut off again.

Lucius faced him. 'We will hear no excuses from you! Reprobate.'

Lucius wore a red domino, lined in black. Somehow the red of his cape was unlike hers. Instead he resembled an image of the devil she'd once seen in the window of Humphrey's Print Shop. Lord Dorman wore white powder and a colourful silk coat and breeches, matching the era of his wife.

At that moment Violet walked up, Mr Raskin in tow. 'We have just this moment heard.' She, too, turned to Anna. 'Is that why you ran off, Anna, and left me all alone?'

Anna gaped at her. 'Violet!'

Violet turned her gaze to Raskin. 'I don't know what I would have done if dear Raskin had not found me!'

Raskin bowed. 'It was my honour, I assure you.'

No one asked where he and Violet had been.

Anna looked at them all in turn. She knew she was of no real importance to them, except in the ways they found her useful. As companion to Lady Dorman and Violet, for example. Someone to fetch for them or carry parcels. But she thought they would at least *listen* to her. She thought they knew her well enough to know she would not indulge in assignations.

Lord Dorman's voice rose. 'We cannot tolerate your cavorting with this—this—sworn enemy, of all people! It is unforgivable, after all we have done for you.' He rubbed his hands together. 'I wash my hands of you!'

Willburgh's voice was even higher. 'I demand that you listen to me. You are mistaken—'

Lord Dorman's face turned red with anger. 'I heed no demands of yours, sir. Out of my way.' He pushed past Willburgh and gestured to the others. 'We are leaving! Now.'

They filed by Anna, each pointedly refusing to look at her.

Even though she remained rooted in place, Lord Dorman turned back to her. 'You may not follow. You are no longer welcome in our home.'

Only Mr Raskin looked back, a smirk on his face. The others walked away without a backward glance.

Anna finally found her voice. 'Well, this is famous. What am I to do now?'

'Damn them,' a voice next to her said. 'Damn them all. *Dormans*.'

Willburgh. She'd forgotten he was there. He was the reason the family had so roundly rejected her. Had she been caught with Raskin's friend and truly compromised, they would not have been so outraged.

He returned her glance. 'Forgive my language,' he murmured. 'And I forgot you were a Dorman.'

She used her stepfather's name, she thought, but she was definitely not a Dorman.

She glanced away, her predicament becoming more real. 'What am I to do?'

He moved so he was in front of her and he caught her gaze. 'Is—is there not a friend I can deliver you to? Someone who would assist you?'

A friend? She'd had no opportunity to make friends. She knew Violet's and Lucius's friends, but she would not dream of asking any of them to take her in.

'There is no one,' she told him with a helpless laugh. 'And I have no money. What I own is in the possession of Lord Dorman.'

'Well, I can give you money,' he responded.

A masked gentleman dressed as a harlequin strolled by, a grin on his face. 'You are in a fine pickle, are you not? Better you than me!'

'Get lost,' Willburgh snarled.

'Someone you know?' she asked.

He shrugged. 'I suppose. Good thing for him he wore a mask.'

People strolling by were slowing as they passed them and obviously talking about them. She'd always worried that Violet would someday be such an object of gossip and scorn. She never dreamed she'd be one.

'We should go,' Willburgh said. 'I've had enough of this place.'

They left the supper box and walked towards the Proprietor's House entrance, passing the orchestra, which had started playing again. Soon a tenor's voice rang out:

The lord said to the lady,
Before he went out:
Beware of false Lamkin,
He's a-walking about...

Willburgh said, 'We'll hire a hackney coach to take us over Vauxhall Bridge.' Vauxhall Bridge had opened the previous year. Otherwise they'd be crossing the Thames by boat. At the entrance he sent a servant to have a coach brought around.

Anna did not know his plan. Was he intending to drop her somewhere in Mayfair and leave her to fend for herself? She was afraid to ask.

As if reading her mind, he said, 'I suppose I could take you to a hotel.'

'A hotel. Yes,' she responded without enthusiasm. At least she'd have a place to sleep for one night.

The hackney coach pulled up.

'Take us to the Pulteney,' Will called to the jarvey.

The jarvey's brows rose knowingly and he answered with a smirk. 'Yes, m'lord. The Pulteney.'

What was this man thinking? The Pulteney was a very respectable hotel. It had been fine enough to house the Tsar of Russia and his sister a few years ago; it should be respectable enough for a Dorman.

Miss Dorman's cheeks flamed red at the driver's comment. She'd obviously understood the driver's reaction.

Will helped her into the coach. He sat in the backward-facing seat, his spirits sinking even further than before. He could not take her to a hotel, he realised. With the spectacle the Dormans created at Vauxhall, there was certain to be plenty of gossip already. If he took her to a hotel at this hour of the night, in the costume she wore, would that not make the situation look worse? Confirm what the Dormans believe happened? What everyone would believe happened?

'Miss Dorman, I do not think it advisable to take you to a hotel. I will tell the driver to take us to my townhouse.'

Her eyes widened in alarm. 'To your townhouse!'

'My mother is in residence. No one can make of it what it is not.' Certainly his mother would not jump to that erroneous conclusion. She knew a Dorman was the last woman he would be caught alone with.

Although that was precisely what happened. They were caught alone, unchaperoned, in one of the shelters at Vauxhall created for 'private parties.'

He stole a glance at Miss Dorman who was absently gazing out the window into the darkness. He admired that she did not go into hysterics, although she certainly had every right to do so. She'd said very few words since they were discovered, but he felt the terrible blow the Dormans inflicted on her. Accusing her. Rejecting her. Abandoning her. He sensed the aloneness they'd created in her. When his father died, Will had felt very alone, even though he'd had family and friends around him. He was alone in becoming the viscount, though. No one else shared that burden.

Will opened the window to call to the jarvey to take them to Park Street instead.

Will and Miss Dorman rode in silence until the hackney coach pulled up to Will's townhouse. He helped her out of the coach and paid the jarvey. As the hackney coach rumbled away, Will hoped no curious eyes were awakened to see him escort her into the house.

Bailey, his butler, roused himself from a chair in the hall.

'M'lord, forgive me. I must have dozed off.' He stumbled in surprise at spying Miss Dorman, who was a sight in her Red Riding Hood costume.

'You needn't have stayed up, Bailey,' Will said. 'But I am glad you did. This is Miss Dorman.'

'Miss Dorman?' The butler sounded even more puzzled.

Bailey was aware, as were all the servants, that the Dormans and Willburghs were sworn enemies. He was, though, an excellent butler and quickly schooled his features back to blankness.

'Can you wake up Mrs White?' Will asked. Mrs White was the housekeeper. 'We need a room made up for Miss Dorman. She will need night clothes, as well. And a dress for the morrow. And any other items essential for her care and comfort.'

'Right away, sir.' Bailey bowed in Miss Dorman's direction. 'Miss Dorman.'

She nodded in return.

In the light of the hall, Miss Dorman looked pale and fatigued, as if she might collapse in a heap at any moment.

Will took her arm. 'Come into the library. You can sit there. I should have asked Bailey for refreshment. You look like you are spent.'

'Thank you,' she managed.

He led her to a comfortable chair and lit a taper from the sconce in the hall, using it to light the library lamps. 'I can have Bailey bring tea later. All I have here is some brandy.'

'Brandy would be most welcome.' She sat on the edge of the comfortable sofa near the fireplace as if wishing to bolt.

He took the decanter from a cabinet and poured two glasses, handing one to her.

She took a sip. 'I should not be here,' she said.

'Lord and Lady Dorman left you no choice,' he countered. 'A hotel would be worse. It would only generate more talk.'

'They would not let us explain.' She held the glass against her cheek for a moment, talking more to herself than to him. 'Do they really think so little of me?'

Will's anger rose again. Yes. How dare they simply leave her like that? He drained his glass and poured them both another. 'I will call upon them tomorrow. I will make them listen. They will have to listen to me.'

The brandy was having no effect on him. Certainly not calming his anger. He paced the room.

Mrs White entered, still in her nightcap, robe wrapped around her thick waist. Bailey stood behind her.

'I am here, m'lord,' Mrs White announced. 'The room is being readied. Everything is being done.'

Will's shoulders relaxed. For the first time this night someone else seemed to take the reins from his hands.

She approached Miss Dorman. 'Miss Dorman, is it? I am Mrs White, the housekeeper. I will show you to your room. You look as if you need a nice rest.'

Bless the woman, Will thought. She knew nothing of what happened but was taking pity anyway. Neither she nor Bailey had asked any questions, even though, as old retainers, they well knew the animosity between the Dormans and the Willburghs. They'd been around when his father was killed by her father. Will owed them an explanation. Later, though.

Mrs White led Miss Dorman to the stairs, right across from the library door. At that moment, though, Will's mother appeared at the top of the stairs.

'I heard voices,' his mother said, then saw Mrs White and Miss Dorman. 'What is this?'

Anna looked up at the woman who, in her eyes, caused her papa to die.

She'd seen Lady Willburgh before at a distance, an always

elegant figure, still beautiful in her fiftieth year even in her nightcap and robe. How Anna resented her! She'd lured her papa into a seduction. If only he had resisted her.

'Who is this creature, Mrs White?' Lady Willburgh demanded. 'Why is she in my house?'

Willburgh came to the doorway. 'I will explain, Mother.' He climbed the steps to her. 'This is Miss Dorman who must stay the night as our guest.'

'Dorman!' Lady Willburgh's voice rose. 'Violet Dorman?'

'Anna,' Anna replied.

'The orphan?' The woman's voice was scornful.

Yes, Anna thought. Orphaned because of you.

Willburgh spoke. 'I will explain, Mother. But let Mrs White show Miss Dorman to her room.'

'I will not have a Dorman in my house!' she responded indignantly.

'It is not your house, Mother,' Willburgh said evenly.

Anna, still at the bottom of the stairway, lifted her gaze to the woman and tried to keep the animosity out of her voice. 'I am sorry to intrude, ma'am. Believe me, it was not by my choice.'

'Not my choice either!' Lady Willburgh sniffed. 'She cannot stay.'

'She *will* stay.' Willburgh took his mother by the arm. 'Come back to your room and I will explain.'

He escorted her away.

'Unhand me, Will.' His mother's arm felt surprisingly frail in his hand.

He led her to her bed and lit a candle from the fireplace.

'She is *his* daughter!' she exclaimed, standing her ground. 'How could you bring her here?'

Will faced her and made her listen while he told the whole story, starting with Miss Dorman's abduction.

When he finished, her eyes flashed. 'Those Dormans. They are nothing but trouble!' She glared at him. 'You should have left her to her fate! Likely she wanted that man to— to—'

'Mother.' Will admonished. 'What sort of man would I be not to intervene? Besides, I had no idea who she was until we were in the shelter. And then it rained.'

She pursed her lips together.

'I will call upon Lord Dorman tomorrow,' he assured her. 'I will straighten this out. Do not fret another moment about it.'

He smoothed her covers and helped her sit on the edge of her bed.

She fussed with her nightdress. 'You say others heard Dorman's accusations?'

'I am afraid so,' he admitted.

Her eyes narrowed. 'Then there will be a scandal. More scandal, because of *them*.'

At the time of the duel, tongues had already been wagging about the younger Dorman's affair with Will's mother. The duel set the scandalmongers on fire. It had taken until he was old enough to take his seat in the Lords for it all to die down enough for his mother to show her face during the London Season.

'I believe we can nip the scandal in the bud. Try not to dwell on it.' It all depended upon Lord Dorman's cooperation.

He lifted the covers and his mother crawled under them. 'I will not sleep a wink, knowing a Dorman is under my roof.'

Will placed a kiss upon her forehead and tucked her in like his nurse used to do for him when he was very young.

He blew out the candle and left the room, hearing her continue to grumble to herself about the Dormans.

Will understood that even knowing about this incident would have set his mother off. Any mention of the Dormans tended to do that. He'd never have mentioned it to her if only the Dormans had been reasonable, which, of course, they were not.

According to family lore, the Dormans had never been reasonable. The feud had existed for generations, beginning with that land dispute, land that abutted the Dormans' property at the Willburgh estate in Buckinghamshire. The land was potentially valuable, but, because of the dispute, it had gone undeveloped for over one hundred years. Before his father's death, Will had thought the dispute a frivolous one, surmising it only required some sort of compromise each side was too stubborn to propose. It was not the land but the death of his father for which Will could never forgive any Dorman. Even *the orphan*, as his mother had called her.

He'd heard that Lord Dorman had initiated another search for a clear deed to the land. Well, now Will would be damned if Dorman would procure rights to it. Will would contest it with all his might. He'd also heard that the Dorman finances were precarious, no doubt due to the excesses of each family member, Lucius especially.

The hypocrite. Lucius was quick to accuse his cousin of indiscretion when it was widely known Lucius spent a fortune on his latest lady-in-keeping—and the other women he saw behind her back.

But Will must damp down these feelings. He must approach the Dormans with a cool head.

He continued down the stairs in search of Bailey to again explain the events of this terrible night.

Chapter Three

Lucius Dorman arose much earlier than was his custom and dressed more quickly, having been summoned by his father *in no uncertain terms*. He entered the breakfast room where his parents were already seated, stern expressions on their faces.

'Good morning, Father. Mother,' he said, gauging that his expression should not be too cheerful.

'About time you got out of bed,' his father barked. 'I swear you'd sleep the day away if you could.'

His father was correct. He'd much rather sleep all day. The night was so much more interesting, but then, he was like his father in that respect. And his mother. But it might be prudent not to make that point at the moment.

'I rose as soon as I heard you needed me, as I would do any time.' Lucius chose a slice of bread and ham from the sideboard. After the evening's festivities, his stomach was not in its finest shape. He poured himself a cup of coffee, adding much cream and only one lump of sugar and settled himself across from his esteemed father and mother. Why they were in a pet was beyond him.

Unless it had to do with the utter betrayal of his cousin. Cavorting with Willburgh. The insult was unbearable.

The Meissen clock on the mantle ticked loudly as he waited for his father to speak.

The man finally roused himself. 'Do you realise what a bramble bush you've landed us in?'

'I?' Lucius was affronted. It was all Anna's doing as he saw it—if that was to what his father referred.

'You know that we need that girl,' his father said. 'You will have to marry her.'

Lucius straightened. 'I'll do no such thing! I'll not marry the leavings of *Viscount* Willburgh. You cannot ask it of me.'

'We will need her money,' his father responded.

Lucius countered. 'I'll marry someone else rich.'

His mother smiled patiently. 'You know you cannot attract an heiress. Your father's title is not so elevated. A wealthy merchant's daughter you might manage, perhaps, and if you find one of those before Anna is twenty-one, you will not have to marry her.' She glanced away thoughtfully. 'Of course, Anna has aristocratic blood and that is very important. And she is so eager to please, she would make an acceptable wife.'

Anna's mother was the daughter of an earl, although the title was now extinct. The family was anything but prolific. All gone now, with only Anna left. The family's considerable fortune was bequeathed to her alone but only if she did not marry until twenty-one, only a few weeks away. If she married before twenty-one, her fortune would go to any children she might bear and with the same restrictions.

Lucius's parents had always let it be known to him that he might need to marry her. He hadn't minded so much—until seeing her with Willburgh.

'You expect me to marry the chit after she's been with Willburgh?' Surely they would not ask that of him.

'It pleases me no more than it does you,' his father responded. 'But we are in dire straits. We must cajole her back to us. If we can find her, that is. I've sent two of the footmen to search for her. We will have to concoct some story to counteract the scandal.'

His mother groaned. 'I am certain tongues are wagging as we speak.'

'She'll come back to us,' his father mused, mostly to himself. 'She has nowhere else to go.'

And she knew nothing of the fortune that awaited her at age twenty-one if she remained unmarried. Lucius's father had kept that information from her so she would feel even more beholden to the family for taking her in. Keeping the secret of her inheritance kept the whip in his father's hand. Besides, the allowance the family trust provided her was a nice boon for the rest of the family. Anna knew nothing of that either.

Lucius and his parents often laughed about Anna being his bride. They joked that she was their secret gold mine, only to be fully mined when she came of age. Lucius had no doubt he could charm her into marriage. He flattered himself he could charm any woman. Besides, it was not like Anna would have any other choices.

Although how the devil had she come into Willburgh's sphere? He must have targeted her somehow. Lucius burned with rage just thinking of Willburgh with her.

Willburgh, his most detestable enemy, had been ahead of him in school, as well as being ahead of him in almost every other way. In contests of strength. In success in his studies. In cleverness and courage. Lucius, though, had always bested him with women. That was why Willburgh seduced Anna, Lucius was sure. To thumb his nose at Lucius.

The droning voices of his parents interrupted these thoughts.

'You must secure her hand, Lucius,' his father was saying. 'Grovel to her if you have to. Put on that charm of yours.'

Lucius would never grovel! Not for Willburgh's used goods.

'Are you heeding your father?' his mother asked.

Lucius glanced from his mother to his father. He'd play along with them for the time being. And if he had to marry Anna, he'd find ways to punish her for letting Willburgh have his way with her.

'I will do as you say,' he told them. 'As I always do.'

Anna did not sleep well, even though the bed was more comfortable than her bed at the Dormans' townhouse, and the nightdress Mrs White provided her was woven of cotton softer than any Anna owned. Even the room was larger than her bed chamber and was beautifully furnished.

A pleasant but obviously very curious maid came to help her dress. Anna had no idea what, if any, explanation of her presence would be given to the servants, so she said nothing. The maid addressed her as Miss Dorman, so the girl knew that much—that she came from the camp of the enemy. The maid was trained well enough that she did not ask any questions of Anna, except regarding what was necessary to help her dress, but, even with that constraint, the girl was chatty.

'Mrs White said I was to bring this day dress for you,' the maid said. 'It was Lady Willburgh's, but she never wore it, really. Said the colour washed her out.'

Anna was to wear a dress of the woman who caused her papa's death? That held little appeal. It was a print fabric, fawn with darker brown vines, leaves and flowers on it. How the woman chose such a fabric in the first place was a mystery, but, at least Anna would not have to wear that awful Red Riding Hood costume. The dress needed stitching here and there to fit her. Anna, apparently, was slimmer than Lady Willburgh. 'Less womanly,' Violet would have said.

Violet.

Last night Violet could have spoken up for her, but, typically, she didn't. Violet usually found ways to blame Anna for her own transgressions. No doubt last night Violet had engaged in an assignation precisely like the one for which Anna had been falsely accused.

The maid piled Anna's hair high atop her head and managed several curls to cascade down, a far cry from the simple chignon Anna usually wore. Somehow the beige and brown of the dress complimented her nondescript brown hair and seemed to emphasise her light brown eyes.

When she walked down the stairs to the first floor a footman greeted her. 'Good morning, miss. They are waiting for you in the breakfast room.'

He directed her to a sitting room at the back of the house and opened the door. Willburgh and his mother were seated at a table. Both looked up at her arrival.

Willburgh rose. 'Miss Dorman. I see Mrs White has found you something to wear. Come have some refreshment.' His tone was devoid of emotion, neither welcoming nor repelling. 'I trust you slept well.'

Of course she did not sleep well! 'The room was very comfortable.' She nodded respectfully towards Lady Willburgh. 'Thank you for the dress.'

The older woman harrumphed. 'I loathe that dress. You might as well keep it. I'll never wear it again.'

Because Anna wore it?

The butler she'd met the night before attended her. 'What may I serve you?'

Anna did not think her stomach was up for the kippers and cold meat on the sideboard. Or even the blackberry preserves or sweet cakes. 'Some bread and butter will do,' she said. 'Thank you.'

After the butler placed the bread and butter on her plate and poured her a cup of tea, he left the room.

When Anna lifted the cup to her lips, Willburgh spoke. 'I will call upon Lord Dorman this morning.'

Anna took a sip and placed the cup back in its saucer. 'I will accompany you.'

His brows knitted. 'That would not be wise. Best to leave it to me.'

She shook her head. 'This is about me. For me, and I will hear what is said of me.'

Tossing and turning all night did not exactly help her decide a specific course of action. She still did not know what she should do.

But deep inside her, she knew what she would not do.

Lady Willburgh's hand shook. 'The scandal will be terrible.'

'Terrible for me, certainly,' Anna responded.

'And for our family!' Lady Willburgh shot back. 'No respectable mother will allow her daughter anywhere near Will after this! And the *ton* will take great delight in the fact that he has compromised *you*.'

Because they were enemies.

Anna faced the woman. 'I presume your son told you the truth of what happened.'

Lady Willburgh waved her hand. 'The truth. The truth does not matter. Society will much prefer the fiction.'

'Mother,' her son admonished. 'This is not helpful. I will go to Lord Dorman and fix this.'

'And I will go with you,' Anna added.

Henrietta Street, where the Dormans' London townhouse was situated, was only a few blocks away, a tad less fashionable and a bit smaller, which meant nothing to Will, but probably rankled Lucius Dorman. Lucius had always made such comparisons, a part of the rivalry between them, Will supposed. Although before the duel, Will had never paid much mind to Lucius, especially at school. Lucius was a nuisance, nothing more. After Will's father was killed, though, Will could not help but despise all things Dorman, including Lucius. It was only then that he noticed Lucius's lack of character, his shirking of responsibility, the excesses of his vices—gambling, drinking, and whoring. Lack of loyalty, too. Lucius had been vicious to his cousin—a Dorman— when he should have been protecting her.

Or was Will merely resentful of Lucius's freedom? Not that Will ever wished to be as dissolute as Lucius. But, after his father's death, Will never had a day without responsibility, never possessed a chance to simply do whatever he wished.

Now he must call upon the Dormans. He'd rather swim in a cesspool than call upon them, but he must.

He ordered his curricle, even though it made more sense to walk the short distance. Riding in the curricle lessened the chance his society neighbours would see him escorting Miss Dorman to Henrietta Street. They would know what that meant.

Will did not want her company on this errand, though. Better he discuss the issue man to man with Lord Dorman, distasteful as that was. Although if they resolved the matter this morning, he could leave her there and have no more to do with the lot of them. That was one advantage he could see. The only one.

Mrs White had somehow found a proper bonnet for Miss Dorman and a paisley shawl that complemented the dress she wore. She'd even found Miss Dorman a reticule. Why the woman needed a reticule was a mystery to Will. She had nothing to carry in it.

As they approached the Dorman townhouse, Will spoke to her. 'I will direct the discussion with Lord Dorman. It is best you leave it to me.'

'I cannot do that.'

He gaped at her reply.

'I will speak for myself. I believe I am the best judge of what I need.'

It was just like a Dorman to counter him.

Will shrugged. 'As you wish, but it will be a mistake not to allow me to handle this.'

They reached the Dorman townhouse and his tiger, who had been riding on the back of the curricle, jumped down to hold the horses.

Miss Dorman faced Will. 'Do you expect me to trust you to have my best interests at heart? How can I trust any of you?'

She had a point, Will conceded, but only to himself. Will *was* trustworthy, though. It was a point of honour with him and it did not matter if you were enemy or friend, if he gave you his word, he would keep it. When countless people depend upon you, like all the people who depended upon the Viscount Willburgh for their livelihoods, their food, clothing, and shelter, it would be dishonourable not to be trustworthy.

Since she was a Dorman, of course, he wanted to have the last word. 'I am a man of my word.'

'As any dishonourable man might say,' she added.

So much for having the last word.

Will climbed down from the curricle and extended his hand to help Miss Dorman.

He called to his tiger, 'Toby, walk the horses if they need it. I am not certain how long we will be.'

Will and Miss Dorman approached the door. Will sounded the knocker.

A butler answered. His face broke into a relieved smile when he spied Miss Dorman. 'Miss Anna! You are safe! What wonderful news!' He glanced at Will and frowned. Recognised him, no doubt.

Will handed the man his hat and gloves. 'Announce us, please. I wish to speak with Lord Dorman.'

The butler sputtered, as if uncertain of what to do.

Anna stepped forwards. 'Announce us, Sedley. We will wait in the drawing room.'

'Yes, Miss Anna.' The butler bowed and headed for the breakfast room where she presumed Lord and Lady Dorman would still be, lingering over their tea.

She gestured for Willburgh to follow her up the stairs to the drawing room.

They entered the familiar room, which for some odd reason seemed foreign to her. 'You may sit, if you wish,' she told Willburgh, but neither of them did.

Anna walked to a window and peered out to where Willburgh's tiger held the horses. From behind her she could hear Willburgh drumming his fingers on some piece of furniture. Anna's insides twisted in anticipation. What would it feel like to be in their presence again? After the things they'd said to her the previous night. After they'd walked away leaving her at Vauxhall Gardens alone?

Except for the company of the enemy.

The Dormans did not keep them waiting. After only a few minutes Lord and Lady Dorman burst into the room, followed by Lucius.

'Anna! My dear child! You've come home!' Lady Dorman embraced her.

Anna stiffened. An embrace from Lady Dorman was the last thing she expected.

Uncle Dorman also came to her, taking one of her hands in his. 'Our prayers have been answered. You are here. We are much relieved. I sent all the footmen out to search for you. Was it one of them who found you?'

'No one found her. We came on our own,' Willburgh said.

Her uncle ignored him and kept hold of her hand. 'I think we went a bit mad last night. Were we not, Lucius?' He turned to his son.

'Indeed,' Lucius replied, although his voice was dry.

What game were they playing? Acting so glad to see her? Their words from the night before echoed in her ears. She believed in their rejection, not their welcome.

She pulled her hand away.

Dorman patted her on the shoulder. 'We will not speak again of your little indiscretion, my dear. Fear not.' He glared at Will. 'We know who is to blame.'

Willburgh stood impressively tall and strong as he faced Lord Dorman. 'You have no idea who is to blame, sir, as you refused to hear us. The only indiscretion was your own, sir, to unfairly accuse your niece. You will hear us now—'

Dorman waved his hand dismissively. 'Whose ever fault it was matters not, I assure you. The important thing is that our dear Anna is in the bosom of our family again.'

'You gave us such a fright!' added Lady Dorman.

'So you left her all alone at Vauxhall?' Will protested.

'Not alone, my dear fellow,' Lucius drawled. 'She was in *your* company.' He turned to Anna. 'I suppose you spent the night with him, Anna.'

Anna had heard rumours of Lucius's conquests of women— actresses and the like. How dare he accuse her of loose morals!

'She spent the night at my townhouse,' Willburgh answered Lucius. 'With my mother in residence.'

Anna's anger rose. Lord and Lady Dorman and Lucius offered no apology. No acceptance of their responsibility in the event.

'You gave her no other choice.' Willburgh sounded angry, now, as angry as she felt.

Lady Dorman put her arm around Anna. 'Come sit, my dear. I've ordered some tea.'

Her touch felt revolting. Anna pulled away. 'I prefer to stand.'

'Then come with me to your room,' the woman persisted. 'I am certain you are eager to change that atrocious dress. I suppose it was one of Honoria's.' This last was said in a disdainful tone.

Anna supposed Honoria was Will's mother.

'I will stay here until this is sorted out, ma'am,' Anna retorted.

'Here. Here,' Lord Dorman broke in. 'There is nothing to sort out. You are home. That is all that matters.'

She swung around to face him. 'Home? Home?' Her eyes flashed. 'The place I am no longer welcome? That was what you said last night, was it not, sir?'

The man's expression turned ingratiating. 'Now, now. You know I did not mean it. Heat of the moment and all that.'

'You called me a trollop.' Anna, her temper lost, turned towards Lady Dorman. 'You accused me of having an assignation with this gentleman.'

'But you did have an assignation!' cried Lady Dorman.

Ever since Willburgh's father killed her papa, Anna knew her welcome at the Dormans' was on thin ice. She coped by being of service in any way they required. She always knew they valued her only because she was useful as Violet's companion, someone they could trust to behave in a moral and upright manner and who could try to make Violet behave so.

It took nothing at all, though, for them to think the worst of her.

Violet appeared at the door. 'What is all this talking? You woke me up.'

Anna strode over to her. Violet could have defended her the night before. She knew Anna was not sneaking off to bed Lord Willburgh. 'And you, Violet. You said I'd run off when you of all people knew I'd done no such thing.'

Violet, still in her dressing gown, looked at her haughtily. 'But you did run off, Anna.'

Lucius broke into this confrontation, his voice placating. 'Anna, it makes no difference to us if you ran off or if you were enticed away.' He tossed a scathing look at Willburgh. 'You know how fond we all are of you. This family cannot do without you. It was merely who you chose to be private with that shocked and surprised us so. You cannot put yourself in a compromising position with a Willburgh and expect us not to lose our senses. But we forgive you. We care about you so very much that we do forgive you.'

'You gave us such a turn!' cried his mother.

Lord Dorman readily agreed. 'That is so.'

Violet Dorman rolled her eyes.

Anna was appalled. Not one apology. From any of them. Not one acknowledgement of the wrong they'd done her.

Violet's gaze swept over her parents and brother. 'Have you all become beetle-headed? She's been with *him*.' She pointed to Willburgh. 'You disowned her for good reason.'

Lucius took Violet's arm and led her a few steps away. 'We have welcomed her back *for good reason*,' he said, enunciating each word.

But Anna could not fathom what that reason might be,

especially after all the horrid things they'd said to her the night before. It did not matter, though. Nothing would entice her to spend another day under their roof.

She drew an audible breath. 'Enough. I am done with this. I came to pack my belongings and leave. Please have a trunk brought to my room immediately.'

'Pack your belongings?' cried Lady Dorman. 'You are leaving?'

'Come now,' Lucius cajoled. 'Where will you go?'

Violet laughed dryly. 'Do not be a dunderhead. She's going with *him*.'

'You are correct, Violet,' If they persisted in believing the worst of her, Anna would not disappoint them. 'I *am* going with Lord Willburgh. You stated it all so publicly last night, right near the Turkish Tent in Vauxhall Gardens. Loud enough for everyone to hear. You said that I have been compromised with Viscount Willburgh. What other choice do I have?' She walked up to Willburgh and threaded her arm through his. 'What must a compromised lady do? I must marry him.'

Chapter Four

Will stiffened in shock. What the devil? Who said anything about marrying? She was the last woman in existence he would ever marry.

The Dormans reacted more loudly. Shouts of 'No!' and 'You must never!' and 'Traitor!' and 'Turncoat!' sounded in his ears.

This was not what Will had expected. He'd expected to see Lord Dorman alone. He'd expected Lord Dorman would listen to the account of what really happened, then the man would apologise to his niece and agree to her return. Once that was done Will expected they would discuss how to minimise the scandal they'd created.

He should have known the Dormans would muddle up everything.

In a guise of being reasonable, they'd persisted in blaming her. They still had not allowed Will to tell them what really happened. Instead they'd thought the worst and refused to acknowledge that they left that young woman at Vauxhall Gardens, alone and friendless.

Except for himself, that was. He was no friend, though. It was only because he was a man of honour that he'd not deserted her, as well.

This was how she thanked him? By threatening to marry him?

Well, he would see about that.

'You ungrateful wretch!' cried Lady Dorman. 'After all we have done for you, you betray us this way? Marrying a Willburgh? You could do nothing worse!'

Will agreed. There could be nothing worse than a Willburgh marrying a Dorman.

Miss Dorman stood firm. 'The trunk to my room, please.'

Lord Dorman's face turned bright red and his hands were curled into fists. 'I will not allow you to dishonour our family in this manner. You will not marry him.'

Lucius scowled, but his expression suddenly brightened. 'Father. You can stop her. She is your ward. She cannot marry without your permission.'

Lord Dorman brightened. 'That is right. My permission.' He glared at his niece. 'I will never give my permission. You will never marry this Willburgh.'

Good. That much was settled.

She shot back. 'Then we will elope.'

No! Will cried silently.

'No!' Lord Dorman shouted. 'I'll keep you prisoner here. I won't let you out. I swear I won't.'

This was getting way out of hand.

Will held up a quelling hand. 'Lord Dorman, you will not keep her prisoner. That will make more trouble for yourself than you can imagine. Just have the trunk brought to her room so she can pack her things and leave.'

Will supposed he would have to take her back to his townhouse and after that he did not know what he would do with her.

Amidst protests from the others, Lord Dorman summoned the butler and made the arrangement.

Will walked at Miss Dorman's side up the stairs. He was angry with her—angrier at the rest of the Dormans—but definitely angry at her.

'Don't get in a lather, Willburgh,' she whispered.

What did she expect of him? To be happy?

Marriage was indeed the usual solution when a gentleman compromised a lady. If the gentleman did not marry the lady, the lady would be ruined. Not much happened to the gentleman in such a case, though. But he and Miss Dorman could not marry. They despised each other.

They entered a small bed chamber, little more than a closet. Miss Dorman retrieved a key from a hiding place and unlocked a drawer in the dressing table.

She took out a small box. 'My mother's pearls and locket.' She slipped the box in the reticule.

A servant brought in a very small trunk and a maid came to help Miss Dorman pack a few dresses and other necessary items. She left a good deal behind.

'What about the other dresses?' The maid lifted a ball gown, the same one Will had admired her in weeks ago. Before he'd learned who she was.

'I do not want them, Mary,' Miss Dorman said.

The girl set it aside. 'But you've only four dresses!'

'They will be enough.' Miss Dorman looked around the room. 'I think we are done.' She turned to Will. 'What shall I say to do with the trunk?'

This was her plan; she should know, he thought, but said, 'It should fit on the curricle. We may need ropes to secure it.'

She turned to the maid again. 'Will you get one of the footmen to carry it down to the curricle and get ropes, if needed?'

'Yes, miss.' The maid curtsied and started for the door. Before she reached it, she spun around and rushed back to Miss Dorman, giving her a heartfelt hug. 'I will miss you, Miss Anna,' the maid cried. 'I do not know what it will be like without you!'

'Oh, Mary!' She returned the hug. 'I will miss you, too. You have been such a treasure.'

The girl rushed out of the room.

Miss Dorman gave the room one more look. 'I am ready.'

Will let her pass through the doorway ahead of him. 'Did you foresee all this?' he asked. It seemed well thought out.

She shook her head. 'No, but I knew I could never return. Anything would be better.'

Even marrying him, he supposed. But that would never do. Every day the mere sight of her would remind him that her father killed his father.

They walked down the stairs together. The Dormans appeared in the hall and yelled curses at them until they were out the door.

Will stood with her on the pavement as the footman and his tiger fastened the trunk on the back of the curricle.

'I will not marry you,' Will said through gritted teeth.

She responded without facing him. 'And I will not marry you.'

Now he was truly puzzled. 'Then why announce that you would—we would? To *them*?'

She smiled. 'Petty revenge, I'm afraid. Me, marrying you. Lord Willburgh. The enemy. They will be at sixes and sevens for days.'

Will could not help returning a smile. 'Well, it serves them right. If they'd had an ounce of sense, they would have listened to us and kept the whole matter quiet. We could have gone on as before.'

'I could never have gone on as before,' she said.

The trunk was secured and Will helped Miss Dorman into the curricle.

He called down to his tiger, 'I am driving back to Park

Street. Not a far walk for you.' There was no room for the tiger to ride with them.

'I expect I will arrive there before you, sir,' the tiger, a small but spry man in his forties, responded. He set off on foot. Will signalled the horses to start moving.

'You are taking me back to your townhouse?' She sounded surprised.

'Until we can figure out what to do next.' Of which he had no idea.

'Take me to a jeweller,' she insisted. 'Or somewhere I might sell my mother's pearls and locket. So I have funds to find a room to let somewhere.'

'A room to let?' What the devil was she talking about now.

She stared ahead. 'I need money. My jewellery will give me funds until I can secure some sort of employment.'

Employment? What sort of employment could she find? Impoverished ladies might become a lady's companion or a governess, but this whole Vauxhall Gardens event was certain to cause talk. Who would recommend her? Who would hire her?

He blew out a breath. 'You do not have to sell your jewels.' She seemed to have pitifully few of them. 'I will give you whatever funds you need.'

She turned to him. 'I am not asking you to do that.'

He turned onto Duke Street. 'Believe me. The money is of no consequence to me.'

As a youth he'd had little regard for money. There always seemed to be an abundance of it, always more than he needed. After his father was killed, though, he'd learned that finances were not that simple. He'd managed to preserve his father's wealth and to build upon it, but the lessons he'd been forced to learn so quickly took their toll. At least he could honestly say that supporting her would indeed be of no consequence to him.

There was more traffic on the streets than when they'd left for the Dormans', men on horses, people in carriages, people walking on the pavement. Mayfair was too much like the village back in Buckinghamshire. Small enough that everyone knew everyone else, and they all could see that Lord Willburgh drove Miss Dorman in his curricle.

When they pulled up to Will's townhouse, he noticed the neighbour's curtains move. No doubt it would be noticed that he brought her to his house, trunk and all. Toby, his tiger, was indeed waiting to take the horses and as Will alighted, two footmen came out to get the trunk.

Will helped her down and they hurried into the house.

His mother was in the hall waving a newspaper in her hands. 'Did you see this? Did you see this? It is in the newspapers!'

He ought to have guessed. Spreading the tale word of mouth was not enough. 'Well, let us go to the drawing room.' The butler was attending the hall. 'Bring some tea, Bailey.'

'We are ruined!' his mother wailed. 'What are we to do?'

He was not about to discuss it on the stairs.

They entered the drawing room.

Having just been in the Dormans' drawing room, Will could not help but note the contrast. He'd resisted his mother's desire to remodel the principal rooms of the townhouse. This room remained much like it had been when he was a youth—before his father died—serene with its pale green walls, plasterwork and striped upholstery. The Dormans' drawing room was all that was new in garish shades of red, gold, and blue.

Will needed this serenity today.

'Mother. Miss Dorman. Please sit.' He gestured to the

chairs and sofas. 'I cannot bear all of us pacing the room.' Like they had at the Dormans'.

Miss Dorman chose an armchair. His mother perched on the edge of an adjacent sofa, as far away from the young woman as possible. Will chose the sofa opposite his mother, placing himself in between.

'Here.' His mother shoved the newspaper into his hands. 'Read it.'

It took him some time to find it.

At Vauxhall Gardens last night, Miss D— was caught by her guardian, Lord D and his son, in a private as-signation with their sworn enemy Lord W—. A loud altercation ensued, Lord D— leaving his ward with W—, disowning her.

That left nothing out.

But the truth.

'May I see it?' Miss Dorman extended her hand.

He handed the paper to her, pointing to where the words were on the page.

She handed it back to him.

His mother glared at her. 'This is all your fault! I cannot bear it.'

'Leave it, Mother.' He put his head in his hands.

He did not know what to do. What solution was a good one?

Miss Dorman spoke. 'I'll accept your offer of money. I will move away.'

'Oh, that will be lovely,' his mother said scathingly. 'Then everyone will say you disappeared because Will got you with child.'

'Then I won't move away,' she countered. 'We can pre-tend to be betrothed and after several months, I'll cry off.'

Society said a woman could break an engagement to be married, but if a man did so it would be considered a breach of promise.

Will brightened. 'That might work. My reputation might suffer a little, but the *ton* will get over it.' A man with a title and money rarely stayed outside the *ton*'s good graces for long.

Of course. *His* reputation might survive, but what about hers? With scandal, no funds, and no family to back her, what prospects would her future hold? She'd indeed be ruined.

He wished he hadn't realised this.

'It is not you whose reputation concerns me the most!' his mother wailed. 'No match you make will ever be as good as it would be without this scandal, but you will recover. A man always recovers. It is your sister I am worried about.'

His sister, Ellen, was sixteen, on the cusp of being presented to society and entering the marriage mart.

His mother's voice rose. 'She already suffers from the scandal your father created—this will put her beyond the pale. How will she ever make a good match now?'

He might remind his mother that it was her affair with Miss Dorman's father that started the whole thing. True, she'd only wanted to get his father's attention by inviting Dorman's addresses. Indeed, his father had noticed and the result was disastrous.

Bailey, the butler, appeared at the door with the tea service and a plate of biscuits. He set them on the table, then quietly spoke to Will. 'May I see you outside for a moment, m'lord?'

'Certainly.' Will rose, asking leave of his mother and Miss Dorman. He stepped outside the room. 'What is it?'

His butler pulled a piece of paper from his pocket and handed it to Will. 'One of the footmen discovered this handbill being sold.'

Will skimmed the paper. It was a scandal sheet showing a drawing of two people, looking vaguely like him and Miss Dorman, *in flagrante* and a very embellished account of what happened at Vauxhall Gardens.

'It was selling quite well, I am afraid,' Bailey said.

'Deuce.' It had taken no time at all for someone to profit from the event. Will inclined his head towards the door. 'I'll have to tell them before someone else does.'

He re-entered the drawing room.

'More bad news, I fear.' He showed them the scandal sheet.

His mother dropped her head into her hands. 'We will never recover from this! This is the end of all for us.'

Will walked over to the window and looked out. He knew what he must do. The clarity of it struck him like a blow to the chest. He ought to have known it from the moment he opened the door to Lucius and Lord Dorman at Vauxhall Gardens. Will must do what any gentleman of honour would do to salvage his reputation and the reputation of the lady. Miss Dorman herself had hit upon it. Only one way society would forgive this imagined transgression.

Will turned to Miss Dorman. 'We must marry.'

'No!' Anna shot up from her chair. She would not marry him. She would not! 'Just tell me where I might sell my jewellery. I'll find a room to let and trouble you no more.'

Was it her impulsive threat to marry Willburgh at her uncle's house that gave him this idea? That she was willing to marry him? She would never do so. She'd despised him for ten years, even without knowing him. If only she'd never met him!

If she had not met him, though, what would have happened to her at the hands of that vile creature at Vauxhall Gardens?

'Do not be foolish,' Willburgh said. 'Money from two pieces of jewellery will never be sufficient. You'll say you'll find employment. What employment? Who would employ you? You have no one to recommend you. Even a servant needs references.'

His words rang true, but she did not want to heed them. She lifted her chin. 'I will find something.'

He stood toe-to-toe with her, glaring into her face. 'Do you know the sort of employment left to a single woman of no means and no references? Such women walk the streets at night.'

Violet's governess had told them stories about street-walkers, women reduced to selling their bodies in order to survive. These were meant as cautionary tales of what can happen if a young lady does not protect her virtue.

But Anna had done nothing unvirtuous.

'Then pay to support me,' she snapped. 'You said the money would be of no consequence!'

'It would not be—' he began.

His mother interrupted. 'No, Will! You mustn't. Having her in your keeping will only cause more talk. Consider your sister...'

His face stiffened in pain. With his back to his mother, he spoke only to Anna. 'My sister. Ellen is sixteen. An innocent. Most of her life has been tainted by scandal. My mother is right. This does not affect only you and me. I must consider her.'

Anna knew of Ellen Willburgh, but never gave the girl a moment's thought. But she remembered herself at sixteen. So worried for what the future might bring. Could her ha-

tred of the Willburghs extend to this innocent girl? Anna
remembered the scandal the duel caused.

She could imagine ladies of the *ton* whispering together
of how Willburgh had to send away that poor ward of Lord
Dorman's, how it must mean there was a baby. After her
papa was killed she'd overheard ladies whispering about him.
She remembered suddenly that they'd speculated about her,
too—and her mother. She'd made certain, then, to always
behave with complete decorum.

Even so, the sins of one member of a family always tainted
the whole family.

Anna raised her gaze, looked into Willburgh's face, and
spoke in a pained voice. 'I do not want to marry you.'

'I do not want to marry you either.' His voice reflected hers.

'Must we elope?' she asked.

'Without your uncle's permission, it is the only way,' he
responded.

Chapter Five

They set off the next day in a post-chaise.

The decision to hire a post-chaise rather than take one of Willburgh's own carriages had been a topic of much debate, mostly with his mother—Anna's opinion was not sought, not that she had one in this particular matter, except that she'd rather not go at all.

His mother prevailed.

'Good gracious,' she had exclaimed. 'Is there not enough gossip? Someone is bound to recognise the crest on your carriage. They will know you are going to Gretna Green and soon it will be in papers all over the country.'

Anna doubted that much interest in them existed.

In any event, Willburgh, Anna's future husband, opted for the post-chaise. To make the changes at coaching inns as simple as possible, they each brought luggage small enough to carry by hand. Anna's portmanteau was reluctantly lent to her by Lady Willburgh and contained one change of clothing. Toby, the tiger who'd ridden with them to Henrietta Street two days ago, was the only servant to come with them. He rode on the outside of the chaise.

The fastest route apparently was the mail route. Mail coaches with their ability to travel day and night could make the trip in three days. Anna and Willburgh did not require that level of speed, however. It would take them seven days.

The longer the better, thought Anna. More time meant more of a chance to come up with a different way out of this predicament.

They had little conversation as the streets of London opened into country scenes and glimpses of small villages. Anna could not simply gaze at the fields and hedgerows they passed and pretend Willburgh was not with her, though. He sat next to her on the one seat and Anna could not ignore how tall and broad-shouldered he was. Every bump in the road pressed his body against hers. His long legs knocked into hers. His warmth and strength had its effect on her. When had she ever been so close to a man and for so long a time? And such a man. The sort who would turn heads wherever he went.

Except for short breaks to change teams and one longer one for a midday meal, Anna spent eight hours enveloped by Willburgh's presence, yet raging against being forced to marry him. It was exhausting and unsettling.

When dusk fell, they pulled into a red brick, thatched roof inn with a sign posted of a fox and hound.

'Where are we?' Anna asked.

'Northampton,' Willburgh responded tersely. 'We'll spend the night.'

An ostler opened the door of the chaise and Willburgh disembarked first. He turned and offered Anna his hand to assist her.

Her legs were stiff and aching from sitting, but she managed to descend from the chaise. Toby spoke to the stable workers then followed them carrying their luggage.

'Remember who you are,' Willburgh whispered to her as they entered the inn.

He had decided they should travel under false names to protect them from more gossip should the handbills and newspapers have reached this far.

'Welcome,' the innkeeper greeted them.

'I am Mr Fisher,' Willburgh announced. 'I would like two rooms. One for me and one for my sister. And accommodations for my coachman.'

The innkeeper's brows rose at the word *sister* and his mouth twitched. 'Very good, Mr Fisher. We can accommodate you and your *sister*.' The man cast a meaningful look at Anna. 'And your coachman.'

She managed to appear composed, pretending she hadn't noticed. It was discomfiting, to say the least.

Willburgh signed the register. 'May we arrange a private room for dining as well?'

'It will be done, sir,' the innkeeper said.

'We will freshen up and desire our meal in one hour. Will that be possible?'

Anna thought Willburgh sounded every bit a viscount in his imposing tone. The innkeeper had already tagged her as not being a sister; the man likely figured out Willburgh was not a mere mister.

'It will indeed, sir,' the innkeeper said. 'I will show you to your rooms directly. Do you need servants to attend you?'

Willburgh turned to Anna. 'You will likely desire a maid to assist you at bedtime. Do you want assistance now?'

'No,' she replied. 'I will manage.'

The innkeeper gave them rooms right next to each other. Toby carried their luggage to the rooms and excused himself, assuring Willburgh all would be ready in the morning to continue their trip.

Anna luxuriated in the sensation of being entirely alone, away from Willburgh—except she could hear him moving around in the other room. She sighed and walked over to the basin to wash her hands and face and ready herself for dinner.

Will paced his room trying to release the pent-up tension of being cooped up in the chaise for long spells of time. And sitting next to Miss Dorman.

He was well aware of crowding her, though she did not complain and did not try to shirk away. Her scent filled his nostrils, and it was impossible to miss the loveliness of her profile, the soft femininity of her figure, especially when his body was jostled against hers. His senses were filled with her. How was he to endure a week of this close proximity?

A lifetime.

He shook off that thought. It did no good to think about marrying her. He'd learned after his father's death that it was best to think about the next task in front of him. The enormity of the whole picture always froze him in place.

He washed his face and hands and shaved the stubble off his chin, brushed off his clothes and waited until an hour had passed, then left his room to knock on her door.

'I am ready,' she said.

They ate a typical coaching inn meal of mutton stew and bread and drank ale instead of wine. Perhaps after she retired for the night Will would come down to the public rooms and have something stronger. They hardly spoke.

They'd hardly spoken to each other all day. What was there to say, after all? They both knew they did not want to marry.

But Will forced that thought away. Handle the next task. Only the next task.

He escorted her back to her room after dinner. A maid awaited her there to attend her.

At her door, he said, 'We'll leave early in the morning.

Breakfast at seven. Order a maid to wake you early and help you dress.'

'As you wish,' she responded.

As soon as her door closed Will returned to the public room and ordered a glass of whisky. And a second.

The next day of travel was much like the first. Passing towns and villages. Stopping to change teams. Enduring the close quarters and desolate silences. As the sun dipped lower in the sky, they entered a town larger than the ones they'd passed through.

Will broke the silence. 'We'll stay the night here.'

'What town is this?' Miss Dorman looked out the window with some interest instead of blankly staring at nothing in particular.

'Loughborough,' he responded.

'Loughborough?' Her interest seemed to increase. 'The Loughborough where the Luddites attacked the lace factory?'

'Yes.' He was impressed that she'd heard of it. As a member of the House of Lords Will had been completely informed. 'The attackers came from Nottingham, not from Loughborough. They attacked the watchmen, destroyed fifty-five frames, and burned the lace.'

Their chaise passed by a three-storey building with the name *Heathcoat and Boden* on it. The building looked empty and neglected.

'That is the lace factory, I suppose.' Miss Dorman gestured to the building, an imposing structure made of the same red brick as their inn the previous night. She added, 'I do not know to whom I should owe sympathy. The owners and workers in the factory or the men whose livelihoods disappeared because of the machines.'

'There was a great deal of suffering on both sides,' Will agreed.

They stopped at the Old Bull Inn and their evening was much like the previous one, although their discussion of the Luddite attack and the economic hardships that spawned it gave them conversation across the dinner table. Miss Dorman asked many questions and seemed interested in hearing how the Lords had discussed the situation. They debated the suspension of the Habeas Corpus Act which allowed persons to be imprisoned without bail, in Will's view the most important issue of the day.

The third day brought them into Nottingham and led to conversations about Robin Hood and debate about stealing from the rich to give to the poor and whether there had indeed been a Robin Hood or had he been a fictitious legend.

In addition to being almost irresistibly alluring, Miss Dorman was also an intelligent woman of good education and thoughtful opinions. Many of the young women thrown in his path to court had little to say of substance at all. Miss Dorman told him she, along with her cousin Violet, had been given typical lessons in proper behaviour, stitchery, piano, and other feminine skills. She also loved to read and had been permitted to read whatever was in Lord Dorman's library.

As long as she was in no one's way.

When Will settled down to sleep that night, he allowed himself to be a tiny bit hopeful about marrying her. Perhaps there could be something more between them than the grievances of the past.

Will had just fallen asleep when a knock on the door awakened him. It was Toby, looking alarmed.

He gestured for the man to come in. 'What is it, Toby?'

'Sir.' His tiger was out of breath. 'I was in the public

rooms having a pint when three men came in, asking the innkeeper and others if there was a Lord Willburgh staying here. I believe it was young Mr Dorman, sir. And a fellow he called Raskin and another fellow.' He swallowed. 'I lay low in case they'd recognise me, but they wouldn't. That sort don't take notice of men like me. Any road, I decided I'd better tell you right away.'

Lucius. Looking for him. Planning to thwart their elopement, Will was certain. He was glad he'd used a different name, but they'd figure out who Will and Miss Dorman were quickly enough. Dorman had obviously guessed that they would head to Gretna Green using the quickest route, the mail route.

Will would be damned if he'd allow Lucius to stop him.

He paced the room, thinking, then stopped and turned to his groom. 'Here's what we will do, Toby.'

The knock on Anna's door woke her. It took a moment for her to remember where she was. And why.

She went to the door. 'Who is it?'

'It's Will. I need to talk to you.' He used the name his mother called him. Will. He'd never done that before.

'One moment.' She hadn't packed a robe but did have a shawl, so she wrapped that around her, almost covering all of her shift, which she wore to sleep in so as not to pack a nightdress. She opened the door.

He was dressed more like his groom than a viscount. Before she could ask why, he burst into the room and shoved a dress at her. 'Put this on. We have to leave now.'

How dare he order her like that. 'Leave? What time is it?'

'I do not know,' he answered. 'Five, perhaps. Heed me. Lucius is here, staying in this inn. And Raskin and some other fellow. My groom heard them asking for us.'

Anna felt the blood drain from her face. 'Lucius? Why would he?'

'It foxes me,' Willburgh replied. 'To stop us, can be the only reason. We have to leave. Are you able to dress yourself?'

Would Lucius truly want to stop her? Why? After the things he said to her—that all the Dormans said to her—why were they not glad she was gone?

'I am able to dress myself,' she responded. 'But why this dress?' The dress was plain, like a maid's dress.

'Toby has hired a man and woman to impersonate us. One of the ostlers agreed to do it. With his wife. This is her dress. They will dress in our clothes, carry our luggage, and ride in our post-chaise. Toby will go with them. With any luck Lucius will believe they are us.' He shoved a cap into her hands. 'Wear this, too.'

'But I need things from my portmanteau,' she protested.

'We'll purchase whatever we need. It is a market day, I'm told, so all we need should be available.' He made it sound so easy. 'Hurry. I'll wait outside your door.'

Good thing she'd left anything she cared about in London at Willburgh's townhouse.

Anna dressed as quickly as she could. Fixed her hair in a simple chignon, covered it with the cap, and opened the door.

He gestured her to come with him. They walked quietly down the hallway and the stairs and out into the yard. Willburgh's groom was waiting for them. He and Willburgh spoke again about the arrangements and the groom directed them to the market square.

As they set off, the sun was sending its first rays into the new day. Even though it was June there was a breeze that chilled the air. The market was not open, of course but they found a place to sit out of the wind. They sat on the stone pavement which sent cold right through Anna's clothes.

She shivered. 'The first item I wish to buy is a shawl.'

Willburgh gazed at her. 'You are cold.' He changed positions. 'Here. Come sit in front of me. I'll warm you.'

He sat cross-legged so that she wound up sitting on his legs instead of the cold stone. He leaned her back against him and put his arms around her.

His body did indeed warm her, but also sent a strange thrill throughout. Her cheeks flamed. It was scandalous for him to hold her like this, but since they were dressed as they were, the few people who arrived to set out their wares paid them no heed. When the food booths opened Willburgh bought them loaves of brown bread and hot salop, a sweetened sassafras tea.

'I've never tasted such things,' Anna remarked. 'They are lovely.'

Willburgh smiled, which only made his handsome face more handsome. 'I am glad.'

By the time they'd finished eating and returned the wooden bowls to the vendor, more and more booths were filling with wares. They wandered through them until discovering one selling shawls. Some were beautiful paisley shawls worthy of a Bond Street shop, but Anna chose a plain woollen one in a brown shade not unlike the dress Lady Willburgh had lent her.

Had that only been three days ago?

'Good choice.' Willburgh nodded.

'The plan is to not be noticed, correct?' she responded.

'You have grasped it.'

Surprisingly, his approval pleased her.

Next they purchased two portmanteaux, one for each of them and spent another hour or more finding toiletries and used clothing. In the end they looked very much like a labourer and his wife and nothing like Viscount Willburgh and the lady he was to marry.

They sought respite in The Bell Inn, right on Market Square.

'What now?' Anna asked as they sat drinking tea and eating pasties. 'How do we proceed?'

'That is what I am turning over in my mind.' He pulled out a map and a copy of *Cary's Coach Directory*, two items he'd just purchased. He laid the map on the table. 'We should not follow the mail route, that is certain.'

Using the mail route must have been how Lucius almost found them.

'We'll stay east.' He pointed to the map. 'It will take longer, but we can avoid Lucius and his companions that way.' He looked up. 'There was a third man with Lucius and Raskin. I wonder who he was.'

She curled her hand into a fist. 'A—a companion of Raskin's abducted me. Could he be the third man?'

He blinked in surprise. 'I assumed that man had been a stranger. He was someone Raskin knew?'

'I was not given his name.' Her heart pounded with the memory. 'I do not think I was supposed to.'

'Lucius knew him as well?' His voice deepened.

'I cannot say.' She glanced away. 'I would hate to think Lucius would…'

But she feared both he and Violet had set her up. Perhaps without knowing what the man would do or perhaps it was their idea of a joke. Lucius did seem to know precisely where to find her after the rain.

What horrible men they all were. So unlike this man whom she'd called her enemy. Even though he despised her, he'd protected her. And was doing so still.

She met Willburgh's gaze again and held it.

Chapter Six

Will's anger flamed. He'd half a mind to seek out Lucius and show the man precisely what he thought of him. With bare fists, preferably. The lady seated across from him surely did not deserve such treatment.

She was proving more game than he'd anticipated. Uttering not one word of complaint the entire trip, even through this morning's trials. Not a word about wearing plain clothes, nor of giving up her own dresses. He knew she could not be happy about any of this.

He needed to get back to the task.

'How we should travel, I cannot decide,' he said, breaking the silence that followed talk of Lucius. 'Whether to hire another post-chaise, or take the stage coach, or even purchase a vehicle and horse.'

Her brows rose. 'You have enough funds with you to purchase a vehicle and horse?'

He cocked his head. 'I might arrange it.'

At that moment a youth approached their table. Will glanced up at him.

'Are you Mr Fisher, guv'nor?' The boy could not have been more than fourteen.

Willburgh looked at him suspiciously. 'Who asks, if you please?'

If Willburgh wished to portray a labourer, he sounded precisely like a viscount.

'Name's John.' The boy gave a little bow. 'I am to tell you that the gentlemen have gone.'

Willburgh nodded, but still looked askance. 'And why did you think I was Mr Fisher?'

The boy pointed to the hat Willburgh had placed on the chair next to him. 'M'brother's hat. M'brother's the one you hired to be you and his wife to be your wife.'

Miss Dorman winced when the boy called her Will's wife.

The boy went on. 'Yer groom paid me to find you after he left with m'brother and the gentlemen left soon after.'

Willburgh relaxed. 'Thank you, John.' He reached in a pocket and pulled out a coin to hand to the boy.

The youth took it and wrapped his fist around it. 'If you do not mind me asking, sir, if you have any other work to be done? I'm good around horses and I'm clever in a pinch, if you get my meaning.'

Willburgh stared at him, obviously thinking.

Finally he said, 'I have need of a groom to accompany us the rest of the way to Scotland.'

The boy hopped from one foot to the other. 'I am your man, sir. I can be a groom. I've been around horses all m'life. M'father was an ostler. And m'brother.'

Willburgh gestured to a chair. 'Sit, John, and hear what I have in mind.'

The boy sat. Willburgh called to the servant to bring the boy some tea and a pasty, which the servant brought right away.

When the servant was out of earshot, Willburgh said, 'I wish to hire another post-chaise, but to take a different route to Scotland. I do not want those gentlemen to know where we are or where we are heading. They must not find us.'

'Do not worry, guv,' the boy said after biting into the pasty. 'M'brother will fool them.'

'Can you assist in hiring the post-chaise? Or any available vehicle?' Willburgh asked.

'Yes, sir,' the boy replied, his mouth full. 'But if you do not mind me saying, you are not dressed like riders of a post-chaise usually are dressed.'

'Because labourers would not hire a carriage like that,' Miss Dorman broke in. 'We will have to dress more prosperously.'

So she and Will returned to Market Square and the clothes dealers and found clothes that were not too rich, nor too poor. John, Will's new groom, went to talk to the head ostler at The Bell Inn, to hire a carriage for them.

By noon Anna and Willburgh were riding in another post-chaise with their luggage secured and Willburgh's new groom, John, on the outside. The forests made so famous in the Robin Hood legends gave way to rolling countryside with stone fences and sheep grazing. They also glimpsed tall chimneys of smelt mills and spied mining villages.

The seat to this carriage was more spacious so Anna did not have to sit with Willburgh's body touching hers, except when the road caused the carriage to ram them together. Perhaps she was getting used to it, because it did not bother her as much as before.

They had more conversation than before, as well, conferring on the route they were taking, commenting on what they saw outside the carriage window. By sitting in the Lords, Willburgh knew things, such as the state of the mining industry, the challenges to farming, the hardship the war had caused some of these villages, the fomenting of unrest in the country. Anna liked learning of such things.

At dusk they entered Sheffield, a town unlike any Anna had seen before, dirty, grimy, its streets ill paved. It was a town full of industry, known for making cutlery, the place silver plate was created, a lead mill, a cotton mill. Smoke. Poverty.

And yet they passed by a beautiful church with a tall spire.

Willburgh seemed as aghast at the conditions as Anna was.

'I will remember this town,' he murmured, although she did not think he was speaking to her.

The chaise pulled into the King's Head Inn and ostlers jumped to tend to them. John carried their luggage like a proper groom, although he did not have the livery. Anna thought that befitted the roles they were playing—shopkeepers, if anyone asked.

They entered the inn and met the innkeeper who asked their name.

'Oldham,' Willburgh said.

'Mr and Mrs Oldham,' repeated the innkeeper handing the register to Willburgh.

Anna waited until they were standing in the room and John and the innkeeper had left. 'You put us in the same room!'

He faced her. 'It is best.'

'It is not best for me!' she scoffed. 'We are not married yet!'

'Heed me.' He sounded angry now, too. 'We have Lucius and—and his disreputable friends chasing us. Maybe there are others. This is better for our disguise. Besides, this town looks dangerous. I can protect you.'

'I can take care of myself,' she huffed.

They went to dinner in silence.

Anna declined a maid even for after dinner. He left when she was readying herself for bed. Only one bed in the room.

Where was he going to sleep? He had better not take any liberties with her. When they were married, she'd endure it, but not now.

Although his arms around her that morning to keep her warm were extremely pleasant. Even thrilling.

She needn't have worried, though. When he returned to the room she pretended to be asleep. He approached the bed but all he did was remove a blanket. He stripped down to his shirt and drawers, a sight she could not help watching. She also watched him settle into a chair, his legs on another chair, the blanket around him.

How was he to sleep in that position? And, even if he could sleep, how would it be for him to feel cooped up in the carriage all day tomorrow?

'Willburgh?' she cried softly.

He startled at the sound of her voice. 'What?' He tried to straighten in the chair, scraping the one that held his legs on the wooden floor.

'You cannot sleep on that chair,' she said. 'I should. It will fit me so much better.' She sat up to trade places with him.

'You will not sleep on the chair.' His voice was firm in the darkness, the sort that brooked no argument.

She argued anyway. 'You will be miserable and cross in the carriage. Not to mention aching bones.'

'No matter. You will not sleep on the chair.' His voice grew louder.

She persisted. 'The floor, then. I should do nicely on the floor with a blanket and pillow.'

He sat up. 'Are you daft, woman? I would not take the bed and leave you on the floor or a chair or wherever else you contrive. Leave it.'

'As you wish, then,' she retorted in clipped tones.

Anna lay back down under the covers, turning her back

to him, but the creak of the chairs every time he moved kept her from sleeping. It was impossible to endure another person's discomfort. Totally against her nature.

She rolled over to face him. 'Willburgh?'

'What now?' he snapped.

She could not believe what she was about to say. 'This bed is big enough. We can both sleep in it.'

His silence was palpable.

'I have given up propriety, if that is your concern.' She swallowed. 'They took that away from us days ago.'

'Propriety is not the only concern,' he responded, his voice quieter.

She forged on. 'You must not touch me, though. I draw the line there.'

The chairs scraped and she watched him stand up. Blanket in tow, he walked towards the bed. She scooted to the far side tucking some of the bed linens around her like a shield. The bed dipped as he climbed in. They were face-to-face for a moment before they each rolled away. Anna was more awake than before, acutely aware of the warmth of his body so near to hers, of the cadence of his breathing. Of the scent of his soap and of him, now becoming so familiar to her.

Of that strange thrill she'd experienced when his arms were around her that morning.

When Will woke the next morning his arm was around her and she was nestled against his chest. His first impulse was to push away from her, but he checked himself in time, not wanting to wake her.

And she felt so good against him, so soft and round and smelling like the lavender water they'd purchased the day before.

He closed his eyes and tried to bring back the memory of

pistols firing and his father falling to the ground. Her father stood a moment longer, a look of triumph on his face, before he, too, collapsed. The emotion of that day came back, but when he opened his eyes he could not attach any of it to her.

He did not mind her company. Could no longer blame her for their predicament. No. It seemed as if they were facing this together. The two of them against the world.

Her eyelids fluttered and soon he was looking into her eyes, the colour of a fine brandy, still warm and sleepy. Her eyes widened, though, and she pulled away from him. He moved away as well, climbing out of the bed and gathering his trousers.

She rose and wrapped her shawl around her. They'd replaced the drab brown one they'd chosen at first with this muted green one, embellished with embroidered flowers. Neither of them spoke until they were dressed and ready for breakfast.

Before they sat down to eat, Will sent a servant to alert John to ready their carriage. They breakfasted in a private dining room, attended by one servant girl.

When they were alone, she broke their silence with each other. 'Did you sleep well?'

He felt his face flush. He actually had slept better than any night since Vauxhall Gardens. Even before. 'Quite well,' he responded. 'And you?'

Her eyelids fluttered. 'Very well.'

The stiffness between them was unlike when they'd started this journey, but Will missed the growing ease between them.

The servant returned. 'Mr Oldham, your groom wishes to inform you the carriage will be ready within an hour.'

'Thank you,' Will replied.

After the servant left, the silence between him and Miss Dorman filled the room again.

Will broke it. 'I was thinking that we should agree on how I should call you, should I need to use a name. I do not wish to slip and call you Miss Dorman.'

She looked up at him over her cup of tea. 'I cringe when you say Dorman. Call me Anna.'

'Anna,' he repeated, liking the sound on his tongue.

He ought to tell her to call him Will. But, no. Not yet.

Travel the next two days and nights was as pleasant as could be expected. John proved adept at finding the equipage needed when the post they hired could not continue any longer. Some carriages were more comfortable than others, but Miss Dorman—Anna—was as uncomplaining as ever.

Their days were filled with the changing scenery. Fields. Mountains. Lakes and rivers. Villages and towns of all sizes, each with its unique character. Their nights grew more comfortable. They shared a room and a bed and slept snuggled next to each other.

As much as Will tried to tell himself their physical closeness was no different than it had been when he'd used his body to warm her in Nottingham, his senses demanded more. In the darkness he was consumed with the desire to join her body to his, but he'd somehow kept to his promise. He held her but no further liberties. Will did not know what their nights would be like after marriage; he could only trust that eventually he could make love to her the way his body demanded. That she seemed to welcome his arms at night and smiled at him more during the day, fed that trust. He could almost believe their marriage could be more than tolerable. It might even bring great pleasure.

Then he'd remember who she was and how it came to be that they shared a bed together. Then hope vanished.

They'd spent those two nights first in Skipton; then, Orton

and before Will knew it their latest post-chaise was pulling into the Bush Inn in Carlisle. The Scottish border was less than ten miles away.

This was the most vulnerable part of their journey thus far, though. They were back on the mail coach route where they'd sent their decoys. If there was anywhere to encounter Lucius and his companions, this would be the place.

'We'll stay in the carriage until we know,' he told Anna.

'And be ready to leave quickly if Lucius is here.' She was always quick to comprehend.

Will sent John to make enquiries and to look around the inn and stable yard. He'd seen Lucius, Raskin, and the other man back in Nottingham. He would recognise them.

Not more than a half hour later John walked back to the carriage with none other than Toby!

'Toby is here,' Will prepared to exit the carriage.

'I hope that is good news,' she said as he helped her out.

John spoke straight away. 'Those gentlemen are not here.'

'But they are waiting for you,' Toby added. 'At the border.' He turned to Anna and tipped his hat. 'G'day, miss.'

'I am glad to see you are in one piece,' she responded.

They settled into a private dining room Toby had arranged. Refreshment was ordered and Will, Anna, and Toby sat down to plan the next step while John saw to their luggage.

Toby filled them in on his part of the journey.

He and John's brother and the wife managed to remain a few hours ahead of Lucius. They avoided the coaching inns that the mail coaches used but once had to make a run for it when Lucius showed up asking for them. They reached Gretna Green before they were discovered, but since they had no information of Will and Anna's plans, there was nothing Lucius could learn from them.

'Mr Dorman was hopping mad, too,' Toby said. 'Cursing and pounding his fists. The ostlers ordered him to compose himself or leave. Right before I slipped away, I heard him say they would wait for you at the border and hire more men to stop you. I wouldn't put it past him to have followed me, though, so you cannot stay here.'

Will spread his maps on the table. 'Then we must find another way. Another route. Gretna Green is not the only Scottish town where we can marry.'

It was too late in the day to try to make it into Scotland if they had to go farther out of their way.

'We could take another day,' Anna said. 'Find the next best place to cross the border west of here. No matter what, I do not want to encounter Lucius.'

The map showed a route to a village called Canonbie that was right over the border but east of Gretna Green.

'What if they guess we have gone east? Canonbie would be the first place they would look.' Anna pointed to a town marked a bit north of there. 'We should go a little farther still. Here, perhaps.'

She pointed to Langholm.

There was a knock on the door and John entered.

He was out of breath. 'A post boy coming from Moss-band told me a gentleman was looking for Lord Willburgh's groom, supposedly who'd been on horseback. That'd be you, right?' he asked Toby.

'Me.' Toby frowned.

Will started to fold up the maps. 'John, get us something to take us out of here right away, but we won't leave from the yard. Meet us somewhere.'

'There's another coaching inn on this street,' John said, although how he knew, Will could not guess. 'The Angel

Inn. I'll run ahead and get something from there. You can meet me there.' He started for the door.

'Wait,' Will said. 'Let us make them think we are staying the night here. I'll procure a room and you can make a pretence of taking the luggage there. Then go to the inn. We'll meet you at the other inn as soon as we can sneak out of here.'

'I'll stay here,' Toby said. 'If they find me, I'll make it seem you are here, as well.'

Will and Anna went with John to arrange the room. Will went so far as to order dinner and paid for it all right away. After John brought the luggage and left, Will and Anna were out on English Street within a half hour. Will carried their luggage.

By the time they made it to the inn, John had a post-chaise ready for them and they set out east for Brampton, a market town about nine miles east of Carlisle. They pulled into a white stucco inn, The String of Horses.

Thwarting whatever plan Lucius had for chasing them to Scotland drove out of Will's mind the realisation that he would be married on the morrow. *Focus only on the next task.* When he settled in the bed next to Anna, though, the thought came back to him, both with anticipation and misgiving. What would bedding her be like next he lay beside her?

For that alone he hoped he'd keep Lucius at bay.

Chapter Seven

$\mathcal{A}$nna woke as the first rays of daylight shone through the window. This would be her wedding day.

She gazed at the sleeping face of the man who would be her husband. It was a handsome face, almost boyish in repose. It had also become a familiar one over these few tumultuous days since he removed his mask at Vauxhall Gardens.

But she did not know him, really. She knew the Dormans' version of him, especially Lucius's version. A haughty man. A selfish one. One who could not be trusted. That version had been ingrained in her over the last decade.

Ever since his father killed her papa.

She supposed she could call him haughty, but could that merely be his anger over being forced to marry her? He was not selfish, though. His own interests seemed to never count in any action he undertook. That was true from the moment he rescued her in Vauxhall.

Could he be trusted? All she could say was he'd not given her any reason not to trust him.

If only she could forget what his father did, she might even look forward to marrying him. She knew the *ton* would consider him a catch. He was a viscount, after all.

He murmured in his sleep and rolled over. Anna slipped out of the bed without disturbing him. She padded over to the wash basin and poured fresh water. Taking advantage of his sleep, she washed herself as thoroughly as she could and splashed on the lavender water. Its scent calmed her. Reminded her of her mother. Of when she had a home, when the three of them, she, her mother, and her papa lived together in an exotic house in India. She remembered the warm breezes, the scent of spice in the air. And her mother's lavender water.

She was a far cry from that idyllic childhood. When her mother caught a fever and died, Anna and Papa took the long trip to England, where she'd been told she was *from*, but had never set foot. She'd lost everything but Papa and, then, within a year, she'd lost him, too.

That wound was still painfully deep.

Blinking away tears, she dried herself and checked to see if Willburgh was still sleeping. She changed into a clean shift and put on her corset, tying her strings as best she could. She'd been wearing the same dress since Nottingham, but the night before had unpacked her only other dress, a carriage dress of dark blue. Most of the wrinkles were out of it this morning. Such a dress would have been fashionable over five years ago. It was made of corded muslin which gave it the effect of white fabric with thin blue stripes running on the bias. Its collar nearly touched her chin, but the buttons down the front made it easy to put on herself. The ribbon sash at her natural waist made it particularly old-fashioned.

Anna held her breath as she put it on, hoping it would fit. She released a relieved sigh when she was able to button every button. She checked herself in the dressing mirror. The sleeves were a bit too long and the bodice a little loose, but it would do.

Willburgh's voice came from behind her. 'The dress looks well on you.'

Anna turned around, surprised he was awake and even

more surprised at how pleased she was at the compliment. 'I did not know you were awake.'

'I just woke up.' He swung his legs over the side of the bed and continued to gaze at her. 'You made a good choice on that dress.'

It would not do to grin in gratification of his words, but she could not suppress a small smile. 'It is hardly *à la mode*.' Lady Dorman and Violet would have perished before wearing such a garment.

As he rose from the bed, Anna's memory flashed with how warm and comforting it was to sleep next to him. As if she were not alone in the world.

Would they sleep together as a married couple? Would he wish to perform the marriage act with her? Her senses flared at that thought. Did that mean she wanted him to or she did not want him to?

While he washed and shaved and dressed, she brushed out her hair and, to be a bit fancier, braided it first before winding it into a chignon. Not that it mattered, though. She covered her hair with a bonnet.

Willburgh had arranged a private dining room for their breakfast. The less they showed themselves the better, in case Lucius had tracked them this far. John reported that there had been no sign of them, however.

After a quick breakfast they were again on the road, this time on the final leg of their journey. John called down to them when they neared the Scottish border. Anna held her breath. Both she and Willburgh scanned the surroundings to see if Lucius would appear or if anyone would try to stop them, but their passing the border was uneventful.

Willburgh turned to Anna at that moment. 'We've made it to Scotland.'

She could not tell if he were pleased or disappointed.

'Willburgh, this is what we must do, is it not? We have no choice, do we?'

He looked deeply into her eyes. 'We have no good choices. This is what we decided was the best of them.'

She held his gaze. 'I am sorry it has come to this.'

Will glanced away.

Was he sorry? When he woke that morning and watched her buttoning her dress and looking at her image in the mirror, he'd been aroused by the intimacy of the sight and the situation. She was lovely and he wanted nothing more in that moment than to remove that dress and take her back to bed. As the coach rumbled on, though, the old feelings of resentment and frustration crept back in. He was not marrying by choice. He was marrying the enemy.

By noon they entered Langholm, the destination they'd chosen. Most of its buildings were built of a grey stone that lent the town a dismal, depressing air. What's more, the sky was also grey and the air heavy with signs that rain was imminent.

How fitting that rain should have forced them together both now and at Vauxhall.

When they pulled into the Crown Inn, fat droplets started to fall. John went off to sort the post-chaise and the luggage, Will and Anna dodged raindrops to dash into the inn.

And found nobody.

Will paced the hall, waiting for the innkeeper to appear, to no avail. This was exasperating. 'Where is the innkeeper?'

Laughter sounded from another room. Will followed it with Anna right behind him.

They entered the tavern where a half dozen men were drinking, three seated and two leaning against a bar behind which one was wiping a glass. Every single one of them turned their heads to look at them.

The man behind the bar gestured for them to approach. 'Well, now, I dinna hear you enter the inn. I'm the innkeeper. You'll want a room, I expect.'

'We do.' Will wasted no time. 'We also want to be married—'

Collective laughter responded to that.

'Do y' now.' The innkeeper thrust out his hand for Will to shake. 'Name's Armstrong. There are plenty of us Armstrongs about, so they call me Armstrong of the Crown.' The man laughed as if he'd said something funny.

'A pleasure, Mr Armstrong,' Will accepted the handshake. It would have been an impudence for Armstrong to presume such familiarity of a viscount, but the man could not know Will was a viscount. That had been the whole point of their disguises. 'Can you please tell us where we might find someone to marry us?' Will's patience was wearing thin. Better to get this over with as soon as possible.

The man came out from behind the bar, with a bottle and two glasses. 'Come sit and have a drink and I might tell you.'

This was annoying, but so the Scots could be to Englishmen. Will pulled out a chair for Anna to sit. He sat next to her. Chairs scraped as everyone turned to face them.

Was an Englishman such a novelty? In a border town?

Armstrong poured them each a glass. 'Have a whisky.' He waited for them each to take a sip. 'Now, for a guinea each for my friends here and me, I'll tell you what you want to know.'

Will had been told to expect to show his coin to anyone even peripherally involved in a Scottish wedding. He reached in his pocket and paid the outrageous amount.

'Who is it who is after being married?' the innkeeper asked.

'We are.' Will gritted his teeth.

Armstrong rolled his eyes. 'I meant your names, lad.'

All Will wanted was directions to where to find someone to marry them, but he felt he had no choice but to play along.

'I am Neal Willburgh.' He gestured to Anna. 'This is Anna Dorman.'

Anna spoke up then. 'Anna Edgerton. I am Anna Edgerton.'

Will gaped. This was the first he had heard of this. 'Not Anna Dorman?'

'No.'

The innkeeper quipped. 'Have the two of you met, by any chance?'

The room broke out in laughter.

She wasn't a Dorman? Not a real Dorman? Something loosened inside Will, like a knot untwisting.

The innkeeper went on. 'And I gather the two of you are of age.'

'I am twenty,' Anna said.

'Twenty-eight,' Will added, pointing to himself.

Armstrong grinned. 'And you truly want to be married?'

One of the men seated at the other table shouted, 'Heed what you are doing, lad! Before it is too late!'

The others laughed.

The innkeeper chuckled, but turned to Anna. 'Miss, do you truly want this man to be your husband?' He spoke as if it was a poor idea indeed.

'Yes,' said Anna.

Will's patience was lost. 'Perhaps you could merely tell us where we might find someone to marry us?'

The innkeeper held up a hand. 'Do you truly want her as a wife?'

'Do not do it!' another patron called out.

'Yes, I want to marry her,' he snapped.

'And nobody's forcing you?' the man asked.

Anna looked as if she was suppressing a smile. 'No one.'

Will was less amused. 'Of course no one is forcing us. Can you direct me to the proper person—'

The other men snickered.

'First I must fetch a piece of paper.' The man disappeared behind the bar again.

To bring them directions, Will hoped.

When Armstrong returned he placed the paper on the table along with an ink pot and pen. 'Fill this in, my lad and lassie. As soon as I sign, and two of these witnesses sign, you are married!'

The room broke out in guffaws and the innkeeper filled everyone's glass from the bottle. 'Let's drink to their health!'

Will glanced at Anna whose eyes were sparkling. 'You guessed.'

'Not at first.' She smiled.

Will dipped the pen in the ink pot and filled in his name. He handed it to Anna.

'We do not fuss about in Scotland,' Armstrong explained. 'All you need is to be of age and to declare you want to be married of your own free will. Simple, eh, lad?'

Will managed a smile. 'Simple indeed.' He downed his glass of whisky and the innkeeper poured him another.

All the signatures were completed and the paper returned to Will. He folded it and placed it in his pocket. He was not certain if what he felt was relief or bewilderment. He downed the second glass of whisky.

'I'll record it in my ledger, as well,' Armstrong said.

The other men came up and clapped him on the back, giving him various warnings about married life.

'Do as she says, whatever she says,' one man told him. 'Won't never go wrong.'

The others groaned at that one.

They were more gallant towards Anna, bowing to her or kissing her hand, all of which she accepted with good humour.

John entered the tavern, looking stunned at the revelry. 'I've brought your bags, sir.'

Will managed a smile. 'Congratulate us, John,' he said. 'We are married.'

Anna smiled through the impromptu celebration. The Scots in the tavern seemed very ready to be joyous and their merriment was infectious. The whisky helped as well, its warmth spreading through her chest and making her mellow.

She was glad it was done, the marriage. No more uncertainty. The die was cast. She was even happier at her impulsive reclaiming of her name. Her real name; the name given at birth.

She'd used the Dorman name since a baby, her mother had explained. Now, after how the Dormans had treated her, she was glad to claim another, even for only a few minutes.

Because now she would ever be a Willburgh, the name she'd once learned to hate. Armstrong poured her another drink. The lovely whisky floated all her tension away, all the tension of the last ten days when her life again changed for ever. She watched the Scotsmen tease Willburgh about being a married man and about not knowing her name. It made her laugh.

The innkeeper wagged his eyebrows. 'I ken it is time to show you to your room.'

The other men hooted.

Anna finished her third glass of whisky and stood. And swayed. 'Oh. Goodness,' she said. 'I felt dizzy for a moment.'

The innkeeper pushed Willburgh towards her and he put his arm around her to steady her.

'Follow me,' the man ordered. He turned to John who had also consumed a glass or two. 'Bring the bags.'

'Yessir. They're in the hall.' John walked ahead of them.

In the hall, Armstrong had Willburgh sign the register. 'Be sure to write Mr and Mrs Willburgh,' he bantered.

When they started up the stairs, the man looked over his shoulder. 'I'll be giving you the best room in the inn.'

Anna's legs felt like jelly. She held on fast to Willburgh's arm. Behind her John tripped on a step and dropped their portmanteaux.

'Pardon,' he said.

The room was tucked away at the far end of a hallway. Armstrong opened the door with a key and they entered. Anna noticed a large bed with four carved posts and an intricately carved headboard. It was made of the same dark wood that panelled the tavern. There was also a dressing table and other tables and chairs.

Armstrong lit a fire in the fireplace and took John by his collar and pushed him out of the room, closing the door behind the two of them.

'I think you had better sit.' Willburgh guided her, not to a chair but to the bed. He sat her on the edge. He unlaced her half boots. 'Your shoes are still wet.'

And it still rained. She could hear the rain patter against the window.

'It was a funny wedding, was it not?' Her head felt so light. In fact her whole body felt as if it might easily float to the ceiling.

'If we are married, perhaps you should call me Will.'

Anna took his head in her hands and lifted his face, looking into his eyes. How had she never noticed his eyes were a piercing blue?

'We are married, Will.' She blinked. Gazing at him left her feeling giddy inside. And wary. Was he happy about being married to her?

Of course he was not.

Chapter Eight

Will was drawn closer to her, closer to tasting her lips, but she pulled her hands away as if she'd touched a hot poker.

As the innkeeper had led them up to the room, Will's excitement grew. He knew what Armstrong and his friends teased him about. They expected him to consummate this marriage. Post haste.

And he wanted to consummate this marriage. He was on fire to do so. The whisky had stripped away all his resolve. His mind could not keep hold of family enemies and duels and death. All he could think of was how she felt in his arms at night and how that delight promised greater delights. Now that he could bed her. Should bed her. Wanted to bed her.

He'd drunk too much and so had she.

He slipped off her half boots and stood.

'I know what is supposed to happen between a husband and wife,' she said, slurring her words. 'And I know you do not want to do it. You did not want to marry me, but you had to and you are angry at me. You do not like me. *Sins of my father* and all that.' Her upset was building with each word.

He sat beside her and turned her to face him. 'You, Anna, have had too much whisky.'

She lifted her chin. 'I've only had three.'

He nodded. 'Three.' That was sufficient for her good sense

to fail her. 'And I have had a great deal more than that. I know precisely what we should do.'

'What?' She sounded combative.

He took off his coat and waistcoat and pulled off his boots. 'We should rest.'

She blinked at him. 'In bed?'

'In bed.'

A grin grew on her face. She tried to unbutton her dress, but could not manage it. Will was not certain he could either, but he managed the first one, then the next. Excitement grew inside him. Arousal.

He undid all her buttons and pulled the dress over her head.

She turned her back on him. 'Unlace me,' she murmured.

He managed to untie her laces and she slipped out of her corset. He recalled how she felt wearing only her shift and he yearned to rid himself of that flimsy barrier, to throw off his shirt and feel her naked skin against his.

But he wouldn't. Instead he lay her down in the bed and moved next to her, to hold her like he'd done the past two nights.

With a sigh she settled against him. And fell asleep.

When Will woke the room was dark except for the glow of the coals in the fireplace. They'd slept until night apparently, the whisky and the several days of acute stress knocking them out. The day before was a blur, but he remembered one thing. They were married.

They'd thwarted Lucius's efforts to stop them and they were married. They'd achieved that goal. Never mind that it was a goal neither of them wanted; it was still a goal achieved. He was glad of that.

He tried to recall the wedding ceremony, but it was a

jumble, possibly because he had not known it was happening until it was all done.

She'd caught on much before him. She was clever. Uncomplaining.

And not a Dorman.

Will laughed at himself for being glad of that.

He rose from the bed and poured some water to rinse the foul taste from his mouth. Another gift from the whisky, along with his foggy mind. He turned to look for a lamp or a candle to light before he crashed into something and woke her. Lord, he was hungry. They had not eaten since breakfast. Perhaps there was a lamp on a table.

There was a table right inside the door, in a particularly dark corner. He gingerly felt his way to it, hoping he would not topple a chair or something in its path. He groped the surface of the table. His fingers touched a candlestick. Excellent. He groped his way to the fireplace and rubbed his hand on the mantle. A taper, as he expected. Will lit the taper from the one glowing coal in the fireplace and touched it to the candle, blinking as the flame came to life.

He could now see the room better. To his relief, the candle illuminated a plate of bread and cheese and a teapot on the table by the door. He placed the candle on the table and helped himself to a piece of hearty oat bread and a generous slice of Caboc cheese.

He poured a cup of tea and gulped it down, not bothering with milk or sugar. The tea was tepid. Will did not care. He poured himself another cup and drank it, as well.

The refreshments had not been there when they first entered the room, Will would swear. That meant Armstrong or someone else must have come into the room while they were sleeping. That was distressing. Someone had entered and he did not wake.

What if it had been Lucius?

Lucius was no longer a threat, though. Will and Anna were married.

Will helped himself to more bread and cheese and washed it down with a third cup of tepid tea.

Anna stirred and Will turned towards her, just able to make out her face.

Her eyes opened. 'Willburgh?'

'Will,' he corrected. Who else did she expect?

'Will,' she repeated. 'I could not see you in the dark. What time is it?'

'I am not certain.' There wasn't a clock in the room, not that he'd found at least. 'Middle of the night.'

She sat up and groaned. 'My head aches.'

Why did he feel disquieted around her suddenly? Why sound so churlish?

He tried to soften his voice. 'That's the whisky.'

She pressed her fingers against her temple. 'How much did I have?'

'Plenty.' He'd lost track of how many times his glass was filled. 'You said three, I believe.'

She sighed. 'I don't remember that. I don't remember coming up to this room. Did we miss dinner?'

'We did,' he responded. 'Are you hungry? There is bread and cheese and tea.'

She groped around until finding her shawl. She wrapped it around her and walked over to him.

He pulled out a chair for her. 'Have a seat and I will cut you some.'

'Some tea first please.' She sat in the chair. 'My mouth is so dry.'

He poured her tea and handed it to her. 'It is no longer hot.'

'I do not care.' She drank it as quickly as he had done.

He cut her a piece of bread and a slice of cheese and sat across from her. She ate as eagerly as he had.

She took a sip of her second cup of tea and lifted her gaze to his. The candlelight softened her face. She looked vulnerable. And alluring.

'Did—did we—?' she asked.

He knew what she meant. 'No. We didn't.'

She glanced away. 'I—I want you to know that I will understand if you do not want to. I—I know you did not want this marriage. I know you may not want to bed me.'

Will's first impulse was to snap back at her and accuse *her* of not wanting to bed *him*, but she looked so forlorn, he pushed that impulse away, remembering her growing distress the day before, saying that he did not like her and that he blamed her for her father's actions. He did like her—or was growing to.

He lowered his voice. 'We are man and wife. To think of what we wanted before is useless now. I expect us to have—marital relations.'

She faced him again.

He went on. 'We—we do not have to—to consummate our marriage tonight, though. I make you a promise that I will not touch you until you are ready.'

She peered at him. 'I cannot tell if your words mean you want to or you do not want to, because I certainly do not wish it if it is abhorrent to you.'

He met her eye. 'It is not abhorrent to me.' Good God, his body was already humming with desire for her.

She glanced away again. 'I—I am not sure if it is abhorrent to me.'

Who might have discussed such matters with her? Young women might have such instruction right before their wedding day. No one would have had that conversation with her, though.

'What do you know of it?' he asked.

She gave a wan smile. 'Cautionary tales from the governess. Titillating tales from some of the maids. I know what happens.' Her brows knitted. 'I believe it must give pleasure, otherwise would men seek it out so; would women engage in affairs?'

That was an intelligent deduction. 'I will do my best to give you pleasure, Anna.' He meant that. 'Whenever you wish to try.'

She inhaled a deep breath. 'Tonight? Best not to wait, I think.'

Will stood and extended his hand.

Anna put her hand in his and let him lead her to the bed.

Her knees trembled. She was afraid, yes, but it was a fear she was eager to face, much like when she was young and afraid to ride horses but wanted to more than anything. Of course, riding a horse was exhilarating, something that gave her great pleasure. Could she trust that the marital act brought pleasure? Having heard a description of what happens between the man and the woman, and having seen animals copulate, she could not imagine pleasure from it. Perhaps it would merely be gratification from conquering the fear.

When they neared the bed, he swooped her into his arms and gently placed her on it. Anna felt giddy. It was so unexpected. So playful.

She'd not imagined that Willburgh could be playful. She sat on the edge of the bed and watched while, in the same playful spirit, he removed his trousers. Only his drawers remained. She was used to seeing his drawers. He'd kept them on when they'd shared a bed.

She smiled. 'Did you fall sleep in your trousers?'

'I must have.' He took off his drawers, as well.

Now he wore only his shirt, but it covered his body nearly to his knees.

He undid the ribbon at the collar, but paused and his expression sobered. 'We may do this clothed or not. What do you prefer?'

She hardly knew. Except, once she'd learned to properly mount a horse, she'd wanted to gallop.

'Unclothed,' she said.

He crossed his arms and grasped the hem of his shirt. In one fluid motion, he lifted the shirt over his head. He was naked.

Anna could not take her eyes off him.

'Have you seen a man unclothed before?' He tossed the shirt aside.

'I've seen statues.' But statues did not prepare her for this male physique.

He was broad-shouldered with rippling muscles all the way to his waist, like a statue of Hercules she'd once seen in Lord Lansdowne's house. His waist was narrower, though, and his skin was spattered with hair and glowed in the dim light in a way cold marble could never do.

Would she ever tell him that he compared favourably with Hercules? She doubted it, but it made her smile.

Standing naked in front of her, he twirled a finger in her direction. 'And your clothes?'

Her breath came faster. She wore only her shift.

'I'll take it off for you, if you like,' he murmured.

She'd never heard his voice sound like that. Like a purring cat. It added to the thrill.

'Very well,' she managed.

He came closer and took the thin fabric in his hands, easing it up her legs. As his hands came close to her female parts, her body seemed to throb. She wriggled, freeing the garment from beneath her. He'd moved slowly before, but now pulled the shift over her head as swiftly as he'd removed his shirt.

His gaze swept up and down her body, his blue eyes darkening.

The modiste that dressed Lady Dorman and Violet and altered their castaways for her always complained that her breasts were not large enough to fill a dress properly and that she was too tall. She was not round and luscious like Violet.

'I am a disappointment, I know.' She scooted onto the bed and covered herself with the bed linens.

He peeled them away. 'Not a disappointment at all.'

He was being kind.

He climbed in the bed next to her and she rolled on her side to face him.

Her nervousness returned and she could hardly get a breath to speak. 'How do we start, then?'

How was he to start? Will wondered. How was a man to give a woman her first experience of the marital act, especially when she'd been forced to marry?

It had been a long time since he'd lain with a woman, but the lack had not overly bothered him. There always seemed to be too much to do and too much required of him to pursue any amorous adventures like his old schoolmates were fond of doing, the friends who'd convinced him to go to Vauxhall Gardens that night.

That lifetime ago.

His head might not have felt the lack of female company,

but his body certainly did. He'd kept it in check the three nights he'd shared a bed with Anna.

But just barely.

Now, with barriers gone and expectations high, his body wanted nothing more than to surge on, the fastest and hardest that he could go.

But he would not do that to Anna.

Their truce was fragile. The trip to Scotland had given them time to become acquainted with each other. She proved herself more intelligent, more resourceful and more forbearing than he ever would have imagined. And she seemed as willing as he to see if they could make something good out of this forced marriage.

He could ruin that by rutting like some bull in a field of cows.

Which was precisely what his body wanted to do.

Will began carefully by touching her cheek. She tensed, but he simply stroked her skin with the back of his hand. She relaxed. He put his hand on the back of her head and lowered his lips to hers.

Gentle kiss, he told himself. *Barely touch her.*

When he moved away, she sighed.

'I'm going to touch you,' he said. 'I'll tell you what I'm going to do before I do it.'

She nodded.

'You can tell me to stop any time.'

She nodded again.

He stroked her cheek again and her neck and slid his hands down her arms.

'Now your breasts.' He started by stroking the skin above her breasts.

'They are too small, I'm told.' Her voice was forlorn.

He guided her face so she would have to look him in the

eye. 'Your breasts are lovely.' He covered one with his hand. 'See? They fit perfectly.'

She laughed. 'Now you are making sport of me.'

He made her look at him again. 'No, I am not.'

He caressed her breasts again, but instead of relaxing her, her back arched and eager sounds escaped her mouth.

Could she be aroused?

'A kiss,' he murmured and placed his lips on her nipple, then dared to taste it with his tongue.

She writhed in response, but she did not say no.

He continued caressing her, running his fingers down her abdomen, sweeping his fingers down her legs. The force of his arousal intensified, becoming more and more painful and demanding by the moment. He could not wait much longer.

'I must prepare you now,' he told her. 'If you feel you are ready—'

'For goodness' sake, Willburgh,' she rasped.

'Will,' he corrected.

'Will,' she repeated. 'I am not made of glass. Gallop already.'

He eased up enough to look at her. 'Gallop?'

'I meant I am ready.' She pulled him down.

That was all the permission he needed. He moved atop her and she opened her legs and arched her back. He knew she was unschooled in this; her body must be doing its own demanding. His body urged him to thrust into her, but he had enough restraint to go slow. When his male member touched her, she flinched, but immediately rose to him.

'This—this might cause you pain,' he managed.

'I assure you, I will deal with it,' she responded.

As you wish, he thought. He wanted to give her pleasure this first time—or at least not cause her too much pain. He eased himself in slowly.

She gasped and tensed around him. He moved slowly at first, creating a rhythm that she quickly matched. They moved faster and faster together.

Galloping, he thought, right before crossing the border between reason and desire.

Anna had not thought it would be like this. She had not imagined the want, the need, that propelled her forward, to ride with him as far and as fast as he could take her. Into some unknown place that she suddenly was desperate to discover.

His kiss had surprised her with its gentleness. His touch had soothed and excited her. His consideration of her, though, unsettled her. When, since her papa had died, had another person been concerned about how she would feel?

The only sound in the room was the clapping of their bodies coming together and their gasping breaths. His thrusts came faster and with more force, but that only intensified the need inside her. That first stab of pain quickly became inconsequential in light of the ride he was taking her on. She did not know the destination, where want and need would be fulfilled.

But she wanted to get there as rapidly as possible.

When her pleasure burst, she cried out. She had not expected this.

His came right after. He tensed and trembled inside her. Spilling his seed? It must be.

The next moment he collapsed on top of her and rolled off to lie beside her, panting.

'So that was all?' she said, as if disappointed.

'What do you mean, "that was all?"' he shot back, rising enough to glare at her.

Anna laughed. 'I am jesting with you. It was really quite—'
How to describe it? 'Quite nice.'

He lay back again. 'Nice. That is damning with faint praise.'

'Indeed it is not,' she countered. 'If so, I would be implying it had fault.' She turned to face him. 'And it really was quite perfect.'

Her gaze captured his and held, perhaps saying more than words could convey.

He closed the distance between them and touched his lips to hers again, as gently as he had done before, but not tentative.

Affirming.

He tucked an arm around her and pulled her against him. His skin was warm against hers and slightly damp. With her head against his chest she counted his heartbeats. And reprised every moment of the lovemaking in her mind. He'd been her enemy for so long, but now she could not imagine any other man touching her, kissing her, joining with her.

She pressed her lips to his skin. 'A fortnight ago would you have dreamed you would be here? With me?'

When he responded she felt the words rumble in his chest. 'I would have wagered a fortune against such an idea. I would have lost.'

She dared another question. 'Are you sorry about it?'

He laughed. 'Not at the moment.'

Chapter Nine

The next morning Will woke when sunlight poured in the window. He glanced at Anna, still asleep, looking young and innocent and beautiful.

He'd bedded her. Twice. And had found it a profound experience, so why were his emotions in a jumble this morning?

He closed his eyes, but instead of sleep, visions of his father's duel with her father flew into his mind. He again saw them lifting their arms and firing, the smoke bursting from the barrels of both pistols. His father fell, his shirt turning red with his blood.

A mere fortnight ago, Will could go weeks without remembering—reliving—that scene. Since that night at Vauxhall he'd relived the memory nearly every day. Was he doomed to think of it every time he looked at her? He was married to her. Bound to her for the rest of their lives.

But he had not relived the memory the day before. Or the past night. That was a puzzle. From the moment he married her, in that manner so casual he almost missed it, he'd been caught up in revelry. Making love to her had been—he had no words to describe it. Only that he'd felt—whole. As if he did love her and wanted to marry her. As if they belonged together.

But her father killed his father.

The memory returned.

He rolled over in bed and sat up, too restless to remain there.

She woke up and stretched. 'Good morning,' she murmured and he remembered the delights of the night they shared together.

He remembered how good it felt to touch her, to teach her about lovemaking, to make it comfortable for her, to make certain to give her pleasure. Gazing at her and remembering, he wanted to repeat the experience.

But it was madness to care for her. To actually like her. To want her comfort and happiness. Her father killed his father.

But no. The day before she'd given a different name.

'Tell me something,' he said as he picked up his clothing from the floor. 'Tell me why you said your name was Edgerton.' His voice had an edge to it.

She covered herself with the bed linens. 'The man who fathered me was named Edgerton.'

'He was not Dorman?' He put on his drawers.

'No.' There was tension in her voice.

Because he was sounding churlish, no doubt. 'But you were called Dorman. Lucius's cousin.'

'It was the only name I knew.' She paused. 'Until my mother told me my real name. On her deathbed.'

Will knew her mother had died when Dorman and she came to stay with Lord and Lady Dorman.

Her expression turned pained. 'My mother told me about Edgerton. She'd been married to him before she married Bertram Dorman.'

He tried to mollify his tone. 'What happened to him?'

'He died,' she said. 'When I was a baby. He was a soldier in the East India Company army. He was killed at Seringapatam. In the battle.'

'In India?'

'In India.' Her voice was taut, as if her words were difficult to speak. 'That was where I was born and lived until my mother died.'

How little he knew of her. She'd been born in India? Lived there before coming to the Dormans? Of course, he'd been at Oxford at that time and had been totally absorbed in his own interests and desires.

'I called Dorman Papa,' she went on. 'He was the only father I knew. When my mother died, I was afraid, because I did not really belong to him. I dared not talk to him or to anyone about it. What if he would leave me as well?'

The Bertram Dorman Will knew of was reputed to gamble and drink to excess. Worse, he was a womaniser who loved to toy with a woman's affections, as he had done with Will's mother. Her fears had merit.

'A vile man,' Will muttered as he completed dressing.

She got out of bed and put on her shift and corset before speaking again. 'He was not a vile man,' she said with feeling. 'He was generous and fun and kind to me. It was a blow to learn he was not my father. A worse blow when he was killed. I will not hear ill spoken of him!'

Will would not hear him praised. 'He seduced my mother.'

'The Dormans said your mother seduced him!' she cried. 'I do not care. He was good to me and when he died I had no one.'

Will could not stop himself. 'You obviously had the Dormans.'

She turned her back to him, stepped into her dress, pulled it up, and buttoned it.

She faced him again. 'Eventually Lord and Lady Dorman decided I could stay, but after my—my papa—was killed, it was not a certainty. You might say I was *allowed* to live with the Dormans. They found many ways to let me know I was there only out of the goodness of their hearts.

The Dormans had always let Anna know she did not truly belong there, but lived with them at their whim. Did she belong anywhere, to anyone?

Last night, when Will so gently and daringly made love to her, she'd felt perhaps she'd found where she truly belonged. This morning, though, he became like the man with whom she'd been caught in the rain at Vauxhall. Disagreeable. Disdainful. Despising her.

She put on her stockings and sat at the dressing table to comb her hair into some semblance of order. She could hear him moving around behind her but she was hurt and angry and wished he would leave.

She plaited her hair, wound it into a chignon and covered it with a cap. Married women wore caps, did they not? Even if married to a disagreeable man.

He became so quiet that she wondered if he had left the room.

She jumped when he did speak, but his voice was still clipped.

'Forgive me,' he said. 'I spoke unkindly.'

She turned around to look at him and their eyes met. Her senses leapt at the sight of him. She could not help it. How was she to guard her emotions when the mere sight, sound, and scent of him affected her so?

Perhaps he apologised out of duty. He'd married her out of duty, had he not? Had he made love to her out of duty? No. No. That must have been real. It had to be real.

A knock at the door broke into her thoughts.

'Who is it?' he asked.

'The maid, sir.'

He glanced at Anna as if to ask if the maid should enter. She nodded.

'Come in,' he called through the door.

The maid looked no more than a girl. She wore a crisp, clean apron and a plain dress.

'My da—Mr Armstrong—sent me to tell you there are three gentlemen to see you.'

She was the innkeeper's daughter, then.

'Gentlemen?' Will frowned. 'What are their names?'

'I do not know, sir,' the maid replied. 'My da dinna tell me. They are *English*, though.' She spoke the word *English* as if it left a bad taste in her mouth.

'Is it Lucius, do you think?' A new worry. Anna shoved Willburgh's manner aside. Who else could it be? 'Or perhaps Toby or John?'

'Not Toby or John,' he replied, his brow knitted. 'They would not dress as gentlemen and there would not be three of them.' He turned back to the maid. 'Tell them I will come directly.'

'Yes, sir.' The maid curtsied. 'Da says they will be waiting in the tavern.' She left the room.

Anna's heart raced. 'It must be Lucius. And—and—what if the other one is—is *that man*.'

'The one who abducted you? Why do you think so?' he asked.

'I—I am just afraid that he is. The man spoke to Raskin before Raskin disappeared with Violet.'

'Raskin and Violet ran off together?' Willburgh's expression darkened. 'I will see what they want.'

'Wait.' She hurriedly put on her half boots. 'I will go with you.'

* * *

Will thought it unwise for her to go. If it was Lucius and the others, they were likely up to nothing good. But after he'd acted so churlish towards her, he could not deny her wishes.

He did not like himself very much at the moment. She'd done nothing to deserve his ill manners. Her behaviour had been faultless this whole trip. She deserved better than him snapping at her.

He suspected it was not memories of his father's duel that made him pull away from her. He knew she was not at fault. God help him, though, he was petty enough to be glad she was not really a Dorman. The man who fathered *her* was not the man who killed his father. He could no longer use that as an excuse.

What was it, then? Was it that he'd told himself—and his mother when she pushed—that he was not ready for marriage. He needed to master being a viscount first and he was far from perfecting that role. It consumed him. He did not want to be like his father, so enveloped in other duties that he neglected a duty to a wife.

He opened the door for her and the two of them walked down to the tavern.

When they entered, Armstrong was behind the bar.

He broke into a grin at the sight of them and wagged his brows. 'Well, well, well. Mr and Mrs Willburgh, good morning to you.'

How pleasant it was to be greeted by a friendly face. 'Good morning, Armstrong. I hope you are well.'

'No' too poorly, thank you.' He winked at Anna. 'And you, Mrs Willburgh? How do you fare?'

Anna's cheeks turned pink, but she smiled at him. 'No' too poorly, sir.'

Armstrong laughed.

'I understand we have visitors,' Will said.

The innkeeper frowned. 'That lot. *English*, y'know.' He sounded just like his daughter.

'We are English, you realise,' Will reminded him.

'Aye,' Armstrong cocked his head. 'But there are English and then there are *English*.'

Will thought he could agree with that statement, although he'd been acting the disagreeable type to Anna.

'I put them in the private dining room,' Armstrong said. 'So they won't upset the guests.'

His hand swept the room, but only three men were seated at a table who might have been disturbed, the same three men who had been present at the wedding and celebration after.

They all lifted their glasses and Will gave them a friendly wave.

He turned back to Armstrong. 'Show us the way.'

Armstrong draped a towel over his shoulder and led them to the dining room door and opened it.

Will stepped in before Anna.

It was Lucius, Raskin, and another man seated at a table, tankards of ale in front of them. The third man, Will recognised as one of Lucius's old schoolmates. Millman. Millman was precisely the sort of degenerate who would force himself on a lady. Will clenched his fist, wanting nothing more than to plant it in Millman's face.

They looked up, but none of them stood.

'This is a surprise,' Will said, although he was not surprised. 'You are a long way from London. What are you doing here, Lucius?'

Lucius looked from Will to Anna. 'I see we are too late.' He looked daggers at Anna. 'We came to bring you home, Anna. Where you belong. But you have betrayed the family thoroughly, I see. With a Willburgh. You've had your Scottish wedding, I presume.'

'I have.' Anna lifted her chin. 'But you have it wrong, Lucius. I am where I belong now. It was you, your parents, and Violet who betrayed *me*.' She glared at Raskin. 'You and Violet left me alone at Vauxhall, so you are a part of it as well, Raskin.'

'Me?' Raskin put on an innocent face. 'I would never do such a thing.'

Millman leaned on the back two legs of his chair, smirking at everyone. Before Will knew it Anna walked around the table and yanked the back of his chair. The man fell sprawling to the floor with a loud crash.

Well done, Anna, Will said to himself.

He had to admit he liked that fire in her.

'That is for what *you* did,' Anna cried.

The man protested as he fumbled to his feet. 'I did nothing.'

She leaned into his face. 'I know what you did. What you tried to do.'

His face turned a guilty and angry red. He lifted his hand as if to strike her, but Will was there in a flash. He seized the man's arm and twisted it behind his back.

'See here!' Lucius protested.

Gripping the man closely, Will spoke into his ear. 'You stay out of my sight, Millman. And if I hear of you repeating with any woman what you tried to do to *my wife*, I'll be coming for you.'

Millman scurried out of the room.

'Not too hospitable of you,' Raskin drawled.

Will whirled on him. 'Do not get me started on you.'

'There you go, Willburgh,' Lucius piped up. 'Always throwing around your superiority. Here we've raced across the country, trying to save Anna from you, and this is how you treat us.'

'Your efforts would have been unnecessary if your father would have cooperated,' Will said. 'Or if any member of your family had had the decency to listen to her.'

'It was dear Anna who did not cooperate,' Lucius countered. 'Who would not listen. We were willing for her to come back to the family with all forgiven, but look how she thanked my parents for all those years of taking care of her. Marrying the enemy.'

Anna broke in. 'Do not speak of me as if I am not here.'

Lucius made a conciliatory wave of his hand.

Anna's eyes flashed and she pointed towards the door. 'You both left me with that worm. And then your parents abandoned me altogether. I want nothing to do with you.'

Lucius gave a slimy smile.

'This is a waste of our time,' Will said. 'Come to the point of why you wanted to speak to us. You could have guessed you were too late to stop us.'

'Oh, yes.' Raskin sneered. 'That delightful barbarian, Armstrong, told us.'

Lucius stood. 'You are right, Willburgh. Although I cannot believe I am saying that. This is a waste of time. I only wish I could be there when you both discover just how foolish this elopement was.' He glowered at Anna again. 'My dear, you will regret choosing a Willburgh.'

Raskin rose as well and gave them an exaggerated bow. With one final glare Lucius and Raskin left the room.

Anna lowered herself into a chair. Her knees were shaking with anger.

Willburgh leaned against the back of another chair. 'You were magnificent, by the way.'

She glanced at him.

Some of the anger inside her could be laid at his feet.

But he did defend her.

She took a breath. 'It was *him*, was it not? Millman?'

'Guilt was written all over him,' Willburgh responded. 'Lucius and Raskin knew his reputation. Everyone did. And yet they left you with him?'

'Lucius had left already, before Raskin came with—with *him*.' She pressed her fingers into the table. 'After Violet and Raskin disappeared, he approached and offered to escort me back to my aunt and uncle. Well, you know what happened after that.'

Willburgh blew out a breath. 'I hope we are rid of them for good.' He pushed himself away from the chair and walked to the window.

It seemed he stood there a long time, before he turned back to her. His expression had softened. 'Shall I arrange breakfast?'

Any appetite she'd possessed had been swallowed up with emotion—starting with her waking to a colder Willburgh. 'If you so wish.'

'I do wish. I am famished.' His brows rose. 'Are you not hungry?'

She shrugged.

'We should eat. I'll let Armstrong know.' He left the room.

When the door closed, she moved the tankards of ale to a sideboard. She did not want to think of whose hands and lips had touched them. She opened a window as if to release the room of their every essence.

The air was crisp and clean and a breeze did its job of scouring out old smells. The sky was a vivid blue, a beautiful day so in contrast with her mood.

What had Lucius meant when he said she and Willburgh

would discover what a mistake this elopement was? Had Willburgh already discovered the mistake?

Willburgh returned with two generously large bowls of porridge. He ate greedily, precisely how you'd expect a famished man to eat. Anna forced herself to eat a spoonful or two, and it sparked her hunger. She finished the whole bowl and looked up at him, waiting for him to make some scathing remark.

Instead, he asked, 'Do you wish to travel back today?'

Be trapped in a post-chaise with him?

Her answer must have shown on her face, because he quickly answered his own question. 'No travel today, then.'

She felt her cheeks flush. She'd thought she was more skilled at hiding her thoughts. 'Did you wish to start back?' she asked.

He held up a hand. 'Believe me, I have no need to be cooped up in a small carriage if it is not absolutely necessary.'

So he did not want to be trapped with her either. Yes. Their lovemaking must have been a fluke.

She rose and walked over to the window.

He joined her. 'What would you wish to do if you could do anything?'

Her mind went blank. Who'd ever asked her such a question since her papa died?

She flung it back to him. 'What would you do?'

He stared out the window for a moment before speaking, 'It is a fine day for riding.'

She gaped at him. Again her face betrayed her.

He smiled. 'Ah. You agree with me.'

She turned away. 'It is impossible. We have no horses. No saddles. I have no riding habit or proper boots or a proper hat.'

He cocked his head. 'We are in a large enough town. What

did I hear Armstrong call it? *Muckle Toon*. Such problems might be easily remedied in a town of this size.'

She peered at him. 'I do not understand what you mean.'

'Anna.' He met her gaze. 'I have the funds. We merely purchase what we need.'

Willburgh was true to his word. He purchased everything they needed.

A visit to a bank provided the funds. Mr Armstrong directed them to where they could find what they needed. Armstrong even knew a horse breeder with stock to sell.

Willburgh purchased *three* horses. *Three*, when he probably had a stable full of horses on his estate.

Anna found it difficult to fathom.

It took the rest of the day and visits to several establishments to accomplish everything else. Anna was able to see much of Langholm and to assist in each aspect. Goodness! Willburgh even sought her counsel on selecting the horses. She picked the horse she would ride. Imagine. Before this she'd ridden whatever steed Violet or Lucius did not want to ride.

Anna selected a lovely and very sweet grey Highland pony she named Seraphina. Willburgh chose a brown pony for John and a bay dun for himself. Anna named his pony as well as John's. She could not resist naming Will's Armstrong and John's Crown, after Armstrong's inn. Amazingly, they had no difficulty finding saddles that fit them, a riding habit that fit her well enough, and boots, hats, and gloves.

As they left the last shop, Willburgh said, 'I was thinking. Since we purchased the horses, we might as well ride them as far as we are able. Would you agree? We could ride them all the way to London if we so desired.'

She stared at him, astonished. Not to be jostled in a post-chaise with no room to move? Instead to be on horseback in the fresh air? Every day?

Again her face must have shown her thoughts.

He smiled. 'There it is, then. We ride all the way to London if we like.'

'Is it what you desire?' she asked.

He was confusing her again. Why would he go to such lengths merely to please her? He had turned kind and generous again. Like the night before. Why would he do so, when he woke so unhappy with her?

It must be that this was what *he* wished to do. She just happened to desire it, as well. That would make sense.

The day, really, in spite of how it started, had been a joy.

They ate dinner in the tavern and all the men who had been there the day before, the ones who witnessed their wedding, were gathered there again. It felt like they were among old friends.

And then the day was over.

And they were faced with going to bed.

Chapter Ten

When they readied for bed, the air was filled with tension, such a contrast to how the day had been after they'd rid themselves of Lucius and his cohorts.

Will could not remember when he'd last had such an enjoyable day not spoiled by some burdensome task or another hanging over his head. How could he feel guilty for giving himself over to the pleasure of the moment, when she'd been giddy with excitement when choosing her horse?

'A horse of my own!' she'd cried. 'I've never had anything so grand!'

His chest had burst with joy at her words.

And why should he not feel joyful? Purchasing whatever they wanted—whatever *she* wanted—had been a delight, even more of a delight, perhaps, than their passion-filled night before. Will did not want these feelings to end.

Now that they were back in the room in the inn, though, it was as if all his disagreeableness of the morning had returned.

Will wanted the joy back.

Anna climbed into bed much as she'd done when they stayed at the other inns and he'd promised not to touch her. Will joined her. He moved close to her, spooning her in front of him. But her body did not quite melt under his touch as it had the night before. She felt distant even though she was in his arms.

He gathered his courage and whispered in her ear, 'I want to make love with you again. Will you permit it?'

He felt her muscles tense, but she said, 'If you wish it.'

'I do wish,' he replied with feeling. 'But only if you wish it, too.'

She needed to share in the pleasure, like when they'd purchased the horse, or it meant nothing.

It seemed a long time before she answered. 'I wish it.'

He removed his drawers and threw them aside. She sat up and he lifted her shift over her head. One candle was still burning, bathing her lovely skin in a soft glow. His need for her flared, but he touched her carefully, relishing in the silkiness and warmth of her skin.

She was not indifferent to his touch, stirring beneath his fingers. He leaned forward and placed his lips against hers, hoping he could erase the words with which his lips had wounded her. She softened.

They lay down then, but he contented himself with the pleasure of stroking her skin. What harm to give himself to this pleasure? To give her this pleasure as well? They had no difficulties to face, no plans that needed to be made, and none of his duties back home could press him here. Was this not what he'd once lost? To simply enjoy himself?

His body's needs grew stronger and her response urged him on. He rose above her and entered her with ease. Her body was ready and it felt like a welcome, like forgiveness. All Will could think at the moment was that he loved her and was glad he was married to her.

In the next moment his primitive urges drove all thought and emotion from his mind. He moved faster and faster and she met him, stroke for stroke. Together they came to the brink of pleasure and carried each other over it. He felt her release burst and his followed. He slid off her and held her in his arms. They did not speak. Eventually her breathing became even. She was asleep.

Sleep came later for him as he savoured the joy for as long as he could.

They rose early in the morning and dressed for riding. While they ate breakfast John saw to the horses. Their portmanteaux had been exchanged for saddlebags, now all packed and ready to go.

Mr Armstrong insisted on wrapping up bread and cheese— and three bottles of cider—for their trip. He and his daughter and the tavern regulars were there to wave them off as if they were old and dear friends.

Will helped Anna onto her horse, but turned to shake Armstrong's hand before mounting his own.

'Thank you, Armstrong.' He handed the man his card. 'If I may ever be of service to you or your family, write to me.'

Armstrong glanced at the card. 'I'll be a—you are a lord?' He turned to his friends. 'The lad's a lord!'

'G'wan!' they cried.

Will clapped him on the shoulder. 'Do not hold it against me.'

Armstrong shook his head in disbelief. 'First one I met who wasn't *English*.'

Will laughed. 'I am English but, from you, I will take that as a compliment.'

Armstrong turned to Anna. 'So you are a lady, then, lass?'

Anna smiled graciously. 'Ever since you married us, sir.'

Armstrong waved his arms. 'Be off with ye before I charge you an extra guinea or two for the room.' Will had already paid him generously.

They said their final goodbyes and were on the road.

As the inn receded in their sight, Anna said, 'I believe I will miss them.'

Will thought she said this more to herself than to him but he responded, 'As will I. They were decent people, the lot of them.'

It was another fine, clear day, not too hot for June. A perfect day for a ride and Will was determined to enjoy it.

John rode a few feet behind Will and Anna. Will rode next to her, but they did not talk much.

It was difficult to endure her distant silence, especially since he wanted her to share in the freedom from all responsibility that he felt. On this ride back to London, they could take all the time they wished. They could indulge every whim without any care. He'd be patient with her. He could not expect Anna to trust he would not turn churlish again merely because he felt the opposite.

He was determined to be amiable, though.

'You ride well,' he said as they left the town and entered the countryside.

She turned to him and he was gratified to see her smile. 'I enjoy it.'

He smiled, as well. 'Then I am glad we are making this trip on horseback.' He wanted to keep the conversation going. 'We should make it to Carlisle by noon, I should think.'

Their first destination was Carlisle, to find Toby.

She merely nodded.

Once out of the town they rode past fields rich with crops and green pastures dotted with sheep or cattle. Stone fences or thick hedgerows crisscrossed the lands. Will wondered how many of the barriers were a result of the Clearances, where large landowners took over the land, driving off the tenants whose animals had grazed over the pastures for generations.

Another topic Will met with ambivalence. He also was a landowner who needed to increase the productivity of his farms, but he could not help feeling more was owed to the common people who were displaced.

There was nothing he could do about it at the moment, though. He filed such thoughts away for a later date and merely relished how beautiful was the land.

Anna took in a deep breath of the crisp countryside air. Coils of tension deep inside her since Vauxhall Gardens loosened a bit. The scenery itself was calming. To be riding, even at this sedate pace was a joy. She was already in love with her pony, who seemed completely at ease.

She glanced at the man riding beside her, so tall and comfortable in the saddle. She smiled to herself. He looked too big for his Highland pony although the animal seemed perfectly content to be carrying him on its back.

She thought of the night before. His lovemaking had been as gentle and kind as the first time, and she'd given in to the pleasure of it. He'd been exceptionally kind the whole of this trip, but in a sudden instant he'd turned back into the enemy—antagonistic, disagreeable, churlish—much like he'd been when they first removed their masks at Vauxhall Gardens. She did not know what to trust. The kind man or the ill-natured one?

At least riding her lovely pony amidst the beauty of the countryside and breathing the fresh country air mollified her emotions. She could forget for long stretches of time that he might not be the strong, handsome, loving man that first night of lovemaking—and the one following—promised him to be.

Whatever he was, though, the die was cast and she must lie in the bed she'd made for herself. Or what had been made for her.

They reached Carlisle when the sun was high in the sky. Noon or near to it, and they found Toby at the Bush Inn where they had left him. With him were John's brother and his wife, Lottie.

Willburgh requested a private dining room and they gathered there as equals for refreshment and to trade tales of their separate experiences.

'You should have seen when the gentlemen discovered us was us,' John's brother, Adams, said. 'The one was hopping mad.' He grimaced. 'They thought they could get the better of me, but I was bigger and stronger.'

Anna gasped. 'Did they fight you? Did you get hurt?' She had not wanted anyone to come to harm because of her.

John's brother grinned. 'No, ma'am. They did some pushing and shoving, but I put a stop to that right off.'

His wife gave him a proud look.

'I am so very grateful to both of you,' Anna said.

The brother's wife waved her words away, then said, 'I have your dresses packed for you.'

Anna touched the young woman's arm. 'I would like for you to have them, Lottie.' They had come from the Dormans and Anna did not want them anyway.

Her eyes brightened. 'Thank you, ma'am.'

Their meal was leisurely and pleasant, but as it went on, Willburgh asked Adams, 'Are we keeping you from your work?'

The young man shrugged. 'The stable let me go. But you paid me plenty. We'll be all right and something will come up.'

Willburgh looked towards Toby. 'We should have something at Willburgh House, do you not think?'

Toby nodded. 'Looks to me like you have three more horses need tending to. An extra hand will be welcome.'

'And there is always need for an extra pair of hands in the house.' He glanced at Lottie. 'If you like. It means leaving your home, though.'

'This isn't our home, sir,' John said. 'We came for the work.'

'We'll gladly work for you, m'lord,' his brother said.

While they discussed arrangements, Anna watched Willburgh. Here was another surprise. Such a generous offer. He hadn't been required to make it; he'd paid them well, after all. He offered them security.

When the horses were rested and their repast over, she and Will returned to the road. Toby, Adams, and his wife were to travel by coach directly to Buckinghamshire where Willburgh's country estate was located. Anna knew the house and property, of course. She'd glimpsed it many times while riding with Violet and Lucius. It was grander than Dorman Hall, the Dormans' country house. The Dormans' property abutted Willburgh's at that parcel of wooded land to which each claimed ownership. Part of the feud between the families.

When she and Will left Carlisle behind and were back in the open countryside, Will had ridden ahead. Anna urged her horse to catch up to him.

'Willburgh?' she called.

He turned around and waited for her. Her horse came to Willburgh's side.

He smiled—a bit sadly, she thought. 'It's Will,' he said.

She felt guilty for deliberately not calling him by his preferred name. 'Will,' she repeated. 'I wanted to say—' She didn't know how to say it. 'I wanted to say that it was good of you to hire John and his brother and wife.'

His smile brightened. 'A mere trifle.'

She remained next to him, while John rode behind. She made an effort to talk to him, to comment on the sites they passed or the other travellers on the road. They avoided the busy routes with their wagons of goods and speeding coaches. They were no longer dependent upon coaching inns and post horses and could stop and rest their horses at any village inn they wished. They rode the smaller roads and were often the only ones in sight. It was quiet and peaceful and her coils of tension loosened even more.

They stopped at one such village inn to spend the night, registering as Mr and Mrs Willburgh. Their room was small and Anna's legs were aching from the day in the saddle. The bed, though, was comfortable enough to make love. After Anna again experienced that exquisite burst of pleasure, she relaxed in Will's arms. The wall she'd constructed over her heart cracked a little. Anna fell asleep as the crack allowed a glimmer of hope to seep into her heart.

The next day Anna's heart opened a little more, each time Will treated her or someone else well. He was truly the best man she'd ever known and her heart leapt at the mere sight of him.

The frantic travel by post to reach Scotland could not have been more different than the leisurely return trip. They stopped as often as they wished or whenever the horses needed rest. They avoided the larger towns but happily explored whatever smaller village they fancied, villages with names like Newbiggin, Bollington, and Goosnargh. When staying at inns, Will always signed them in as Mr and Mrs Willburgh and no one questioned that. They wore ordinary clothes and rode ordinary horses and were simply assumed to be ordinary people.

On fair days they picnicked by clear blue lakes and explored crumbling ruins. They rested in the inns on rainy days, playing cards and making love during the day. When the roads were dry and the air was fine, they let the horses gallop, the wind tugging at her hat. It felt like flying.

Anna told Will about India, about her *ayah* and the other beloved servants she left behind, about the sights and sounds and smells. Will regaled her with stories about his school days, about the mischief he and his friends engaged in, about the oddities of his tutors. They remarked on what they saw along the road and the people they met. At night they let their bodies speak and the lovemaking only got better and better.

Throughout the trip neither of them spoke about fathers or duels or Dormans or duties or even what arriving in London would bring.

After almost a fortnight, though, they faced the end of their idyll. The roads became thick with wagons, horsemen, and carriages. The fields and woods and tiny villages gave way to factories and workshops and crowded tenements. Finally they reached the neat streets, shops, and townhouses of Mayfair where passers-by dressed in fine fashions eyed them with curiosity and dismay. Anna suddenly saw herself through their eyes. Her clothes, full of the dust of the road, were the worse for wear after almost two weeks of travel.

When they turned onto Park Street, Anna's spirits sank. They were at the end. At the door of Will's townhouse.

Anna, dirty and shabby, looked like she ought to be using the servant's entrance; Will, like a labourer seeking work. John appeared more like his companion than his groom.

Will helped her dismount and John held the horses while Will sounded the knocker. Bailey answered the door.

The butler's shocked expression quickly became composed when he welcomed Will's return and quickly summoned a footman to tend to the horses and another to collect their bags.

Before leaving her pony, Anna stroked the horse's neck. 'Thank you, Seraphina, for carrying me so far,' she murmured.

She was rewarded with a nuzzle back.

Anna reluctantly stepped away. 'See she's taken good care of,' she pleaded.

The footman bowed. 'Yes, m'lady.'

Anna blinked. Right... *M'lady*. She was Lady Willburgh now.

Will introduced John to the footman. 'He is our new groom,' Will explained. 'Show him the stables and introduce him to the head groom. He is to be welcomed and given every consideration. Let them know. He can be in charge of these horses.'

'Yes, m'lord,' the footman said.

Anna approached John before he was led away. She clasped his hand. 'Thank you, John. You must let us know if you need anything at all.'

'I will, ma'am,' the youth said.

Will escorted Anna into the hall where the butler eyed her with some distress. She hoped it was merely due to her dress.

'Bailey, you saw John, our new groom,' Will said.

'I did indeed, sir,' the butler replied.

'Check on him later, if you will,' he went on. 'I want to make certain he is treated well. He was invaluable to us.'

How like Will to be concerned about John, Anna thought. The young man *had* been invaluable to them.

'I will, sir,' the butler replied. 'And Toby? Is he with you?'

'I sent him on to Willburgh House.' He handed Bailey his old hat and worn gloves. 'Is my mother at home?'

'She retired to the country a few days after you left, m'lord,' Bailey responded.

'Probably for the best,' Will said, as if to himself.

Anna could just imagine what her new mother-in-law would have thought of her present appearance.

'Are there rooms ready for us?' Will's voice sounded different. Like a viscount's. He even stood differently. Stiffer. With an air of command.

Had her affable, relaxed new husband disappeared?

'Yes. Your room and the one adjoining it for the viscountess.' The butler looked a little disturbed. 'Some of the servants have the day off, it being Sunday and we did not know to expect you today, but I will find your valet, sir, and a maid to tend to—to the viscountess.' He turned to Anna. 'The belongings you left here are in the room, unpacked, m'lady.'

At least they'd thought of her.

'Very good, Bailey.' Will spoke before Anna could acknowledge him.

Will offered his arm and walked with her up the stairs to the bed chamber that had been Lady Willburgh's. His mother must not have been pleased at being so displaced, Anna thought.

'There is a connecting door to my room.' Will opened it to show her. 'Is there anything I can do for you before a maid appears?' His voice sounded so formal.

Anna looked around at the beautifully decorated room. How could his mother not resent her use of it?

'I will not need you.' She echoed his formal tone.

What she did need was for it to be only the two of them in a simple room in an inn, helping each other, not waiting for valets and maids. Those days—and nights—would never return.

She removed her hat and pulled off gloves, placing them both on a chair. Still feeling like an intruder, she opened drawers and discovered her clothes were indeed there, as

Bailey had said. She took out a clean shift and corset. It would be glorious to change into them. It would be glorious to clean off the dirt of the road.

In a corner of the room behind a spectacular hand-painted screen was a lovely French wash stand with ornate marquetry. Inside its cabinet were soap and towels. The pitcher was filled with water. It did not matter to Anna if it was fresh or not. She stripped off her riding habit and underclothes and washed the dirt of travel off her body. It would be lovely to wash her hair as well, and even to have a tub bath, a nice long tub bath with nice hot water. Would it be offered to her? she wondered.

Or could she, now Lady Willburgh, simply order it done?

This she could not imagine.

After she dried herself and put on her clean shift and stockings, there was a tap at the door.

'It is the maid, m'lady.' It was the chatty maid who had served her before. She entered the room carrying Anna's saddlebags. 'I've brought your luggage. Mr Bailey also said I was to help you dress or whatever you wish me to do. I'm not a lady's maid, though.'

'You helped me well enough before,' Anna said. 'What is your name?'

'I am Hester, m'lady.' Hester was little more than a girl, smaller than Anna with a riot of blond curls escaping her cap.

Anna nodded. 'Hester, I found my underclothes, but I have not yet found my dresses.'

The girl walked over to the wall covered with Chinese wallpaper. She found knobs cleverly blending in with the wallpaper and opened a cabinet, a clothes press built into the wall. 'Your dresses are in here, m'lady.'

Anna could not help but laugh. 'I would never have found them.'

'Which dress, ma'am?' Hester asked.

Anna glanced inside the cabinet where three dresses were neatly folded on shelves, one of which was the dress Will's mother gave her. She selected that one.

'This is the one Lady Willburgh gave you,' Hester exclaimed. 'I must say it looked better on you than it did on her.'

'It wasn't her colour,' Anna said diplomatically. She touched her hair. 'Before I dress, I should like to brush my hair. I have a brush and comb in the bags over there.'

Hester went to the dressing table and opened a drawer. 'There is one here, as well.'

Anna joined her. 'Someone thought of everything.'

'His Lordship wrote a letter saying you would come soon,' Hester said. 'He told Mr Bailey to tell Mrs White to make sure you had everything you would need.'

Anna had not known that.

'But you need more dresses,' Hester added as Anna sat at the dressing table and she removed the pins from her hair. 'You don't have nearly enough.'

When her hair was arranged, the maid said, 'Before I forget, I am to tell you to meet His Lordship in the drawing room when you are ready.'

Yes. She'd be meeting *His Lordship*, not her Will.

Chapter Eleven

Will sat at his desk in the library, piles of mail and other papers in front of him. It would take an age to attend to it all. A quick riffling through the pile showed many notes from his peers in the Lords. Two or three letters from his mother. Bills from various shopkeepers. Letters from the managers of his various estates. A summons to come see his men of business. Charities seeking donations. Relatives seeking funds. Relatives writing to chastise him for compromising Anna. Others warning him not to marry her.

He wanted to chuck the lot into the fireplace and watch it burn to ashes. He wanted to be with Anna, free to ride down country lanes, explore new villages, revel in the delights of sharing her bed. His mind refused to focus, yet all this correspondence was vitally important. Countless people depended upon him meeting his responsibilities.

His idyll was over.

Staring at the endless piles was achieving nothing, though, and he'd told Anna to meet with him. Will left most of the letters unopened and walked out of the library to go to the drawing room where Bailey was just setting down a tray of tea, biscuits, and sandwiches.

'Thank you, Bailey.' Will took two of the sandwiches off the tray. 'I did not realise how hungry I was.'

'I suspected it, sir,' the man replied.

Will sank down in one of the chairs. 'Before you go, tell me. What has it been like here?'

'Well, sir.' The butler straightened. 'About as dreadful as one could imagine.'

Will groaned. 'Tell me.'

'The printers seemed to be attempting to outdo each other. Several handbills were released embellishing the tale. Some made you out to be a terrible villain, preying on an innocent. One could have been written by Lord Dorman, all about how his ungrateful ward betrayed the family by consorting with you, merely to hurt them.' He dipped his head. 'I saved them for you. They are on your desk.'

They must have been at the very bottom of the piles.

'Your mother received some nasty letters,' he went on. 'And all the invitations she'd received hitherto were withdrawn.'

'She was wise to leave town, then.' And Will had been glad she'd gone.

His feelings towards his mother were ambivalent at best. Although he'd resolved not to ignore her as his father had done, he did not believe she was wholly innocent in the affair that caused his father's death even though she attempted to paint herself as ill-used. Especially when she tried to manipulate him to get her own way. She was often the most burdensome of his chores.

Bailey added, 'She was quite distressed.'

As well she would be. Will was glad he and Anna were spared that at least. It would all die down now they were married.

'Is that all, sir?' Bailey asked.

Will stood and walked over to the cabinet. 'Is there brandy here?'

'There is, sir.'

Will opened it and took out the carafe of brandy and a glass. 'Then nothing more. Thank you, Bailey.'

The butler bowed and left the room.

Will poured himself a glass of brandy and drank it in two swallows. He wished he had taken Anna straight to Dover and hopped on a packet to the Continent. Think how exciting it would be to explore France, Italy, Spain, and Greece with her?

If only he could. He'd merely neglected his duties for three weeks and his work had turned mountainous. Payment for choosing enjoyment over a rush back to duty.

He poured himself a second glass of brandy.

Anna entered the room.

It had been almost two weeks since Will had seen her dressed in anything but her riding habit, a simple dress—or her shift. She took his breath. She wore that dress his mother gave her, the one that complemented her colouring so well. Her skin glowed with the health a week spent in fresh air would do. Her light brown eyes captivated him. She looked stunningly beautiful.

All he wanted was to take her in his arms and carry her back to his bed chamber. And remove that lovely dress.

Instead he stood. 'There is tea. And refreshments.'

She gestured to his glass. 'What are you drinking?'

He lifted the glass and peered at it as if noticing it for the first time. 'Brandy. Would you prefer a glass?'

She looked at him with questions in her eyes, but merely said, 'Please.'

Did she realise he sought out brandy when stressed?

He put his glass down and turned to the cabinet to get one for her. 'Is the room and service meeting your satisfaction?' Lord. He sounded stiff-necked.

She took the glass from his hand. 'Of course it is.' She spoke with a touch of irritation.

At him, he supposed.

She lowered herself into a chair. 'Hester has been a help.'

Will sat, too, and passed a plate of sandwiches to her. 'I am glad. She is a good worker.'

He took a couple of biscuits and berated himself. This was not what he wished to say to her. It was as if they were strangers again.

His thoughts were consumed with her. How was he to accomplish all that needed doing?

She sipped her brandy and seemed to be watching him carefully. 'Hester tells me I need a new wardrobe.'

He remembered the urgency of their purchasing old garments from the market in Nottingham as well as the pleasure of shopping for her riding habit in Langholm. Think how delightful it would be to comb the second-hand clothing shops on Petticoat Lane with her.

But, no. A viscountess must have her clothing made by a modiste.

'Buy whatever you want,' he said. 'Have the charges sent to me.'

'And a new riding habit?' She smiled wanly.

'Of course. A new habit.' He answered automatically, thinking how deprived of enjoyment he felt not to be ordinary enough to shop on Petticoat Lane.

A minute later he realised she'd meant him to remember how excited they'd both been when the garment fit her. The moment had passed.

He also realised he'd answered her exactly how his father answered his mother when she attempted to talk to him about something she desired to buy. '*Buy whatever you need,*' his father would say, as if he'd wished not to be bothered.

Or maybe his father was simply preoccupied by work. Will could understand now. Will was overwhelmed at how much he needed to do.

But somehow his father never seemed to yearn to be free of responsibility. When his father said duty comes first, he almost always sounded glad.

Anna finished the glass of brandy. She might as well have been alone. Will was preoccupied. He was also almost formal with her, more like he'd been those first days when they were nothing but enemies. It was as if he'd turned from being her Will of their travels into the viscount as soon as they crossed this house's threshold.

She put her glass on the table. 'What is it, Will? You are not attending.'

He shook his head as if dislodging more important thoughts. 'Forgive me. You said a new habit. New clothes. I could unearth the name of my mother and sister's modiste, but you may not want to use her.'

'I'd rather not,' she admitted. 'I certainly do not want to use Lady Dorman's modiste.'

'No, indeed,' Will looked distracted again.

She tried again. 'Will, what is wrong?'

He met her gaze. 'Wrong? Nothing.' But he finished his brandy and stood. 'I am sorry to do this, but I must leave you.' He seemed in a hurry to do so. 'I need to tend to a desk full of correspondence in the library.'

'Oh.' He was leaving her alone? 'Is there anything I might do to assist?' Anna wanted his company, even if he seemed a million miles away.

He shook his head. 'You are free to do as you wish, though. If you need anything, call a servant.' That felt like a dismissal. 'I will see you at dinner.'

He left.

He left? How could he leave her so abruptly? Not that he seemed like much company the last few minutes. What had happened?

The room turned deadly quiet except for the ticking clock. She must do something at the moment or go mad.

She placed the empty plates and the glasses on the tray that held the untouched tea things. She could at least carry the tray down to the kitchen.

As she descended the stairs to the lower floor and emerged in the hallway to the kitchen, Mrs White, the housekeeper, met her. 'M'lady! I was coming to you. You are not to be carrying trays. I will take that.' She almost pulled the tray out of Anna's hands.

'I thought I would help,' Anna explained. 'I knew some of the servants had the day off.'

At the Dormans' she'd often perform servants' tasks when asked.

'You are not to help, m'lady,' the housekeeper scolded. 'You must ring and we will come to see what you need.' The woman started to walk away.

'Mrs White?' Anna called. 'What were you coming to see me for?'

'The dinner menu. I will meet with you in a moment.' She turned away again.

'Shall I follow you?' Anna called after her.

The housekeeper turned back. 'Goodness, no.' Her voice softened. 'Lady Willburgh never came down to the kitchen. I will come to you.'

'Where shall I meet you?' asked Anna.

Mrs White looked a bit pitying. 'M'lady, you must tell me where you wish me to be.'

There was nowhere in this house Anna felt comfortable.

'Would the bed chamber do?' She could not call it *her* bed chamber.

'That will do nicely,' the housekeeper said. She bustled away with the tray.

Anna paced the bed chamber until the housekeeper came. There was very little to discuss about dinner, as it was obvious Mrs White and the cook knew precisely what they wished to serve.

'What else might you need, m'lady?' Mrs White asked as she readied to leave the room.

'Nothing at the moment. Thank you.' What she really needed and wanted was a return to the gambol of the past two weeks with Will.

After the housekeeper left, Anna paced the room again, until she could stand it no longer. She wanted to be with Will even if he was busy. She'd go down to the library and park herself there. Read a book. Or even better, assist him.

She descended the stairs and entered the library without knocking.

Will stood. 'Anna!' He did not sound overly glad to see her. 'I was just about to come to you.' He straightened a pile of papers on his desk. 'I just this moment learned I must leave you. Lord Lansdowne and Lord Brougham have sent for me to meet them and others at Brook's. There is to be a vote tomorrow to suspend habeas corpus. It is important we discuss the matter beforehand. I must go.'

'You must go now?' she asked.

'I must.' He straightened another pile.

'And you will be gone tomorrow?' she managed.

'Tomorrow. Yes.' He hurried past her. 'I am sorry. I will miss dinner. And I may be late. These things take time.' He turned back to her. 'Choose any book you like. The library is yours.'

And he was gone.

And she was alone.

She stood at the window and watched him rush out of the house and hurry down the street.

The vote on habeas corpus was important, she knew. It protected citizens from imprisonment without proof that they had committed a crime. The government thought its suspension would help control the unrest that was fomenting across the country and to prevent the sort of revolution France had endured.

If Will had simply spent a few minutes talking with her about it, Anna might be more forgiving of his abandoning her. She'd have felt important to him, not excluded. Instead, it seemed like he'd been eager to be away from her.

She was mystified at this change in him, but had she not experienced this once before? He'd become haughty and disagreeable the morning after their wedding. She was mystified but also angry. She had done nothing to deserve this treatment, to be left alone with virtually no regard for her feelings. She might as well be back with the Dormans for all the consideration she received from him.

One thing was different, though. She was not entirely powerless. She was Viscountess Willburgh now and a viscountess could sometimes have her way.

Anna turned on her heel and strode out to the hall, but it was unattended at the moment. She wasn't about to ring bells and wait, no matter what Mrs White thought of her. She marched down to the lower floor and found Mrs White and Bailey conversing in the servants' hall.

'M'lady,' Mrs White began. 'I said you must ring—'

Anna interrupted her. 'I did not wish to wait for bells. This is what I want. I want a bath. As soon as it might be accomplished. I want to wash my hair. Bring dinner to my room when it is convenient and I do not care what Cook fixes. She need not fuss. Anything will do.'

Without waiting for a response, Anna turned around and hurried off, before her emotions exploded. On her way to her bed chamber, she stopped by the library and pulled three books at random.

'*Choose any book*,' he'd said, as if that made amends.

Anna's bath was arranged right away and Hester attended her. Since Anna was not intending to leave her room, she dressed in night clothes afterwards. She sat at the dressing table while Hester combed the tangles from her hair.

The maid remarked, 'M'lady, your hair curls nicely.'

'Curls?' Anna remembered that this maid had arranged curls in her hair before, when Anna had first stayed here.

'Yes, m'lady. Especially if you bunch it up in your hands as it dries.' Hester took a lock of Anna's hair and demonstrated. 'See? It curls.'

Indeed when she released her hair, the curls remained. Anna was used to pulling her hair straight, although she did remember having curls when she'd been a little girl.

Hester bunched up another lock of hair.

'You made my hair curl before,' Anna remarked.

'Those weren't what I call curls. Want to see curls?' Hester removed her cap. 'See my hair? It is too curly. But yours will be nice curls.'

'Hester, your curls are lovely,' Anna said.

The girl sighed. 'More like a trial, ma'am.'

Hester's good-natured company was giving Anna some comfort. She certainly needed it.

'Hester, you said I need new clothes. Do you know where

I might find a good modiste? I do not want to use the one the Dormans used.'

Hester sniffed. 'You certainly can do better than that one. My cousin says she is not very skilled and she charges too much. And she is not really French.'

Anna suppressed a laugh. 'I suspected that. Your cousin knows her?'

The maid stopped with the comb in mid-air. 'My cousin sews for a modiste who dresses the daughters of merchants and cits. She wants to have her own shop someday.'

'Do you think your cousin might sew for me?' Anna asked.

Hester dropped the locks of hair she was bunching. 'Do you mean that, m'lady? I'm sure she would love to. My goodness! She'd be making clothes for a viscountess!'

'I'm not sure she would want to advertise that it was me,' Anna responded. 'Not with the scandal, but Lord Willburgh would pay her well, I am certain, especially if she could make some clothes quickly. Could she see me tomorrow, do you think?'

Hester put the comb down and bunched more curls into Anna's hair. 'I could go to her now and arrange it. If I have permission to leave, that is.'

'Who should I speak to arrange permission for you?' Anna asked.

Hester giggled. 'M'lady, you need not seek permission. If you say I can leave, I can leave.'

The meeting at Brook's dragged on until near midnight. Will might as well have missed it. He could barely attend to the discussion let alone contribute. His mind was filled with Anna. He missed her company. His body ached for her.

This would not do. He needed to pay attention in meetings like this. He needed to contribute.

Lord Lansdowne offered him a ride home in his carriage and Will was forced to continue their discussion as the carriage made its way to Park Street.

How was he to go on? He had his responsibilities. His duty. He could not spend his hours mooning over her like a lovesick calf.

The carriage stopped and a groom opened the door. With Lansdowne still making one more point, Will paused before climbing out and bidding the man goodnight.

He entered the house. The hall was being attended by a sleepy footman who took his hat and gloves. Everything was dark and quiet.

Will hurried directly upstairs to his bed chamber, catching his valet dozing in a chair.

'Beg pardon, sir.' The man jumped to his feet.

'No need,' Will responded. 'It's late, I know. Is everyone asleep?' He meant had Anna retired or was she waiting for him?

'I expect so, sir,' The valet helped him off with his coat and boots.

'I'll tend to myself from here, Carter,' Will said. 'You can go to bed.'

'Very good, m'lord.' Carter bowed and, carrying Will's coat and boots, left the room.

As soon as he left, Will went to the door connecting his room with Anna's. He opened it a crack and listened, but all was quiet. There was a light, though, so he entered. It was a candle on a table near the bed, burning itself almost to a nub.

It left enough light, though, to see that Anna was in bed, eyes closed, breathing evenly.

'Anna?' he whispered, but she did not stir.

He stood watching her for a long time, yearning to strip off the rest of his clothes and join her, but reluctant to disturb her peaceful sleep. Eventually, he turned around and returned to his own bed chamber.

Anna opened her eyes and watched him walk away.

She'd already heard a clock strike twelve so she knew it was later than that. Had he thought her asleep? Why did he not come to her anyway?

It wounded. And angered her.

If he had only joined her in her bed, she might have forgiven him for staying away so long. Instead he walked away.

She rolled over and hugged a pillow, but sleep did not come easily.

Chapter Twelve

The next morning Will woke early, acutely aware that he was alone in the bed, alone for the first time in over a fortnight. He missed her. He greatly missed her.

His valet was as prompt as ever in appearing to help him dress. Will had half a mind to send Carter away and see if Anna was still abed. Perhaps there was still time to make love in the morning like they'd done on their journey, but if he did that he'd keep his valet waiting and the maid serving Anna might have to wait, as well. Will made it a point of honour to be considerate of the servants and to appreciate the services they performed for him.

So he let his valet dress him, and as soon as Carter left, Will went to the connecting door. He opened it and listened, but all was quiet. He walked in as quietly as he could.

The bed's linens were smoothed and everything appeared neatly in order.

She had arisen early. Earlier than he.

He hurried down to the breakfast room and found Anna there, sipping tea and reading the *Morning Post*. She wore the same dress as the day before, the one his mother had given her, but her hair had been transformed into cascading curls that framed her face and bounced at her slightest movement. He was entranced.

She looked up. 'Good morning, Will.' Her voice was flat. And chill.

'Good morning.' What was he to say to her?

He wanted to tell her she looked beautiful. Wanted to beg her forgiveness for leaving her alone the day before and tell her they could spend this entire day together. But that would mean neglecting some correspondence that must be answered this day and missing the meeting his men of business had deemed of the greatest importance. Afterwards he must make his way to the Old Palace of Westminster for the House of Lords session and the vote. His day was filled.

He gestured to the newspaper. 'I arranged to have a notice of our marriage put in the papers.' One of the tasks he'd accomplished the previous day. 'It will be printed tomorrow.'

She lowered the newspaper and simply stared at him. Or perhaps *glared* was a better word, although no specific emotion seemed to be reflected in her expression.

None that he could read, at least. He selected his food from the sideboard and sat across from her. 'I am afraid I will be gone most of the day today.'

She stared at him again, pausing before she spoke. 'And what shall I tell Cook about dinner?'

He hated his reply. 'I will not be here for dinner.'

She returned to the newspaper.

By the time Will finished his breakfast, he'd convinced himself her coolness towards him was a good thing. He needed to do his work and the sooner she realised that took precedence over everything else, the better. His could not be a life of enjoyment and spontaneity. The mountain of papers on his desk was testimony to that.

Because he wanted what he could not have. The freedom to enjoy her company.

* * *

Before Will settled down to his pile of papers, he wrote out letters with his seal indicating that the shopkeepers could bill him for any purchases Anna made. He could have had Bailey or one of the footmen bring her the letters, but he chose to deliver them to her himself.

He found her in her bed chamber, surprising her, apparently.

'Will!' She shut the drawer she'd been looking through. 'I—I did not expect to see you.'

He handed her the letters. 'Show these letters at any of the shops,' he told her. 'They will allow you to purchase whatever you like.'

She took them from him. 'Thank you,' she said in a low voice, but raised her head to meet his gaze. 'Because I will need clothing quickly, I expect to be asked to pay more than what is customary.'

He held her gaze and felt his resolve waver. He wanted to take her in his arms. Instead he said, 'Cost does not matter. Buy what you like.'

A faint smile flitted across her face. 'As you have often told me.'

He wished she'd not reminded him of their time together shopping. He'd never had such pleasure spending his money.

He hesitated a moment, still gazing at her, but then glanced towards the door. 'I have work to do,' he said. 'I wish you a good day.'

He left.

Will holed himself up in the library, putting pen to paper, hardly looking up until he heard voices in the hall. He rose and walked to the door, opening it a crack to see Anna and the maid leave by the front door. From the library window he watched them walk down the street. It lowered his spirits even more.

By noon he was forced to stop working on his correspondence and called for his carriage. As he climbed in he thought he ought to have told Anna to take the carriage. He could have caught a hackney coach. Too late.

His coachman drove him to Fleet Street and the offices of his men of business. Whatever they'd deemed so urgent wound up taking a little more than an hour. He had time to kill until he must appear at Westminster. He strolled up and down the street waiting for his carriage and stopped when a shop window caught his eye.

The shop was Rundell and Bridge, goldsmiths and jewellers to the king.

He went inside. Until this moment he'd not given it a thought. Anna had no wedding ring. He'd fix that forthwith.

The next morning Anna's humour was improved. The meeting with Hester's cousin had been unexpectedly diverting and productive. Anna even left with two new dresses she could wear right away. She and Hester also managed to buy two hats, three pairs of gloves, several pairs of stockings, and countless ribbons. They'd even gone to a tailor to be fitted for a riding habit and to a corset maker.

Hester and her cousin devised a brilliant way for Anna to build a complete new wardrobe quickly. Her cousin would ask as many modistes as she could think of if they had any dresses that were not paid for or not finished for any reason. If they would be of a near size to Anna's, Hester's cousin would propose buying the dress for her unnamed customer. Then the cousin and her seamstresses would alter the dresses so they would not be recognisable as the originals. 'So m'lady wouldn't be talked of for wearing someone else's discards,' Hester's cousin explained.

As if she would not be talked of for other reasons, Anna thought.

After Anna dressed and Hester arranged her hair she examined herself in the mirror. The pale lilac dress complemented her well. She looked the best she'd ever looked in her life.

Not that Will would notice.

He hardly took the time to say hello to her. What plans would take him away this day? she wondered.

This morning Will arrived for breakfast first. He stood when she entered the room.

She managed, 'Good morning.'

He stared at her, finally saying, 'Is that a new dress already?'

'It is.' Although the pleasure of it was diminished by his lukewarm response. 'Do you approve of it?'

His gaze flicked up and down her body. 'I do approve. You look very well in it.'

That was better, but not by much.

'Did you manage to buy all you needed?' he asked.

'Not in one day.' She sat across from him. 'I did order a new riding habit, though.'

He sat, as well. 'Very good.'

Even mention of riding did not elicit more from him.

She'd heard of marriages like this—or perhaps read of them in a novel—the courtship all filled with declarations of love only to turn into coldness or abuse after the wedding.

But she and Will had no courtship and she was confident he would never hurt her, at least not in a physical way.

After filling her plate, the footman left the room.

Will rose. 'I bought something for you.'

'Oh?' She poured her tea.

He walked over to the chair next to hers and took a small box from his pocket.

He placed the box in her hand. 'You should have had this on our wedding day.'

Anna opened the box and gasped. It was a ring. A beautiful ring with one large diamond in the centre and smaller ones encircling it. The diamonds were set in a gold band fashioned in a floral filigree design.

Her eyes flew to his face.

He took the ring from its box and slipped it on the third finger of her left hand.

Her heart beat so fast it took a long while before she could speak. 'You—you should not have—it must have cost a great deal—'

He continued to hold her hand. 'I wanted you to have it.'

She was awed. 'It is beautiful, Will.' Even more so because he troubled himself to buy it for her.

He smiled. 'Now our marriage is official.'

She leaned over and kissed him on the cheek. He gazed at her and reached up, touching her cheek so gently it sent waves of sensation throughout her body. She yearned to have him share her bed again.

He moved back to his original seat and handed her the *Morning Post*. 'The announcement is in it.'

She scanned the page until she found it.

'Does the wording suit you?' he asked.

'It seems adequate,' she responded.

She was more puzzled than ever. Right when she'd resolved herself to think him turning cold, he did something so lovely. Buying her a ring. Why was he so cold and formal with her? Why did he not come to her bed?

Bailey entered the room. 'Pardon, sir, this missive just

arrived for you. The messenger said it was important. He awaits your reply.'

Will read it. 'Tell the messenger I will come within the hour.'

Bailey left.

Will handed the message to Anna. 'This is from a man at Coutts Bank. It is about your trust.'

She looked up in surprise. 'My trust? I have no trust.'

'He says that you do and insists that I call upon him immediately.'

She perused the message. 'There must be some mistake. How would I have a trust, when I have no money?'

Will stood. 'I will go right now.'

She rose, too. 'I will go with you.'

'Women are not typically expected to go to—'

Was he going to say women were not welcome at Coutts? She cut him off and was adamant. 'I will go with you.'

'Very well.' He started for the door. 'I will call for the curricle.'

Within a half hour Will's curricle was brought around. He was surprised to see who held the horses.

'Toby, you are back from the country.' Will helped Anna into the seat and climbed up himself, taking the ribbons.

'I am, sir. All is well there.' He jumped into the groom's seat.

Anna turned towards him. 'How are John's brother and his wife settling in?'

The groom shrugged. 'As best they can. You know how it can be if you're from a different place.'

More to worry over, thought Will.

As they reached the Strand, Will wondered at the urgency of the summons to Coutts. What could be so urgent? And why did Anna know nothing about a trust in her name?

'Could the trust have been set up by your relatives?' Will asked her.

'My mother said we hadn't any relatives,' she replied.

'But there was your father.' Perhaps this was about her father.

'None on my father's side, my mother said. Or on her side.'

They passed Somerset House and St Clements and pulled up in front of Coutts Bank. Toby jumped down and held the horses.

Will helped Anna down. 'I do not know how long we will be,' he said to Toby.

'I'll walk 'em if need be, sir,' the groom replied.

Will escorted Anna into the building. He announced himself to the attendant at the door. Several men within earshot turned to look when they heard 'Lord and Lady Willburgh.' Anna was the only woman present.

'We are here to see Sir Edmund Antrobus,' Will said.

'Lord Willburgh,' the attendant said too loudly. 'Yes. Follow me. I am certain Sir Edmund will see you.'

As they followed the man, Anna whispered to Will, 'We are attracting a great deal of notice.'

'I can see,' Will responded.

They had to wait only a few moments for Sir Edmund, who was one of the partners at Coutts, second in importance to Thomas Coutts himself. To come without an appointment and be seen right away? What did it mean?

Sir Edmund bowed to Anna. 'Lady Willburgh. It is a pleasure. I did not expect you.'

'Indeed, sir?' responded Anna. 'This apparently concerns me.'

'Yes. Yes.' He gestured to some chairs. 'Please do sit. May I serve you tea?'

'Thank you, no.' Will glanced at Anna who shook her head. 'Tell us. What is of such importance?'

Sir Edmund did not sit until they both took their chairs. 'It was the announcement of your marriage that prompted me to contact you, sir. From the—um—information made available to us before this, we did not know for certain that you would be married.' That information being from the handbills, he meant? 'I must say that I would have strongly advised you to consult with us before taking that step—'

'Why would we consult with you?' Will asked.

'Why? Because of the trust.' He looked dumbfounded.

'What trust?' The man was making no sense.

'Why, Lady Willburgh's trust,' Sir Edmund said.

Anna spoke up. 'I have no trust!'

Sir Edmund turned to her. 'Oh, but you do, my dear lady. It was set up by your grandparents.'

'But I have no grandparents!' she cried.

'No.' Sir Edmund gave her a sympathetic look. 'Not now, because they died shortly after your poor mother. Your grandfather set this up before their deaths.'

'So what of this trust?' Will asked.

Sir Edmund turned back to him. 'What have you heard of her grandparents?'

'Nothing,' Will replied.

Anna broke in. 'That is because I know nothing!'

Sir Edmund continued to address Will. 'The grandfather was Norman Lyman, a nabob. Made a fortune in India, then retired to Croydon in Surrey. It broke their hearts when their only daughter eloped with that soldier, especially when she went with him to India. Her parents disowned her, but settled some money on her when she had the child.' He inclined his head towards Anna.

Will glanced at Anna. Her face was pinched with distress. No wonder. Sir Edmund told it in a manner so oblivious of her feelings.

Sir Edmund went on. 'Then Edgerton died and she married Dorman. Mind you, this is all before her twentieth year.' He grimaced. 'Dorman must have been the only Englishman to lose a fortune rather than make one in India. He went through her money like water through a sieve.' Sir Edmund chuckled. 'Dorman begged Lyman for more money after she died, but Lyman set up the trust instead, providing the child with an allowance, but no more.'

Will interrupted him. 'So Lady Willburgh inherits this trust?'

'No,' Sir Edmund said. 'That is why I wished to see you. To explain.'

'Then tell us.' Anna's voice was strained.

'Well,' Sir Edmund went on. 'The Lymans did not approve of either of the marriages. They blamed their daughter's age. They were determined to prevent the same mistakes being made by their granddaughter.' Again the man gestured to Anna as if Will would not know to whom he referred without pointing her out. 'So the will has a stipulation. If the heir marries before age twenty-one she forfeits the inheritance entirely and it reverts to her children when she dies, with the same stipulation and so on.'

Will leaned forwards, unwilling to believe his ears. 'Do you mean there is a fortune to be inherited, but Anna—Lady Willburgh—cannot inherit because she married—'

Anna broke in. 'I will be twenty-one within months.'

Sir Edmund attempted to look sympathetic. 'I am afraid you do not inherit, but your children, if you have any, will.'

'And what happens if she does not have any children?' Will asked, his voice rising.

'Then it defaults to a charity. I would have to look up which. The Church, I believe.'

Will turned to Anna who looked as if she was struggling to control her emotions.

'How much of a fortune is this?' Will asked.

Sir Edmund held up a finger. 'I looked it up this morning after I read the marriage announcement. Ninety-six thousand, five hundred and thirty-six pounds.'

Will saw Anna grip the arms of her chair. It was an astounding figure. Enough wealth to live very, very well.

Will swallowed. 'Is there any property?'

Sir Edmund shook his head. 'As the will directed, the property was sold upon the death of both Mr and Mrs Lyman.'

Will glanced at Anna again. She looked about done.

He felt a knot twisting in his stomach.

She would have been only a month away from a fortune large enough for her to live on her own terms no matter how much gossip flew around her.

If only he hadn't married her.

Will stood. 'There is nothing else to say.'

Sir Edmund rose, as well. 'We will continue to manage the trust and you are certainly welcome to ask for an accounting at any time.'

Will offered his hand to Anna. She let him help her from the chair, but she did not look at him.

Sir Edmund walked them to the lobby. 'You must tell us if you have children, of course. Each child will receive fifty pounds a year.'

'Fifty pounds,' repeated Will.

'Yes,' responded Sir Edmund. 'Each child—as long as they do not marry before age twenty-one.'

'But not me,' Anna said, her voice wounded.

'Oh, but you received it,' he said. 'Did you not know?'

She shook her head.

'Was it paid to Lord Dorman?' Will's tone was tense.

'Well, he was her guardian.'

So Dorman knew all this and did not tell her? Will fumed.

Sir Edmund's hand covered his mouth. 'We gave him the money not two weeks ago.'

Will's lips thinned. 'We were married by then.'

Sir Edmund nervously wrung his hands. 'I suppose we should try to get the money back.'

'It belongs to the trust,' Will responded.

They reached the lobby. Sir Edmund bowed politely, bade them farewell and quickly turned away, hurrying back to his desk.

Will and Anna walked outside.

'Anna—' Will began.

She interrupted him. 'I want to go back to the townhouse.'

He did not know what to say to her. It was his fault they married so quickly. They could easily have waited for her to come of age. What had he done?

Chapter Thirteen

Toby came with the curricle and Will helped Anna into the seat. She could not speak. She felt as if someone had struck her in the face.

Betrayal. More betrayal.

By the Dormans, certainly. They could have told her she was an heiress. They could have let her know that she was not wholly dependent upon them. Fifty pounds was a great deal of money, enough for her clothing, pin money, food. She'd never been a burden on them.

Her stepfather—Anna could no longer think of him as her papa—could have told her, too. Why had he not if he'd truly cared for her?

Even her mother. Why had she not told Anna about her father and her grandparents long before she died?

And these grandparents she'd never known—they betrayed her, as well. They sent money after she was born, true, but they'd cruelly rejected her mother when she married her father. How her mother must have felt, no more than sixteen years old, to be shunned by her own parents? What if they had helped her instead? Maybe her father would not have had to stay in the army. Maybe he would not have had to go to India. Maybe he would still be alive. Her mother, too. Maybe she would not have caught the fever that took her life. Maybe Anna could have had a family who loved her.

And if her father had never died and her mother never married her stepfather, perhaps her stepfather could have found someone he truly loved. Maybe he would not have dallied with Will's mother and the duel would never have taken place. Perhaps Will's father would still be alive and Will would not have been so wounded.

She glanced at him. He was totally in control of the horses and was driving them skilfully through the busy traffic on the Strand. His expression was grim, though.

And why would it not be? Because of her he was trapped into a marriage that had been completely unnecessary.

Those days on the ride back to London were mere illusion. They were pretending they led other lives, lives without care, lives in which they could be happy, but all the while they'd not known the mistakes they were making.

The curricle pulled up to the Park Street townhouse. Will helped her down and she immediately rushed into the house. She passed the footman who attended the hall and hurried up the stairs to her bed chamber. The bed chamber that should have remained Will's mother's. She removed her shawl, her bonnet, and her gloves and flung herself onto the bed.

But she would not let tears fall. Some hurts were beyond weeping.

There was a knock at the door and Hester entered. 'Oh, my lady. Pardon me. I did not think you were napping.'

Anna sat up in the bed. 'I wasn't napping.'

Hester was clearly excited. 'I came to tell you that my cousin finished another dress and she has located several others for you to look at if you can come for fittings tomorrow.'

At least the search for a complete wardrobe was an exciting distraction. Even though she could have afforded three wardrobes if…if…

Anna blinked away those tears she refused to have fall. 'I am certain I can go to a fitting. Will you be able to accompany me?'

'Goodness.' Hester laughed. 'We'll merely tell Mrs White you need me.'

Anna managed a smile. 'Then let us go in the morning.'

Will sat at his desk and tried to look through the mail that had arrived that day. When he could not concentrate, he paced the room.

It was no use. He strode out of the library and into the hall.

'My hat and gloves,' he said to the footman. 'I'm going out.'

'Yes, m'lord.' The footman rushed off and returned in a trice.

Will put them on. 'I shouldn't be gone long.'

He walked the few blocks to Henrietta Street and sounded the knocker at the Dorman townhouse.

When he was admitted by their butler, he demanded, 'I wish to see Lord Dorman.'

'One moment, m'lord,' the butler said.

Will cooled his heels in the hall until the man returned. 'Lord Dorman will see you.'

The butler led him to the same drawing room where Will and Anna had spoken to him before.

'Lord Willburgh,' the butler announced.

Will faced them all. Lord Dorman, Lady Dorman, Lucius, and Violet. None of them looked pleased to see him. None of them rose when he entered.

'What now, Willburgh?' Lord Dorman snapped.

'I have been to see Sir Edmund Antrobus at Coutts.' Will did not need to tell them Anna had come with him. 'I know what you have concealed from Anna all these years, what you knew when we called upon you before.'

Lucius laughed. 'Did I not tell you the elopement was foolish?'

Will glared at each of them in turn. 'Do you know how exceptionally cruel it is to have deprived Anna of her rightful inheritance? What sort of gentlemanly behaviour is that?'

Again it was Lucius who spoke. 'We did nothing of the sort. It was *you* who deprived her. By compromising her. By eloping with her. We tried to stop you. Why do you suppose I tore off to Scotland?'

'Do not say so, Lucius,' Will shot back. 'A word from any of you would have stopped it.' He turned his glare to Lord and Lady Dorman. 'And how badly done of you to conceal the truth of her fortune? She had a right to know. You made her believe she was accepting your charity. Her expenses were paid and you knew it.'

'She cost us more than a paltry fifty pounds!' Lady Dorman cried.

Violet laughed. 'It is such a joke, though, is it not? She was only a few short weeks from being rich.'

Lucius grinned at her.

Will regarded them all with disgust. 'I do not know more detestable people than you lot.'

Lord Dorman half rose. 'See here, Willburgh. I will not be insulted in my own house. You may leave.'

Will turned to go, but turned back again when he was in the doorway. 'I wonder how well a handbill will sell with the story of how Lord and Lady D fraudulently kept fifty pounds belonging to the trust when they knew Anna was married and they were not entitled to it?'

Lucius vaulted from his chair. 'You would not dare!'

Will gave them a sinister smile. 'Oh, wouldn't I? Give

me the name of the printer you used for the handbills you had printed—'

'We won't tell you!' Lady Dorman was red-faced with anger.

Will kept his smile. 'Thank you for confirming that suspicion.'

'Why you—' Lucius came at him, but Will walked out before he even got close.

That evening Anna half expected Will to have arranged some meeting or other so he would miss dinner, but he didn't. She'd hoped to eat alone in her room again. She really did not wish to see him, to see the disappointment on his face. For marrying her.

Hester had convinced her to wear the new dress for dinner and to put her pearl earrings in her ears. It pleased the young woman, so Anna did as she requested. The dress was a Sardinian blue silk, but what Anna loved about it was that Hester's cousin had replaced the full sleeves with white satin inset with lace. She'd added matching lace to the neckline and at the hem. It was versatile as well, appropriate for afternoon or for less formal events such as the theatre or dinner parties.

Not that Anna expected to be invited to dinner parties.

Besides the fact that Will was not going out, the dinner was already planned. Mrs White had dutifully consulted with Anna on the menu that morning which meant, really, teasing out what dishes Cook wished to prepare.

Morning seemed so long ago. Before their visit to Coutts.

Will had just stepped out of the library door when Anna entered the hall.

'Will,' she said, feeling she must greet him.

'Anna,' he returned.

They walked into the dining room together. The long table had been set with a place at each end, far enough away from each other that Anna might as well have dined alone.

Will frowned when he saw it. 'This seems odd.'

When Anna dined with Will and his mother, they'd been seated on each side of Will who sat on the end.

Bailey was attending the room. 'Is there a problem, sir?'

Will twirled his finger. 'Move the settings so we sit closer to each other.'

Bailey moved Anna's place to a chair adjacent to Will's.

As soon as they sat, wine was poured and soup was served.

Having Bailey in the room and a footman bringing the food put even more of a damper on conversation than had become typical with them. What did they have to say to each other that they would not mind the servants knowing? Surely nothing about the fortune she'd lost.

How was she to ever get through this?

'Were—were you able to address the piles of papers on your desk?' she asked. Might as well pretend to be a viscount and viscountess having a quiet meal at home—Pretending worked so well on their ride back from Scotland.

'Everything urgent is done,' he replied.

They fell silent for a while, except for the sounds of their chewing and swallowing and the crackling of the chandelier above them.

Will looked up from his plate and took a sip of wine. 'Your dress is quite nice. One of the new ones?'

'It is,' she replied. 'Hester's cousin sent it over today.'

His brows rose. 'Hester's cousin is the modiste?'

'No, she is a seamstress,' Anna responded. 'She sews for a modiste, but she is helping me and, I must say, she's ingenious about it.'

'Is she?'

Anna did not have any illusions that Will was truly interested in dresses or the cousin of one of his maids, but she described how clever Hester's cousin was in gathering a brand-new wardrobe for her. It passed the time until the meal was almost done.

As they were finishing their pudding, Will said, 'Hester's cousin ought to have a business of her own. There must be others who need clothes quickly or at less cost.'

'She is very clever,' Anna agreed.

'Have Hester come speak to me,' he added. 'Perhaps her cousin merely needs some investment to get started.'

Anna gaped at him. He truly was an extraordinary man.

When the meal was done they retired to the drawing room for tea. As soon as Bailey left them after bringing in the tea service, Will went immediately to the cabinet in the corner of the room and took out the decanter of brandy. Tea simply would not do for him, not after the day they'd had.

He held up a glass and gestured an offer of brandy.

'Yes. Please,' she replied with feeling.

He poured them each a glass and handed hers to her before seating himself in a chair near hers.

This had been one horrible day. First the visit to Coutts, then the one to the Dormans. That had been foolish. Useless. Although he did confirm that they were behind some of the printing of the handbills.

That had not surprised him.

He should not have called on Dorman, but he'd been so angry he had to do something. He needed to get a hold on his emotions or he'd never be clear-headed.

He glanced at Anna sipping her brandy, looking abstracted.

No need to tell her about calling upon the Dormans and distress her more.

But he had to say something about what they'd been through. 'What Sir Edmund told us. It does not change anything.'

He meant he would still do his duty by her, try to make her life as pleasant as possible. He understood, though, that it must change how she felt about this marriage. About him. She must resent him for pushing the idea of marriage. How could she not?

She took another sip. 'It does change things,' she insisted. 'It makes everything worse.'

He had to agree with her. He'd not rescued her. He'd not saved her reputation. If he'd simply agreed to what she wanted—to live free from the Dormans—she'd have a fortune in a few weeks and then could do whatever she wished.

He finished his brandy and poured another one. 'If we had waited a few weeks...'

'You would be free,' she finished for him.

She had it wrong. 'No, you would be free,' Will said. 'You would be a wealthy heiress.'

Anna emptied her glass and extended it for Will to refill. She put it to her lips and let the amber liquid warm her mouth and chest.

She stared into her glass for a long moment before raising her eyes to his. 'What is it about me that no one saw fit to tell me about this will?'

He didn't answer, but she did not really expect him to.

She twirled the glass in her hand. 'I thought my stepfather cared about me. But if he did why did he not tell me I could be rich someday?'

'Perhaps he thought you were too young,' Will responded.

'I was ten. That seems old enough to me.'

'Perhaps he would have told you in time.' If he'd not first been killed by his father, she figured he meant.

It had been a long time since Anna had thought about that and she'd rather not think on it now. 'Lord and Lady Dorman should have told me, then.'

He nodded. 'Indeed they should have.'

She fell silent, sipping her brandy. When she finished it, she placed the glass on the table next to her.

'No one was honest with me,' she said with feeling. 'My mother was not an orphan. I was not a charity case that the Dormans needed to care for. Even my pa—' She stopped herself when a sudden thought intruded. She turned to Will. 'Did my stepfather keep me with him because of the money?' Did he not care for her at all? Had anyone besides her mother cared for her?

Will looked at her with what seemed like sincere sympathy, but could Anna trust in him? Did he truly care for her or was he merely trying to be kind? He changed so unpredictably even before this revelation—that he need not have married her at all. It was nonsensical to believe he would not resent her.

An ache grew in her heart that all the brandy in the world could not soothe. She wanted him to love her. Desperately wanted it. Because he was truly the finest man she'd ever known and, briefly, she'd felt cherished and safe in his arms. As if she belonged with him always and yet their being together was merely a fluke. A mistake.

A mistake that need not have happened. She felt sick with grief. The magical life of her early childhood, her unhappy life as a Dorman, the illusion of a home with Will, all were lost to her. What was she to do?

Anna stood, unable to contain her emotions any longer

and not wishing to impose them on Will. 'I should like to retire now. If you will excuse me.'

'Of course.' He rose to his feet and appeared for a second as if he thought he must accompany her. She did not want him to, not out of obligation.

She walked out alone.

Chapter Fourteen

The next day's visit to Hester's cousin was not as diverting as the one before, but Anna made an effort to hide the swirl of emotion that threatened to consume her. Odd how she could both actively engage about the dresses and, at the same time, puzzle out how she was to go on in her marriage.

These two young women were filled with enthusiasm about providing her with a wardrobe the likes of which neither of them could ever afford. Yet so much could go wrong for them. What if Will refused to pay for the dresses? What if he let Hester go without a reference? Will, of course, would do none of those dishonourable things, but other men did. Anna remembered Lady Dorman's modiste insisting on payment before making another gown for her. Or Lady Dorman nearly turning out one of the maids because Violet accused her of stealing an item Violet had merely misplaced.

Anna was so much luckier than they were. And luckier than many other women who'd been forced to marry. Will might not care for her; he might resent her, but he would never shirk his duty to her. She would always have everything she needed.

Except those glorious times when they were simply Mr and Mrs Willburgh.

She squared her shoulders and lifted her chin as Hester

and her cousin altered the dress to fit her. It was a muslin carriage dress in pale yellow with a matching spencer of corded silk. The lace that had festooned the original dress had been removed when Anna deemed it much too fussy.

After the fittings Anna and the two cousins visited several other shops and Anna purchased hats and gloves and scarves. Anna found a beautiful paisley shawl that Hester's cousin said would match all her new clothes. They even stopped at a shoemaker's shop to order shoes and a boot-maker where Anna was measured for some very fine riding boots and walking boots.

By the time Anna and Hester returned to the townhouse, it was late afternoon and Anna had spent a great deal of Will's money. She'd taken him at his word and he'd better not complain.

They stepped into the hall, the poor footman tasked with carrying their packages stumbling in behind them.

Will appeared in the doorway of the library. 'I would speak with you, Anna.' He sounded grim.

Anna turned to the footman. 'Please take the packages up to the bed chamber.'

'I had better go with you,' Hester said to the young man.

She gave the footman attending the door her hat and gloves and followed Will into the library.

He didn't ask her to sit, but put a handbill into her hand.

'A new handbill. Out today,' he said.

She read it immediately.

The handbill spoke about how she had lost her inheritance by only a month by marrying Will. It went on to make up a story about a violent fight between the two of them because he'd caused her to lose a fortune.

She crushed a corner of it in her hand. 'How did they even know of this?' She looked down at the handbill again.

'They must have known we spoke with Sir Edmund. Would Sir Edmund have told them?'

Will had a pained expression. 'Not Sir Edmund. Me.'

'You?'

'I called upon Lord Dorman yesterday,' he admitted. 'They were all there. I didn't tell you—'

She searched his face. 'But, why? Why call upon them?'

He averted his gaze. 'I was angry at them for what they'd done to you.'

Or what they'd done to him, perhaps. Getting him trapped into marrying her.

She felt sick.

On her shopping spree, she'd seen boys hawking handbills. Were those handbills about her? She'd also spied people staring at her and whispering behind her back. Shopkeepers' brows rose in recognition when they learned her name.

It was discomfiting to be talked about, to have one's personal affairs exposed to all.

'I am sorry, Anna.' Will's voice turned low.

She tried to shrug it off. 'Nothing to be done about it now.'

'We should go to the country,' he said. 'Leave London. We never should have come here in the first place.'

She looked at him. 'What about your duties in Parliament?'

He paced in front of her. 'I'll have to shirk that responsibility. In any event, I might prove a distraction from the real work that must go on.'

Surely they were not that important.

'We can leave tomorrow morning,' he went on.

A full day in a carriage with him? Anna imagined silence between them. And distance, trying not to sit too close. Like that excruciating first day on the trip to Scotland.

Before she fell in love with him.

'Very well.' She spoke firmly. 'But I want to ride. I want to ride Seraphina.'

He seemed to consider the idea. 'Have you your new riding habit?'

She shook her head. 'I'll wear the old one. I do not care. They can print a handbill about it, if they like.'

'Very well,' he said. 'We'll ride the ponies. It is not more than forty miles. We should be able to reach Willburgh House before dinner.'

They rose at dawn and were ready to leave an hour later.

Anna suspected the town servants were happy to see them go. She'd invited Hester to come with her and be her lady's maid, but Hester declined. She had family in London...and there was a certain footman in the house four doors away she had her eye on.

Anna would miss her.

Hester had mended and brushed her riding habit so that it looked as good as it could. Putting it on was like reuniting with an old friend. And like being enveloped in happy memories.

Hester promised to ship the new riding habit and all her new dresses to her when they were done. She had all the accessories they'd purchased and four dresses to take with her, including the blue one which could be worn at an evening party or even a ball. Anna did not think there would be any of those, though.

True to his word, Will rode his Highland pony even though Anna was certain he had a finer horse he could have ridden. Anna rode Seraphina and John accompanied them on the brown pony.

Just as they had done when leaving Scotland.

Will's coachman would carry both Anna's and Will's

trunks as well as Bailey, the valet, and the two footmen. The other grooms, including Toby, would bring the curricle and the other horses Will had stabled in Town. Luckily Will said he and Anna needn't stay with the carriages. They could ride as freely as they'd done before.

Except the pall of reality shrouded the journey. They'd been run out of town by gossip.

It was nearly five o'clock by the time they reached the wrought iron gate that led to Willburgh House. When Anna had been a girl, she'd passed by this gate and glimpsed the house a few times. The Dormans had filled her ears with disparaging remarks about the unfashionable baroque architecture and inferior red brickwork which they said had been made on the estate itself.

John dismounted to open the gate and closed it again after they passed through. The avenue leading to the house was lined with lime trees standing like soldiers on review. Off to one side she glimpsed an octagonal dovecote. On the other side, she could barely see a small lake behind cultivated landscaping.

As Anna rode closer, the house appeared even more impressive. Certainly it was not of the classical style that Lady Dorman insisted was the height of good taste, but it had tall, paned windows in abundance, a lovely symmetry and its red brick showed well, with Corinthian pilasters setting off the centre of the house from the two wings at its side.

Will slowed until his horse was next to hers. 'You've seen the house before?'

'Not properly,' Anna responded.

'What do you think of it?' He sounded uncertain.

'It is very pleasing,' she answered honestly. And daunting.

A satisfied smile flitted across his face and he rode ahead again.

John followed a little behind Anna. 'That's a big house, m'lady.'

She turned her head to answer. 'It is indeed.'

They'd given no forewarning of their arrival so undoubtedly the household would be in a dither. Will's mother was supposed to be in residence. What sort of reception would Anna receive from her? Anna doubted it would be welcoming.

Shouting could be heard from the house as they rode closer. Servants began to pour out of the doorway and line themselves in order of precedence to receive the return of their viscount. And their new viscountess.

Her appearance was certainly not typical of a viscountess, in her worn, ill-fitting riding habit that she was so fond of. She hadn't thought ahead about it.

Too late for regrets.

Will rode up to the front of the house and one of the footmen promptly took the reins of his pony, giving the animal a quizzical look. A servant Anna assumed was an under-butler spoke to Will as she reached the house. The servants were all eyeing her, but trying not to appear to be doing so. Anna knew she looked a fright and the expressions on the maids confirmed it.

Will quickly took her in hand and presented his staff to her, their names washing through her mind like water through sand. How was she to remember them all?

One face was familiar. John's brother's wife, who smiled shyly at Anna.

'My double!' Anna shook her hand. 'It is good to see you again, Lottie. I hope you are well and happy here.'

The young woman's smile faltered. 'I am quite well, ma'am.' She did not answer Anna's second question.

John stood awkwardly with the ponies who seemed to

receive the same disapproving looks as Anna had. Will noticed and introduced John to them.

He called over John's sister-in-law. 'Would you like to take John to your husband, Lottie? Tell the others that John is to care for these ponies.'

Anna's heart lurched. How good of him. To notice John. And to care.

He rejoined her at the door. The under-butler opened it and they entered a fine panelled hall, the painted ceiling two stories high depicting some classical scene and leading to an arcade of marble columns. But Anna could not take it all in. In the hall stood Will's mother looking like thunder and a very pretty young girl who looked sixteen. Will's sister, she presumed. Will walked straight to them.

'Mother.' He gave her a dutiful peck on the cheek.

'You could have let us know you were arriving today,' she complained.

'No, we could not,' he said casually, then turned to his sister with a grin. 'Hello, Lambkin.' He took her in his arms and swung her around. 'I've missed you.'

Anna approached Will's mother. 'How are you, Lady Willburgh?'

The older woman looked her up and down, but rather than return the greeting, turned to her son. 'This is very inconvenient, Will. You have put the house in an uproar.'

'We do not require a fuss, Mother,' he responded, leading his sister over to Anna. 'Let me present you to my wife, Anna.' He presented his sister proudly. 'My little sister, Ellen.'

Anna, still stinging from Lady Willburgh's blatant rebuff, smiled. 'I am delighted to meet you, Ellen.'

'Why are you dressed that way?' Ellen asked, eyes wide.

It was so spontaneous and what everyone else must have

wanted to ask that Anna laughed. 'These are the only riding clothes I had.'

'There is a tale about that,' Will interjected. 'We'll tell you all of it later.'

'Did you really elope to Gretna Green?' the girl asked.

'Not Gretna Green,' he responded. 'But we did elope to Scotland.'

The servants filed back in and hurried to their tasks. One footman held their saddlebags awaiting instructions. The housekeeper, whose name Anna could not remember, stood a few steps away. She was a formidable, thin-lipped woman with narrowed eyes that seemed to miss nothing.

'What rooms should we prepare, ma'am?' the housekeeper asked Lady Willburgh.

Will answered. 'We will occupy the lord and lady's chambers, Mrs Greaves.'

'As you wish, my lord,' she replied. 'It will take some time, though, to ready the lady's chamber. In what room do you wish us to put Lady Willburgh's belongings?'

'You mean the Dowager Lady Willburgh's belongings,' he corrected. 'Lady Willburgh's belongings will be placed in the lady's chamber.'

The housekeeper and Will's mother exchanged glances. 'I did understand you, sir.'

Anna was to displace Will's mother again.

Will blew out a breath. 'Really, Mother. Could you not have selected another room before this?'

She sniffed. 'I would have had you told us when you were coming.'

Anna broke into this. 'Please. At the moment all I need is a place to tidy myself and change clothes.'

'You may use my room,' Will's sister offered.

'Excellent idea, Ellen,' Will said. 'Will you show Anna where it is?' He gestured to the footman to follow them.

Ellen led her through the marble columns to an impressive oak staircase. 'My room is on the second floor,' she said. 'Mama's room—the one you will have—is on the first floor. They both face the garden, which you will like.'

When they entered her room, the huge windows revealed a lovely garden and park.

The footman waited at the doorway. 'Which…bag… m'lady?'

Anna indicated which was hers.

The footman brought it in and turned to leave.

'Would you summon my maid, please?' Ellen called after him.

One of the footmen helped Will change from his riding clothes to home attire. When he was done he asked the man to have his mother meet him in the parlour and to have tea served there. Now Will was seated in one of the more comfortable chairs in the parlour, eyes closed, weary from the long ride.

He heard his mother enter and rose.

'Really, Will,' his mother began. 'I am much put out with you, coming with no warning like this. This whole quagmire has taken a terrible toll on my nerves and it does not help that you spring all this on me without even a how do you do.'

Will was too weary for this. 'You make too much of it, Mother,'

She presented her cheek and he kissed it.

She glanced around and sighed. 'Do I need to ring for tea?'

He gestured for her to sit. 'I have already arranged it.' She selected a chair and Will sank back into his. 'Tell me how you have been,' he said. 'How are matters here?'

She fussed with her skirt. 'Well, it has been difficult to manage without Bailey. And Ellen has asked me why you had to marry if you had done nothing wrong. What was I to say?'

'What did you say?' he asked.

'Only that it would ruin all of us if you did not marry.'

'That was the truth of it.' Right. There had been some urgency to marry—to prevent the scandal from affecting Ellen. But they could have waited. Should have waited.

He certainly was not going to tell his mother that they need not have married at all.

His mother rubbed her brow. 'I cannot bear it that you had to marry into *that* family?' She gestured in the general direction of the Dorman property which abutted theirs, albeit acres away.

'Actually she is not a Dorman.' Perhaps it would ease his mother's nerves to know this. 'She had a different father. Her mother was widowed before marrying Dorman.'

She averted her face. 'That is not what he told me,' she said in a barely audible voice.

'What did you say?' Will demanded.

She faced him. 'That is not what Bertram Dorman told me. He said she was his daughter.'

The will proved her parentage, if necessary, but Will believed Anna even before that.

He waved a hand. 'It does not matter. We are married and we must make the best of it.'

'I know.' She sighed again. 'I just wish it were different.'

'We all wish it were different,' he said.

At that moment Anna and Ellen appeared in the doorway. Anna's face told Will she'd overheard him.

He stood. 'Come sit, Anna. We've ordered tea.'

She nodded a greeting to Will's mother who said, 'Well, you look better.'

Anna did indeed look better than the travel-weary rider she'd been. She looked beautiful.

'Thank you for the compliment, Lady Willburgh,' Anna replied.

Will directed her to the sofa and he sat beside her, briefly touching her hand as he did so. She moved her hand away.

Ellen sat facing them. 'You said you had a tale to tell about eloping. Tell it now, Will!'

He glanced at Anna, not certain if she'd wish their story told. He'd no intention of telling all of it anyway.

Not about their passion-filled nights and joyful days.

Anna's expression was impassive.

He was saved for the moment by the under-butler bringing in the tea. Without consulting Anna, his mother poured for everyone.

Will took the opportunity to directly ask Anna. 'Shall I tell of our adventure?' He tried to keep his voice light.

'As you wish,' she replied, giving away none of what she really might wish.

Still, Will went ahead and told the tale anyway, starting with how Lucius tried to stop them and how they foiled him.

'Do you mean that groom and maid that turned up here, when, honestly, we had no work for them? They pretended to be you? You let them wear your clothes?'

'They did a fine job,' Will insisted. 'It was not until Lucius saw them that he realised they were not us.'

'And you wore old clothes that were once worn by who knows who?' his mother continued sounding outraged.

Will ignored her and continued from where he left off, telling how they detoured to Langholm and how Armstrong, the innkeeper married them.

'Anna caught on right away,' Will said. 'But I confess, I was married before I even realised.'

Ellen laughed. 'So clever of you, Anna!'

His mother huffed. 'How dreadful! No proper vows at all. And in a tavern!'

'It suited us,' Will said. 'Did it not, Anna?'

Anna picked up her cup of tea for a sip. 'It was perfect,' she said. Her ring caught the light from a nearby lamp and sparkled. At least she was still wearing it.

'What is that on your finger?' his mother asked.

'My wedding ring,' Anna replied.

'You wore that ring in Scotland?' His mother sounded horrified.

'I bought it in London two days ago,' Will responded.

Ellen broke in. 'You didn't explain why you were riding today or where those funny horses came from.'

Will made a quelling gesture with his hand. 'We are just coming to that part of the story. And those are not "funny horses." Those are Highland ponies. I bought them so we could ride home.'

His mother shook her head. 'Who ever would want to ride that distance?'

Anna spoke up. 'It was my request. As was riding today.'

Will told about their riding back to London, which explained Anna's riding habit, even though his mother continued to purse her lips in disapproval. Telling of those days filled him with melancholy. It brought back the pleasure of their nights together, the joyfulness of their days, and how freeing it had been to not be a viscount. Anna's head was bowed during this part of the story. Was she remembering too? Or was she thinking that she need not have married him and that he was responsible for all of London knowing why.

He glanced at his mother, the very picture of incivility. If he wanted to assign blame for them marrying so quickly, he could give some to his mother.

But he knew the blame rested on him.

At that moment the coach carrying their trunks and Bailey and the footmen arrived. Will excused himself to be certain all was in order.

'More commotion.' Lady Willburgh sighed and turned to Anna. 'I suppose we must find a maid to attend you, although I do not know who that will be. I assumed you would hire your own person from London.'

Anna did not miss the criticism in Lady Willburgh's statement. 'There was no time,' she explained.

She was still reeling from hearing Will's words—'*We all wish it were different.*' They should not have surprised Will's mother. The woman had always made it very clear she was not happy that Anna had to marry her son. Anna even wished she had not married Will, did she not?

No. What she wished was that they could again be simply Mr and Mrs Willburgh traveling from Scotland indulging their every whim.

Loving each other.

'Let her use my maid,' Ellen suggested.

Yet another sigh from Lady Willburgh. 'I suppose that will do, although it does put an extra burden on the girl.'

All Anna wanted at the moment was to be alone, unattended by anybody. 'I do understand that the unexpected nature of our arrival has created problems for you, Lady Willburgh. For that I am sorry, but I assure you, I do not need much assistance. I do not need to be moved into the lady's chamber right away. Any room will do.'

Lady Willburgh waved a dismissive hand. 'It is too late for that. Mrs Greaves already has the servants tearing my room apart.'

'At your son's direction,' Anna clarified. 'Not mine.'

Ellen passed the plate of biscuits to Anna who selected one.

'What was Scotland like?' Ellen asked. 'Did you meet Highlanders and Jacobites?'

'She has been reading novels,' Lady Willburgh explained in an exasperated tone.

Anna set her biscuit on her saucer. 'I do not know if we met any Highlanders. We were only in the Lowlands. We might have met a Jacobite or two.' Those, like Armstrong who disdained the English. 'But they did not say that they were. They seemed indistinguishable from the sort of people you would see in a tavern in England, except they spoke like Scotsmen.'

'I certainly hope *my* daughter does not see *anyone* in a tavern!' huffed the girl's mother.

Anna regarded Lady Willburgh over her cup of tea. Would she not say one favourable thing?

The woman was still a beauty, even as she must approach fifty years. Her full head of hair still had more blond in it than grey, and the only lines on her face were at the corners of her eyes. Her daughter had the same dark hair as her brother, but had inherited her mother's flawless skin and delicate features.

In contrast, Anna had always been told her own looks were 'passable'—this by Lady Dorman and Violet, primarily. Indeed, her hair could only be called brown and her features were too big for her face. And she was taller than was fashionable and lacked sufficient curves.

For this alone she could understand Lady Willburgh's disappointment in her. At least, though, she knew precisely where she stood with the woman. She surely could never be duped into thinking Lady Willburgh cared about her.

Unable to think of a polite way to escape, Anna asked Ellen what books she had read. Anna had read many of them and Ellen delighted in discussing all aspects of her favourite novels, which seemed to include those of the author of *Waverley*. No wonder she asked about Highlanders and Jacobites.

'Wait until you see our library,' Ellen exclaimed. 'There is none like it in all of England!'

'I should like to see it,' Anna responded.

Ellen turned to her mother. 'Mama, may I show Anna the library now?'

Lady Willburgh waved her hand. 'Do. I need some solitude for my nerves.'

Chattering all the way, Ellen led Anna up the oak stairway to a drawing room that was panelled with the same sort of wood that was on the staircase. Once in the room Ellen stopped.

Anna looked for another doorway. 'Where is the library?'

'Here!' Ellen swept her arms to encompass the whole room. She laughed at Anna's confusion and rushed around the room somehow opening the panelling to reveal bookshelf after bookshelf.

Anna smiled. 'What a surprise!'

Ellen twirled around. 'It is my favourite room.'

Anna thought it might become her favourite room, as well. She was reasonably certain that Lady Willburgh did not spend much time here. The room also seemed to be absent a desk—unless it, too, was hidden behind panelling—so Will probably did not spend much time here either. And if Ellen was her only company?

At least she did not convey disappointment or disapproval.

Chapter Fifteen

Will's valet could be trusted to unpack for him, but he thought he ought to make certain Anna's trunk would be taken care of. He doubted his mother would do it. He'd hardly said more than two words to the housekeeper about it before his estate manager sent word that he needed to speak to Will urgently.

The manager's office was in an outbuilding. Will took the back stairs and went out one of the doors leading to the garden. He crossed the lawn to the building. The door was open and he saw the manager seated at a desk, looking at a paper.

'Parker?' Will entered the office. 'You need to speak to me?'

Parker, a robust man with thinning hair and a restless energy, was only a few years older than Will. His father had been estate manager when Will's father was alive and his son learned the job at his side.

He rose and strode over to Will, extending his hand to shake. 'Good to see you, Will. I hear you've managed to scandalise all of London and get married. My best wishes to you and your wife.'

Will accepted his hand, the informality normal between them. They'd grown up together as boys and Parker had always looked out for the younger Will.

Parker went on, 'My apologies for asking for you when

you've hardly set foot in the place, but there are a few things that best not wait.'

They sat while Parker detailed several problems and they discussed the solutions and made the needed decisions. That done, Will rose to leave and Parker walked with him to the doorway.

'One more thing,' Parker said. 'I thought I'd give you warning. Jones and Keen have complained to me that they do not know what to do with now two new grooms, since you brought another one today.'

Jones was the stable master; Keen, the head groom.

Why was this so difficult? 'Surely there is enough work to keep two more men busy. There are three new horses to tend, after all.'

'Seems that one of the men heard that Adams and his wife came from Lord Dorman's London house to cause trouble here.' Parker explained.

Will pressed his hand on his forehead. 'That is nonsense. Who would say such a thing?'

'I wouldn't be surprised if it was one of the Dorman servants who told him that,' Parker said. 'They've heard all the London gossip just as we have.'

Will shook his head. 'It could not be further from the truth. John, Adams, and Lottie prevented Lucius Dorman from thwarting the elopement.'

Although if Lucius had succeeded, then Anna would have been able to inherit her fortune.

'Walk with me to the stables,' Will asked. 'I'll speak to Jones and Keen.'

They walked the distance to the stables where there was plenty of activity since the carriages and horses had arrived. Will noticed right away that the Highland ponies were unnecessarily tucked away in the farthest stalls. He could just glimpse John and Adams tending to them. Toby was sitting nearby.

Will strode through the stable to purposely greet the two brothers, Parker in tow. Will did not bother to ask how they were settling in, because he knew the answer. Instead he asked Adams if the accommodations for him and his wife were adequate.

'They'll do, sir,' the young man said unenthusiastically.

'They were given a room above the stables,' John said. 'It's separate from the other men, but only by a wall.'

Will turned to Parker and frowned. 'That was the best you could do?'

'I left it to Keen, sir,' the manager said.

'Well, we must do better,' Will insisted. 'Find them a little cottage. I know we have some vacant.'

'Yes, sir,' Parker said.

'Thank you, sir,' Adams said.

Keen, apparently having heard that the Viscount was in the stables came bustling through. 'Welcome back, sir,' the man said.

Will did not mince words. 'I do not like what I see here, Keen, nor what I've heard. I expect these two men and Adams's wife to be treated in a fair manner. They are not spies from the Dorman estate. Quite the reverse.' Will inclined his head towards Toby. 'Toby can tell you all that they have done for me and for my wife. I expect you to make certain every man knows the truth.' Will did not usually show his anger so plainly. 'If in the future there are any rumours about the Dormans or about my workers, I want to be informed immediately.'

Before he walked out, he made certain to shake Adams's hand and to clap John on the back. He knew every worker in the stables was watching him and he wanted them to know these two men were in his favour.

Will and Parker went on to the carriage house and imparted the same information to Jones, the stable master. When Will finally returned to the house it was time for dinner. He didn't feel like changing clothes for dinner, but did not want to risk coming to the table smelling like horse.

His valet helped him make quick work of dressing for dinner. Afterwards he knocked on the door connecting his room to the lady's chamber, hoping to find Anna. When there was no answer, he opened the door and entered the room.

It appeared that all his mother's things had been removed, but Anna's trunk still sat in the middle of the room. Had it even been unpacked? Will did not want to snoop that far.

Instead he went to the drawing room where his mother typically waited for dinner to be announced. Anna was there. And his mother.

He greeted them all and walked over to the carafe of claret. He noticed Anna did not have a glass.

'Would you like some claret, Anna?' he asked.

'I would,' she responded.

He poured and handed the glass to her.

He turned to his mother. 'Mother?'

'I have some.' She lifted her glass.

He frowned as he poured his own claret. Had his mother not offered any to Anna?

He went to sit by her. 'I was called away,' he said. 'How has it been for you?'

He hoped to hear that his mother had graciously shown her around or had made certain her room was readied for her.

Instead Anna said, 'Your sister was kind enough to show me your library. Very unusual.' Her tone was polite. Disguising much.

He was dismayed. 'Yes. It is unique. You must feel free to treat it as your own.' He wanted her to feel welcome. She was bound to him. He had spoiled her chances to determine her own fate, had she become an heiress. It was his duty to do right by her.

He hated being so formal with her. They'd not been formal at all on their ride back from Scotland. He wanted to tell her what was on his mind—how John and Adams and Adams's wife were treated for one thing—but it felt like a wall between them, one made of molasses perhaps because he felt like he could slog through it with time and effort.

At least he hoped so.

Ellen came rushing in. 'Am I late? I was afraid I would be late.'

She and Will did a pantomime of her asking for claret and him pouring her only a short glass.

Their mother took a sip of her wine. 'Had Betty been delayed in helping you?'

Ellen looked puzzled. 'No. Why would she be?'

'I thought—' She inclined her head towards Anna. 'I thought she might have been busy.'

'Oh,' Ellen exclaimed. 'Anna said she did not need Betty.'

Their mother lifted a brow. 'Indeed?'

Anna smiled graciously. 'As you can see, I did not change clothes so I needed no maid.'

Their mother formed a stiffer smile. 'I did notice.'

Bailey appeared at the door. 'Dinner is served in the dining room.'

'The dining room?' Will was baffled. 'For only the four of us?'

His mother stood. 'I thought you would desire a formal dinner for your first…' Her voice trailed off so he didn't know to what *first* she was referring.

He offered Anna his arm and she accepted it. If his mother wished to be formal than he would lead the party to the dining room with Anna on his arm. His mother and sister would need to follow.

In the dining room the long table was set oddly, with Will and Anna at each end and his mother and Ellen on each side at the table's centre. At least it seemed odd to Will, because conversation was more difficult, nearly impossible between Anna and him. So the dinner was a stress to him and he worried that it was even worse for Anna. If not for Ellen's conversation, it would have been unbearable.

After dinner Will hung back while Anna, his mother, and Ellen retired to the drawing room for tea.

He stayed only to speak with Bailey. 'The table setting was not comfortable. It put us all at a distance from each other.'

'It was as your mother requested,' Bailey explained.

'I realise that,' Will said. 'But we do not need the long table.'

'I offered to remove some of the leaves, but your mother—'

Will put up his hand. 'Say no more. I understand. But do remove the leaves for tomorrow's dinner. We do not need them unless we have guests.'

'It will be done, sir.' Bailey bowed.

Will left to join the others in the drawing room, but only his mother and Ellen were there.

'Where is Anna?' he asked.

Ellen answered him. 'She begged off, saying she was fatigued from the journey.'

He was losing patience with his mother's unwelcoming treatment of Anna. 'I hope you sent Betty to attend her.'

'She said she did not need Betty tonight,' his mother responded.

He sat facing his mother. 'You need to be more cordial to Anna, Mother. No matter what you wish, I am married to her and she is my wife. This will not change.'

'I am very cordial to her,' his mother protested.

'No, you are not,' he countered. 'I expect you to do better.'

His mother pursed her lips and did not respond.

'I'll do my best,' Ellen added.

He had not been faulting her. He smiled at her. 'I know, Lambkin. I can count on you.'

He stood and excused himself.

His valet was surprised that he had come to the room so early. Will told him he wished to retire. When the man finally left, Will went to the door connecting his room with Anna's. He opened it a crack.

The room was dark and it was clear she was in bed.

He closed the door again and returned to his room.

The next morning Anna woke early and, having no confidence that a maid would come to assist her, dressed herself. She made her way down to where she supposed the breakfast room would be, somewhere near that small sitting room she'd seen when first arriving.

A footman with a dour expression pointed to the proper room. She entered and was the only one there.

After a couple of minutes the footman reappeared. 'Breakfast is still being prepared, ma'am. We are not accustomed to serving so early.'

Goodness. Did she hear disapproval in the footman's voice? 'I am well able to wait,' she responded, her tone sharper than usual. 'I will learn these things in time, but this is my first morning here.'

Which ought to have been obvious to the young man.

He did not respond directly to the statement but asked, 'Would you like tea or coffee?'

'Tea, please.'

She expected him to ask what she preferred for breakfast, but he bowed and left.

It seemed like she waited a lot longer for tea than she had even at the Dormans' when it was only her making the request. She was considering going on a search of the kitchen when the door opened and Will entered.

He looked surprised to see her. 'Good morning.'

'You've been riding.' She could tell. He carried the scent of the out of doors on him.

'I have,' he admitted. 'I usually ride in the morning when here. Take a look at the land.'

He might have asked her to ride as well, knowing how much she loved it. She averted her gaze, not wanting to reveal her disappointment.

He glanced around the room and frowned. 'Has no one seen to your breakfast?'

'One of the footmen is seeing to it.' She did not tell him that she'd been waiting nearly half an hour.

One moment later the door opened and in came footmen carrying warming dishes of red herring, baked eggs, and sausages, bowls of porridge, and plates of bread and cheese. One footman brought a pot of coffee, cream, and sugar and poured for Will. Last came Anna's tea. The under-butler asked Will what he wished to be put on his plate.

'Serve Lady Willburgh first,' Will told him.

The man dutifully asked Anna.

'Bread and cheese and an egg, please,' she responded.

When they both were served, the servants left and they were alone.

Will leaned towards her. 'How was your night, Anna?'

Lonely, she wanted to say.

But if she revealed how much she yearned for him next to her in bed, he might do so out of duty. She had no wish to be bedded out of obligation.

'I slept well enough,' she answered perfunctorily.

'You retired early,' he went on. 'I feared you might be ill.'

She felt many things—lonely, estranged, unwelcome. Angry—but not ill. 'No,' she told him. 'I am not ill.'

They ate in silence until Will said, 'You know if there is anything you need, you have merely to ask?'

Ask who? she wondered. The servants? His mother? Him? At least if she asked him, he would see to it. It would be his duty.

Very well. She would ask. 'I would like a tour of the house and grounds. So I know my way about.' And she would not have to wander around to find where she was supposed to go. 'Who should I ask to show it to me?'

He didn't answer right away. 'I will give you the tour.'

She'd expected him to assign Bailey to the task, not himself. She did not know what to say.

'We can begin after breakfast,' he went on. 'If that suits you.'

Heaven help her, she could not resist his company even if he offered it out of duty. Even if he was *disappointed* she was here at all.

When they were finished eating, Will stood and extended his hand to help her up. 'Where would you like to start?'

His tone turned stiff and formal, but the warmth of his hand in hers seeped through her whole body. She was disturbed by this visceral reaction.

'You know the house,' she managed.

'We'll start on this floor, then.'

He walked her through the sitting room where they'd first gathered with Lady Willburgh and Ellen, to another sitting room, to the dining room where he told her about the ancestors whose portraits were on the wall. He pointed out that the huge painting of fruits and nuts, oysters, and a lobster was by a Flemish artist and had been in the family for over a hundred years.

On the other side of the hall was a drawing room that led to another room filled with classical statues and a bust of Pitt and other important men. Beyond the sculpture room was Will's office.

'My duties require me to spend a great deal of time here,' he said.

The room was dominated by a large desk stacked with papers and ledgers. Behind the desk were shelves of books and other ledgers. It was saved from looking dismal by the large windows opening onto the beautiful garden outside and two comfortable chairs facing the fireplace. Above the fireplace was a portrait of a young man with powdered hair and a blue velvet coat with a red collar. She stared at it. It resembled Will.

'My father,' Will muttered, turning away from it.

She wished she hadn't stared at it. The mood grew sombre instead of merely stilted.

'Shall we tour the first floor?' Will strode to the doorway.

Anna hurried after him.

He explained who the portraits were on the stairway. There were four. His grandparents. His mother—dazzlingly beautiful as a young woman—and another of his father, older this time. Would Will look as stern as this, in ten or twenty years?

She'd seen the drawing room before, of course, but Will pointed out some special family items there. A Pembroke table and some ribbon-back chairs, both by Chippendale and acquired by his grandparents. This most formal room had the plasterwork and pale colours of years ago when Robert Adam's neoclassical style was popular. The Dormans had preferred the more modern furnishings, brighter colours on the walls and fabrics, tables and cabinets of ebonised wood or embellished with gold paint or Egyptian details.

They toured the library. She thought Will almost looked pleased that it captivated her. There was also a lovely music room brightened by the windows with a pianoforte, a harp, and a chest she presumed held sheets of music.

'Do you play?' he asked.

'A little.' She'd learned along with Violet, but never had as much time to practice as she wished.

'Use it whenever you like.'

He showed her his room, but he said little about its adornments or furniture. For some reason, Anna felt the spectre of his father strongly there. She wondered if he'd moved into the room without changing what his father had left.

They walked through the connecting doorway to her room.

He glanced at the bare walls. 'There were paintings I wanted to tell you about, but my mother has had everything taken out of the room.' He frowned. 'I'll have some more paintings brought in to be hung. There are several in the attic.'

'May I select them?' Anna asked.

He looked surprised she'd asked. 'Of course.' He then noticed her trunk, still in the middle of the room where the footman had left it.

'What is your trunk doing here? Did you not call for a footman to take it away?'

'It is not unpacked yet,' she responded.

He countered in a chiding tone. 'You must ask the maids who attend you to unpack for you and see the trunk stored away.'

'No maid attended me,' she replied.

'Why not?' He sounded disapproving.

'Betty was assigned the task, but I did not want her to do it,' she told him.

'Why?'

'It was clear she found it a burden.'

'*She* found it a burden?' He turned to face her. 'You are the Viscountess, Anna. They are employed to meet your needs.'

'Really, Will,' she shot back, annoyed now. 'My first days here I should order the servants about?'

'Unpacking your trunk was hardly an unreasonable demand,' he responded.

Should she tell him that the servants already displayed a reluctance to help her, if not animosity towards her? Following his mother's lead, no doubt.

'I prefer to tread carefully,' she said instead.

He shrugged but added. 'You need a lady's maid to attend you.' He still sounded as if he was admonishing her.

She agreed. 'I do, but I should very much want a lady's maid to want to serve me.'

They left this room to go up to the second floor. Muffled voices came from one bed chamber.

Will inclined his head towards that door. 'My mother.' There was an edge to his voice. 'That is the room she selected. It used to be mine.'

The door to a different room opened and the maid, Betty, appeared. She sent a guilty glance towards Anna and Will before disappearing around the corner.

'The servants' stairs are back there,' Will explained.

Ellen walked out of the room Betty had left and stopped

abruptly upon encountering them. 'Good morning! What are you doing?'

Will gave her a playful, endearing hug, making Anna's heart ache. Towards his sister, he acted like her old Will. 'I'm showing Anna the house, Lambkin.'

Anna smiled. 'The grand tour.'

'Oh.' The girl's brow creased. 'I am famished or I'd come with you.'

'Join us later,' Anna told her. Ellen was the only person in the household with whom Anna felt welcomed.

'I will!' Ellen hurried to the stairs.

Will smiled as he watched her disappear, then his expression sobered. 'Shall we continue?'

Was showing her the house merely another chore for him? He seemed to be taking little pleasure in it. Or was it her company he disliked?

Perhaps he could not get over the disappointment of marrying her when he had not really needed to.

They toured the children's wing and some guest bedrooms. He pointed to the door leading to the servants' rooms at the top of the house.

'That is about everything.' He headed back to the stairway.

All? 'What about below stairs? The kitchen and the rooms around it?'

His brows rose. 'You want to see that? My mother never goes down there.'

Lady Dorman never went down to the kitchen either. 'I would like to see it.' Anna wanted to know what the servants' areas were like.

'Let us use the servants' stairway, then.'

Chapter Sixteen

They reached the lower level of the house where the servants' hall, the kitchen, scullery, still room, housekeeper's room, butler's pantry, and such were located.

Will greeted each servant they encountered by name and presented them to Anna. Anna was certain each one of them greeted her suspiciously and with disfavour.

Mrs Greaves, the housekeeper, appeared and stuck to them like a plaster to a wound. She was deferential and cordial to Will, but cool and curt with Anna, and her demeanour was mirrored in all the others they encountered.

Did Will notice? She was not sure he had.

When they toured the laundry, which was in a wing off the kitchen, Anna found Adams's wife there. 'Lottie! I am surprised to see you in the laundry. I thought you worked in the house.'

Lottie curtsied. 'Mrs Greaves moves me around, ma'am.'

Will's brows furrowed. 'Is this the best place for you? What work did you do in the inn?'

'Tended the rooms, mostly, sir,' she responded. 'I helped serve in the tavern some, as well.'

'But not the laundry?' he asked.

'No, sir. Not the kitchen either.'

He touched her arm in a reassuring manner. 'I am certain

the house needs you more than the laundry. We will speak to Mrs Greaves.'

'Thank you, sir.' She curtsied again.

He nodded in acknowledgment. 'Did your husband tell you we are locating a cottage for you?'

'We are grateful, sir.'

'What was that about a cottage?' Anna asked him when they left the laundry.

'I was not satisfied with the rooms they were given over at the stable,' was all he said.

They walked up the stairs and back to the hall.

Will gestured towards the door. 'I must meet with Parker, my estate manager, who is in one of the outer buildings. He is expecting me.'

'Do those buildings include the stables?' she asked. 'I would like to know how to find the stables.'

He hesitated. 'You can accompany me, then.'

'Thank you,' she replied. 'I will just get my hat and shawl?'

'I'll wait here.'

Anna dashed up the stairs and retrieved her shawl, still packed in the trunk in her room. She put on her hat and was out the door again, approaching the stairs.

Voices sounded from the floor above. Anna stepped out of sight.

It was Lady Willburgh. 'Remember, she is a Dorman and can be up to no good for us here.'

'Do not fear, my lady,' Mrs Greaves responded. 'We will take our direction from you.'

Anna's stomach dropped. She had suspected Lady Willburgh wanted to make her feel unwelcome. To what end? What choice did any of them have that she was here? Certainly Anna had none.

A wave of loneliness washed over her. She was the outsider here just as she'd been the outsider at the Dormans'.

Ellen seemed happy enough to have her here, but Anna would not ever put that sweet child in the middle of this muddle. The only others she knew—John, his brother, and wife—possessed even less power than she. Anna would not risk them being damaged, not after they'd helped so.

No, she was alone, as alone as she had ever been.

She listened to be sure Mrs Greaves and Lady Willburgh had retreated and, squaring her shoulders, strode back down the stairs.

Will paced the hall waiting for Anna.

Why had he volunteered to show her the house? He had mounds of work to do and he was already late to see Parker.

He simply could not resist the chance to spend time with her. He was proud of his house, his heritage and it did not want to cede the pleasure of showing it off to her to anyone else. But they were so distant from each other, as if a wall had been erected between them that was too high and too thick to breach.

That news about her lost trust sounded a death knell on their marriage.

He should tell himself it was good they were distant. He could get his work done then.

But watching her descend the stairs with that special grace of hers took his breath away. She was strong, not delicate and did not pretend to be otherwise. Her lovemaking had been strong, as well. It aroused him to think of it and he thought of it far too often.

Like right now.

'I'm ready,' she said as she reached the bottom step and wrapped the shawl around her.

He offered his arm, knowing he'd be affected by her touch. 'We can leave by the garden door. It is quicker.'

When they stepped out into the fresh country air, Will was proud anew at the beauty his grandfather and father created in the gardens and grounds. A great expanse of green lawn, a formal garden behind the house, and pathways leading to the picturesque gardens beyond.

'What do you think, Anna?' he asked.

'About the gardens?' She took in the view. 'Lovely.'

'Perhaps tomorrow I'll give you a proper tour of them.' Could they find in that cultivated wilderness a respite from what separated them? Could he get over himself? He feared he was the wall between them.

The outer buildings were beyond the gardens and the stables, past them.

She'd been quiet through most of the walk, but suddenly spoke. 'You told Lottie that *we* will speak to Mrs Greaves on her behalf. I hope you meant you would do it.'

That was what was on her mind? 'I will, if that is what you wish.'

'Good. Mrs Greaves will have to listen to you.'

Will had chided Anna about not seeking the servants' assistance, but when they toured below stairs, he noticed how the house servants reacted to Anna. If they believed Anna was a Dorman spy like they'd thought of the Adamses, he'd have to set them straight.

Anna went on. 'I want to look for a lady's maid for myself from outside the household. Perhaps from some agency in London.'

He thought that was best, too. 'Whatever makes you happy.'

She averted her face but not before he spied a cynical smile on her lips.

'Will! Anna!' Ellen ran to catch up to them. 'Did you finish the tour of the house?'

'We did,' Will said. 'I'm on my way to meet Parker.'

Ellen turned to Anna. 'Would you like me to show you the garden? I'll wager I can show you places Will doesn't even know about.'

'I'll wager you can't,' Will quipped.

'Will was going to introduce me to the estate manager and show me the stables,' Anna said.

'Oh, you can meet Parker any time.' She pulled on Anna's arm. 'Let me show you the garden, then we can go to the stables.'

Anna had the grace to turn to Will raising her brows in question.

'Go with Ellen,' Will said, disappointed to lose her, even though he ought to be relieved. He could get back to work. 'I'll see you both at dinner.'

That evening dinner was a bit more comfortable for Anna. For one thing, the table had been made smaller so she was not banished to the far end.

When Lady Willburgh saw the room, though, she'd exclaimed. 'Who did this? The room is unbalanced with the table that way!' She shot a scathing look towards Anna.

But Will answered, 'I ordered it, Mother. As long as it is only the four of us dining, it stays this way.'

His mother had pursed her lips, but she said no more. Ellen, who was becoming more dear to Anna, carried the conversation again, chattering about her and Anna's tour of the garden and asking Anna all kinds of questions about her impression of the house.

Lady Willburgh asked Will about Lottie and if it was his place to involve himself in the running of the house. Obviously she'd heard from Mrs Greaves of his request that Lottie be used in the house. Will answered that as long as he was Viscount he could involve himself wherever he wished.

Lady Willburgh said little after that and was quiet even when they'd finished dinner and had retired to the sitting room for tea.

'Play cards with me, Anna,' Ellen begged.

After some hesitation, Anna replied, 'Oh, very well. What do you want to play?'

Ellen opened a baize-covered card table. 'Piquet?'

'Piquet.' Anna pulled up a chair. 'Although I warn you I am not very good at it.

It did not help that Will watched them while he sipped his brandy. It made her heart beat faster and she lost attention to the cards.

After losing the second game to Ellen, Anna declared a desire to go to bed. 'Before I lose another,' she said, smiling.

Will stood. 'I'll go with you.'

Her heart skittered even faster.

As they walked up the stairs, he asked, 'Do you want a maid to attend you?'

'It isn't necessary,' she responded. Actually she'd rather he helped her, like he'd done in those first days of their marriage.

'I promise we'll find a lady's maid for you,' he went on. 'I'll write to an agency tomorrow.'

She thought she would be the one writing.

He opened her door but stopped her from going in right away.

'May I come to you later?' he asked softly.

She searched his face. His eyes looked sincere and a bit wary.

'If you wish,' she replied, wary as well.

They made love that night, but in a sad way, it seemed to Anna. As if they both mourned the loss of joy they'd once shared together. Their pleasure came, though, but to Anna it seemed melancholy. Still, she wanted him in her bed. Perhaps with time they could regain some of what they'd lost.

The next morning Anna woke when the first light of dawn was peeking over the horizon. Will was gone.

Her spirits plummeted. Once again she'd let herself believe he cared about her, but once again she was alone. Was he using her like a bandalore, reeling her in, then rolling her away, over and over?

She rose from the bed and donned her riding habit. She plaited her hair and tucked it into the old hat she'd worn on the travels. The footman attending the hall was dozing. She did not wake him but walked past him and through Will's office to the doors to the garden.

A milky mist carpeted the lawn and swirled at her feet as she hurried to the stables, hoping at least one of the grooms was awake. When Ellen showed her the stables she merely pointed to them; they never walked close to them.

The doors to the stable were open and, to her relief, several grooms were at work. She spied John and hurried over to him.

'Could you saddle Seraphina for me?' she asked.

The other grooms eyed her curiously—or perhaps suspiciously. When Seraphina was saddled and ready, John helped Anna mount her. Anna leaned over and hugged the pony's neck.

'I am so glad to be riding you,' she whispered.

As she rode out, Will walked in.

'Anna!' He looked surprised.

She took in a breath. He was at his most handsome,

in comfortable riding clothes and boots, almost like he'd dressed on their travels. And the sight of him brought back the night before, the lovemaking she'd so desperately missed.

She blinked, unable to meet his eye. 'Good morning, Will.'

He paused before responding. 'Wait. I'll ride with you.'

Every morning the next week Anna rose early to ride. Sometimes Will rode with her. She never waited for him, but, more often than not, he left the house when she did and they walked together to the stables. They rode together, then, too, rarely talking more than necessary. For Anna, though, it increased the pain. Riding together had once been her delight, but now a reminder of what must have been an illusion.

It was clear to her he rode with her out of obligation, what was expected of him.

He no longer joined her at night, which only intensified the pain.

His days were busy otherwise and she rarely saw him after breakfast until dinner. Lady Willburgh and Mrs Greaves continued to run the household without involving her and any time Anna tried to broach the subject with her mother-in-law, she was put off. Lady Willburgh often kept Ellen busy at her side, as well.

So during the day, Anna was very much alone. She occupied herself by reading or walking in the garden. Or tidying her room, because she did not have a lady's maid and had not yet received a response from the agency she'd written to.

Anna was accustomed to taking care of herself, so this was not a huge hardship. Requesting the service of a maid when she needed one continued to be difficult. Her requests were never promptly filled unless Lottie was available, but

Lottie could do little more than clean her room and take her clothes to the laundry and bring them back.

A trunk carrying her new clothing from London had arrived the day before. Anna had not fully unpacked her first trunk and she debated whether she should make a fuss to be given some help in unpacking this new one. This one included her new riding habit. Discovering it made her rather sad.

She was laying the riding habit across her bed when Will stuck his head in the doorway. 'I have an errand in the village. Is there anything I might do for you there?'

She closed the trunk's lid. 'I would like to come along.'

He paused as he always did when she asked for something from him. 'Very well. I am leaving within half an hour.'

Anna made certain she was ready on time and soon they were on the road in the curricle, with Toby riding on the back. Anna had not visited the village since the scandal and elopement. She supposed the villagers knew all about it. They certainly knew more about the generational feud between the Willburghs and the Dormans than did members of the *ton* in London.

She sighed at the thought of facing them.

Will noticed. 'What is it, Anna?'

She regretted revealing that much to him. 'Nothing of consequence. The villagers know me and will have knowledge of all the gossip.'

He glanced at her. 'Perhaps they will simply wish us well.' He turned his eyes back to the road. 'They will also want the Viscountess to spend money in their shops.'

Oh, yes. She carried a title now. One would not know it by how it was for her at Willburgh House.

The village was about five miles from Willburgh House and it took them less than an hour to reach the familiar streets and buildings that she had not seen since accompanying the Dormans to London months ago. Will stopped the curricle in front of the mercantile shop. Toby hopped down and held the horses. Will helped Anna climb down. She left him to his errands and entered the mercantile shop.

The shopkeeper there knew her from when she lived with the Dormans. He was welcoming and eager to assist her. Other customers in the shop nodded politely and did not leer or whisper behind her back as they had in London. But then, she was the Viscountess Willburgh, the highest-ranking woman in the area.

After making her purchases in the mercantile shop, Anna walked towards the milliner. She needed a hat with a wide brim to shield her face from the sun when she took her walks. The village milliner always had such hats for sale.

Before she reached the shop, she spied a familiar figure seated on a bench, her head in her hands.

'Mary?' Mary was Violet Dorman's lady's maid, the maid who'd been so helpful in packing her things that awful day.

The young woman looked up. 'Oh, Miss Anna!' She dissolved into tears.

Anna sat down next to her. 'What troubles you? Tell me.'

If Mary was in the village, then the Dormans were back in the country. Anna was not happy about that. It also meant that Violet was near.

The maid leaned against Anna as she wept. Passers-by were noticing and looked concerned, but Anna could not worry about that now.

Finally Mary spoke with shuddering breaths. 'Miss Dorman gave me such a scold! She pushed me out of the shop and told me to stay out of her way!'

Anna had seen many of Violet's outbursts. It used to be her task to calm Violet down.

'I—I tripped and knocked against her,' Mary said. 'I did not mean to!'

'Of course you did not,' Anna responded soothingly. 'She should not have lost her temper with you.'

'She is losing her temper all the time now!' cried Mary. 'They all are! I wish you were back, Miss Anna. It was better when you were there. Now all they do is yell at each other! I hate it there! I don't want to go back!'

Mary was distraught or she would never be saying such things to anyone, especially Anna—Anna who was now in the enemy camp. Mary never talked about the family. Anna was fond of her. She was young but sweet-tempered and talented at her job. She loved clothes and hairstyles and all of it.

'I wish you were still there, Miss Anna.' The maid whimpered.

Anna put an arm around her. 'It is Lady Willburgh now, you know.'

Mary straightened. 'I beg your pardon, miss—I mean—ma'am.'

An idea was forming in Anna's mind, one that grew stronger by the moment.

She faced Mary. 'What if—? What if you came to Willburgh House? I am in need of a lady's maid. You could work for me.'

The young woman's jaw dropped. 'Me? Work for the Willburghs?'

Anna knew what she meant. They'd all been trained to consider the Willburghs the enemy.

'It might be difficult at first,' Anna admitted. 'The servants will see you as a Dorman. They will not be welcoming, but there is one young woman there who is also new and she will look out for you. As will I.'

Mary gaped at her. 'Do you think I could?'

'I would like you to work for me.' That was the truth. It would be like having an ally there.

Mary's eyes grew wide. 'Will it not cause trouble?'

Anna laughed. 'A great deal of trouble in both households, but you know I will not scold you or push you and I will not let the others in the house mistreat you. Lord Willburgh will deal with any fuss the Dormans make. They cannot force you to stay.'

The young woman glanced away and back again. This time her expression appeared resolved. 'I'll sneak away and walk to Willburgh House. Do you not think that a good plan?'

'We will have to follow up with a letter, but that will work well enough.' Anna hoped anyway. 'Come whenever you can.' Anna stood. 'Now I am off to the milliner.'

Mary's expression turned grave. 'Miss Dorman is in there.'

Anna patted her hand. 'All the better.'

Anna did encounter Violet in the hat shop. The shop girls took notice.

Anna decided to be cordial. 'Good day, Violet. I hope you are well.'

Violet's eyes flashed before she turned away without a word.

The cut direct. Anna expected no less from Violet, who no longer outranked her. If that did not put Violet in a rage then certainly stealing her lady's maid would.

Yes, Violet would be in a rage.

Chapter Seventeen

Will finished his errands and waited with the curricle. He, of course, had been treated well by the villagers. He could only hope that Anna experienced the same.

His senses flared when he saw her approach, laden with packages, her face glowing with excitement, wearing something he'd not seen much of lately. A smile.

Her smile fled when she saw him. 'Am I late?'

He reached for her packages. 'Not at all.' He stowed the packages beneath the seat and a hatbox behind it. 'You had some success shopping I see.'

'I purchased what I needed.'

The stiffness between them returned.

He helped her onto the curricle and climbed in beside her. Toby let go of the horses and hopped on the back.

'I have something to tell you.' Her voice sounded different.

He lifted his brows.

She settled herself in the seat. 'When we are out of the village.'

Will drove through the busy village streets until the traffic cleared and the village buildings receded behind them.

He did not want to wait longer. 'What do you need to tell me?'

'Well.' She sounded cautious. 'As I left the mercantile

shop I saw Mary sitting on the bench. Mary, Violet's lady's maid. She helped me pack my trunk that day in London.'

'Wait. *Violet's* lady's maid.' He shot her a glance. 'The Dormans have returned from Town?'

'Yes. Apparently they are not very happy. Mary said they are arguing all the time.'

Will frowned. 'They usually do not leave Town until later in the summer. I wonder what brought them back?'

'She did not tell me the reason.' Anna shifted in her seat.

Will's mind whirled. Had the Dormans come to cause trouble for them? He had enough to contend with without that.

She continued. 'Apparently Violet had a fit of temper and pushed Mary away. Mary wished she did not have to go back with Violet—'

Or had Dorman left too many debts in London? Will had heard rumours about gambling losses.

'So I offered her the position of lady's maid. For me.'

Will almost pulled on the reins and halted the horses. 'You did what?'

'I hired her to be my lady's maid.' She spoke as if it were the most normal thing in the world.

'No!' His voice rose. 'I'll not have a Dorman servant in my house. That is like putting the fox in with the hens. No.'

'Will.' She spoke very deliberately. 'I hired her. I am not going to tell her no. She is going to come to Willburgh House and I am not sending her away.'

Was she mad? 'I absolutely forbid it.'

'You *forbid* it?' Her voice was raised now. 'You forbid it? You told me I could hire my own lady's maid. I choose to hire Mary.'

'I said you could select from an agency. Not from the Dorman household.' The two sets of servants were as hostile to each other as the families were.

'I do not recall that conversation.' Her voice was clipped.

'Hear me now,' he said. 'You are not hiring a Dorman servant as your lady's maid.'

'Hear *me* now,' she countered. 'You may be *disappointed* in marrying me, but recall that I had as little choice in the matter as you did.'

Disappointed in marrying her? He'd never said that to her!

Then he remembered she'd overheard him say something like that to his mother.

She pointed to his hands. 'You hold all the reins.' She held up her reticule. 'You possess all the money. I am completely at your mercy. If I had refused to marry you, you would have gone on much as you do now. Perhaps your sister would have suffered, because she is a woman, too, but not you. So if you refuse to allow me this one request, I have no power to change the decision. Does that seem fair to you? I was as innocent of any indiscretion as you were, but this time it is not society who turns its back on me, it is you.'

That arrow hit its mark. 'You do not understand what is at issue here.'

'I do not understand?' Her eyes shot daggers. 'I know all about the silly feud over land. And you forget that I loved my—my stepfather. So do not tell me I do not understand. It is you who do not understand. I lost everything. I even lost a fortune I never knew I had. You lost the opportunity to select your own wife. I am asking for one thing for myself. To help Mary. I know her. She has no family. She has few choices as do I. If she becomes my maid, she has something. She has me to watch out for her. If she does indeed leave the Dormans' house, as she plans to do, and you refuse her, she cannot go back.'

Arrows. Daggers. He was full of pain. He did not want to hurt her or the poor maid, but this was an unreasonable request. Was it not? She should have asked him before she made the offer.

They spoke no more during the rest of the trip. When he pulled up to the door of Willburgh House, she did not wait for assistance. She climbed down from the curricle herself and hurried inside just as the footman was opening the door. Toby jumped down and took the horses in hand.

Will was frozen for a moment. Then he directed the footman to gather Anna's packages and to deliver them to her bed chamber. He did not go inside but turned to walk away from the house.

That evening Anna sent word she had a headache and would not be at dinner. Will knew better what was troubling her. When he retired for the night, he peeked into her room to try to talk some sense into her. She was in bed and still. He had to assume she was asleep or that she wished he'd go to the devil.

She simply did not understand the rift between the Dormans and the Willburghs. Could a servant from the other house ever be trusted? Or would they betray the family to their rivals?

He ought to have told her more about what happened to Adams, John, and Lottie simply because of a rumour that they were Dorman spies. Perhaps then she would have realised why they could not hire a Dorman servant as her lady's maid. *Especially* as *her* lady's maid. Of all the servants, the lady's maid and the valet were most likely to become privy to the private affairs of their employers. What could happen if that servant told all to the enemy?

No. He must stay resolved. She must accept that he knew best in this matter.

Will did not have a very restful night's sleep, though,

tossing and turning and continuing to see Anna's outraged expression and hearing her tell how wrong he was.

But he wasn't wrong.

He dared to knock on her door and enter her room early the next day, thinking to catch her before she rose to ride. Maybe they could talk about this in a more civilised manner on horseback. Today, though, her curtains were drawn and she sat in the dark staring into the fireplace.

'Are you not riding today, Anna?' He tried to sound like yesterday's angry words had never happened.

'I am not riding.' She did not even look at him.

He opened his mouth to tell her how ridiculously she was behaving, but he closed it again. He could sense her despondency as if it were an open, bleeding wound and he had no wish to hurt her further. Instead he turned around and made his way out of the house and over to the stables.

John had the white Highland pony saddled and ready for Anna.

'Lady Willburgh is not riding today,' Will told him.

'She is not?' John was surprised. 'I do hope she is not ill.'

'Not ill.' But sick at heart, he feared.

Will started across the field feeling aimless, but soon realised he was riding to the disputed patch of land where his property bordered the Dormans'. Sheep were grazing in his field, their bleats sounding like conversations between them.

Anna would have laughed at them, he thought.

In the distance he saw something moving. As he rode closer he could see it was not a sheep but a small, thin young woman carting a very large sack, so large that she was almost dragging it.

He knew instantly who it was and rode to her. 'Mary, is it?'

She dropped the sack and gave him a wary, frightened look as if he might be the devil himself. 'My lord.' She curtsied.

She looked very young and vulnerable standing below him, reaching for the sack again and clutching it like it contained all her worldly belongings.

Which it probably did.

How much courage must it have taken for her to make this trip, to sneak away in the dark and know she could never return? How much faith in Anna, as well.

'You are headed to Willburgh House?' Where else might she be going?

'To Lady Willburgh,' she responded. 'I—I am to be her lady's maid.' She caught herself and lowered her head. 'If it please Your Lordship, that is.'

He dismounted. 'We've been expecting you,' he heard himself saying. 'Let me relieve you of your burden.'

Had he gone daft now?

Tossing the bag onto his horse, he gestured for her to proceed on her way and fell in step with her. She was shy and frightened and very determined and nothing like a Dorman spy might appear.

'I—I am grateful to you, m'lord,' she stammered. 'Miss Anna—Lady Willburgh, I mean—was always very kind to me. It will be an honour to be of service to her.'

He asked her about her family. Her parents when they had been alive had worked for the Dormans so she worked for them, too, but, she told him, she'd always liked Anna the best. And now the family did nothing but argue and Miss Dorman had become very prone to scolds and slaps across the face.

'M'lord,' she asked as the house came into view. 'Will you ask your servants not to hate me?'

That was a shaft to his heart indeed. 'I will. But you must come tell me if any of them treat you badly.'

'Oh, no!' she exclaimed. 'I could never do that. I would never tell on them. It just isn't done!'

The young maid might do very well here after all, Will thought.

Anna sat at her dressing table combing out her hair, although why she bothered she could not say. She had no intention of leaving this room all day.

Desolation threatened to engulf her. It was one thing for Will to distance himself from her, but it was quite another for him to think he ruled her.

Although what was marriage but a woman ruled by a man? By common law a husband and wife were one person, although that never meant they were equal. A woman's property and fortune became her husband's upon marriage, and any children born to them belonged to the husband. So Will could rule her and she had no recourse.

It was just that their early days and fleeting moments afterwards had convinced her that Will was different, that he wanted to respect her, wanted her to have some say in what happened to her. It was shattering what he said to her about hiring Mary. '*I absolutely forbid it.*' How could she ever again trust his kindness when he could be so cruel?

But then, how could she trust anyone really? They all betrayed her eventually.

As she tugged at a knot with the comb, she remembered the pleasure of Will brushing her hair. And the pleasure of his lovemaking. Tears stung her eyes and she blinked them away.

She'd thought he loved her. He did not love her any more than the Dormans did. Or, perhaps, any more than her stepfather had. Will's mother loathed her and the servants loathed her. She was surrounded by people who despised her.

She put down the comb and lifted her chin.

Well, she could not care that they all despised her. She had done nothing wrong, nothing to deserve their ire. She'd hold her head up and go toe-to-toe with any of them.

The door opened and Will stuck his head in. 'Anna?'

She did not want to see him! She turned away.

'I've brought you a maid.' He made it sound like this would be welcome news. 'To help you—'

How dare he!

She swung around. 'I told you I did not want a—'

Mary had entered her room. 'G'morning, Miss Anna—I mean, Lady Willburgh.'

Anna jumped from her chair and rushed over to the young woman. She wrapped the maid in a hug. Not how a lady treated her lady's maid, but Anna did not care. She was so happy to see her.

Her gaze caught Will's. He stood in the doorway smiling and her heart swelled at the sight of him. He had brought Mary to her! He had given her something that she wanted, simply because she wanted it, even though he'd been thoroughly against it.

He took a step back. 'If you will pardon me, I must speak to a few people about our new lady's maid.' He addressed himself to Mary in the kindest voice possible. 'We'll get you settled.'

Anna wanted to pull him back to embrace him, to tell him how grateful she was, but he left too quickly.

Mary stared at where he'd disappeared. 'My goodness, Miss Anna—I mean, m'lady—I don't know why Miss Dorman and Mr Lucius said he was such a villain. Lord Willburgh was ever so kind to me.'

'He is a very kind man.' Anna blinked back tears of happiness. She took Mary's hand in hers and squeezed it. 'I am so glad you are here, Mary.'

The maid looked around the room with its two trunks in the middle of the floor and complete lack of embellishments. 'It is a pretty room, but not fancy at all, is it?'

'You can help me decorate it,' Anna said, her spirits brightening considerably.

'Perhaps I might unpack your trunks for you first.'

Will did not relish the task of telling the household about the new lady's maid. He expected them to react as he had; his mother, worse. He would tell her first.

He climbed the stairs to his old room, her new bed chamber.

Ellen caught him in the hallway. 'Good morning, Will.' She frowned. 'What is it? Has something happened?'

His expression must have given away his trepidation. 'Oh, Lambkin. I am about to cause an uproar.' He explained it all to her—except for the angry discord he'd made Anna endure.

'Violet's lady's maid?' Ellen shook her head. 'The uproar is going to be at the Dormans', I should think.'

'I'm afraid our servants will not be happy to have her,' he confessed.

She seemed to consider that. 'Probably not, but think how nice it is for Anna to have someone familiar to her as her lady's maid.'

He gave his sister a hug. 'Thank you for saying that.'

'I'll encourage Betty to be kind to her,' she said.

'That would be very good.' He took a bracing breath. 'Wish me luck. I am going to tell Mother.'

Her eyes widened. 'Good luck.'

He knocked on his mother's door and heard her tell him to come in.

He opened the door. 'Good morning, Mother.'

Luckily she was alone, seated by her window, sipping

a cup of chocolate. 'You never visit me in my room.' She glanced around. 'Such as it is. What is it now?'

He told her.

Her expression turned thunderous and she gripped the cup handle so hard he feared it would break.

'No, Will.' She spoke through gritted teeth. 'This is unacceptable. Willburghs never hire Dorman servants. You know that.'

'Anna chose her, Mother,' he said.

'Well, she might have considered my nerves.' She put her cup down and fussed with the collar of her morning dress. 'You know how distressing it is for me to have anything to do with the Dormans. They killed your father, remember!'

His anger flared. 'If you wish to add Father's death to the discussion, do not forget to include the part you played in it.'

'Oh, that is too cruel!' she wailed. 'It is unfair of you to say this to me. You know how completely I was taken in! That is why I despise the Dormans so. Look how ill they treated me.'

Oddly he hadn't specifically thought of his father's death when he'd forbidden Anna to have this servant as her lady's maid. He'd reacted to the generations-long feud, the conviction that Willburghs and Dormans did not mix. He hadn't been reliving the duel every time he looked at Anna, as he'd feared.

But he thought of his father dying in his arms now and sadness engulfed him. Sadness. Not anger.

He hardened his voice to his mother. 'This little maid did not kill my father. Neither she nor Anna had any part in that. Anna wants her to be her lady's maid. She knows her and feels comfortable with her. Anna has the right to choose her own lady's maid, after all.'

'We could find one she might like from an agency,' his mother pleaded. 'Anyone but a Dorman servant. Tell her she may have anyone she chooses from an agency. You can insist upon it.'

Obviously he would not insist. Could not insist. Nor had he been able to turn away that young maid. It had made him hate himself that he thought to even try.

He answered his mother. 'I will not insist Anna do something against her wishes. It would be cruel to her and to that maid for me to insist. Anna has made her choice and I will support it.' He raised his voice and spoke even more firmly. 'I will also expect the servants to accept this young maid. I will not brook anyone treating her ill. That includes you, Mother.'

'I will have nothing to do with her!' his mother cried. 'This is all your fault. If you hadn't compromised a Dorman we would not be in this fix! You have ruined everything!'

'Perhaps I have, Mother,' Will countered. 'But remember these decisions are mine to make, not yours, not anyone else's.' Such was the burden of being viscount.

'Mark my words, Will. That maid will do nothing but report all our business back to the Dormans. You've let a spy into our household.'

Will simply left the room.

Ellen waited in the hallway. 'I heard that.'

He blew out a breath. 'I wish you had not.'

Her expression was all sympathy, though. 'Would you like me to come with you when you tell the servants?'

'Yes.' As Viscount this was his problem alone. But he had an idea of what he would face and really felt the need of support. 'I'd be grateful if you would,' he told Ellen and straightened his spine. 'Let us do that now.'

Chapter Eighteen

Lucius Dorman was lounging in the drawing room while his mother and Violet sat whispering together on the sofa. Violet was in a snit because no one could find her maid and she was threatening to send the girl packing. Lucius could not care less about the maid. He was fuming about Willburgh and Anna. He'd heard rumours in the village that they were getting along very well. Humph! The very least Willburgh could do after thwarting all of Lucius's plans was to be miserable. There must be some way to make the man suffer. Apparently the loss of Anna's fortune meant nothing to Willburgh. Or maybe to Anna

The loss of Anna's fortune meant a lot to Lucius. It would have paid his debts and his father's debts and set them up rather nicely.

He and his family had botched things rather thoroughly, Lucius had to admit, but he'd been so furious to find Anna with Willburgh that all rational thought went out of his head. Not that he held a *tendre* for her, exactly, but she was supposed to be his family's ticket to the lap of luxury and Willburgh had foiled that plan.

The thing was, what to do now? How to get revenge on Willburgh and Anna and restore the family fortune?

Lucius was still musing over this problem when his father stormed into the room waving a piece of paper.

'This was just delivered. From Willburgh House!' He flung the letter at Lucius. 'Read it!'

Lucius read aloud.

'Dear Lord Dorman,
I write to you this day to inform you that I have hired the maid Mary Jones to be Viscountess Willburgh's lady's maid—'

Lucius looked up. 'Well, that solves the mystery of where Violet's maid disappeared to.'

He read on:

'I assure you, Dorman, that I will assume the payment of any wages you owe Miss Jones, so there will be no need for you to correspond with her or to concern yourselves with any of her affairs.

Lady Willburgh and I realise this loss in your household is very sudden and we regret any inconvenience it may cause you. I am confident that you realise what an improvement in status this is for Miss Jones and that you will forgive her need to leave without notice.
Yours, etc.
Willburgh'

'Improvement in status.' Lucius threw the letter down in disgust. 'That is just like Willburgh to lord it over us.'

Violet nearly vaulted out of her seat. 'Anna has stolen Mary from me! She cannot do that! Mary is *my* lady's maid.'

'What a dirty trick!' their mother cried. 'Anna goes too far. She's completely crossed over to the enemy.'

'Papa,' Violet begged. 'You must do something! Get her back!'

Their father shook his head. 'I can do nothing! The maid was free to leave her employment at any time. She had better not ask us for a letter of reference, however. I'd make certain no one would hire her.'

Lucius vowed he'd get back at Willburgh and Anna somehow. He'd make them regret ever trifling with the Dormans.

After Mary helped Anna dress and unpacked her trunks, Anna left the maid in the hands of Ellen's lady's maid, who seemed cordial enough, and went in search of Will. To thank him.

She hurried down the stairs, through the hall and the sculpture room to Will's office.

She walked in without knocking.

He was not there.

His desk was still stacked with papers and ledgers and now two chairs also had papers on them. Poor Will! He intended to tackle this all himself? Even Lord Dorman employed a secretary. Mr Bisley. A thin, intense man who seemed delighted to spend his days with papers and ledgers much like these.

She smiled to herself. Perhaps Will could hire Mr Bisley away from Lord Dorman.

She made her way back to the hall and asked the footman there, 'Do you know where Lord Willburgh has gone?'

'To see Mr Parker, the estate manager, ma'am,' the footman told her with only a hint of the usual antipathy.

'Thank you so much,' she replied, climbing the stairs again. She'd have to wait until Will returned.

As she reached the landing, a voice from above her demanded, 'I would speak with you, Anna.'

It was Will's mother. Calling her by name? It must be the first time.

Anna made no reply until she reached the floor. 'Yes, Lady Willburgh?'

Will's change of heart had filled Anna with renewed strength. She'd stood up to him! And he'd done right by her. At that moment Anna felt she could do anything.

Even face her mother-in-law.

The older woman's eyes flashed. 'My son tells me you have manipulated him into hiring a maid—a lady's maid, no less—from the Dormans. I will not have it.'

Anna should have expected this. '*You* will not have it?' she retorted.

'I insist you send the girl packing. This very instant!' She stomped her foot for emphasis.

Anna burned with anger which she could barely keep in check. 'I will not do that.'

'You will do that!' Lady's Willburgh's face flushed. 'Our family cannot have a Dorman servant in our household. She'll be privy to all our affairs!'

Somehow Anna knew Lady Willburgh did not include her when she said *our family*. 'This is my household, too, and, as Will's wife, I am family. I have every right to select what servants I wish. Mary Jones stays.'

'You wretch!' the older woman cried. 'I knew you were a Dorman. Manipulative! Selfish! Like the lot of them. I wish that Will had never married you! You have disrupted all our lives.'

Anna could hold her temper no longer. 'I may be a *disappointment* to you, Lady Willburgh. I may be a disruption, but I am not a Dorman! What I am is Will's wife, whether you like it or not. I am the Viscountess. I have allowed you to run the house, because I did not wish to take everything away from you. Your room. Your title. I thought you would be generous enough to teach me how to manage the house and gradually pass the responsibilities on to me, but instead you accuse me of being manipulative and selfish when you know I did not choose any of this! I *am* a part of this family now, however. In fact, I am second only to Will, and you must accept this.'

Lady Willburgh's lips thinned and her chest heaved.

Anna went on. 'From now on Mrs Greaves will take instructions from me, not you. I will plan the menus. I will instruct the servants. Me. Not you. You are the dowager. I am Lady Willburgh. If I make mistakes, then it will be because you decided to oppose me rather than help me.'

Will's mother seemed to collect herself. Her eyes flashed. 'You are nobody in my eyes! A clever maneuverer, I would say. You tricked my son into marrying you—'

Anna shot back. 'You know that is not true. You were the one who said we should marry. You are no better than the Dormans. Creating your own version of how you prefer to see things rather than the way they are.'

The older woman's face turned red. 'Do not compare me to the Dormans! I am nothing like them! My son will not allow you to speak to me that way! You might have tricked him into marrying you, but I will not give over the running of this house until he tells me to and Mrs Greaves will not listen to you. My son will not hear of you usurping my authority.'

'We will see about that!' Anna whirled around and strode down two flights of stairs, through the hall and out the door. Her anger propelled her along, to the outbuildings and Parker's office.

She walked in without knocking.

Both Will and Parker looked up, stunned by her entrance.

She was panting. 'I need to talk to you right now, Will.' She walked out the door again.

He followed, looking alarmed. 'What is it, Anna?'

She paced in front of him, still so angry she could not stand still. 'Your mother!'

Will released an exasperated breath. 'What has she done now?'

'She has insisted I get rid of Mary!' Anna cried.

'Wait. What?' He pressed his fingers to his temple. 'I spoke to my mother about this. And to the servants, as well.'

Anna went on. 'She said I had no right to hire her and that I manipulated you and that *she* will not have it—' He glanced away and Anna was not certain he was listening. 'She also accused me of being selfish and a disruption!'

Will nodded, rather absently, Anna thought. 'Let's walk back to the house.'

She wrested her temper under control as they neared the house. 'I never wanted a feud with your mother. I know I am nothing she would choose for you to marry, but I will not be accused of it being my fault.'

He blew out a breath as he opened the door off the garden. 'Why does this have to be so difficult?'

Anna flared again. 'I am not being difficult! I have tried to deal fairly with your mother! I know this is a hard change for her!'

They entered his office.

She swept her arm across the room. 'And this, Will. Really. All this paper!' She could not stop herself now.

'What has my work to do with it?' he snapped.

'Nothing at all,' she shot back. 'It is just that—I came looking for you, to thank you properly for hiring Mary. When I came in here—well—I never see you asking anyone for help. Any other gentleman of means would simply hire a secretary!'

He halted and looked like he was seeing the piles of paper for the first time.

He shook his head. 'One thing at a time. I'll speak with my mother.'

But she was not sure what he would say to his mother. He might take her side, for all Anna knew.

Or he might support her, like he did in hiring Mary.

'I should tell you,' she added in a calmer tone. 'I lost my temper with your mother. I told her I was taking over all her duties.'

'Taking over her duties,' he repeated absently. He straightened. 'I will speak with her now.'

'Thank you, Will,' Anna said.

She truly hoped this would be something for which she'd be thankful.

Will found his mother in a sitting room on the other side of the house. Mrs Greaves stood near her chair. The two had obviously been talking.

'Will, thank goodness you are here,' his mother said, reaching up from her chair to clasp his hands. 'Has *she* spoken to you? Did she tell you she threatened me? She threatened to turn me out of my home!'

Will pulled his hands away. 'Cut line, Mother.' He glanced at Mrs Greaves who suddenly was examining the Aubusson carpet. 'I have had enough of this.'

His mother blinked.

Will towered over her. 'Heed me now, Mother, because you will not be given a second chance. You will treat Anna respectfully. She is the Viscountess now, not you. She has every right to take over your duties and to hire whatever servants she wishes.'

His mother turned away.

'Look at me, Mother,' Will demanded. 'A kind thing would have been if you'd taken Anna under your wing and taught her how you've run the house, but you and Mrs Greaves have shown yourselves to be unkind. That will stop now. You will respect Anna's wishes even if they disagree with yours. You will not interfere or obstruct. If she asks for your help, you will help her. Or—'

'Or what?' she asked defiantly.

'Or you will live in the dower-house.' He turned to Mrs Greaves. 'You, Mrs Greaves, will work cooperatively with Lady Willburgh and her lady's maid and you will instruct all the servants to do the same. If I hear of any of them disrespecting my wife or her maid or causing any sort of trouble, they will be terminated and you with them.'

'But—but I cannot control—' the housekeeper stammered.

'If you cannot control your servants, then perhaps you are in the wrong job.' He glared from one to the other. 'You two have made difficulties where none needed to exist. You will stop doing so right now.'

'It's that Dorman maid she hired,' his mother protested. 'She's causing the difficulties!'

Will gave a dry laugh. 'Come now, Mother. The girl has not been here even a full day.'

'The Dormans sent her to spy on us,' cried his mother. 'It is the Dormans' fault.'

'That excuse will no longer work.' He glared at her. 'Your choice, Mother. Be decent or be gone.'

Anna was not privy to what Will said to his mother, She did not see either of them until dinner. Lady Willburgh was much subdued and avoided any direct looks at either Anna or Will. When she did speak, Anna had the sense of a great deal of anger repressed, but she did not toss any of the barbs towards Anna that had been her custom.

Something had changed. Even the servants she encountered cast their eyes down at her approach and spoke carefully to her. What had Will said to them?

He spoke little, though. If it had not been for Ellen the dinner would have resembled a wake. The girl's happy mood and cheerful conversation lifted the pall over the rest of them.

After dinner Anna excused herself early without offering any excuse.

Mary came to her after finishing her meal with the other servants. 'Do you want me to help you get ready for bed?'

'I do not need much help,' Anna replied, but let the girl untie the ribbons of her dress and slip her out of it.

Anna washed herself and donned her nightdress before sitting at the dressing table and taking the pins from her hair. Mary skipped over to help her.

'How have things been for you today?' Anna asked.

Mary smiled. 'Betty has been such a help to me and she even fixed it so we can share a bedroom. Was that not nice?'

'What of the others?' Anna was not worried about how Betty would treat her.

Mary turned pensive. 'I am not sure. Mr Bailey was nice. Nobody else said much to me at the meal, but they were not mean to me.'

'And Mrs Greaves?' Greaves's treatment was perhaps the most important.

'I admit she scares me a little.' That Anna could well understand. 'She just told me what to do and things like that.'

No one had chided her for being a Dorman servant? That must have been Will's doing.

Mary put away her dress and bid Anna goodnight, but Anna did not retire. Instead she sat up listening for Will to come up the stairs and open his door. She heard his mother and Ellen come up before she heard Will's door open. She hurried to the connecting door and opened it a crack. It was Will's valet.

She left the door open a crack and waited some more until finally Will's footsteps sounded on the stairs and in the hallway. She could tell it was Will, because the footsteps sounded burdened and weary.

She'd been so angry at him that morning—until he brought her Mary—and now she felt such sympathy. He'd obviously faced his mother and that could not have been pleasant.

A wave of guilt washed over her. The Willburgh household had probably been running smoothly and comfortably until she came to disrupt everyone.

She'd planned to go to Will that night, to crawl into bed with him, tell him how grateful she was to him. Make love with him.

She quietly closed the connecting door and walked back to her bed. Alone.

The next morning Anna rose as early as usual. She was halfway dressed when Mary came in the room.

'Miss Anna—m'lady, I mean! I did not think you would be up so early. I am so sorry I was not here.'

'Mary, I did not think to tell you,' Anna responded apologetically. 'I am so used to rising on my own, but, now you are here, you can help me put on my new riding habit.'

With Mary's help she dressed quickly and was out the door and on her way to the stables. She hoped she was in time to catch Will.

From a distance, she spied him entering the stable door and she quickened her step.

The grooms were used to both of them riding at this hour and had the horses ready. Will typically rode his thoroughbred and Anna always rode Seraphina. By the time Anna entered the stable, Will was already mounted.

He nodded a greeting.

She looked up at him. 'May I ride with you a little, Will?'

'I'll wait for you outside,' he said.

Her heart beat faster as she mounted Seraphina quickly and rode out the door.

They headed in the direction of the farm fields.

'I want to check on the planting,' he explained.

Why had she not realised before? Will did not only ride in the morning for pleasure. He rode to oversee the work on his land.

They went awhile without talking. Finally Anna said, 'I gather by the mood at dinner last night and the behaviour of the servants, that you supported my keeping Mary?'

He shrugged. 'It was the right thing to do. You ought to select the servants you want.'

'That is what you told your mother?' She wanted to keep him talking.

'That and more.' He did not look at her, but kept his eyes straight ahead, on the road. 'I also addressed the managing of the household. I apologise for being remiss. I thought my mother would take care of that. Show you how to run the household. Help you. I thought she would know her place.'

'She is very strong-willed,' Anna said.

He laughed. 'Indeed.'

'What did you say to her?' she asked.

Still looking straight ahead, he answered, 'I told her she'd better stop this foolishness or I'd send her to the dower-house.'

'You didn't.' Goodness! Anna truly had caused a disruption. 'Your poor mother! First I boot her out of her bed chambers and next out of her own home.'

'Not you,' he said. 'Me. Anyway, she can stay if she behaves herself.'

Now her mother-in-law would be required to stand on pins and needles because of Anna.

They reached some of the fields where farm workers were already at work.

'Good,' Will spoke more to himself than to Anna. 'We are catching up.'

When they returned to the house, they entered by the garden door.

'I had an idea,' Anna said, as they walked through his office. 'I thought perhaps I could help you with your piles of papers. Perhaps organise them for you or put things in ledgers.'

He paused contemplating the array of work before him.

'Until you hire a secretary, that is,' she added. 'You really should use some of your money that way.'

His brow furrowed. 'My father did not have a secretary.'

'That does not mean you couldn't have one.' She swept her hand over his desk. 'In any event, I would like to help.'

He paused again, then answered, 'Come to me after breakfast.'

Chapter Nineteen

The next few days were at least productive for Will, even though he felt far from composed.

Anna turned out to be very efficient and organised and quicker than he at performing some of the more tedious tasks, like putting all the receipts and bills in order and recording the expenditures in the ledger. He hated to admit it, but she rather proved a secretary would be useful.

For certain some eager younger son would not be as distracting. Will had the greatest difficulty concentrating when Anna was present. He was distracted by the way the sunlight from the windows illuminated her face and put streaks of gold in her hair. When she moved to shelve a ledger, or bent over to pick up papers that fell, or simply stretched the kinks from her neck, he was thrown into memories of stroking her skin or moving inside her.

He took to using the time she worked to meet with Parker and the other men who helped run his estate, especially his dairy manager. Their dairy cows were older and producing less milk each day. His manager found a farmer, not too far away, who had two young dairy cows for sale. The farmer agreed on Will's offer to buy them. They fixed on the morrow to make the purchase.

Will hoped his absence would not cause any difficulty.

He mostly hoped his mother would continue behaving herself. She could cause a good deal of trouble even though he'd only be gone a day. He knew that Anna had asked his mother to be present in her meetings with Mrs Greaves. He did not know how that was going. In any event, he hoped his mother knew he was serious about sending her to the dower-house if she caused any more trouble.

Having Anna's new lady's maid was turning out better than Will expected. Mrs Greaves must have reinforced what Will had told the other servants himself so they'd been civil to her.

At least he did not have to worry about Ellen. She was always so refreshingly happy.

Will walked back from Parker's office and entered his office, knowing Anna would still be there. She sat at a table near his desk writing figures in a ledger. She looked up and smiled, which always reached right into his very essence.

He sat in a chair near her. 'I will be accompanying Parker and the dairy manager to that farmer I told you about, the one selling the cows.'

'Oh?' She turned to face him. 'When?'

'Tomorrow.'

'How long will you be gone?' She looked disappointed.

'Only a day.' He tried not to get distracted by how lovely she looked in her dress, even though she wore an apron over it to protect it from the ink. 'But we'll leave very early and are likely not to make it back before dinner.'

'Is there anything you would like of me in your absence?' she asked.

Will feared that if he indulged in what he'd like of her, he might forget all about cows and ledgers, and everything but her. And then what would happen?

He glanced around the room, more orderly now that Anna

had helped him, but still stacks of papers, things to attend to. All would tumble like a house of cards.

He pretended he'd been thinking of her question. 'I believe you know enough what to do.'

Anna did not ride the next morning, but rose even earlier, wanting to see Will off. She'd arranged an early breakfast for him and insisted he eat something before he left. She also had Cook pack them some bread and cheese for later in the day.

He was dressed for riding, the attire that reminded her of their travels, even though this coat and breeches were impeccably tailored and of the finest quality cloth. Merely seeing him dressed this way always filled her with longing for what they so briefly shared. Things were more comfortable with him than they had been before their altercation about Mary, but she still feared he treated her well out of duty.

'You did not have to rise so early, Anna,' he said to her, still cool and distant.

'I wanted to.' Even if he did not want her to.

When he'd hired Mary against his own wishes, Anna had hoped it would bring them closer. It seemed like such a loving thing he'd done, just because she wished it. Then he'd allowed her to help him in his office. Should that not have brought them closer?

He simply spent most of the time out of the room, claiming other tasks and all the time her heart ached to be with him.

She'd forged a sort of truce with Lady Willburgh, but she had no illusions that the woman had any less dislike for her. Mrs Greaves and the other servants were overtly more solicitous of her, but she hated that fear of losing their employment made them that way. Even Ellen, who she thought might become a friend, seemed to prefer her solitary pursuits to spending time with Anna.

She was as alone as she'd ever been—except for Mary. Mary was the one ray of sunshine that made the rest tolerable.

And it had been Will who'd brought Mary to her. It simply made her love for him grow to even more painful proportions.

She watched him while she sipped her tea, her handsome Will, her champion, the husband who must still regret marrying her.

Anna asked him a couple of questions about his paperwork merely to dispel the silence between them. When he finished breakfast she walked with him to the hall. Outside the front door a groom waited with his horse.

When Parker and the dairy manager rode up, Will turned to her and she hoped for some sign he might miss her, at least a little. For a moment she thought she saw some softness in his eyes, but he merely put on his hat.

'I will be late returning. After dinner,' was all he said.

She knew that already. 'Safe travels, Will,' she told him.

He nodded and went out the door.

Anna climbed the steps to the drawing room which looked over the road to the house. She watched him ride away until she could see him no more.

'Safe travels, my dearest Will,' she whispered.

That afternoon Anna felt too restless to sit and write figures in ledgers. She missed Will, even though he was probably happy enough to be absent from her. She put away her pen and ink and called for Mary to help her change into her riding habit.

Riding Seraphina would calm her down. The pony always did.

It was a lovely day with blue skies and white clouds like

cotton wool. The sun was high in the sky brightening the green foliage and wild flowers and warming the air. Anna rode aimlessly and found herself at the edge of Will's property, near the land that had been the source of the Willburgh feud with the Dormans. Because of the feud the families had never resolved the land's ownership, it was left uncultivated; the wooded areas, untended. Such a waste.

How like this land Anna was, caught in some unresolvable place, belonging to no one. Left to her own devices. Untended.

She rode Seraphina carefully through the wooded part of the property. The thick green foliage parted only enough to allow shafts of sunlight to pierce the ground where ferns and flowers of the underbrush bloomed white and purple against the green. The cawing of the rooks protecting their rookeries broke the silence.

Anna could almost forget her anguish in this wild, but peaceful place.

As she rode on, the rooks' cries faded into the distance, but the blackbirds, chaffinches, and robins took over the song. Then suddenly she heard human voices.

Through the trees she could see them. In a clearing. Embracing.

Ellen and Lucius.

Anna gasped.

They parted and Lucius walked Ellen to her horse. He lifted her into the saddle and pulled her down for a light kiss on the lips. She laughed and turned her horse to ride away.

Anna backed Seraphina deeper into the woods until she knew she would not be seen, then she turned and rode faster to escape the woods and intercept Ellen.

Ellen and Lucius.

At least she knew now why Ellen preferred solitary afternoon pursuits. That embrace. That kiss. No wonder Ellen seemed so incandescently happy lately. She fancied herself in love.

With Lucius.

No doubt he had manipulated her into thinking so. To toy with her? To achieve some revenge upon Will or Anna herself? Why would he do such a despicable thing?

Anna waited on the path she knew Ellen must take to return to the house until she saw her sister-in-law approaching her.

'Hello, Anna,' Ellen cried cheerfully. 'I did not know you would be riding, too. We could have ridden together.'

Anna decided not to spare words. 'I saw you with Lucius.'

The girl inadvertently tugged on the reins. Her horse faltered. 'I—I do not know what you mean.'

'I saw you with Lucius,' she repeated while Ellen regained control of the horse. 'I saw him take liberties with you. You were in the glen at the edge of the woods. I know what I saw.'

Ellen's horse was next to Anna's now. Ellen, on a taller horse, leaned over and touched her shoulder. 'Oh, Anna! Do not tell Will. Please do not tell him.'

'That you've been secretly meeting Lucius? How long has this gone on?'

'Oh…' Ellen's eyes took on a dreamy look. 'Five days. We are in love, Anna.'

In love?

Anna could believe Ellen thought so, but Anna knew Lucius better. He'd either manoeuvred to encounter her or had taken advantage of an accidental meeting. Whichever it was, Lucius was up to no good.

'Ellen, do you realise how improper this is?' Anna spoke insistently. 'You cannot be meeting a man alone like this. Think of your reputation. You will be ruined. I have already seen him behave in ways with you more compromising than what happened between Will and me. Look at what happened to us.'

'You had to get married.' Ellen sounded petulant now. 'But you were not in love, Anna! Lucius and I are in love.'

'I know Lucius.' Anna persisted. 'He is not in love with you. He is dallying with you. You are a conquest, nothing more. He is merely using his charm on you.'

Anna knew Lucius to be very capable of trifling with a woman's feelings or even of seducing her, but he usually confined himself to opera dancers and actresses, not respectable young ladies who'd not yet been presented. Not the sister of his biggest rival.

Ellen pursed her lips together and lifted her chin.

'You must heed me,' Anna insisted. 'This puts you in great peril. You must not see him again. He is not a man of good character. He will ruin your reputation and walk away from you.'

'He would never do that!' Ellen cried. 'I told you. He loves me. He told me all about the other women, but he has never met anyone like me. He said I make him want to be a better man.'

Lucius knew what to say to get what he wanted. Ellen had fallen for his nonsense and was being primed for—what? Complete ruin?

She needed to be protected from him.

'What if I do tell Will?' Anna asked.

'You can't tell Will!' Ellen pleaded. 'He will become angry with me and pack me off to some school somewhere! You do not know how angry he can become.'

Did she not?

'Then will you agree to stop meeting Lucius?'

The house was coming into view. They did not have much farther to ride before reaching home.

'That is my bargain,' Anna stressed. 'You stop meeting Lucius or I tell Will exactly what I saw.'

Ellen glanced away.

Anna pressed her. 'Ellen, you must agree. Believe me, I will do what I say. I'll even encourage Will to send you away if that is what it takes to save you from Lucius.'

Ellen rode a little ahead of Anna and did not answer for what seemed like several minutes. When she finally slowed enough to allow Anna to catch up to her, she said, 'Very well. I'll stop seeing him.'

Was she telling the truth? Anna hoped so. In any event she would keep a close eye on her sister-in-law.

Anna did not find sleep easy that night. Half of her was listening for Will to safely return; the other half wrestling with her promise not to tell Will about Ellen meeting with Lucius.

She regretted making that agreement. Will really ought to know. He'd want to protect his sister. Anna had no doubt Will would do anything for his sister.

He'd married Anna because of Ellen, had he not? To save her from a scandal that could ruin her chances to make a good match. What Lucius was up to could be so much more ruinous to Ellen's reputation.

She resolved to tell Will, no matter her promise to Ellen. It might make Anna one more enemy in the household, but it seemed the only decision that let her settle down to sleep.

Just as she was drifting off, Will returned, making more of a clatter than she'd heard him make before. She rose from her bed intending to tell him about Ellen right away when she thought better of it. Let him rest. Tomorrow would be time enough.

* * *

The next morning Anna thought she would catch Will when he went on his morning ride, but he'd told the grooms he wasn't riding today. It was disappointing. Talking while on horseback always seemed to go better between the two of them, but he was probably tired and needed the rest.

On her solitary ride she returned to where she'd seen Ellen and Lucius the previous day. Not that she expected to find them, but more to reassure herself that she indeed must tell Will. She would catch him at breakfast.

But when she came back in to the house through the garden, he stood waiting at the office door.

'I would speak with you, Anna.' He looked thunderous.

She was taken aback. 'Now?' Before she changed her clothes?

'Now.' He stepped aside to let her in the room.

She'd been proud of how she'd left his office the day before. Only two piles of papers needing correspondence on his desk. The ledgers neatly set in order on the bookshelf and the unrecorded receipts hidden in his bottom desk drawer. Had he noticed?

His angry glare made her doubt it.

And it roused her anger, as well. Why this change in him again?

She turned to face him. 'What is it, Will? What is so pressing that I cannot change out of my riding habit and into clean clothes?'

'The devil with clean clothes,' he shot back. 'I will tell you what is pressing. Our trip to purchase the dairy cows—the ones we needed so much—was wasted because someone outbid us.'

Anna was puzzled. 'That is unfortunate, but…'

'But nothing!' He glared at her. 'Do you know who outbid us? The bid we offered privately?' He didn't leave her a chance to answer. 'Lucius Dorman.'

'Lucius?' This made no sense. 'Lucius never bothered with tasks like that.' Something made even less sense. 'Why yell at me for something Lucius did?'

His eyes flashed. 'Because the farmer said Lucius knew of our bid, knew to offer more.'

'But how did Lucius know—?'

Will raised his voice. 'I will tell you how Lucius knew! *Your maid* told him.'

'Mary? No.' Impossible. 'Mary could not have told him! When would she have done so?'

He started pacing in front of her. 'She obviously slipped away.'

'I refuse to believe it!' Mary would never have done such a thing.

'One of the grooms saw her. With Lucius,' Will insisted.

'It couldn't have been!' Anna countered. 'It must have been somebody else.'

Will clenched his fists. 'He said it looked like Mary Jones. Who else could it have been? She came to spy on us. Just as I feared.'

'Mary is no spy!' She could not be. If Mary was a spy, then it meant even sweet, timid Mary had betrayed her.

'She goes, Anna,' Will glared into her eyes. 'I cannot have a Dorman spy in this house. She goes today!'

'No!' Anna straightened her spine and met his gaze with a blazing one of her own. 'I do not believe for one minute that Mary acted as a Dorman spy. You are judging her unfairly.'

'This is precisely why I did not want to hire her,' he said, leaving the rest unspoken—that Anna had insisted.

She ignored that. 'Think about it, Will. How would a lady's maid even know about the purchase of dairy cows?'

'You must have talked to her about it.' His glare turned accusing.

She gave a sarcastic laugh. 'I did not talk about dairy cows with my maid.'

'Then she found the letters in the office,' he asserted.

That was possible, Anna supposed, but very unlikely. 'Why would she go in your office?'

His voice grew louder. 'To find out our business so she could tell the Dormans.'

'No. Not Mary. It could not have been her!' Anna shot back.

He raised his brows indignantly. 'Are you are accusing one of my grooms, who has been in my employ for years, of lying?'

'Not of lying.' He was twisting her words. 'Of being mistaken.' She turned towards the door. 'Come with me back to the stables. Let's ask this groom. I want to hear for myself.'

Chapter Twenty

Will strode out of the room with her and they walked briskly to the stables.

He wasn't sure why the poaching of dairy cows angered him so. He knew they would find others eventually. It was because it was Lucius who had done it.

In a way he blamed himself. He knew it was not a good idea to hire a Dorman servant. He knew what would happen. The servant would talk and the Dormans would know all their private affairs and would interfere whenever they could. Will wanted the Dormans out of their lives. He wanted rid of the foolish rivalry that was a credit to neither of them.

Instead, he all but invited a Dorman into the most private parts of his home. All because he could not convince Anna he knew best in this matter and, as a result, he could not refuse her.

Well, this time he intended to stand by what he knew was right. The Dorman maid had to go.

He would not be heartless, though. He'd give the girl a good reference and plenty of money for a new start. But she would never be able to spy on him and his family for the Dormans again.

When they reached the stable Will asked for the groom who'd told him about seeing the maid with Lucius. The man was out in the field and it took several minutes for him to be brought back to the stables. While they waited, Anna stood apart from Will. She stood with her arms crossed and refused to look at him.

The groom finally hurried over to him. 'You asked for me, m'lord?'

Anna joined them, then.

'Yes,' Will responded. 'Would you please tell Lady Willburgh about seeing the maid with Mr Dorman?'

The groom turned to her. 'I saw them. You see, one of the horses got spooked and ran off and I tracked him into that part of the woods. And I saw them through the trees.'

'Are you certain it was Mary Jones, my new lady's maid?' Anna asked.

'Well, yes,' the groom replied. 'I think so anyway.'

'Did you see her face?' Anna persisted.

'Well, no, ma'am.' He looked sheepish. 'She wore a red cloak, but it looked like your maid, ma'am. She was with the young Dorman.'

'Thank you,' Anna said.

She walked out.

Will caught up with her.

'That was not proof it was Mary.' She spoke firmly.

Will had to admit, the groom was less convincing this time. 'Who else would it have been?'

'Not a maid who's only been here a few days and has been busy learning her tasks.' She quickened her pace.

Will stopped her outside the garden door. 'It does not matter, Anna. I can never trust her now. I cannot have the worry that whatever I do or say might become known to the Dormans and be fodder for their mischief.'

'But she's done nothing wrong!' Anna cried.

Will needed to hold fast to his position. 'I never wanted

a Dorman servant here in the first place. She's an outsider. She needs to go.'

'An outsider?' Anna sounded outraged. 'Like me, do you mean?'

'A Dorman outsider,' he clarified.

'Oh?' Her brow lifted. 'You mean someone who spent years in the Dorman household because she had nowhere else to go?'

He caught her point, but needed to stay firm. That was one thing his father did teach him. To be firm. 'This sort of betrayal never happened before your maid came. I simply cannot have her here. She must go.'

'No!' She pleaded now. 'She will have no place to go. I will not let you be so unkind to her. I will not let you!'

Will felt her pain and regretted being the cause. 'I've no intention of being unkind, Anna.' He lowered his voice and spoke kindly. 'I'll pay her generously and provide her with good references. I will also give her time to make arrangements, whatever time you see fit. Will that do?'

Her eyes narrowed. 'It will not do. But you will not listen to reason.'

'I'm not debating it, Anna.' He was getting impatient now. 'I am serious. And I will not change my mind. So leave now. I'm done talking.'

Leave, because he was not feeling very good about the decision, but could not waver.

Anna opened the garden door and rushed in, so angry at him she could not see straight. She hurried up to her room. Mary was there, putting her clean laundry in drawers.

The maid's eyes grew wide. 'Miss Anna—ma'am—what is wrong? You look upset!'

'Oh, Mary!' Anna turned to her, her only ally in this

house, but she needed to know for herself. She looked directly into Mary's eyes. 'I need to ask you something. And I want you to be very honest with me.'

'Of course I will, m'lady.' She looked earnest. And wary.

'I need to know if you have met with anyone from the Dorman house and if you told them anything about us. About Willburgh family business. Anything, even something small.'

Mary looked as if Anna had struck her. 'I would never, Miss Anna. Never. Why would I do such a thing? When you've been so kind?' Her eyes filled with tears. 'Who said I did?'

Anna could not bear to tell her it was Will. 'That does not matter. Is there any way someone might have seen you with someone and thought it was a Dorman or a Dorman servant?'

A tear rolled down Mary's cheek. 'Do you mean here in the house? I haven't been anywhere else, except maybe in the yard. I don't want to talk to anyone from there!'

That was what Anna thought, but she had been fooled so many times before and Mary could have slipped away when Anna was helping Will in his office.

'I don't talk about what I hear, not to anybody,' Mary went on, her lip quivering. 'Am I being sacked?'

Anna enfolded the girl in her arms. 'What will become of me?' Mary wailed.

Anna knew that pain, that panic. She'd felt it many times before.

'Do not fear,' she reassured the girl. 'I will not allow anything bad to happen to you.'

But Will had been adamant and Anna had no power at all. She never did.

Anna was shocked at Will's unreasonableness and his sudden anger. He was completely unwilling to consider any other explanation of the events. He'd made up his mind it was Mary, merely because Mary had been a Dorman servant. An outsider. Well, Anna was an outsider, too. How could she trust that he would not be unreasonable with her as well? And how was she to predict when he'd erupt in these irrational outbursts?

Mary helped her change out of her riding habit. After Anna had washed off the dirt of the road and donned a day dress, she calmed a little. Only then did it strike her that she'd not told him about Ellen. Well, she certainly was not going to tell him now, not when he was in this unreasonable mood.

She felt the blood drain from her face. Anna knew who had told Lucius about the sale of the cows! It had been Ellen. It was Ellen the groom saw and mistook for Mary. They were about the same height and figure and who would ever believe a Willburgh would secretly meet with a Dorman?

Could she tell Will? He'd been so angry at her when he suspected Mary; how angry would he be if he knew it was his own sister who spilled family business to the enemy? And how much angrier still to discover she fancied herself in love with that enemy?

But she had to tell him. Ellen's future was at stake. When, though?

Will expected Anna to isolate herself in her room and avoid him and the rest of the family. That was her typical behaviour when upset. Instead she seemed to spend a lot of time with Ellen who had somehow contracted a spell of the blue devils. Anna's company did not seem to help Ellen's mood, though.

Will knew what troubled Anna, but Ellen's Gordian knots were a mystery. Just the other day she'd been full of cheer. Now she acted like she'd lost her best friend. And it was clear her best friend was not Anna. Ellen seemed as peeved at Anna as Will was.

From his office, he overheard an exchange between Ellen and Anna in the hall.

'I'm not going riding,' Ellen said petulantly. 'I'm going for a walk.'

'I'll go with you,' Anna responded.

'I do not want you to go with me,' Ellen cried. 'I'm just walking to the road and back.'

'To the road and back. Alone.' Anna sounded sceptical, but why would she care?

'Very well, not alone,' retorted Ellen. 'I'll take Betty with me. You can watch from the front of the house if you like.'

'I will,' Anna said.

Will checked and that is what they did. Ellen walked with Betty and Anna watched them closely.

The whole incident did not make sense to him. What did Anna care if Ellen took a walk alone? Ellen was used to walking and riding alone. He refused to ask Anna, though. He'd only spark another argument.

That night's dinner was tortuous. Anna spoke little and avoided talking to him, and Ellen was sullen. Only his mother seemed pleased, possibly because it was clear something had happened between him and Anna.

Anna excused herself after the meal was done. In the drawing room afterwards Will was alone with his mother and Ellen.

Will decided to ask Ellen about the walk.

'I overheard you and Anna arguing about you going for a walk,' he began. 'What was that all about?'

His mother perked up in interest, presumably because this was about Anna.

Ellen looked distressed for a moment, but quickly composed herself. 'I do not know why she all of a sudden does not think I should walk alone. I've walked or ridden alone a lot since she's been here. I refuse to heed what she thinks. She has no authority over me.'

'Indeed she does not,' their mother readily—and somewhat happily—agreed. 'She is behaving very oddly, I must say.' She turned to Will. 'Are we to expect this always?'

'I do not know,' he responded.

His mother leaned towards him. 'You know how much I hate to pry—' Oh, yes, his mother *never* interfered, *never* pried. 'But what did happen between you and Anna to make her behave so oddly?'

He supposed he owed her an explanation. He picked the easiest one. 'We had a disagreement about her lady's maid.'

His mother looked smug. 'I told you that girl would be trouble. What did she do?'

Will took a sip of brandy. 'Remember I told you we were out bid for the dairy cows?'

She nodded.

'It was Lucius Dorman who outbid us.'

Ellen's head perked up.

'Lucius Dorman!' his mother cried.

'Someone tipped him off,' Will went on. 'I believe it was Anna's lady's maid and Anna insists it was not. But who else would have done it?'

'Indeed,' his mother agreed. 'I am certain you are correct. I told you that maid would spy on us. You might have listened to me.'

Ellen broke in. 'The cows were that important?'

'Not the cows,' Will explained. 'It was that our personal family information was told to a Dorman. We cannot have that. We cannot trust them.'

'Indeed we cannot,' his mother expounded. 'So Anna takes the maid's side against us? That is disloyal!'

'This is because of the feud,' Ellen said with derision. 'The feud that you think is so important.'

'It is important.' His mother shook a finger at Ellen. 'Remember that feud led to your father's death.'

Ellen sobered. 'No one ever told me how.'

Remind Ellen of Father's death, Mother, thought Will. *That will cheer her up.*

Her mother eagerly explained, 'Because of the feud, your father and Bertram Dorman, Baron Dorman's younger brother—Anna's father—fought a duel and they killed each other.'

'Anna's stepfather,' Will corrected.

'Stepfather, then,' sniffed his mother.

'How come they fought a duel over the feud?' Ellen persisted.

Will broke in. 'Because they were foolish.'

Ellen did not need to know of her mother's fling with Bertram Dorman. That certainly would not cheer her up. He could at least count on his mother not to tell her that.

'And the feud was about that land?' she asked.

'Yes. The disputed land.' That was all she needed to know.

'Well.' Ellen stood. 'I think it is all very silly!' She walked out.

At the moment Will agreed with her. How much havoc over generations had this feud created? Was he perpetuating the havoc?

Had the feud not existed would Bertram Dorman have bothered to seduce his mother? Would his father have fought a duel with anyone but a Dorman? Would the Dormans have acted so outraged when Will was caught in the rain with Anna? Nothing good ever came from the damned feud.

A few days ago he would have hoped that marrying Anna

would turn into the one good thing that came from the feud, but look how that hope was dashed.

That night Will could not sleep.

His head told him he'd been right when he'd refused to hire the Dorman maid. So now he was right to let her go, was he not? He'd expected trouble and trouble came. Was that not right?

Anna's arguments on behalf of the maid were compelling, though. They nagged at him.

Who else could it have been? No one else made sense. He wanted Anna to see his way, though she seemed determined not to.

Everything seemed wrong. What tortured Will the most was he feared he was wrong. Was he the one who made a mess of everything?

He heard the door connecting his room to Anna's open and he turned to face it.

She was framed in the doorway. 'Will? Are you awake?'

'I am awake,' he responded.

'I would speak with you,' she said. Not *may* she speak. She was not asking for permission but making a command.

He rose from the bed as she walked towards him, the flame of the candle in her hand illuminating her face, her curls loose around her head like an aura, her nightdress flowing as she walked, giving him glimpses of her womanly shape beneath. He was naked save his drawers and he yearned to pull off her nightdress and feel her warm, smooth skin against his.

Suddenly it seemed like there was no air for him to breathe, only this otherworldly spectre coming closer and his desire growing stronger. Was she his weakness?

He managed to answer her. 'Then speak, Anna.'

She stopped a mere three feet away. 'I have a plan that will remove Mary in mere days and will avoid further *disruption* to the family.' She emphasised the word *disruption* and sounded sad, but resigned.

It had been a word he'd used, he realised. 'What is the plan?'

She took a breath. 'Mary will leave here, but I will leave with her.'

'What?' Will was shocked.

She held up a hand. 'Hear me out.' She placed the candle on a nearby table and faced him again. 'Before we decided to marry, we'd contemplated you simply supporting me, giving me enough money to live on.'

That had been what she'd wanted, and if they'd done that, she'd have wound up wealthy. His fault she wasn't.

She went on. 'It was what we should have done all along. Set me up with some sort of settlement or stipend or something—nothing extravagant—and I will take Mary as my maid. We can live very simply, except I should like to afford to keep Seraphina.'

No! He wanted to protest. She would leave him? Wanted her horse, but not him? No!

'Where would you go?' he asked, keeping the emotion out of his voice.

She shrugged. 'Oh, I don't know. Perhaps a village near Reading. Reading sounds like a nice town.'

Reading? With its iron works and a ruined abbey? What could appeal there?

'Reading,' he repeated. 'You want to leave and take the maid and go to Reading.'

'And Seraphina,' she added. 'It solves everything, do you see? Think on it.' She picked up the candle again and turned to walk away, but paused and spoke over her shoulder. 'Except I've not given you an heir. I do regret that.'

The mention of an heir sent his mind back to tangled sheets and passion and pleasure unlike he'd ever experienced before. That was what he wanted back. That and the easy camaraderie they'd once shared.

She walked back to the door, a silhouette now, even more spectre-like. As she walked away his spirits plummeted even deeper than before. He was left feeling a dislike of himself that rational thought disdained.

And beyond that, emptiness.

The next day Anna avoided Will.

It was too painful to be near him, not because of his temper, but because she loved him so. He was a good man on the whole, trying to do the right thing by everyone. Everyone but her.

When he brought Mary to her, Anna thought it the most loving act, even though she could not say he loved her. It bitterly disappointed Anna, though, that Will could so cruelly take Mary away, with such baseless accusations. He might wrap her banishment in gold ribbons, but it was the fact of being unwanted that was so deeply wounding. How could Will do that? How could he not see that Anna needed to make Mary know that she was wanted, that she belonged somewhere and that someone cared for her? Could Will not see that Anna needed him to tell her she belonged with him, that he wanted her, cared for her?

Anna might be a disappointment to him, but, in this, Anna was disappointed in Will. It was best she and Mary leave.

At the moment, though, Anna had Ellen to worry about. She stayed close to Ellen the whole day and still agonised over whether she should tell Will about her and Lucius. Even though Ellen had given Anna her word that she would not see Lucius again, every instinct told Anna she could not trust Ellen not to slip away and run to him.

So when Ellen went to the library to select a book, Anna selected a book. When Ellen settled in one of the sunniest parlours to read, Anna sat in the same room with her own book.

Anna had selected one volume of *England's Gazetteer* to read of the places she and Mary might settle. She'd not set on Reading for certain, but mentioned it to Will so he'd know she was serious about leaving. Reading was as good a place as any.

The more she read of other villages and towns, the more her spirits dipped. Living in this area since her childhood made it familiar to her. She was used to the village, the church, the people. Even more, Anna had come to love this house. Even in the short time she'd lived in Willburgh House, it felt more like home than Dorman Hall. At Dorman Hall she'd been treated as if she were Violet's lady's companion instead of a member of the family. As if she did not truly belong.

She glanced over at Ellen who was gazing out the window instead of reading her book. Those first days here Anna had hoped she and Ellen could be friends. Now Ellen despised her.

Ellen glanced over at her. 'You do not have to watch me every second, Anna. I gave you my word I would not see Lucius. Do you not trust me?'

'I would like to trust you,' Anna answered.

Was it useless to keep such a close eye on Ellen? When Anna left, Ellen could continue her secret trysts.

That was why Anna must tell Will. So Anna's word could not be trusted either, could it?

Lucius would lose interest eventually, of course, but it was the harm he could do to Ellen beforehand that Anna worried about. No, Anna would have to tell Will and tell him soon.

But not today.

In the meantime Anna could try to convince Ellen that Lucius was not of good character.

'Let me tell you a little more about Lucius,' she said to Ellen. 'About the kind of person he is.'

She told Ellen about Lucius abandoning her at Vauxhall and leaving her to the mercy of his friend, Millman, and exactly what Millman tried to do to her.

Ellen listened with a defiant expression. 'You cannot convince me that he knew Millman would try to molest you.'

Actually Anna did not believe that of Lucius. 'No, but he remained friends with him after he knew what happened.'

'Are you sure?' Ellen countered. 'You were not with him after Scotland.'

'True, but I would wager any amount of money that Lucius would care more about his friendship than about what the man tried to do to me.'

'By then he was probably very angry at you,' Ellen said. 'You ran off and married Will. That was like a betrayal to him. That silly feud, you know.'

Anna did not know what to say in response.

Ellen rose and faced her. 'I cannot bear to be inside this stuffy old house for another moment. I am going for a walk.'

Anna opened her mouth to say she would walk with her.

Ellen waved her hand dismissively. 'I do not want your company. I will take Betty. We will walk to the road and back and you can watch from the front of the house like you did before.'

'I will be watching,' Anna said.

Chapter Twenty-One

After another tension-filled dinner that evening Anna retired to her room and had Mary help her get ready for bed. She'd hardly slept the past two nights. She hadn't told Mary about needing to leave. Why upset the girl until Anna had all the details set? Mary was happy here at Willburgh House, Anna could tell. Betty had become her friend and the two could be found together at every spare moment. Let Mary have her friendship for as long as possible.

When Mary left her, Anna crawled into bed and burrowed beneath the covers, but, instead of sleep, Anna's emotions spilled over and she wept. She'd held back tears long enough, and now the dam had broken. Her grief at all she'd lost—especially Will—flooded her. When she finally slept, though, her sleep was peaceful and deep.

Until she was jarred awake by someone shaking her, telling her to wake. 'M'lady! M'lady! Wake up!'

She opened her eyes.

Betty and Mary stood over her.

'You must wake up, m'lady!' Betty cried.

Anna sat up. 'What? What has happened?'

Mary held the candle while Betty shook her shoulder, a breach of proper servant behaviour, but Betty was distraught.

'She's gone, m'lady!' Betty cried. 'Not long ago. Maybe half an hour? Less.'

Anna brushed the hair out of her eyes. 'Who is gone?'

'Miss Willburgh!' Betty cried.

'Ellen?' Anna straightened, wide awake now.

'She's run away!' Betty stifled a sob. 'She took some clothes! What shall we do?'

Anna bounded out of bed. 'We must go after her!' She turned to Mary. 'Quick. My old riding habit!'

Mary shoved the candle into Betty's hand.

Anna ran to the connecting door to Will's room, burst in his room and in the dim light, found his bed.

'Will! Wake up!' She shook him like Betty had shaken her.

He shot up so quickly she jumped back.

'What is it?' He seemed even more awake than she was.

'Ellen has eloped!' she said. 'I'll explain later. We must go after her! Right now.'

He got out of bed, wearing only his drawers. Betty had followed her and lit a candle in his room.

'Get dressed now!' Anna cried. 'Hurry!' She ran back to her room.

While Mary helped her dress, Betty explained. 'She told me not to tell, but on those walks, she left a letter for someone in a knot in a tree that was on the road. Then yesterday she found a letter there for her.' Betty shook her head. 'That's all I know. Do you think that has something to do with her running away?'

'I'm sure it has,' Anna responded.

Betty went on. 'I thought something was up so Mary and I got up early. The clock struck four. She was in bed then, but something seemed strange so we went back and she was gone. We could not have been more than a quarter hour. Or a half hour.'

Perhaps she'd been dressed and ready to leave but pretending to sleep. But with the letters, there was no doubt that she planned this.

Will came into her room as she was putting on her boots. She gave quick embraces to both Betty and Mary and rushed out with him.

Their clatter on the stairs roused the footman monitoring the hall. He was barely awake when Will called to him. 'Tell no one we've gone!'

Then they were out the door hurrying to the stables. By this time the first rays of dawn had appeared on the horizon, enough to light their way.

'She's been meeting Lucius in secret,' Anna explained. 'And Lucius has convinced her she is in love with him. I thought I stopped it, but they were passing letters on those walks. I think he is planning a terrible revenge. I think he is eloping with her!'

'Lucius!' Will growled. 'I'll kill him.'

Will's anger alarmed her. 'We just need to stop them in time.'

When they reached the stable door and opened it, Will's voice boomed. 'Grooms! Now! To saddle horses!'

He'd already picked up the saddles and brought them to the horses when John and Toby appeared, hastily.

'Saddle Anna's pony and my thoroughbred,' he ordered and turned to Anna. 'My thoroughbred is the fastest.'

The two grooms asked no questions, but made quick work of it. Will and Anna were soon mounted and ready to ride.

'Be ready if I need you,' Will shouted to John and Toby. 'I do not know how long it will be.'

Will galloped off and Anna followed him. He had the gate open for her by the time she reached it and he was standing in the middle of the road, looking down.

He looked over at her and pointed. 'They went that way.' He remounted.

'Ride ahead, Will,' she told him. 'I'll come as fast as I can.'

Will needed to keep his wits about him.

He needed to conserve his horse's strength. How long before he could catch up to them? He didn't want his horse blown.

Will was reasonably sure Lucius and Ellen were headed to Aylesbury to a coaching inn. The tracks looked like Lucius drove his curricle. Lucius was not likely to take his curricle all the way to Scotland.

If Scotland was where he intended to go.

Will would not let himself think of the alternative—to merely ruin her thoroughly. Just in case, Will kept his eye on the road to make sure their trail did not turn off this main road.

As Will rode, the puzzle pieces fell into place. While he and Anna were working together on his papers and ledgers, Ellen was happily riding or taking walks alone. Meeting Lucius. It was Ellen, not the poor maid, who'd told Lucius about the sale of the cows, probably innocently, but still... Had it not occurred to her that Lucius would take advantage of the information? Why had she allowed the maid to take the blame?

Anna discovered this and was making certain Ellen did not meet him again. That was why Ellen turned sullen and why she turned against Anna.

Everything fit.

What a fool Will had been. He'd been as much a prisoner of the feud as Lucius was, as their ancestors were. Would he have been so unfair to Anna, if not for the feud? Would he have been so harsh on poor Mary Jones? Would Lucius have bothered to trifle with a respectable sixteen-year-old?

He must have ridden at a good pace for at least an hour. They'd started out in near darkness and now the new day had dawned. Sheep appeared on the hillsides, birds sounded in the bushes and took to flight when he rode by. He saw farm workers making their way to the fields. The road was still empty of traffic, though. He was not too far from Aylesbury. Another hour, perhaps. He wanted to overtake them before they reached the town. It would be the very devil to find the coaching inn at which they would stop.

Will finally spied a vehicle in the distance, but it was coming towards him. As it got closer, he could see it was a farm wagon carrying hay and pulled by a sturdy farm horse. A grizzled man drove the wagon and a young boy sat next to him on the wagon's bench.

When Will came close enough, he asked them, 'Did you pass a gentleman and lady in a curricle, by any chance?'

'I did, sir.' The man answered in a very unhurried manner. 'Thought it odd they were up so early, but you can never tell.'

Will could barely contain himself. 'How long ago did you see them? Are they far? Are they still on this road?'

'Oh, they were on this road all right. Not too many side roads worth bothering with around here.'

'How far?' Will pressed.

'Not too far.' The farmer turned around in his seat and gestured to the road behind him. 'I passed them just over this hill here. Not too many minutes before seeing you. You can't see over the hill but if you could, you'd see it is not too far.'

'What is your name, my good man?' Will intended to send him a reward for his help.

'Name's Begum,' the farmer replied.

'Thank you, Begum.' Will rode on increasing his speed.

He did not see them over the hill but galloped over the next hill.

And he saw them!

He gave his horse its head and he closed the distance between them.

Lucius turned at the sound of Will's approaching horse. 'Blast it! It's your brother.'

He drove his horses faster, but Will caught up and brought his horse next to one of the curricle's horses. He took hold of the reins. Lucius stood up and thrashed Will with his whip, but Will kept hold, slowing his horse and the curricle.

Ellen pulled on Lucius's coat, yelling, 'Stop! Stop!'

There was a tiger riding on the back, a youth barely breeched who looked terrified.

With the curricle stopped, Will seized the whip and pulled it. Lucius kept his grip, but lost his balance and tumbled out of the seat onto the road.

Ellen shrieked, 'Lucius!'

The tiger had the presence of mind to hop off and run around to hold the horses. Will dismounted and was striding towards Lucius as he was getting to his feet. As soon as Lucius stood, Will pulled his arm back and punched him in the face. Lucius spun around and fell again.

'Will, no!' Will was close enough to the curricle that Ellen pounded him with her fists. 'Don't hurt him.'

Lucius got to his feet again, rubbing his chin. 'Always the brute, Willburgh,' he snarled.

'That's what you deserve and more,' Will shot back. 'Good God, man. My sister is only sixteen years old!'

'I'm old enough to know my own mind!' cried Ellen. 'We are to be married! Just like you and Anna.'

'That's it, isn't it, Lucius?' Will approached him again, fists clenched. 'The perfect revenge. I married Anna and your family could no longer steal her fortune, so you take my sister. Did you not realise that I could prevent you from having her dowry?'

Lucius raised his own fists but backed away. 'You wouldn't do that, though, would you, Willburgh? You'd never deny your sister. I'll bet her dowry rivals Anna's wealth.'

It didn't, but Ellen was worth a sizable amount.

'Stop this talk of money!' Ellen cried. 'Let us be on our way!'

'He's not taking you to Scotland,' Will told her. 'You are coming home.'

'No!' She closed her arms over her chest. 'We love each other and we will be married.'

'No you won't!' Will advanced on Lucius and threw another punch.

This one Lucius dodged. He was clearly trying to avoid Will.

'You will let me marry your sister,' Lucius said. 'Unless you want a scandal that goes beyond all scandals. A scandal so terrible your sister will be ruined.'

'By God if you've violated her!' Will charged him and seized the front of his coat, lifting him off the ground and thrusting him away.

Lucius fell again but laughed. 'Not *violated* because she was willing. Very willing and there are consequences for being willing.'

'I was willing!' Ellen insisted. 'Very willing.'

Will's anger surged so high his vision turned red. 'You've got her with child!'

'Do not insult me, Will!' Ellen cried. 'Of course he did not get me with child.'

Lucius laughed again. 'No, I am not that depraved, but you know the truth matters little to a London gossip rag.'

Ellen looked perplexed. 'What are you talking about, Lucius?'

Will took a step towards Lucius again. 'I swear I would gladly kill you!'

Lucius walked to the other side of the curricle, with Ellen in between Will and him now. 'You would not kill me, Willburgh,' he said. 'Not unless you could do so with honour. Would you like to kill me with honour?'

Will was so angry he could not think. He raged, not only about Lucius Dorman running off with his sister, but about all the Dormans had done to Anna, what they'd done to his father. And even his mother. Will was engulfed in his emotions. Reason had fled.

Lucius reached under the seat of the curricle and took out a box. 'Here is how you can get your revenge with honour.' He lifted up the box. 'These are my duelling pistols. I challenge you to a duel for the honour of your sister.'

'I accept,' Will said.

Anna knew she was near to catching up with Will. And with Ellen and Lucius. The farmer in the wagon told her. Already she felt relieved. Will would stop them. He would save Ellen from making a terrible mistake.

She rode Seraphina a little faster.

When she came over the crest of the hill she saw the curricle and horses stopped in the road. She glanced to the right and gasped.

In the field, two men stood back to back and began to pace away from each other.

Will and Lucius.

A duel.

'No, no, no, no, no,' she cried.

She urged her horse into a gallop, sailed over the hedgerow on the side of the road and, right when both men turned to fire, rode straight in between them.

The sound of the shots exploded in her ears. Seraphina squealed and toppled to the ground, throwing Anna off. She landed hard in a heap.

She could see the field. Saw Lucius run over to Ellen, seize her by the waist and run towards the curricle. They were getting away! Will ran towards her, calling her name. Seraphina writhed on the ground near to her and incongruously a youth in livery stood stunned a few feet away.

Will reached her just as she regained her breath. He slid to the ground. 'Anna!'

'I'm—I'm not hurt,' she managed, hoping it was true. She sat up. 'Go after them, Will.'

Lucius and Ellen were in the curricle, driving off.

'I'll come back for you.' He ran to his horse.

Anna crawled to her pony. 'Poor Seraphina.' She stroked the pony's neck.

To her surprise, Seraphina rose to her feet. She'd been certain the pony had been shot. Anna gripped her mane to help her stand, as well. She checked the pony all over, felt its legs for breaks, but found none. There was a gash on the horse's shoulder, not very deep, not even bleeding much.

'Poor Seraphina!' Anna laughed in relief. 'The shot just startled you.' She turned to the liveried servant, recognising him as Lucius's tiger. 'Nick, is it? Come help me mount.'

The poor lad roused himself enough to come to her side and help her into the saddle. She rode away leaving him befuddled and alone. They'd come back for him, but she didn't have time to reassure him.

Chapter Twenty-Two

Will rode as fast as he dared. Lucius was driving his horses at a dangerous pace. Ellen looked like she was hanging on for dear life.

If anything happened to her, how could Will forgive himself? He'd managed everyone and everything into complete disaster. He could not have possibly made more mistakes.

The road was rough in some places where rain and wagon wheels had dug ruts. The curricle bounced and shimmied over the surface and Will feared it would simply come apart.

When the road made an abrupt turn to the left, Will held his breath.

The curricle horses scrambled to keep their footing. The curricle tipped onto one wheel which hit a rock in the road. It flew in the air and Ellen's screams filled Will's ears. The curricle crashed onto its side tossing Lucius onto the road. Ellen hung on while the horses dragged the curricle several feet. Will caught up and brought the horses under control.

He helped a shaking Ellen to the side of the road, seating her there, and ran back to Lucius's still body.

Had Will succeeded in killing him? God, he prayed. Please. No.

'Is he dead?' Ellen wailed. She rocked back and forth.

Will felt for a heartbeat.

And found it.

'He's alive.'

But Lucius was unconscious. He'd hit his head when he fell. What's more, his shoulder looked broken. Will eased him onto his back and held him up, hoping to ease his breathing. Lucius moaned when Will moved him.

'Ellen!' Will called. 'Find something in the curricle to elevate his back.'

She simply rocked back and forth.

'Ellen!'

But she was insensible. What was he to do?

At that moment, though, Will saw Anna riding towards them. Intrepid Anna. He should have known he could count on her.

Before she could ask, he said, 'He's alive. Unconscious, but alive. Can you find something to put behind his back?'

She rode over to the curricle and dismounted. First she went over to Ellen and spoke quietly to her, putting a comforting hand on her shoulder. Then she dashed to the curricle and ran back to Will carrying a blanket and Ellen's portmanteau which had fallen out.

Will propped Lucius up and, after making certain he was as comfortable as possible, got to his feet and embraced Anna.

'I am sorry for it all, Anna.' His voice cracked. 'All my fault. All my fault.'

'Nonsense,' she murmured. 'You are not responsible, but we need to figure out what to do.'

He released her. 'Yes. Yes. Help me turn the curricle.'

Anna held the horses, while Will tried to set the curricle on its wheels, which seemed intact. Lucius had purchased a high-quality vehicle so that made sense. It would roll if Will could only set it to rights.

But he could not do it, not after several tries. He sat down near Lucius to catch his breath.

'Maybe tie one of the horses to it and have them pull?' Anna suggested.

Will nodded. It was a good idea.

He tied his thoroughbred to the curricle and led him away, but they still could not set the curricle back on its wheels.

'Should I ride for help?' Anna asked.

'We're about halfway between Aylesbury and home,' Will said. 'I do not know which way you should go.'

Anna looked towards Ellen. 'I'm worried about her, too.'

Ellen had curled herself into a ball and was shaking. Lucius moaned and tried to stand up.

Will went over to him. 'Stay down, Lucius. You are injured. Best not to move.'

Lucius shoved off Will's attempt to help him. 'Guh 'way,' he slurred. 'Hate you. Always did.'

He went down on his knees and vomited, clutching his injured shoulder as he did so.

Will eased him back against the blanket and he moaned in pain.

What was best to do? They could wait for the ordinary traffic to come down the road, but Will was afraid they needed help sooner. He was reluctant to let Anna go for help, though. She'd suffered a fall, too. She said she was not injured, but he was not sure. The horses were getting restless. Lucius's horses were already spooked. Who knew what might set them off again?

'Someone's coming!' Anna cried.

Two men on horses approached from the direction in which they'd come. One of the men had Lucius's tiger riding behind him.

Will stood. 'It is Toby and John!'

They rode up to him.

'We thought it best to come after you, m'lord,' Toby said. 'In case you needed help.'

With Toby and John's help, they soon righted the curricle and sorted out the horses' harnesses. They put Lucius and Ellen in the curricle with John driving. The tiger rode John's horse.

'Let's take them back home,' Will said.

He rode next to Anna. 'Are you certain you are not injured?'

She smiled at him. 'I will probably ache tomorrow, but, no—nothing broken.'

They rode a while in silence.

Will spoke, needing to tell her and to hear himself speak aloud. 'I was angry enough to kill him. Angry enough to agree to the duel.'

'Stealing Ellen away was reprehensible,' she said.

She did not reproach him for it? Will could not believe it. 'When I turned to fire—in that instant I saw my father's duel—I could not do it, Anna. I could not fire at him. I deloped.'

She looked over at him but he could not read her expression. Was it understanding? Admiration? He could not believe either one.

'Maybe that's the only thing I got right,' he murmured.

John called back to him. 'The gentleman's delirious!'

Will rode up to the curricle.

Anna watched him.

Will ordered Ellen to hold on to Lucius. When she did not respond, he rode closer so she could not fail to see him. 'Buck up, Ellen!' he demanded. 'He needs you. Hold on to him!'

She did as she was told.

Anna was filled with emotion.

Will was doubting himself, blaming himself, and yet he was handling all of this. Her heart burst with pride for him, but also ached with his suffering. She wished she belonged with him, because she loved him. If anyone was at fault for all that happened it was Anna. Her presence had caused him and his family all this trouble.

The ride back was fraught with tension and seemed endless, but finally they neared the gates of Willburgh House.

Will sprang into action again. 'Toby, ride to the village. Get the surgeon. Bring him here. We will take Dorman to the house.'

Toby nodded and galloped off.

To Lucius's tiger Will said, 'Ride to Lord Dorman. Tell them their son is injured and they must come.'

The youth cried, 'Yes, m'lord!'

The household must have been watching for them, because the door opened before they pulled up. Lady Willburgh took charge, immediately having Lucius carried to a guest room, and taking Ellen under her wing while listening to Will's explanation of what happened.

Anna was not surprised that she went unnoticed. She did not need anything, after all. She went to her room with Mary who helped her to quickly wash and dress in clean clothes.

It was Anna who was there to greet Lord and Lady Dorman and Violet, to fill them in on what happened. She took them up to Lucius's room.

The surgeon arrived and examined Lucius thoroughly. He was most concerned about the injury to Lucius's head. It was bad enough for Lucius to go in and out of consciousness. If Lucius survived the night, the surgeon said, his chance of recovery was good, but the next twenty-four hours would be crucial.

Lady Willburgh and Will told the Dormans they were welcome to stay. They could use the drawing room to rest when not with Lucius. Or they could sleep in the guest bedrooms. Lady Willburgh said refreshments would be provided for them.

The Dormans said they would stay in the drawing room for the whole day and night. Anna went to the kitchen herself to make certain Cook would be prepared for the extra guests. Mrs Greaves was there.

'Lady Willburgh gave those directions already, ma'am,' Mrs Greaves said.

For once Anna did not resent being usurped by her mother-in-law. 'She thought of everything,' Anna said with true admiration.

'Yes, m'lady,' Mrs Greaves agreed.

Would Anna ever be able to do even half as well as Lady Willburgh, if she stayed? Anna wondered.

Anna walked back upstairs and decided to check in the drawing room in case she might be useful there. When she approached the door, she heard Will's voice.

'I know this is not the time, Dorman,' he said. 'But I want you to know that I believe it is time to settle the land dispute. If you want the land, I can deed it to you. If you would prefer funds, we can negotiate a sale of sorts. Do not tell me now, but think on it when Lucius's health improves.'

Lord Dorman's voice quavered, 'Do you think he will improve?'

Anna peeked in the room to see Will put a comforting hand on Lord Dorman's shoulder. 'I think Lucius is strong. And he certainly is determined. He'll get better.'

Violet came down the stairs. She had a handkerchief in her hand and dabbed at her eyes.

She stopped when she saw Anna.

'How is he?' Anna asked.

Violet blinked before answering. 'The surgeon said he dislocated his shoulder. He put it back in place, but it must have hurt.'

'Must have been hard to witness, as well.' Anna gestured for her to come in the room. 'I'll pour you a cup of tea.'

When Violet saw her father, though, she ran into his arms and wept into his chest.

Will walked over to Anna. 'Come. Let us leave them alone.'

She walked out with him. 'You haven't changed your clothes, Will.'

He was still in the clothes he'd hastily put on before dawn. His face was shadowed with a growth of beard, making him look like a drawing of a pirate she once saw in a book.

He looked down at himself. 'I suppose I should change. That must be why Carter is hovering. Waiting for me.'

She walked with him to the door of his bed chamber. 'I overheard you talking to Lord Dorman about the disputed land.'

He looked surprised, then nodded. 'I want to be rid of it. The dispute, that is. By any means.' He smiled down at her. 'You did well today, Anna. Except for charging into the middle of a duel—'

She interrupted. 'I wanted to stop it.'

He nodded. 'I know.' He lightly touched her cheek. 'You might have saved my life. And I know you saved Ellen's.' He glanced towards the stairway. 'Maybe even Lucius's.'

Lucius's life was saved. By the next day the surgeon declared him out of the woods, but warned that he must stay put. He would need rest and quiet to completely recuperate. So his stay at Willburgh House stretched to a fortnight.

Anna did not press to leave while Lucius was there. That

was enough of a disruption in the family. Her leaving would merely be another one.

It was a very odd two weeks. A member of the Dorman family—or all of them—visited almost every day. Having endured this crisis together, the animosity between the families seemed to dissipate. Will had been true to his word and ended the dispute over the land. He paid Lord Dorman an exorbitant sum for a clear deed to half of the land. Anna suspected it was the sum that would cover Lord Dorman's debts. Certainly that must have eased a great deal of stress in the Dorman house.

Anna was extremely impressed with Lady Willburgh's cordiality to the Dormans. She was especially kind to Lucius who, after all, had tried to elope with her sixteen-year-old daughter. The maids told Anna that Lucius had apologised to Lady Willburgh and to Will for his behaviour. He especially apologised to Ellen, confessed that he'd manipulated her out of a desire for revenge upon her brother, and that she was indeed too young to contemplate marriage with anyone.

Anna avoided Lucius as much as possible, but when she was in his company he seemed changed. He was courteous. Subdued. Completely lacking in sarcasm.

Ellen had changed as well, but in a way that made Anna sad. Her youthful joy and exuberance disappeared and it seemed like she spent as much time alone as Anna did.

Even though the venom that had permeated Anna's relationships with her mother-in-law, sister-in-law, and Will was eased with the more pressing issue of having to attend to the Dormans, Anna felt separate from them all. As if she'd already left. Even though Will was unfailingly polite and kind to her, he also seemed to treat her as if she'd already left.

Except for that one brief moment when she'd reached the

site of the curricle accident, the intimacy they'd so briefly shared was not repeated.

They'd still not told anyone else that Anna was leaving, but when Lucius was almost ready to move back to Dorman Hall, and summer was nearing its end, Anna decided it was time for her to leave. Soon harvest would make more work for Will and she wanted to make this least burdensome to him.

That afternoon Will answered a knock on his office door. It was Anna.

She never came to the office, not since he'd accused her maid of spying for the Dormans. His desk was rapidly returning to the chaos it had been before she'd briefly become the secretary he had yet to hire to help him deal with it.

'Anna!' Will stood. 'What may I do for you?'

She glanced down at his paper-strewn desk, but quickly lifted her gaze back to him. 'I wish to talk with you, is all, Will. For a moment, if you do not mind.'

'Not at all.' He hurried from behind the desk. 'Sit. Shall I call for tea?'

'No. I shouldn't be so long.' She let him lead her to the sofa and chairs.

She sat on the sofa. He chose a chair facing her and felt a cloud of doom engulf him.

She arranged her skirts before speaking. 'I thought this might be the proper time to plan my—my departure.'

Will lowered his head, knowing she'd be able to read his expression. 'There is no hurry, Anna,' he murmured.

'This seems like a good time, though,' she said.

Will's chest began to ache, making it hard to breathe. 'What were you thinking?'

She took a breath. 'I think Mary may want to stay here. Will you be able to keep her on?'

'Of course she may stay.' He dared to reach over and clasp one of her hands in his. 'You don't have to leave either, Anna. You may both stay. Everything is different. I have changed.' He glanced away. 'Or I hope I have. I strive to do better.'

She regarded him with a look of tenderness on her face. 'Oh, Will. Do not take this on as your fault. I've been the disruption. We both know so.'

He knew no such thing. One could just as easily say she was the solution to all the family problems.

She went on. 'We were never meant to be together. Neither of us chose it, remember?'

He may not have chosen it then, but he did now. He wanted to be with her. 'We could keep trying.' He swallowed. 'I want to keep trying. I want you to stay.'

Anna's eyes filled with tears.

'It is no use. I want to leave,' she said.

The first part was true enough; the second a lie. She wanted to stay more than anything, but she was convinced she would only cause more unhappiness. Things were better, because, in so many ways, she was already gone.

He released her hand and spoke sadly. 'If that is what you truly want.'

He was sad now, she thought, but he would be happier without her. She was sorry she did not give him an heir, but how dangerous it would be to make love with him again. She could never leave if they joined together again, flesh to flesh, climbing to that incomparable peak of pleasure.

He cleared his throat. 'But I insist you travel to where you want to live to see if you truly like it. You may wish to live elsewhere.'

He was not arguing with her. Did that make her happy or despondent? She did not know.

'Very well,' she responded. 'I will make a trip to Reading first before arranging to move there.'

'I must accompany you,' he added. 'Since I am paying, I must be certain it is worth the money.'

That made sense. Besides, it would give her more time with him. 'I—I have another request,' she said. 'A silly one, I am sure you will think,' she said.

'What is it?' He seemed to brace himself.

'Might we ride to Reading?' she asked uncertainly. 'On the Highland ponies? Like we did leaving Scotland?'

Like those happy days, did she mean? The ache in his chest grew stronger. 'We can do that.'

Chapter Twenty-Three

They left in two days, telling everyone Will had business in Reading and Anna was accompanying him. They were simply wished safe travel; no one seemed to think anything more about it. Will's estate manager questioned it, but Will told him the business was personal and Parker accepted that. If anyone thought it odd that they rode Highland ponies to Reading, no one said so to them.

They left without fanfare, mounting the ponies and starting on their way. John accompanied them, but after a while, he rode ahead to arrange accommodations for them. Anna and Will rode side by side.

They did not have the beautiful weather that had graced them on their long ride from Scotland. The sky was overcast and the day was one of the warmest of the summer. Reading was a good day's ride and Anna told herself to savour the trip, no matter the weather. It was time with Will and she'd soon be saying goodbye to him for ever.

Will was not pushing the pace, which suited Anna. Mid-morning they stopped at an inn to rest the horses and have some refreshment, but the weather was not improved when they started on their way again. They did not talk much, reminding Anna of those first days when they travelled to Scotland.

Her mind kept wandering to the glorious days and nights she shared with Will on the trip back from Scotland. Especially the glorious nights when everything seemed full of promise. Anna would be alone again. Alone, because she would not be with Will.

The grief of it overwhelmed her. Tears rolled down her cheeks. She slowed enough to ride a little behind him so he could not see. She swallowed the sobs, not wanting him to hear her weeping.

She'd doomed herself with this foolish notion of moving away. At least if she'd stayed at Willburgh House she could see him every day. All she wanted to do was turn around and gallop with him all the way back…home.

She felt a drop on her cheek that was not a tear. Soon more drops fell.

Will turned in his saddle. 'It is about to pour! Look for shelter.'

They rode faster as the raindrops increased.

Finally he pointed. There in a nearby field was a shelter. They left the road and crossed the field to a wooden structure, open on one side, probably meant for exactly this use— shelter from a sudden rainstorm. There was room for the two ponies and them. They dismounted and dried off the horses as best they could and took off their hats and gloves. There was some hay to keep the horses entertained including a bale that they used as a bench.

Anna was acutely aware of the nearness of him. She had not been so close to him since the day of the curricle accident when he embraced her.

He laughed softly.

'What makes you laugh?' she asked.

'The irony of it,' he responded. 'Our first meeting was in a rainstorm and now…' His voice trailed off.

She gazed through the rain across the field. 'This is unlike Vauxhall, though, is it not?'

'And it seems a long time ago,' he said.

'Not even three months.' She turned to him. 'Do you know what else is amusing?'

'What?' he asked without any humour at all.

'Today is my birthday.'

He frowned. 'I should have known that.'

She shrugged. 'I never told you the day. It lacks any importance now.'

'Because I lost you your fortune,' he said.

Impulsively, she grasped his hand. 'Do not think that way, Will,' she pleaded. 'We did not know. Before the Dormans became such *nice people*—' she said this with sarcasm '—they did a very bad thing. A series of bad things.'

He leaned back against the wood of the wall. 'I cannot conjure up the same level of rage as before, but I doubt I will ever trust any of them.'

She sighed. 'They make it easy to blame everything on them. But I made so many mistakes that I regret.'

He sat up straight again. 'You? No. What mistakes did you make?'

She averted her face. She could not speak the biggest mistake. Insisting on leaving. Not accepting Will, his mother, his sister, as the people they were, and staying with them.

He leaned back again and closed his eyes. 'It was me, Anna,' he murmured. 'I let my hatred for the Dormans colour everything. Be my excuse for everything. The truth is I've never forgiven my father for dying in that duel and leaving me to deal with all his duties when I didn't know how. I still don't know how. But then I fought a duel, as well. Was there anyone so foolish?'

She gathered up the skirt of her new riding habit and

turned her whole body to face him. 'But you didn't fire at Lucius.'

'I almost did,' he countered. 'I might have killed you.'

'You chose to delope,' she reminded him. 'You made that choice before you turned, didn't you?'

She moved next to him and put her head on his shoulder. 'The duel was my fault, to be honest. I should have told you about Ellen and Lucius right after I caught them.'

He scoffed. 'And might I have done worse then?'

She threaded her arm through his and laced her fingers with his. 'I wish I could do everything all over again.'

He clasped her fingers in his. 'Do you?'

Will savoured this closeness they fell into, like a habit they'd acquired on the road from Scotland. He liked feeling her hand in his again, liked the easy conversation, the feeling that they were alone in the world, just the two of them. They had everything but the joy of those days.

He did not want to break the spell. 'I'll wager you wish you'd refused to marry me. Think on it. You'd have your fortune today.'

'No,' she said. 'That was not what I was thinking.'

He turned to face her. 'What, then?'

She pulled her hand away and sat up. 'I wish—' she began, then waved the words away.

He wanted to press her, to insist she tell him whatever it was, but, no. That might drive her away. He wanted to bring her closer.

She rose and stood at the open side of the shelter. 'The rain is slowing. Nobody to stop us here like at Vauxhall. We should be able to resume the trip soon.'

'I do not want to,' Will muttered under his breath.

She spun around. 'What did you say?'

'Nothing.' He waved a hand as if to erase his words.

She stepped towards him. 'No. I heard you say something. What was it?' Her voice was turning sharp.

The last thing Will wanted to do on this trip was argue with her. He tried to sound flippant. 'I said I did not want to.'

'Did not want to, what?' she asked.

'Resume the trip.'

She searched his face as if trying to figure it out. 'I did not mean to leave the shelter now.'

'Neither did I.' He inhaled, getting courage. 'I meant I do not want to resume the trip. I do not want to take you to Reading.' He rose and held her by the shoulders. 'I do not want you to live elsewhere. I want you to come home. I love you, Anna. I've been too foolish to always show it, but I've loved you since Scotland.'

She looked up at him, not speaking, until he thought he'd made another terrible blunder. He must release her. Must let her go.

He could not read the expression on her face, but he'd guess it was tenderness.

'Oh, Will!' she exclaimed. 'I have loved you just as long. I want only to stay with you always.'

It took a moment for her words to register. Then he smiled. He whooped with joy, picked her up and spun her around.

And kissed her.

'Then let's go home,' he said.

'I have a better idea,' she said. 'Let's go on to Reading. Meet John as planned. Let's spend the night there, like we did on the way back from Scotland. We can ride home tomorrow.'

He grinned. 'You called it *home*, Anna. Yes, my love. Tomorrow we go home.'

Epilogue

Buckinghamshire,
July 1819

They were all finally home to Willburgh House after a long Season in London—Anna, Will, his mother, and Ellen who'd made her come-out now that she was eighteen. No riding back from London this year for Anna. She was expecting their second child in November. Their darling son, Will's heir, named Henry after Will's father, was a healthy fourteen-month-old who'd accompanied them to London because neither Will nor Anna wished to be parted from him. It made the entourage to London and back more complicated, but they refused to consider leaving the child in the country with only his nurse. They travelled in three carriages. Anna, the nurse, and Mary in one; Lady Willburgh and Ellen in another because Anna's mother-in-law's nerves could not tolerate a crying, fussy toddler filled with energy. The third carriage held the other servants—and Will's secretary. Will rode, the lucky man.

Lucius rode with him. He just happened to be riding back to Dorman Hall at the same time and met them on the road. He kept Will company, although Anna suspected it was Ellen's company he most desired when they stopped for the horses and took refreshment.

Ellen had plenty of suitors for her first Season, many in-vitations, many social outings, but no offers she wanted to accept. Lucius was not one of the suitors, but he often found time to speak with Ellen when they happened to be at the same entertainments. His attentions could be described as brotherly, if you could imagine Lucius as behaving brotherly. The accident did seem to alter him, though.

Lucius continued on his way when they finally arrived at Willburgh House. Little Henry was wailing and flailing his arms and legs as they all piled out of the carriages. Nurse ran him into the house.

'Good gracious! What a racket!' Lady Willburgh huffed as she entered the hall and handed her hat, shawl, and gloves to the under-butler.

'He has good lungs,' Will told her.

Ellen laughed.

She'd not quite returned to the girl she was at sixteen, but some of her *joie de vivre* had returned. Anna thought she was wise not to feel compelled to marry at eighteen. Look at what happened to Violet, who'd married Raskin, the poorest choice of a husband Anna could imagine.

Not so her Will. Anna wrapped her arm through his and he responded with a hug. Will was the best of husbands.

He kissed her. 'How was the last part of your trip?'

Anna savoured the warmth and scent of him. 'I think you heard. Your son indeed has good lungs and great stamina. He is tired and hungry, I expect.'

'Poor you and Nurse,' he responded. 'But how are you?'

They started up the stairway together.

She touched her swelling belly. 'The baby kicked when-ever the road was too bumpy.'

When they got to the doorways of their rooms Will pulled her inside his and kissed her properly and thoroughly and made her wish it was time to retire rather than time to dress for dinner.

'I missed you,' Will murmured.

'You could have shared our carriage,' she replied. 'There was room.'

He laughed. 'I believe I'll content myself with spending more time with you now we are home.'

She leaned against him and felt the beating of his heart beneath her ear. 'Yes.' She smiled. 'The whole family is home.'

* * * * *

COMING SOON!

We really hope you enjoyed reading this book.
If you're looking for more romance
be sure to head to the shops when
new books are available on

Thursday 27th February

To see which titles are coming soon, please visit

millsandboon.co.uk/nextmonth

MILLS & BOON

MILLS & BOON

THE HEART OF ROMANCE

A ROMANCE FOR EVERY READER

MODERN — Prepare to be swept off your feet by sophisticated, sexy and seductive heroes, in some of the world's most glamourous and romantic locations, where power and passion collide.

HISTORICAL — Escape with historical heroes from time gone by. Whether your passion is for wicked Regency Rakes, muscled Vikings or rugged Highlanders, awaken the romance of the past.

MEDICAL — Set your pulse racing with dedicated, delectable doctors in the high-pressure world of medicine, where emotions run high and passion, comfort and love are the best medicine.

True Love — Celebrate true love with tender stories of heartfelt romance, from the rush of falling in love to the joy a new baby can bring, and a focus on the emotional heart of a relationship.

HEROES — The excitement of a gripping thriller, with intense romance at its heart. Resourceful, true-to-life women and strong, fearless men face danger and desire - a killer combination!

 — From showing up to glowing up, these characters are on the path to leading their best lives and finding romance along the way – with plenty of sizzling spice!

To see which titles are coming soon, please visit

millsandboon.co.uk/nextmonth

LET'S TALK

Romance

For exclusive extracts, competitions and special offers, find us online:

- **f** MillsandBoon
- **X** @MillsandBoon
- **⊙** @MillsandBoonUK
- **♪** @MillsandBoonUK

Get in touch on 01413 063 232

Afterglow Books is a trend-led, trope-filled list of books with diverse, authentic and relatable characters, a wide array of voices and representations, plus real world trials and tribulations. Featuring all the tropes you could possibly want (think small-town settings, fake relationships, grumpy vs sunshine, enemies to lovers) and all with a generous dose of spice in every story.

♪ @millsandboonuk
◎ @millsandboonuk
afterglowbooks.co.uk

#AfterglowBooks

For all the latest book news, exclusive content and giveaways scan the QR code below to sign up to the Afterglow newsletter:

afterglow BOOKS

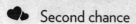 Second chance

 Spicy

Small-town romance

Small-town romance

Fake dating

Forced proximity

OUT NOW

Two stories published every month. Discover more at:
Afterglowbooks.co.uk

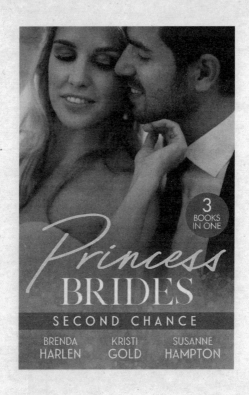